THE MONEY, HONEY

Also by Linda U. Howard

Expecting Miracles

THE MONEY, HONEY

Linda U. Howard

DISCARD

G. P. Putnam's Sons

New York

c./

5465 178

PACIFIC GROVE PUBLIC LIBRARY

Copyright © 1982 by Linda U. Howard
All rights reserved. This book, or parts thereof, must not be
reproduced in any form without permission. Published
simultaneously in Canada by General Publishing Co.
Limited, Toronto.

The author gratefully acknowledges permission from the following
sources to reprint material in this book:
    Chappell Music Company for lines from "Farming" by Cole
Porter, copyright © 1941 by Chappell & Co., Inc. Copyright
renewed, assigned to John F. Wharton, Trustee of the Cole
Porter Musical & Literary Property Trusts, Chappell & Co., Inc.,
Publisher. International copyright secured.
    Peer International Corporation for lines from "If You've Got
the Money, I've Got the Time" by Lefty Frizell and Jim Beck,
copyright 1950 by Peer International Corporation.

Library of Congress Cataloging in Publication Data

Howard, Linda.
  The money, honey.

  I. Title.
PS3558.08822M6   1982   813'.54   82-13693

ISBN 0-399-12694-5

PRINTED IN THE UNITED STATES OF AMERICA

Acknowledgments

I want to thank my friends, my family, my extended family, my editor and my financial advisers for their support, encouragement and great investment tips. Also, thanks to Burt Sugarman for giving me the money and, most especially, to Ned Leavitt for giving me the time.

This book is for
Tucker, Pearle and Duke
with all my love.

Contents

If you've got the money, honey,
I've got the time.

I

Empty Pockets

He was naturally subject to a kind of disease
which at the time they called lack of money.
— Rabelais, *Works*

I

It was on a cold Wednesday in January that Matthew Morganstern discovered the alarming fact that he was a Kept Man.

At thirty-five years of age, in total possession of every required faculty and blessed with a strong and sound constitution, he found he was unable to support himself. Not in the style to which he had become accustomed, albeit tricked into, nor possibly in any previous life-style.

What led him to this realization was a series of unimportant episodes which took place during that day. As unimportant as these incidents seemed, Morganstern still credited them with bringing him thrashing and gasping to his senses; surfacing in the middle of what had come to be known as a Dire Period of Double Digit Inflation and Record High Interest Rates.

Morganstern had no idea what the day had in store for him when he woke at eight A.M. on that January morning. Two things did occur to him: first, that this was the only time in their three-year relationship that he and Ariel had spent the night apart. (She had gone to Chicago on business the day before and was due back that night.) The second thing he realized, upon opening the refrigerator for his morning juice, was that there was no food in the apartment. In getting ready for her trip, Ariel had neglected to make her weekly call to Gristede's.

He had to go out and pick up a tube of paint at the art-supply store anyway, he thought. As long as he was at it he'd stop by Gristede's and pick up whatever groceries they needed. He would surprise Ariel with a special welcome-home dinner.

For Morganstern, shopping was a rare occurrence. He hadn't been inside a grocery store since Ariel started working, and that was over two years ago. In their distribution of duties, she took care of the shopping and Morganstern handled the cooking.

Recently she had taken to shopping by phone. As her job had become more and more demanding and time-consuming, she had opened up a charge account at Gristede's and called in her order every week from the office. The groceries came neatly packaged in cardboard boxes, and Morganstern put them away.

"Why order by phone?" he had asked. "I can do the shopping."

11

Ariel explained: "It saves time. Your time is just as valuable as mine. Besides, I like ordering groceries by phone. It suits my new executive image."

He never did know exactly what their charge at Gristede's ran. The $250 he gave her each month was supposed to cover food, Con Ed, and telephone. He assumed it did.

Morganstern went to the Citibank on the corner and withdrew $75 from his savings account. (He had no need for a checking account, since Ariel wrote all the checks.) He noticed he had a balance of $300 left. It was a good thing he had a big house-painting job coming up, he thought.

As he walked the three blocks to Gristede's, he visualized a menu: something tropical and green, he thought, to take the edge off the dismal winter, with warm red tones to offset the green and a neutral meat to serve as a balancing center. Veal scallopini with avocado-and-tomato sauce. Perfect.

Morganstern was a good, instinctive cook. He never used a cookbook, but prepared his dishes very much like he did his palette, guided by principles of color and consistency. By the time he had reached the store, he had a mental shopping list of the ingredients he needed for dinner plus a few things they were out of at home.

He moved up and down the aisles filling his cart and then he stopped by the butcher counter. Behind the glass display case were photographs of various cuts of beef, pork, and veal placed against a background of shredded green paper. No real meat was to be seen. Three butchers stood around watching *Hollywood Squares* on a portable TV. Morganstern rang the little bell on top of the counter to get someone's attention. All three butchers turned around at once; a look of pleasant expectancy warmed their faces.

"I'd like to get some veal scallopini please," Morganstern said. The butchers eyed one another.

"What?" the oldest butcher asked.

"Veal scallopini," Morganstern repeated.

"Let me do it," the youngest butcher said.

"Nah, nah, me, let me. He got the last one," the middle butcher complained. The oldest butcher ignored the other two.

"How much do you want," he asked, wiping his hands compulsively on his spotless apron.

"Just enough for two people."

The two butchers watched as the senior butcher entered the meat cooler. He returned, carefully carrying in both hands a thin pink piece of veal on white paper as though he were bearing the crown jewels. The other butchers never took their eyes off the scallopini. The butcher placed the meat on the scale and then stepped back. He waited for the scale to settle and then peered closely at the

12

weight, lifting back his glasses to get a clearer view. "About eight ounces. That enough?"

"Sure," Morganstern said, "that's fine. How much is it?" he asked out of curiosity and to make conversation while the butcher carefully wrapped up the meat in three different sheets of paper, sealing each package separately.

"You don't want to know," the butcher said.

"He don't want to know," the youngest butcher echoed.

Morganstern chuckled. "Sure I want to know. I'm paying for it."

"It's going to run you about nine dollars," the butcher said, placing the package on top of the counter.

"Nine dollars! You're kidding," Morganstern laughed.

"I don't kid about veal," the butcher said sternly. "Chopped chuck, maybe. But not veal."

"Forget it," Morganstern said. "Nine dollars for a skinny piece of veal? That's ridiculous!"

He pushed his cart angrily toward the checkout counter. Then he thought: What the hell. He already had all the other ingredients for the recipe. Why should he skimp on food? He turned the cart around and wheeled his way back to the butcher counter.

"I changed my mind," Morganstern said. "I'll take the veal after all."

"Hey, Manny, the big spender's back," the youngest butcher shouted. The meat-cooler door swung open and Manny came out carrying the small package of veal.

"It's a shame you didn't take it the first time," he said.

"Why's that?" Morganstern asked.

"Because now I got to charge you another eighty cents a pound," he said, writing a new figure on the package. "Now it's nine-forty.

"But you said it was nine dollars."

"That was before. The price just went up."

"In two minutes?"

"Hey, man, this is milk-fed veal. This stuff doesn't grow on trees."

Morganstern was tired of arguing. He grabbed the package. "Okay, okay."

"It's a smart investment," the butcher called out after him. "You won't regret it."

It was a good thing that he had taken out the $75, he thought as he stood in line.

Something rolled across his foot. He looked down. An artichoke lay trembling on the floor. Morganstern picked it up and handed it to the woman in the checkout line next to him. She was busy rummaging through her grocery cart, selecting various items and placing them in the magazine rack next to the cash register. In between the

13

slots for the *National Enquirer, People,* and *Us,* she jammed a can of lobster meat, a small canned ham, three artichokes, and a jar of Major Grey's chutney.

"I think this is yours," Morganstern said, handing her the artichoke.

"That's not mine," the woman said.

"I thought you dropped it."

"It's not mine," the woman hissed. "What do I need a ninety-five-cent artichoke for? I'm not Gloria Vanderbilt."

Morganstern placed the artichoke in the magazine rack next to the others the woman had left there. In front of him, a woman in a silver-fox coat was having an argument with the checkout girl.

"The coupon says fifty cents off," the woman said, waving a tattered piece of newspaper in front of the checkout girl's face. "Fifty cents off on Chicken of the Sea tuna."

"I told you," the checkout girl said, not taking her eyes off the tabulator, "it says fifty cents off on chunk light. What you got there is solid white, fancy albacore. That's one-thirty-nine and there's nothing off on that. You want to use your coupon, go back and get chunk light."

"I don't like chunk light," the woman said. "That's inferior tuna fish."

"I don't care what you like, lady. You got fancy-albacore taste, you pay fancy-albacore prices. It's entirely up to you."

"All right, then, what about this?" the woman said, removing another coupon from her Vuitton satchel.

The checkout girl took the coupon. "One free pack of Velamints with the purchase of three," the girl read aloud, "expires November first. It's no good." She handed the coupon back to the woman. "It's expired."

The woman in the fox coat drew back and announced to everyone, "This store does not honor coupons. Buyer beware!" She marched out of the store, leaving her groceries piled up on the checkout counter.

A young boy in a red Gristede's jacket was summoned. It took several minutes to load the woman's groceries into a shopping cart and wheel them away. Morganstern could hear people grumbling behind him.

He carefully arranged his groceries on the movable counter, putting cans in one group, fresh vegetables in another, and paper goods in another. He didn't want any trouble at the checkout point.

The checkout girl never glanced up. With one hand she flung the things past her to the packing area and with the other she played the tabulator, her fingers flying across the keys. The groceries piled up at the end. Morganstern did his own bagging, hurrying to keep up with the girl's furious pace.

14

"Sixty-eight-ten," the girl said, extending her palm toward Morganstern, still not looking at him.

"Sixty-eight-ten!" Morganstern gasped. "It can't be. All I've got is these two bags."

"Sixty-eight-ten," the girl repeated tonelessly. "You want to take everything out and we'll go through it all again? That's okay with me. Or maybe you got a couple of old coupons to cash in."

"No, that's okay. If you say it's sixty-eight-ten, then it's sixty-eight-ten. Just seemed like a lot for two bags of groceries, that's all," he mumbled, handing over the money.

He couldn't understand it. If two bags' worth of groceries came to that much, then Ariel must have been charging well over $100 a week for food. She always got fancy-albacore tuna.

The incident at the art store hit him the hardest and where it hurt the most: in his palette. He hadn't had to buy any art supplies since stocking up at a big going-out-of-business sale two years before. In putting the final touches on a painting he was doing of Ariel, he had noticed he was almost completely out of Cadmium Red.

He stopped by Art Beek-O on his way home.

"I'd like a tube of Cadmium Red please," Morganstern said to the man behind the counter.

"Nine dollars," the man said.

"I just want a small tube."

"You can't get smaller than this," the man said, holding up a three-inch tube of paint. "We've got a special going this week: three tubes of Cadmium Yellow for eight dollars. You can't beat a nice bright Cadmium Yellow."

"I'm painting a red rose. I need red paint."

"Suit yourself, maestro. I was just trying to help you cut corners."

Morganstern had only seven dollars left. He couldn't even afford the Cadmium Yellow special. This was serious. This affected his work. The whole idea of not being able to use the colors he needed just because they were too expensive was something he found appalling. Veal scallopini was one thing. That, he could do without. But Cadmium Red was quite another.

"I could trade you."

"Trade me what?" the man said.

"Veal scallopini for a tube of red."

"Let me see the scallopini," the man said. Morganstern reached inside the bag of groceries and took out the veal. The man unwrapped it, smelled it, held it up to the light. "Okay, it's a deal," he said, dropping the small tube of paint into Morganstern's hand.

Great, he said to himself, walking home. If we had some bacon, we could have bacon and eggs—if we had some eggs. What the hell was he going to do with this fancy avocado-and-tomato sauce now? Maybe he could serve it on a piece of canvas.

And what was going on with prices? It was as if he had left the country on an extended trip, only to discover upon returning that they had changed the currency on him. Dollars no longer had any value or meaning. Megabucks. That's what people were dealing in now. Why hadn't somebody told him his money was practically worthless?

Thank God, he had a big painting job coming up. A nine-room apartment he was scheduled to begin work on the next day. The $1,800 would come in very handy.

The telephone was ringing when he let himself into the apartment. It was Mrs. Kibble, the woman whose apartment he was supposed to paint.

"My husband won't let me do it." She was distraught.

"Do what?"

"The apartment. He says I can't have it painted. After he promised. He says we can't afford it. Oh, I'm so sorry," she cried, "I hate to cancel you like this."

"That's okay, Mrs. Kibble. Don't get so upset. It's only a paint job."

It was only after he hung up that he remembered that it was *his* paint job. His $1,800. Tears were certainly in order. But by all rights, they should have been his. She had just saved herself $1,800. Money he had counted on and now desperately needed.

Where have all my paint jobs gone? When did everything get to be so expensive? Why had Ariel lied about $250 a month being enough to cover his share of their expenses? Why had he believed her?

It hit him: so this is what they meant by economically troubled times. He had seen all the headlines but it hadn't sunk in until now: inflation was on the rise, the dollar was down for the count, recession was right around the corner, and it cost an arm and a leg just to keep your head above water. And what did it all mean to him? Only that he was the biggest, dumbest fool in the world. A thirty-five-year-old Kept Man. Not a man. A child. A thirty-five-year-old baby blindly, totally, ridiculously dependent on his woman.

Forget about the fucking veal scallopini, she was subsidizing his painting, his very life. He simply couldn't afford to live without her. And just how was he going to live with that little fact? he asked himself.

16

2

Morganstern came by his ignorance of money matters quite naturally. It was a sort of genetic defect, the kind that afflicts either the very rich or the very poor. Morganstern's family was the latter.

As the Kennedy family must certainly have felt destined to be great, important, and political, Morganstern's family must have felt destined to be poor. It was a family tradition. A mantle to be worn with pride.

His father, Max, still owned and operated the same notions store in Omaha, Nebraska, that his grandfather had founded. At that point in history when German Jews immigrated to the U.S. and moved across the country to set up great mercantile empires in the Midwest, Grandfather Morganstern opened the wrong kind of shop in the worst part of town.

From all appearances the stock hadn't changed much over the past ninety years. Max Morganstern carried bobbins for old Singer sewing machines (the kind that are pedaled manually), stays for corsets, replacement garters for garter belts. He sold bottles of green setting gel for the hair; also for the hair: hair nets, pin-curl clips, and hair tonic. For the removal of hair: single-edge razors and razor blades and something called lip wax. The things he sold were outdated, unessential, and yet not clever enough or awful enough to qualify as kitsch.

Mr. Morganstern's clientele, the kind of women who still set their hair in pin curls with a dollop of green setting gel or who occasionally needed a new garter replacement, were loyal, senile, and dying off like flies.

Morganstern's mother, Mabel, kept house and saved coupons beyond their expiration date.

They led a simple, quiet life unbothered by the kinds of decisions that plagued so many people in their sunset years: Miami Beach this year or Acapulco? C.D.'s or T-bills? A condo in Ft. Lauderdale or a casa in Phoenix?

They had never suffered from their lack of money. On the contrary, they seemed to find solace in it. As some people find satisfaction and possible salvation in Doing Good, the Morgansterns found peace and happiness in Doing Without.

In their strange scheme of things, the more they deprived themselves (and this was never articulated), the more they had coming to them. This didn't mean that they were looking to cash in on the Hereafter. They were not religious people. It was that by leading their simple life, they were accruing a sort of credit, an equity that increased in proportion to their self-denial. If they were to put it into words (and they couldn't), they would have said that their particular life-style was insurance against tragedy and disaster.

No money in the bank, no tumors of the brain. No stocks and bonds, no angina or aneurisms. No gold jewelry or silver flatware, no divorce or mental breakdowns. No expensive trips abroad, no hit-and-run accidents crossing Elm Street at rush hour.

In both Max's and Mabel's family backgrounds were stories of rich people who came to bad ends. '

Max's grandmother had been run over by an ice wagon on her way to make a big deposit from the then thriving notions store.

Mabel's father, a wealthy washboard manufacturer, had not survived the big crash of '29. While the bodies were still falling on Wall Street, he hanged himself in the basement of his washboard factory. Mabel's mother was left penniless and angry and married the first man who looked like he had money in the bank. The man turned out to be a fraud in a fancy fedora. He left Mabel's mother with a lot of big bills and an irreparable broken heart.

Although Morganstern's parents never alluded to these tragedies, they had put two and two together and come up with the adage that money, either the having of it or the pursuit of it, absolutely guarantees misfortune.

There was another point to their thinking, again unexpressed. It went something like this: the less they had and the more they did without, the greater the chance their boy had of finding true happiness in life. Consequently their measly secondhand car, two-bedroom two-family house, Melmac-dish existence was a certificate of deposit to be cashed in by their one and only.

So as some parents save money for their children's future, the Morgansterns saved up sacrifices. It was a weird form of Jewish asceticism, perhaps the rarest form, but they clung to it as though it were sound economic theory.

As a boy Morganstern was never taught things like: the Value of a Dollar, money doesn't grow on trees, put it away for a rainy day, a penny saved is a penny earned, buy cheap and sell dear. All those real-as-rock maxims which most American boys grow up with were never even uttered in the Morganstern household. The only mention of money ever made, and this was stressed over and over again, was: if you can't pay your own way, you have no business going.

Morganstern's parents never came out and said that money was dirty or evil or dangerous. It just wasn't referred to. In remaining in the unmentionable category (as sex was in some families), it had all the potential of being dirty, evil, *and* dangerous.

Yet Morganstern did not grow up feeling poor. He did not have what he would ever call a deprived childhood. There was, in Omaha, as there is in any good American town, a wrong side and a right side of, if not the tracks, then some other invisible boundary that divides two-car garages from no garages, wall-to-wall carpeting from scatter rugs, country clubs from pitch-'n'-putt ranges. Had he or his family associated with what the rich gentiles called the rich Jews, he might have learned acquisitiveness, he might have experienced the pain of not owning the newest, most elaborate model of fringe-handled, front- and back-bumpered, chrome-plated Schwinn. He might have wept, as many boys had, over the desperate need to have a new or at least nifty refurbished car on his sixteenth birthday, or enough money to take his best girl to the Airport Restaurant and Nightclub, where they charged a cover of ten dollars even if all you drank was Shirley Temples.

As it was, his friends came from the same sort of economically fragile background as he did. They played in the same empty lots, they kicked the same tin cans, they shared the same roller skates. They walked instead of riding bicycles, and later they rode bicycles instead of driving.

Had Morganstern been black, he might have aspired to the rich white way of life. Had he been rich and white, he might have aspired to more of the same. As it was, he was different. And he enjoyed that difference, although he never really pinned it on poverty or the Morgansterns' strange attitude toward money. Morganstern did not want for things as a child. He was lucky. He grew up with the simple assured pleasure of not having anything to speak of and everything to look forward to.

Max and Mabel were able to scrape together a little money over the years. And what they saved they spent on the thing they valued most in their rather mundane, colorless life: the boy's talent. They were delighted with his decision to be an artist. Art was such a quiet, noble, creative, noncommercial pursuit. It simply never occurred to them that if an artist was successful he could very well end up rich. They didn't know any artists, rich or otherwise. The only artists they had ever heard about were the starving ones.

Little Matthew started drawing when he was two years old and never really stopped. And what few pennies his parents had went for paints and brushes and private art lessons.

And that didn't even count as a sacrifice.

So Morganstern grew up to be an artist. But was that an excuse for being blind and stupid about money? he asked himself. No, just another explanation for why he never had any. While many men his age were already planning midlife career changes or devising schemes for early retirement, he was still trying to get to first base with his painting.

He never once thought of giving it up. He knew he was good. He knew he had talent. And he knew it would take time. He just never dreamed it would take this long.

Morganstern's style was a very untrendy but striking blend of realism and classicism. His paintings were meticulously rendered, exquisite in their detail. His subject matter varied, but consistent in each of his works was an extraordinary sense of color, composition, and humor. He always drew from his immediate experience and surroundings. His paintings took commonplace people and things and transformed them into sometimes beautiful, sometimes bizarre, but always joyful expressions of a world that was not quite real, and yet not quite wrong.

His series on bag ladies depicted decrepit old women dressed in the usual garb of soiled blankets and tattered coats, but their shopping bags, on close inspection, held wonderful surprises. Some were filled with jewels, some with exotic foods, some with expensive skin-care products. Morganstern's personal favorite, *Ninth Ave. Bag Lady, 31st of Oct.,* showed a smiling weather-beaten woman dressed in a ragged nightgown accessorized by a shawl made out of an old sleeping bag. Between her knees was a shopping bag filled to the brim with assorted Halloween candy, and dangling from a string around her neck was a mask of a bag lady.

His painting *Portrait of the Young Man as an Artist* showed Morganstern the artist as an old man hunched before an easel with a mirror at his side. The reflection of his face in the mirror was that of a middle-aged Morganstern, and his image translated onto canvas showed Morganstern in his youth.

My Friend, My Dog was a formal portrait of a corpulent man holding an equally corpulent dog on his lap. Both man and dog were smiling. The man wore a baby rosebud in his lapel which picked up the pink of the dog's small erection.

One of his more ambitious works, entitled *Free Concert, Central Park,* showed a crowd of people dressed in formal wear sprawled on the grass sipping champagne, while far off under a shell a rock group performed.

This was one of his larger paintings and yet it was only three by four feet. He wanted to work bigger, but the size of his canvases was restricted by the space in which he lived. Unlike so many successful artists, he had never been able to afford one of the big dingy lofts downtown or the rent on a separate studio.

Currently he was working on a painting of Ariel in the classic nude pose of *The Naked Maja.* Her physical charms were literally translated by Morganstern's brush. Her nipples were baby rosebuds (the reason for the Cadmium Red), her pubic hair was a Boston fern, her hair, parted in the middle, fell to her shoulders in individual strands of corn silk. A hummingbird hovered above her left thigh. In her hand she held a mature, erect asparagus.

It was a typical Morganstern: warm, charming, deftly rendered, and witty.

If I'm so good, how come I haven't made it? Morganstern had asked himself more than once. He knew the business of art was a funny thing. Unlike the movie business, where you're only as big as your last grosses, or the record business, where you're only as good as your next album, Morganstern understood that recognition to an artist can mean that everything from his first Crayola scribblings to his latest, greatest work can suddenly have value. All that he was lacking was the recognition. That chance of ultimate success was one of the things that kept him going. Another was grants.

He had been very fortunate in the grant area. Loved and applauded by his professors at art school (which he attended on full scholarship), he was the recipient of a juicy Fulbright (one year in Paris), a Guggenheim (one year in Venice), and a National Art Endowment (another year in Paris). After completing his studies, he made his way, thumb in palette and head in the clouds, to New York City, art center of the world.

The grants stopped there.

"Our foundation gives financial assistance to promising young artists. It is our hope that this assistance will enable them to succeed in the world of art."

"I appreciate that," Morganstern said. And he did.

"So you'll understand that we are withdrawing our support, based on the fact that you haven't succeeded."

"That doesn't make sense."

"Let me put it another way: you're too old, Mr. Morganstern." Too old, he said to himself. He was, at this time, only twenty-six. Was he a has-been at twenty-six? he wondered.

He applied everywhere, with no luck. Well, to hell with grants, he finally decided. He didn't need anybody's handouts. He could take care of himself. And he did. He supported himself in the usual para-artistic way: Spackling, plastering, and painting/wallpapering other people's apartments. It wasn't bad money when he got the work, and in between jobs he was free to paint.

In the beginning, he worked with Ivan Ludlam, a friend from art school. Between the two of them they could finish a fair-sized apartment in a few days. But Ivan quit after six months. He gave up both the house painting and his own painting and took a job in advertising.

The painting jobs kept coming through for Morganstern. He could work two weeks straight and then have enough money to paint for two weeks. He felt fortunate. He was doing exactly what he wanted to do.

His needs were minimal: a roof over his head, canvases, oils, occasionally food. The one thing he felt he could use more of was time. Even though he didn't mind painting people's walls for a living, he still resented anything that took him away from his easel. He had a million ideas filed away in his head, and never enough time to commit them to canvas.

If he had any interest in money at all, it was only insofar as it could buy time to do nothing but paint. His fondest fantasy was making a big bundle and getting a quiet place in the country, a big reconverted barn where he could work in peace, quiet, and optimum light. He knew that no amount of Spackling, plastering, or painting would earn him that much. Still, he liked to fantasize about what he considered to be the ideal life.

As time passed, Morganstern lost his contacts in the Art World. Many of his friends like Ivan had dropped out of the art scene and into the business sector. Others, who were still struggling as he was, had no desire to get together and compare sob stories. The few who had made it big didn't want to associate with a floundering artist. Failure, they feared, just might be contagious.

Then there were the important contacts, the People to Know: the art dealers, gallery owners, and rich collectors. One could see them at most of the big museum openings and some of the more prestigious galleries. But Morganstern knew it wasn't a question of him seeing them; they had to see him; more specifically, they had to see his work. Anybody could get invited to the openings, but he couldn't exactly drag one of his canvases along with him. What he had to do was talk up his work. Get people interested in seeing it. Get them used to hearing his name. Morganstern had no talent whatsoever in the art-talk area.

"So what kind of stuff do you do?" he was asked on rare occasion.

"Oh . . . uh . . . um . . . oils . . . people, mostly I do people. My things are on the small side and I uh . . . use a lot of color, you know, that sort of thing."

"Fascinating."

After a while, he stopped going to art exhibits and museum openings. It depressed him to see work hanging that he felt was certainly no better than and many times not as good as his.

Once he did come close to a big sale. An art dealer heard about him from an old art-school professor and asked to see his work. He liked what he saw and agreed to handle a few of the paintings on consignment. It was the typical no-risk deal. The paintings, six of them, were picked up almost immediately by a well-known collector, who took them home but never paid for them. When Morganstern asked about the money from the sale, the dealer put him off.

"My client is a very important collector. I can't just call him up like I'm Macy's credit department and he's an overdue account. He'll pay when he pays."

22

The man never paid. A year went by, and Morganstern demanded an advance from the dealer.

"An advance? Out of my own pocket? That just doesn't make good business sense."

What Morganstern did to the dealer's Lucite coffee table didn't make good business sense either. Two weeks later, all his paintings were returned to him plus a bill for the table, which Morganstern never paid. He figured the yearly rental on his paintings should cover the cost of a coffee table.

Apparently the art dealer figured differently. He spread the word about Morganstern. Had he told everyone that Morganstern was a difficult, temperamental artist, a troublemaker who drove a hard bargain and smashed Lucite tables in the process, it probably would have done wonders for Morganstern's name and subsequently his marketability. But the dealer knew exactly what he was doing when he told everyone that Matthew Morganstern was a sweet fellow whose work was inoffensive, imitative, and forgettable.

So the years went by and Morganstern came no closer to succeeding in the world of art. But he stuck to his work, to his dream, and took every house-painting job that came his way.

And although he was never in danger of starving, he never had to worry about high cholesterol either.

So, how did I get myself into this godawful situation? Morganstern asked himself on that cold January day. How did I get from being an independent artist to a Kept Man without even realizing it, for Christ's sake?

It wasn't just his upbringing and it wasn't just his art. The rest of the truth could be traced back to the day when he first met Ariel Hellerman, almost three years before. He knew it was not so much the high cost of living as the high cost of loving that had finally done him in.

3

They had met at the Village Art Show just three years before. It was the only show that anybody could enter. All you had to do was pay a small exhibitor's fee and that was it. It was not exactly one of your more prestigious shows, but Morganstern was desperate for some exposure, any exposure. The Village Art Show was certainly the place to get it. It was held outdoors and covered three city blocks. Thousands of people came. A few were art buyers, more were browsers, and most were just walking their dogs.

Morganstern's space was between a woman who did bulls and matadors in black and red poster paint on one side and a sculptor on the other. The sculptor's work involved taking the prospective buyer's hand and pressing it into a wet pad of quick-drying clay.

The buyer could return within an hour and pick up his handprint, which by then had been individually painted in psychedelic colors.

Morganstern had only one canvas displayed. It was a painting that portrayed a typical art opening in an East Side gallery: twenty people holding plastic champagne glasses, talking animatedly with each other, while off in a corner, totally ignored, the artist stands next to one of his paintings. He is holding an empty bottle of champagne and his fly is open.

It was a beautiful Indian-summer day and Morganstern sat on the grass next to his painting, reading *Life with Picasso* as he enjoyed the warm afternoon sun.

"Fabulous."

He looked up. She was standing with the gold autumn sun backlighting and highlighting her cloud of curly honey-blond hair. Where did she learn about lighting? he wondered. And who taught her posing? One hand rested on a hip and the other held back the hair from her eyes. Her long, slender Levi-covered legs were spread a sexy six inches apart. She wore a man's blue denim shirt, with three buttons open, revealing the contours of a very unmanly chest. She moved her hand away from her hair and pointed at something, her perfect forefinger bent as gracefully as a prima ballerina's.

"Really fabulous," she said. She was talking to his painting, not to him. "Did you do that?" She still hadn't looked at him.

"Oh, yeah, that's mine," he said, getting up. His legs almost buckled underneath him. She turned to him then, her hair blowing forward, softly framing her face. And where did she learn about faces? he wondered. What art school had taught her composition and balance?

Light, luminous eyes. Light green? Light blue? Morganstern's sense of color suddenly failed him. Dark, dark, double-layer, double-thick, double-long lashes. Sable-brush lashes. A classic aquiline nose. And a mouth. A soft, quizzical, magical mouth like that of a French film star. Lips that had a life of their own, that posed and pouted, opened and closed, revealing and then concealing excellent white teeth.

The top of her head, her curly backlit, highlit head, came to the bottom of his chin. With her head tilted slightly back, her eyes were mouth-level to him. Her eyebrows were unpenciled, unplucked. One brow as slightly mussed. He wanted to smooth it into place with his thumb. He wanted to live in that wet, glistening, secret place inside her lower lip. He wanted to reach inside her blue denim shirt to locate the exact spot where the white breast ended and the pink (he knew it had to be pink) nipple began, and consecrate that peak, that beautiful button tip with his tongue.

The mouth was moving. Morganstern came to attention.

"It's an incredible painting. I wish I could afford it."

24

"I'll give it to you. It's yours."

"Don't be silly," she said.

"No, I mean it."

"Asshole. How do you expect to achieve legitimacy as an artist if you give your paintings away to anybody who asks?"

Asshole. She called him an asshole. They were on intimate terms already.

"That's really the stupidest thing I've ever heard."

She was angry. She was beautiful. He took her by the arm (firm, warm upper arm, its perfect circumference affording him a good solid grip) and steered her away from the painting.

Morganstern had a way with women. An easy, attractive, unassuming, but seriously sexy way that women liked. They also liked the way he looked: light gray eyes; handsome, but not too handsome; tall but not towering; lean but not bony. Big hands, big feet; small dimples hidden by a beard that was not too scraggly, not too manicured; a choppy, curly, dark brown head of hair with random skewers of gray mixed in.

"Do you want a cup of coffee?" he asked.

"I'm not much of a coffee drinker," she said. She seemed to be over her anger. Morganstern liked a woman who didn't carry a grudge.

"What I was thinking was, we could go someplace and talk. You don't have to drink coffee. Are you much of a talker?"

"That's why I don't drink coffee. It makes me talk too much."

Ah, she was a quick one, he observed. But he was no slouch either. They spoke a few minutes, going through the quick jabs of any couple who's just met and is probably on the make.

"I'll tell you what I'd like to do," she said. "I'd like to see some more of your work. That is, if you don't mind exposing yourself to a complete stranger."

"A perfect stranger," he corrected her. "And no, I don't mind exposing myself at all." He couldn't believe his good fortune. A beautiful woman interested in looking at his work.

There they were, Morganstern thought. The two of them. Ariel and Matthew, Matthew and Ariel. She, in love with his painting. He with her perfect face. A hell of a good-looking couple already off to an interesting start, after just coinciding in the big city.

His sense of the fortuitous made him unusually articulate and charming. By the time she was halfway through his work, her eye had already started to wander away from his paintings and onto him.

It was as close to love at first sight as you could get in those careful, cautious days.

And they had so much in common. Besides their perfectly

25

matched, exquisitely meshed bodies, she, too, was an idealist, a purist, and a woman with a dream.

Ariel's dream was to be a published novelist. And just as Morganstern, Ariel had made a point of shunning regular steady employment, anything that could ultimately lead and possibly trap her into a career that might stand in the way of her goal. She supported herself by selling bagels and cream cheese from a shopping cart in Central Park.

She had been working on one novel for five years. She had struggled on it in Los Angeles, lugged it to Taos, and satcheled it home to Chicago. (Her family was from Winnetka, her father a well-to-do podiatrist whose practice had grown in direct proportion to the number of middle-aged men pounding the pavements in search of the eight-minute mile.)

She had arrived in New York City only two years before, with the same single-minded fervor as Morganstern. She was determined to struggle it out until she published. Much of this struggle involved resisting the temptation of the monthly checks sent to her by her concerned, cash-heavy father.

One day a few weeks after they began living together Ariel received a letter in the mail which she promptly tore up.

"What was that?" Morganstern asked.

"Oh, just another check from my father."

"He sends you money?"

"Every month," she sighed. "I used to send the checks back, but now I just throw them away."

"Why?" Morganstern asked.

"I can't spend the rest of my life being Daddy's Girl. And he has to get it through his head that he doesn't own me anymore."

"Nobody can own you."

"You don't know my dad. Take my nose, for instance. He owns that outright. He had a plastic-surgeon friend and they had one of those professional-courtesy things: the plastic surgeon's wife had bone spurs in her foot and I had a schnozzola for a nose, so they made a deal. The trouble was that my father hated the nose job the doctor did for me. They had a big fight. 'You call this professional courtesy?' my father said. 'This is just one of your dime-a-dozen Jewish pug noses. I want an aquiline nose. If I have to, I'll pay for it.' So before the swelling had even gone down, I had to have my nose done all over again. It was awful. Afterward my father said to me, 'Ariel, always remember, if it doesn't cost anything, it's not worth the money you pay for it.'" Ariel took a deep breath. "So my dad got his money's worth and I lived in dire fear of the day he would get tired of aquiline noses."

"You poor thing," Morganstern said, putting his arms around her. "It wasn't that I didn't like my new nose," she said, "or my nice clothes or all the things that I had, it's just that it gave him incredible power over me. It's awful when someone has that kind of power. Especially someone you love."

"Well," Morganstern said, holding her to him, "say what you will about your father, but I love your nose."

"You should," Ariel remarked, "it cost enough."

Ariel was in a constant struggle to overcome what she saw as the handicap of her pampered, protected background. The first time they went grocery shopping together, Morganstern was surprised to see her slip a can of smoked oysters into the pocket of her coat.

"Hey, that's stealing," he said.

"It's not like I'm swiping a rib roast or anything," she protested.

"Come on, put them back," Morganstern said. "You don't want to spend the rest of your life behind bars."

Ariel took the can of oysters out of her pocket and looked at it longingly. "I have a confession to make," she said.

"You're a kleptomaniac?"

"No, I'm addicted."

"To smoked oysters?"

"And smoked clams and shrimp and artichoke hearts. My mother was very upwardly mobile in the after-school-snack area. Instead of getting Hostess Twinkies like everybody else, I got hors d'oeuvres. I got hooked on them, just like some kids get hooked on sugar."

"Jesus, a shoplifter *and* an oyster addict," he said, shaking his head. He reached up and removed a box of Carr's water biscuits from the top shelf. He peeled back the flip-top lid of the oysters, took one out, placed it on a cracker, and offered it to her.

"Matthew, what are you doing?"

"Giving you a fix," he said, putting the cracker in her mouth.

Her eyes rolled back as she chewed with relish. "Ooooh, bliss," she sighed.

Thus began a tradition. As they made their way up and down supermarket aisles, browsing through canned goods, comparing ingredients, debating the price advantages of family pack versus regular size, they snacked on smoked oysters and clams, imported crackers, and marinated mushrooms. They never took more than they could finish by the time they reached the checkout line. And nobody ever stopped them. As Morganstern explained, he knew it was against the law to shoplift, but he had never heard of an ordinance against snacking.

At the time they moved in together (she into his apartment because the light was marginally better), they were both earning about the same amount of money. It worked out nicely. On very good days in the park, she could clear $50 to $75. When the weather was bad and bagels were out of the question, Morganstern somehow

27

managed to come through with a painting job. Their combined incomes gave them enough to survive, but just barely. Still, they managed to make do and have a good time at it.

Their first Christmas together, Ariel introduced Morganstern to a new kind of consumerism.

"Let's go Christmas shopping at Bloomingdale's," she said.

"Are you kidding? We barely have enough money to pay the rent."

"It's more fun when you don't have any money. Craving is good for the soul. Come on."

So they went to Bloomingdale's and "played store," as Ariel called it.

The first stop was the designers' floor. Gowns by Balenciaga, de la Renta, Dior, McFadden, and St. Laurent hung in intimidating splendor. Ariel went through the department like a whirlwind.

"I'll take this one, this one, this one, and that one," she announced loudly. "What do you think about this one, honey?" She held up a fabulous black velvet gown heavily encrusted with bugle beads. Morganstern hoped this wasn't an offshoot of her oyster addiction.

He put aside his fears and fell into the game with her. Standing back, he scrutinized the dress.

"Don't you already have one just like that?"

"Sweetheart, you can never have too many bugle beads," she explained. A saleswoman appeared out of nowhere. "Can I help you?" she said.

"Do you deliver?" Ariel asked.

"Certainly," the woman answered.

"Fine. We'll be back with our order before you close."

She dragged him up to the men's department. "Try it on," Ariel said, pointing to a butter-colored sheepskin coat. Morganstern did.

"How much?" Ariel asked.

Morganstern looked at the price tag. "Nine hundred and fifty dollars."

"A steal," Ariel enthused. "We'll have it sent with the dresses."

They hit every floor in the store, attracting much attention from other shoppers and, amazingly, even from the salespeople who were legendary for their lack of interest.

On the escalator down to the first floor Ariel draped herself on his arm and said, "Darling, I think you're being far too extravagant. The silver fox is enough. I don't really need a new mink too."

"It's both or nothing," Morganstern said stubbornly.

"Both, take them both," a woman standing behind them whispered in Ariel's ear.

"Do we have time for Cartier's?" Ariel asked Morganstern.

"We always have time for Cartier's, my dear."

28

On the way out Ariel paused by a counter which featured silk blouses. Morganstern couldn't help noticing the look of longing on her face.

"You'd really like to have one, wouldn't you?"

Ariel slapped herself lightly on the cheek. "Lost control there for a minute. You can't be voted best-dressed girl of Winnetka Junior High and not be somewhat of a sucker for silk blouses. Come on," she said, grabbing his hand, "let's get to Cartier's before they lock up the diamond tiaras."

That Christmas Ariel gave Morganstern a book on David Hockney (reduced from $50 to $7.50 at Barnes and Noble) and he bought her a silk scarf (reduced from $35 to $10 because of a tiny flaw).

They had many ways of enjoying New York without spending any money. On slow, usherless afternoons at the nearby Cinema IV they managed to see 3½ of the four movies for the price of one. They caught many of the big Broadway shows by sneaking in after the first act. Similarly, they could get into most of the major symphony events by charming the ushers into letting them stand in the back and then taking empty seats after the concert had begun.

They did a lot of Madison Avenue art galleries which didn't charge and museums which requested only a small contribution. Morganstern taught Ariel everything he knew about art. She was a complete ingenue, especially in the areas of modern art.

"But it doesn't look like mountains and sea," she protested. They were standing in front of Helen Frankenthaler's seven-by-ten-foot abstract entitled *Mountains and Sea.*

"It doesn't have to look like it. What she is trying to convey is the idea, the essence of nature. Don't pay so much attention to the title. Look at the way she uses the paint. It has a life of its own. Frankenthaler's like Pollock, in the sense that she likes to work directly on raw canvas. She likes to let the paint lead her. See how it stains and spots and spatters. That's a very direct and honest use of oils. She doesn't interfere." He took Ariel back several steps. "The remarkable thing about this work is the delicacy of the colors. They're almost waterlike."

Ariel squinted her eyes. Morganstern pointed to various parts of the canvas. "See how she doesn't fill up the whole canvas. She allows the bare spaces to give the colors room to breathe. Her use of space is as much a part of the painting as the oils are."

Ariel squinted harder. "But I still don't see any mountains or sea."

"Just stay with the painting awhile. Don't try so hard. Let it just be there." Morganstern watched Ariel look at the painting.

Ten minutes later she sighed. "It's really very beautiful. It's very warm and very beautiful."

"Now you're beginning to get it." He smiled. Ariel turned to look at him.

"But what I don't understand is why she didn't call it *Warm and Beautiful* instead of *Mountains and Sea.*" He shook his head and laughed.

During one afternoon of gallery browsing Ariel left Morganstern on the sidewalk while she went into a posh Madison Avenue gallery to ask the price of a painting in the window.

"Do you realize how much your paintings are worth?" she said, coming out of the gallery. "Yours are ten times better than that."

"Ariel, they're only worth something if somebody is willing to pay."

"Why don't you take your work around to some of these galleries?"

"Galleries won't look at work off the streets. You have to make an appointment."

"Well, make some appointments."

"What do you think I've been trying to do for the past ten years?" he said with annoyance.

"I don't understand why they won't see you. You're so damn good."

"Most of these places only handle known painters."

"How do they expect you to be known if nobody will handle you?"

"Now, that is the sixty-four-thousand-dollar question." They walked on.

"Oh, look," Ariel said, pointing to a poster outside of the Guggenheim. "They're having a big gala tomorrow night. A private showing of 150 recent modern acquisitions," she read aloud. "Let's go. We can see what's selling and who's buying. Maybe you can make a few contacts."

Morganstern studied the poster. "Honey, this is a private benefit. It's two hundred dollars per couple."

"That's even better. There'll be a lot of rich collectors there."

"All I need is a tuxedo and two hundred dollars."

"Leave the little details to me," she said.

At Acme Costumes they rented a 1930 tuxedo for Morganstern and for Ariel a slinky spaghetti-strapped satin gown with a silver-fox stole, from the same era, for just $20.

The next night they stopped outside the entrance to the Guggenheim. Just inside the door, a guard checked invitations at a table. A crowd of people was milling around the lobby waiting for the elevators to take them upstairs.

"Okay, beautiful, how do we get in?" Morganstern asked.

"Simple. We just pretend we've already arrived and just stepped out for a breath of fresh air." Ariel took two plastic champagne glasses from a paper bag and filled them from a bottle of ginger ale.

"You would think that just once they might put a limit on their guest lists," Ariel said as they casually strolled past the guard.

"It is dreadfully mobbed," Morganstern agreed.

"And if I see Diana Vreeland one more time this week, I just know I'm going to run out of things to say."

Upstairs, hundreds of people, holding identical champagne glasses, wandered around not looking at the paintings. An elegantly dressed group was gathered around a painting by R. B. Kitaj entitled *If not, not.*

"R. B. Kitaj is the W. H. Auden of modern painting," a woman remarked to her escort.

"You read that in *Time* magazine," the man said disdainfully. The woman looked hurt.

Ariel drew Morganstern closer. "Look, darling, he paints just like you do, only not quite as well."

The woman, who was drenched in diamonds, turned to look at them, obviously interested in Ariel's remark.

"Are you a painter?" she asked Morganstern. He nodded his head.

"He's a brilliant painter," Ariel interjected, "at least to People in the Know."

"Have I ever heard of you," the woman asked.

"You must have heard of Matthew Morganstern," Ariel said haughtily.

"Do we own any Morgansterns?" the woman asked the man. He shook his head. She turned back to Morganstern. "Well, what kind of things do you paint?"

Morganstern turned red. "It's hard to explain," he said.

"I see," said the woman, looking instantly bored.

"Perhaps you'd like to look at some of his work," Ariel offered.

"Oh, where are you being shown?"

"At our apartment," Ariel said.

"Thanks awfully," the woman replied, "but we barely have time to do the museums."

"Pretentious bitch," Ariel said after pulling him away.

They made the rounds of the gala, moving from one group to the next.

"What an astonishing oversight," Ariel said to one tall distinguished-looking man. "What could the selection committee have been thinking?"

"I'm on the selection committee," the man said. "Do you have a problem?"

31

Ariel was unfazed. "Can you tell me why your show doesn't include even one Morganstern?"

"Morganstern? Morganstern? I'm sorry, I'm not familiar with his work."

"You've never heard of Matthew Morganstern?" Ariel gasped.

"Well," she said, turning to Morganstern, "I guess that just illustrates the difference between the Guggenheim and the Modern."

Morganstern doubted that they had done anything to further his career, but he had a wonderful time, nonetheless.

"What a team," he said as they left. "You do the words and I do the pictures."

"And those bastards can do the buying," Ariel said.

They had the perfect fifty-fifty relationship. They split everything: the rent, the food, the Con Ed bill, the chores, and the worries. It was even-steven all the way. Whoever said you have to go more than halfway in a relationship was wrong when it comes to the perfect fifty-fifty split, Morganstern thought. Each carried his own weight, each did his own share, they were equal partners in life and love.

But nothing stays fifty-fifty forever. Given their common dream of living off their artistic endeavors, given their equal determination and drive, there was still one great inequity: Morganstern had demonstrable talent, but as a writer of fiction, Ariel had problems.

She had been working on the one novel on and off ever since she graduated from college. It was the story of unrequited love between a passionate college coed and her ruggedly handsome, very-much-married geology professor; a tale of tragic dimensions set against the backdrop of a Rocky Mountain granite formation. Ever true to a high-school English teacher's advice to write only about what you know, Ariel had made her novel excruciatingly autobiographical.

When she moved in with Morganstern, she was inspired anew. She set aside *Rocks Are Hard* and started work on a second novel, predictably about a young woman who falls in love and moves in with a struggling but talented artist. She wrote of things as they happened, and since there was nothing very compelling or dramatic about their perfect fifty-fifty relationship, *Portrait of Love* was very slow. She never showed Morganstern any of her writing. Whenever he asked about it, she demurred, saying it was still in a rough-draft stage.

Living with Morganstern was fulfilling Ariel's lifelong fantasy: two creative people working side by side in an atmosphere of mutual love, respect, and support. But before long she began to be bothered by his work habits. No, not his work habits, but his habit of working. Working longer, harder, and more enthusiastically than she did.

32

When she mentioned this to him, he laughed. "It's apples and oranges. How can you compare writing a book with painting a picture?"

Ariel was watching him as he painted. "Well, you really have a good time when you work, don't you?"

Morganstern stepped back and squinted his eyes at the canvas. "Yes, of course I do."

"I never have a good time when I'm writing."

"You're just having a bad day."

"No, it's not that. I just can't write," she said tearfully.

"Don't be silly. Of course you can write. You just need to finish the book and send it to a publisher," he said, hugging her.

"Listen, I may not be able to write, but I can read," she cried.

"Come on," he said soothingly, "get back there and get to it. Don't you want the publication of your novel to coincide with the opening night of my first one-man show? We could get another great package deal from Acme Costumes."

Ariel stopped crying and went back to her typewriter. But it got worse. Soon the sounds of his working began to annoy and distract her. The "gurgle-gurgle" of turpentine being poured into an empty coffee can, the "whisk-whisk" of his brush against the canvas actually set her teeth on edge.

"Do you have to paint so loud?" she said to him one day.

"What?"

"Your brush makes funny noises and I can't concentrate."

He laughed. He thought she was kidding. She wished she were. She resented the fact that after a long day's work he was excited and exhilarated while she felt frustrated and tired.

The disillusionment with her writing carried over to the rest of her life. For the first time since she flew the family's Tudor-style coop in Winnetka, poverty began to lose its appeal. Their romantic garret, as Ariel referred to their one-bedroom affair on 110th Street, no longer seemed quite as romantic. True, the two of them were living as cheaply as one, but suddenly it didn't seem like much of a life at all to Ariel. The fun of free snacking at the supermarket or buying underwear at Woolworth's, or of sneaking into Broadway shows during the second act, began to pall.

Of course she never complained to Morganstern about any of this. She felt it would have made her sound like a middle-class Jewish princess from Winnetka, Illinois. But her literary drive floundered, her determination wavered, and her dream suffered accordingly. And so it was that after six months of living the life of Barrett and Browning, Ariel was ready for a change, any kind of change, even a job in the real world.

As luck would have it, the real world was ready for her in the form of Ivan Ludlam, Morganstern's art-school buddy and former house-painting partner who was now "raking in eighty thou a year" as a creative director in a big New York advertising agency. "Eighty thou a year, man, can you fucking believe it?"

Ivan had kept in touch with Morganstern. He dropped by to admire his work, and to try and talk Morganstern into taking a job at his advertising agency.

"You think a real job is going to dull your artistic sensibilities? Blur your vision? Sap your creative energies? You jerk-off. Look at me," Ivan said, holding out his arms and turning to model his $400 Yves St. Laurent blazer. "Do I look like a guy whose creative energies have been sapped?" Ariel couldn't take her eyes off his gold Movado watch. "Listen, pal, I'm just trying to do you a favor. The job I'm talking about would be a piece of cake for you. It practically falls into the hallowed category of manual labor. You wouldn't have to use your so-called brain at all."

"What kind of job?" Morganstern asked.

"You'd work in the bull pen."

"The bull pen?"

"The bull pen is where the artwork is done. You do sketches, lettering, paste-ups, that kind of stuff. It's all mechanical. It's a good steady income. You get overtime. Those guys probably gross about twenty thousand a year."

"Twenty thousand a year," Ariel echoed.

"I appreciate your concern, Ivan. But I'm not looking for a job. Not even a piece of cake. We're not starving."

"You think you're too good to go to work in an advertising agency? You think I sold out? Say it."

That was really what Morganstern thought, but he didn't say it.

"You want Art, I'll show you Art. Look at this." From his pocket Ivan removed a neat folded packet of bills. He peeled off a fifty. "Look at the design on this, the detail. Look at this guy Grant. I mean, get into his eyes. There's a guy who fucking knows something. Who's been places. Who knows where he's going. You tell me that isn't fucking Art. Go on, tell me."

"It's nice, nice composition," Morganstern said, cleaning the oil paint out of his brushes. "You ought to have it framed."

"Tell me what's so awful about a good steady income. What are you so afraid of?"

Morganstern couldn't put it into words. But in fact, Ivan was dead right. Deep down, Morganstern was deathly afraid of anything that smacked of a "good steady income." It was invariably tied to a good steady job. And that meant eight hours a day, five days a week, which would leave him little time for painting. There was an even greater fear: that he would get so used to the steadiness of the income he would never be able to go back to the precariousness of painting.

"So let me see your latest masterpiece," Ivan asked, as usual. He stared for half an hour at Morganstern's most recent work, shaking his head slowly from side to side. Finally he turned and slapped Morganstern on the back. "You got some hell of a talent there. Too bad there's no market for it."

"How come Ivan doesn't buy one of your paintings?" Ariel asked after one of his visits.

"I guess because he's got enough of his own." Morganstern smiled.

"I really don't understand what you two have in common."

"He likes me. I remind him of his artistic past."

"Yes, but what do you see in him?"

"Ivan's the craziest, clearest guy I know. He's the only person I've ever met who can say exactly what's on his mind and get away with it. More important, sometimes he can even say what's on your mind."

"Well, I think he's obnoxious."

"He tries to be. With him it's an art form."

One afternoon Ivan showed up while Morganstern was out working on an apartment. He was wearing a raccoon-lined trench coat.

"How much?" he said, holding open the coat to display the fur.

"How much what?" Ariel asked, knowing exactly what Ivan wanted to hear.

"How much do you think I paid for it?"

"I give up," Ariel said.

"No, guess."

"I don't want to guess."

"Go on."

"If you're dying to tell me, tell me. But please don't make me guess."

"You're jealous."

"Me? Jealous? Why would I be jealous of your five-thousand-dollar raccoon-lined trench coat?" she asked.

"Right on the nose. Actually, it was forty-seven hundred. Look at this. Do you fucking believe this? It's not reversible. The fur is an understatement. Isn't that a killer? You talk about subtle chic!"

"*You* talk about subtle chic, I've got work to do," she said. "Matthew won't be home till about seven."

"Listen, if I'm interrupting the great American novel, I shall take my irreversible raccoon coat and go."

"No, that's okay. I'm sort of at an impasse," she said, plopping down on the blanket-covered foam that served as a couch. "Let me ask you something, Ivan."

"You want to know how much I paid for my Movado?"

"Let's just say I wanted a job. How would I go about getting one?"

"What kind of a job?"

"A writing job, I guess."

"You mean advertising writing? What about your novel?"

"As I said, I'm sort of at an impasse with my novel."

"They're always looking for new talent at the agency. Here's what you do. Put together a sample book, a portfolio of hypothetical ads, and I'll set you up with an interview. We'll see what happens."

Ariel worked on a sample ad book without telling Morganstern about it. Ivan got her an appointment at his agency and she got a job after just one interview. Junior copywriter, starting salary $18,000, which was more than what she and Morganstern together could earn in one year.

"Guess what, I got a job," Ariel said to Morganstern that night.

"What kind of job?"

"At Ivan's agency."

"In the bull pen?" Morganstern asked, his mind instantly turning to snorting, sex-crazed artists pawing the ground at Ariel's drawing board.

"No, as a copywriter, a junior copywriter."

"But what about your novel?"

"I have to get away from it for a while. It's just not going anywhere."

"You don't have to take a job. We don't need the money."

"It has nothing to do with the money. I have to get out of the house, get away from my typewriter, and do something else for a change. But speaking of money, they're paying me eighteen thousand a year."

"That sounds like a lot." In fact, the figure was totally beyond Morganstern's grasp. "Listen, if that's what you really want to do, fine. I just don't want to see you give up something that I know is important to you."

"I'm just going to do it for a while until I work through my block," she said. "It'll be fun for a change."

Ariel was an instant success in her job. The problems of plot and characterization that had plagued her in *Portrait of Love* simply did not apply in the advertising business. Her belief in the autobiographical approach to writing finally paid off. She could relate well to the average consumer. She had been an average consumer herself once. She was good at presenting a product in such a way as to make someone want to buy it.

Ariel had had a major breakthrough on the agency's bra account. Her assignment had been to come up with an advertising campaign that would help the client unload millions of dollars' worth of defective bras. The bra had been intended for large-busted women but had ended up a flop because it didn't offer sufficient support. Ariel's solution: to reposition it as an exercise bra for unathletic women. She turned the minimum support into a plus by promising the consumer "built-in Exer-Action."

"You get the kind of up-and-down movement that you could once only get when running or playing tennis. And you get it without ever having to put on a pair of running shoes or pick up a tennis racket."

After three months as a junior copywriter they promoted her to full copywriter and gave her a raise. She insisted they renegotiate the fifty-fifty split.

"It's only fair," she said. "I'm earning more, why shouldn't I pay a bigger share?" Ariel was a stickler for fairness, especially when it came to money.

"Put it in the bank," Morganstern said. "Save up for something you really want."

"That's a very paternalistic attitude," Ariel remarked. She had nothing specific in mind to save for, but she loved spending it. She took to surprising Matthew with little gifts. Art books, paintbrushes, a camera. She even bought him a blazer like Ivan's, which he seldom wore.

A year passed and a competitive agency tried to woo her away with the promise of yet a larger salary, more responsibility, and a title. She debated over the move for days and finally decided to take the job. In the middle of the night before her first day at the new agency, she woke up screaming.

"What's the matter?" Morganstern asked, gathering her up in his arms.

"I had the most terrible nightmare. I was driving to work in a limousine, a big black—no, a midnight-blue limousine. And there was a man waiting for a bus and I told my driver to stop. I thought it would be nice to give him a lift. Here I am with this big car and everything."

"Did you know the guy?" Morganstern had a tendency to get jealous at the most inappropriate times.

"There was something familiar about him. I told the driver to stop and I opened the door, and that's when I saw it was you. I asked you if you wanted a ride. And you looked at me with the most incredible disgust and then turned away. I felt terrible. And then I looked at myself. Not in a mirror, but you know how you can suddenly see yourself from outside? And I was old and ugly and all bent over. I was wearing gobs of awful makeup, thick Pan-Cake makeup oozing into my lines and wrinkles, and greasy red lipstick, and my eyebrows were penciled in and I had a wig on. I looked like a witch. But like this very wealthy witch. Because I was wearing a beautiful fur coat and there were rings, big diamond rings, on every finger. It was awful."

"It was just a dream," Morganstern said, though he shuddered at the thought of Pan-Cake makeup covering Ariel's lovely fresh face.

"I don't want the job. I don't want to be making so much money. It'll make me old and ugly and nobody will want me."

"Don't worry about it, honey, just go easy with the Pan-Cake makeup. You'll be okay."

"I don't want to be an old-lady executive," she sobbed.

"So don't take the job. You don't have to. Stay home and work with me. Nobody's forcing you to become a big-time copywriter."

"I could be a nowhere novelist," she said.

"Maybe you haven't given it enough of a chance. You could go back to it now with a clearer perspective."

The idea of going back to a novel that was so boring sent a shudder up Ariel's spine. She couldn't even bear to read what she herself had written.

"No, I'll take the job. It'll be okay. But you have to do something for me. Something very important."

"Name it."

"Make love to me," she said urgently. "Please make love to me. Now."

"Hey, sure. No problem. I can do that," Morganstern said. "Yep. That I can do." They made love. Ariel was frantic. Morganstern had a hard time keeping up with her.

Their life-style began to change with the new job. They were going out to dinner, seeing entire Broadway shows from beginning to end, meeting people at fancy bars. Ariel's underwear now came from Henri Bendel's. The shelves were filled with smoked oysters. There was new furniture. A huge three-sided sectional couch that practically filled up the entire living room of their small apartment. A new Sony TV. A complete sound system. All the things that Morganstern couldn't possibly afford to chip in on but Ariel insisted on paying for. Little extras, she called them.

One of the little extras turned out to be a new apartment. Morganstern put his foot down. "What's wrong with where we live right now?"

"Nothing. It's just that the couch is too big."

"You could've bought a smaller couch."

Ariel went on, undeterred. "Besides, if we had a bigger apartment, you would have more room to paint. You could even paint bigger pictures—you've always wanted to paint bigger. You've said so yourself. And big pictures are very big these days. I found a great new apartment. And our lease is almost up here."

"What apartment?" Morganstern asked, not wanting her to get away with slipping it in like that.

"Oh, it's perfect. Please just look at it. If you don't like it, we don't have to move."

It was hard for Morganstern not to like it. It was a bright, modern, two-bedroom-with-dining-area apartment in the East Fifties. The East Fifties were like another world to Morganstern.

"Look how much light you get," Ariel said. "We can use the second bedroom for your studio, and the dining area for dining. We can actually entertain."

"How much?" Morganstern asked.

"There's a doorman and an elevator," she said, as though he had somehow missed the blue-serge stiff who held open the door for them and didn't notice the stainless-steel cubicle that had brought them up to the eighth floor.

"How much?" he asked again.

"We can get a three-year lease and I can walk to work."

"Why would you want to walk to work?" he asked, throwing her a curve.

"It's seven-fifty a month," she answered.

"Forget it. That's almost three times what we're paying now. It's ridiculous."

"Actually, you're going to laugh, but it's a steal. You should see some of the places I've seen."

"Ariel, we can't afford it."

"I can afford it."

"I said, *we* can't afford it. If I can't pay my half, I don't want any part of it."

Ariel took another tack.

"All right. I'll take the apartment by myself. If you want to stay up on 110th Street, be my guest. I'm moving."

"You'd leave me for another apartment?"

"Yes."

"You wouldn't?"

"Yes, I would."

"What would you do with the second bedroom?"

"I'd turn it into a guest room and have guests."

"You're bluffing."

"No, I'm not."

"Okay, I'll help you move."

"Now you're bluffing."

"No, I'll borrow a truck and help you move."

"Great. Maybe you'll come for dinner sometime."

"I might even book the guest room for a weekend. You never know."

Ariel looked at him and then burst into tears.

"I don't want to live anywhere without you. We can stay where we are. It's not where we live that matters. As long as we're together," she sobbed.

Morganstern took her face between his hands. She was beautiful when she was angry, but she was glorious when she cried, he thought. Tears made her light-green/light-blue eyes (he had discovered that they were both and changed according to what she wore) sparkle. She had the ability to shed tears without getting the whites of her eyes red. Another trick was the way the tears stuck to the ends of her extra-long, extra-thick lashes like little diamond chips.

"You really hate our place, don't you?" he said, wiping away her tears with his thumbs.

"No, of course I don't," Ariel sniffled. "How can I hate a place where I've been so happy?" She thought a minute. "I just hate the cockroaches."

"Are you trying to tell me this apartment doesn't have cockroaches?" he asked with amazement.

She laughed. "Cockroaches aren't allowed on this side of Central Park."

"Ariel, this is a perfectly wonderful apartment but I hate the idea of moving into a place I can't even begin to afford. It changes everything."

"What does it change?"

"It makes me feel like a schmuck. With my income so sporadic, I just can't make a commitment like this."

"Switch it around. How would you feel if you had sold a bunch of paintings and wanted to do something like take a trip and I wouldn't go with you because I wasn't able to pay my share?"

"That's different, somehow."

"That's a double standard is what that is."

"You're really set on this apartment?"

"Only if you are. If you don't want to move, we won't move."

The last night in their old apartment, they arrived at the new financial arrangement. Morganstern wanted it all settled before they moved.

"Okay," Ariel had said, "here's how we can work it." She reached under her pillow and took out a small pocket calculator. When did she start sleeping with a pocket calculator? Morganstern wondered. "I'll handle the rent. You can pay for the utilities and food. Which should come to about two-fifty a month," she said, punching the buttons. The calculator had glow-in-the-dark numbers. "That's about what I've been paying all along," he said.

"Is it? Well, that's good. Anyway, the two-fifty will cover food, utilities, and other little extras."

That sounded fair to him. As long as he was contributing the day-to-day living expenses, and in charge of putting food on the table, he didn't feel so badly.

The apartment was sunny, comfortable, modern, and clean. No cockroaches. But it took Morganstern a long time to adjust to his new surroundings. He moved his easel from one spot to another, trying to find the perfect place, like a dog turning round and round in search of the most comfortable corner on a queen-size bed. The wall-to-wall carpeting made him uptight about spilling paint on the floor. He missed his old paint-spattered apartment, the dingy neighborhood, the crazy street people, the garbage and noise. He felt totally out of his element. And Julio the doorman didn't help matters.

Julio was very serious about building security and had taken it upon himself to institute a safety check. He used the password system. Every morning on Morganstern's way out he would tell him the password for the day. Morganstern had to repeat it to him when he returned at night. Morganstern might go out for just a half-hour, and he still had to repeat the password on his way back in.

The password changed each day. And Morganstern had a habit of forgetting it. He'd stand there like a fool, going through the list in his mind (they were usually the names of Puerto Rican baseball players). After a while he noticed that he and some occasional delivery or repairmen were the only ones Julio hassled. The rest of the well-dressed tenants were passed right on through, without any mention of a password.

The new apartment seemed to have pushed some hidden button in Ariel. The woman who had once worn the same winter coat for three years in a row had turned into a compulsive shopper.

"Look at the great sheets I got," she said, holding up a dozen packages.

"But we already have loads of new sheets."

"These were on sale," she explained, annoyed at Morganstern for not understanding the logic of hoarding sheets.

"I want you to do something for me, Ariel," he said to her one day after one of her raiding parties on Bloomingdale's.

"I can't take the curtains back, they were on sale." The curtains she referred to were $1,500 worth of what looked to Morganstern to be burlap.

"I want you to keep a running account of everything you spend. So that I can pay back my half when I have the money."

"Oh, Matthew."

"I mean it. It's the only way I can be comfortable with this setup."

"Of course, if that's what you want," she said, unwrapping the

41

rest of the curtains. But she didn't keep an account. She forgot all about it.

Within the first six months at her second job, Ariel received a big increase in salary. This time, she didn't tell Morganstern about it. She felt guilty. She wondered why she was keeping this information from him. In some strange way she felt as though she were being unfaithful to him. And she stopped talking about money in specific figures. New terms entered her vocabulary instead. Words like "upper percentile," "tax bite," "tax savings," "tax shelter," and "tax cut."

She had gotten herself an accountant. Somebody recommended by Ivan. Apparently he was a very good accountant, Morganstern observed, because she took to quoting him at every opportunity.

"James says that Reagan is on our side."

"James says that I can take all my books, magazines, movie and theater tickets off as a deduction."

"James says the majority of women are still totally unliberated about money."

James was mentioned so often it got to be annoying. Morganstern wondered if he should be jealous, but then he realized he was just an accountant. He had a clear picture of him as a bald guy with gray teeth wearing an eyeshade and sleeve protectors.

And Morganstern viewed Ariel's involvement with high finances a sort of hobby like tap dancing. It was something he had no interest in or talent for, but as long as it amused and involved her, it was fine with him. So as she tip-tapped her way to the office, to the bank, to the accountant's, and through the business section of the New York *Times,* he was content to stay at home and paint with occasional interruptions for his house-painting jobs.

Another six months passed. Ariel got a promotion.

"They're making me a group head," she said, getting into bed that night. She seemed tense.

"What does that mean?" Morganstern asked.

"It means I'll head a group. I'll be responsible for the creative output of three copywriters and three art directors. It also means I'll be in a higher tax bracket," she said with a sigh.

"That's terrific. They're just confirming what I've always said: You give great head. Yuk, yuk."

"Yuk, yuk," Ariel said to the ceiling.

Morganstern ran his hands lightly, lightly over the tips of her breasts, around and around her tight little stomach, and slowly down between her legs.

He pulled her over on top of him. She rolled over him and pulled him on top of her. They repeated this maneuver three times. Morganstern thought it was a game. Ariel had always loved to be on top.

"I want to be on the bottom," she said finally.

"Well, I want to be on the inside. I think we can make a deal," he said, rolling over and entering her. She wasn't ready. She was tight and dry. Her eyes were shut, her mouth set in a firm line.

"My gorgeous little money-maker," he breathed into her warm ear.

"Don't call me that," Ariel said, stiffening and pulling away so abruptly that Morganstern's penis actually twanged out of her. She lay on one side of the bed, her face turned away from his.

"I'm sorry," she said, "I'm not feeling very sexy."

"What's the matter?"

"I don't know," she said, her voice breaking.

"Talk to me, Ariel."

She was quiet for a long time.

"Do you have any idea how much money I'm making right now?"

"Not to the penny, no. I assume it's a lot. You're worth it."

"Do you realize you've never once been impotent with me?"

"Is that a compliment or a complaint?"

"You're always able to get it up."

He leaned toward her. "Only for my friends," he said, carefully enunciating the words around her nipple.

"Most men have episodes of impotency when they're threatened by women."

"Oh? Did you threaten me? Did I miss something?"

"Doesn't my making so much money bother you in the slightest? Doesn't it do anything to your masculine pride?"

"It does a lot for my masculine pride. I have no idea what you're earning, but I'm tickled to death to be fucking someone in the upper percentile."

"Let me put it this way: if I weren't making so much money, would you still love me?"

"Oh, now I get it. She thinks he's after her for her money. May I remind you that I loved you when you were trying to push stale bagels in Central Park. Are you really afraid I'm after you for your money?"

"No. No. No. It's not that. It's just that it doesn't seem to affect you in the slightest. Meanwhile, it's making me crazy."

"Well, if my losing a hard-on will prove to you how threatened I am by your huge income and therefore how much I love you for yourself alone, then observe, in your hand lies the dormant symbol of my love." He placed her hand on his flaccid penis.

"Oh, no, what have I done?"

"You've cured me at last. I'm threatened, impotent, and normal. Mere putty in your hands."

"Oh, sweetheart. I'm such a fool. I'll make it all better," she said, bowing her head to his groin.

"I knew you wouldn't turn your back on a fallen man," he moaned.

They made love. Good love. Ariel on top. Matthew on the bottom. But the money matter wasn't finished.

Afterward she said, "I guess it's me who feels threatened. It scares me to move ahead so fast. I never saw myself as this executive-level career person. It's a lot of pressure. There are so many decisions I'm supposed to make. All this financial stuff just makes me incredibly nervous. And you never show any interest in what I'm doing with my money. How I'm investing it."

"But it's your money. I don't know shit about investments."

"You could learn. I've had to."

"Isn't that what you have your accountant for?"

"I don't live with James. I live with you. You could at least try. It wouldn't kill you to be a little more informed."

Morganstern thought about it. She was right. He should make an effort to learn about money. After all, it was important. Why else would people talk about it so much? He didn't have to be as naive as he was.

Coincidentally, the next day he received an interesting piece of mail from Publishers Clearing House. A combination Super Sweepstakes and Special Introductory Offer. It was the offer that interested him: "Your choice of three magazines at just a fraction of their newsstand price."

Morganstern ordered *Moneysworth*, "brash, ingenious ways to make and save money," *Money-Maker*, "expert advice on how to get rich wisely," and *Income Opportunities*, "boost your earnings, build a second income." And just for the hell of it, he filled out the sweepstakes entry.

The magazines came, but somehow he never got around to reading them. Ariel, however, read them cover to cover.

Whenever the subject of money came up, which was all the time at cocktail parties, most of the time at dinner with friends, and some of the time at home in bed with Ariel, he felt ill-at-ease, out of his element. It was a current event that he hadn't kept up on.

In fact, he had the same feeling about money as he had about the war in Vietnam: it was something he hadn't been able to get a handle on, no matter how much he heard about it. Terms like inflation, consumer price index, prime interest rate, long-term investments, fell into the same disquieting category as escalation, exfoliation, embargo, detente, agent orange, and nuclear proliferation.

With money the great American pastime, Morganstern sometimes felt like he was a visitor from outer space.

44

4

By the time Morganstern got home on that cold Wednesday in January, he was in a state. He'd been to Gristede's and discovered he couldn't afford to eat, he'd been to the art store and found he could barely afford to paint, he was as Kept as Elizabeth Taylor had been in *Butterfield 8*.

He went directly to Ariel's desk. Stuffed inside a recent issue of *Vogue* were some of her unopened bills, which she usually took to the office to pay. He tore them open. The Con Ed bill for that month was $88. The phone bill (mostly to her parents in Winnetka) was $111. The Gristede's bill was $275. Her American Express bill listed many lunches, dinners, and theater tickets. But the thing that caught Morganstern's attention was the charge for the crystal candlesticks they had given his parents for their fortieth anniversary. Ariel had insisted on going in with him on the gift. She had picked out the candlesticks and had them sent from Tiffany's. When he had asked her what he owed her she had told him $12.50. Her American Express bill listed one pair of candlesticks, $90.00.

He had never felt angrier in his life. Even the time he broke the art dealer's Lucite coffee table didn't compare with this. The $250 he gave her every month was supposed to cover the Con Ed bill, the phone bill, and the food. It didn't even make a fucking dent. All the things he felt good about paying for, he wasn't paying for at all. His money was just a token contribution, like a kid donating milk money to the War on Poverty. And all those times he had asked if the $250 was enough, she had said, "Oh, yes, it's more than enough."

He was furious at her and furious at himself. He was the one that had let her handle all the bills. He never really pushed to know the exact price of things. He had only himself to blame. Not true. He had his parents to blame. Hadn't they raised him with total disregard for money and the cost of things? If you can't pay your own way, you have no business going. Terrific. How did that apply when you were being taken for a ride and didn't even know it?

And he had her to blame. Whose fault was it that he had been pulled away from a perfectly fine, easygoing, modest-living, self-sufficient existence to this: artist in residence for a closet capitalist? She had lied to him from the very beginning. She had passed herself off as someone who cared about, or rather didn't care about the same things he didn't care about. Why had she let him go on his merry way, dreaming, painting, protected, like some fucking consort?

So here he was: a thirty-five-year-old fool, living in a fool's dream world. A painter who had never sold a painting, a man who had never earned a decent living, a jerk who didn't even know the price of a lousy cup of coffee.

And what was he going to do about it? Make Ariel give up her job? Her life-style? Could he give her up? Fat chance. As angry as he was, he still loved her. He was as hooked on Ariel as she was on smoked oysters. So where the hell was he going to get enough money to be able to afford living with her, or living at all?

By the time Ariel came home that night, he had reached a decision and had even taken action. But he was still angry. When she walked into the kitchen, he turned away from her.

"Well, hello-hello-hello. How-was-your-day? How-was-my-day? Did-I-have-a-good-trip? Did-you-get-a-lot-of-painting-done? Did-I-miss-you? Did-you-miss-me? Kiss-hug. Kiss-hug." Morganstern walked out of the room. She stood in the kitchen shaking her head. She had never seen him like this. She followed him into his studio.

"Okay, what's the trouble?" she asked.

"You lied to me. You've purposely hidden or lied about our expenses all this time. You've treated me like some sort of schnook."

"Oh, that," Ariel said guiltily.

"Yes, that."

"Well, I didn't want you to get upset. Why should you have to worry about what things cost? Money isn't a problem."

"It is a problem. And it's even more of a problem because you tried to cover it up."

"I don't understand. What's wrong with me spending my money on our life? I don't see what's so terrible about that."

"Oh, it's all so simple. You get to be the Great Provider, the Staunch Supporter, the Responsible One. You know what you're doing? You're playing Daddy. And you know what that makes me, for crying out loud? Daddy's Girl. Next thing I know, you'll be negotiating a nose job for me."

"I never looked at it that way," she said softly.

"How could you? You were so immersed in your own home movies. Hellerman's Happy Family starring Ariel Hellerman as Daddy Warbucks and featuring Matthew Morganstern as Little Orphan Annie."

"But what can I do about it? I make a lot of money. Things cost a lot. What would you have me do? Give up my job? Move back to 110th Street?"

"You don't have to do anything. I've already done it. You are looking at the last of Matthew Morganstern, painter, dreamer, and drain on the budget."

"What are you talking about?"

46

"Starting tomorrow, I am a man with a mission, a man with a job."

"A job? What job?"

"A real job. Working in the bull pen at Ivan's agency."

"Oh, no. You can't. What about your painting?"

"I'll do it in my spare time. Ivan's agency is taking me sight unseen and without any references or previous experience. And I, for one, am giving them my all."

So, for the first time in his life, Morganstern put aside his paints and joined the ranks of the steadily employed.

It was almost exciting that first day. He had never ridden the subway during rush hour before. I always thought rush hour meant the trains ran faster, he thought to himself as he waited for his subway. But that's not it at all. It's the people. He was amazed at the mass of suit-and-tied, newspapered, morning-eyed commuters quickly making their way to somewhere specific, undistracted, undaunted, and, God willing, on time.

When the train came, he was swept up, swept in, and wedged against unknown upright bodies. He shared a metal strap with an anonymous and yet now-intimate hand. No one looked at anyone. Morganstern looked at everyone. He felt as if he were inside one of his own paintings.

Morganstern got off at Grand Central Station and walked the few blocks to Ivan's agency on Forty-first and Madison. People marched right along beside him, staying in some predetermined formation until they peeled off at their various office buildings. Responsible soldiers, good citizens, hearty breadwinners, one and all, Morganstern silently chanted. He felt somewhat pleased to be included in this rush of importance, this momentous hour.

He was told by Ivan's secretary to report directly to the bull pen. The bull pen was not a pen at all, but a large room with fifteen individual drawing boards separated by shoulder-high partitions. The bull-pen supervisor was a short, pudgy Puerto Rican man in his mid-fifties, who wore cowboy boots, Western pants, a hand-tooled belt with a turquoise buckle, and a Roy Rogers shirt.

"Hugh must be the new man," he said, extending his hand and giving Morganstern a big smile. "Hiam the foreman, Martine. Hey, fellows, meet the new skatchman." Fourteen heads looked up, smiled, and bent back to their drawing boards. Next to Martine, Morganstern was by far the oldest man in the bull pen. The rest of them looked to be about twenty.

"Hokay-dokay, this here is your drawing board. And this is your bunk mate, Radky. Radky, say howdy to Matthew Morganstern."

"Howdy," Radky said, smiling. "Whydja tell 'em you could

draw?" Radky was carefully lettering a heading onto a piece of acetate.

"What's wrong with drawing?"

"You'll never get promoted to art director. It's like a woman knowing how to type. Once they find out you can draw, you're finished. When I got out of art school, I could draw like a bandit. Now, I just stick to lettering. Lettering's safe."

"Don't art directors draw?"

"No, man, they think. They do what they call conceptualize. Drawin' takes too much time. They got stiffs like you to sketch up their ideas."

"You want to be an art director?" Morganstern asked.

"Everyone wants to be an art director. You know how much they make a year? What agency you work at before?"

"This is my first agency."

"Geez, you're sort of late getting started, aren't you? What'd you do before?"

"I'm a painter," Morganstern said.

"You mean fine arts?" Morganstern nodded. "I took a painting class in commercial-art school. It's fun, man, but it doesn't pay."

"Hi just got a call from one of the art directors," Martine called from across the room. "Hees comin' over to give you an assignment. Hugh got all the art supplies you need?"

"Just these," Morganstern said, indicating half a dozen boxes of multicolored Magic Markers.

"That's all you need, and a couple of pencils," Martine said.

"You won't need your palette for this job." Radky snickered.

A tall, good-looking man dressed in a blue blazer, cavalry twills, and a white silk shirt came into the bull pen. By the way he was dressed Morganstern deduced that he was the art director.

"Ivan says you know how to draw," the art director said, looking at Morganstern straight in the eyes, his head only inches away.

"Yeah, I can draw."

"Good, because I have a client who has to be able to read the board. Okay, this is it," the art director said as he put four or five large sheets of drawing paper on the table. "First of all, what do you know about dandruff?"

"Nothing. I mean, I know it falls out of your hair and gets on your shoulders."

"That's good. This particular board is for a new product call Danderex. It's an antidandruff shampoo and—keep this under your hat—Danderex is an extra-strength formula. That means we're appealing to the really chronic sufferer. I think you can follow my directions without any problem. They're fairly clear. I need this by two P.M."

Morganstern looked at the clock. It was 10:30. He looked at the

48

drawing paper. There were no drawings. Just TV-shaped frames with little descriptions written inside.

Frame 1: Man and woman talking. She notices dandruff on shoulders. Frame 2: Man brushes furiously at shoulder. Frame 3: Close-up of product. (Note: "Package doesn't exist yet. Fake it.") Frame 4: Dissolve from product to ECU of dandruff particles.

"What's ECU?" Morganstern asked Radky.

"Extreme Close-up."

Frame 5: Show special Danderex XAG action working on dandruff flakes.

"What's XAG action?"

"I don't know. Fake it," Radky said.

Frame 6: Flakes break up and disappear. Frame 7: Woman putting flower in man's buttonhole. She touches his shoulder. (Note: "Make sure suit is dark.") Frame 8: Man bows his head to reveal hair part to woman. Woman kisses part. Frame 9: Cut to product and super: "Danderex, the serious new dandruff-fighter shampoo for serious dandruff sufferers."

"I don't know what any of this stuff is supposed to look like. The product, the dandruff, or the people," Morganstern said to Radky.

"Make it up. Be creative," Radky answered. "Don't worry—if there's something wrong with your drawings, he'll tell you." The art director stopped in at lunchtime to see how Morganstern was progressing.

"What are you trying to do to me?" he said. "You've only done three frames. This isn't an unveiling I'm going to, it's a meeting. Martine," the art director whined, "this guy is slow as molasses."

Morganstern worked through lunch. At five to two the art director picked up the boards and left without saying anything. Late that afternoon he came back, pulled up a chair alongside Morganstern's drawing board, and said, "Do you mind a little criticism?"

"Not at all," Morganstern said, "I'm still learning."

"Well, this board you did was too tight."

"Too tight?"

"I can't show a board like that to my client. He takes things literally. He'll think this is exactly the way the commercial will look when it's shot. In fact, he'll want to shoot the storyboard and forget film altogether. It would save him sixty thousand dollars. You've got to make it more cartoony, looser. Take another crack at it . . . and stay loose . . . you know, like this." He grabbed one of Morganstern's Magic Markers and demonstrated with a wild scribble all over the neatly rendered board that Morganstern had done.

Morganstern grabbed the art director's wrist in a tight grip.

"Listen, fellah," he said through gritted teeth, "I was trained to draw so that people could recognize what it was I was drawing. If you want a scribbler, why don't you get yourself a four-year-old?"

"Hey, no offense," the art director said, pulling away. "Get this back to me first thing tomorrow morning. And remember, loose is the key."

Morganstern picked up his pencil and began to furiously sketch out the first panel of the story board.

"Loose is not the key," Radky said, "slow is the key. Your first big mistake was knowing how to draw. Don't make the mistake of doing it too fast. Slow up, man. You ain't getting paid by the piece. The faster you are, the quicker they want it."

"How's it going?" Ariel asked after the first day.

"Oh, I'm having a hard time loosening up. An art director told me my sketches looked too good. I was thinking I might try drawing with my left hand. I might achieve a more primitive feeling that way."

"You didn't really think you were going to be able to express yourself artistically in the bull pen, did you? This is advertising. I knew you'd hate it. You have no business being in that business."

"Don't worry. I can handle it. I just need time to loosen up."

In the beginning, Morganstern made the mistake of asking about the work.

"How did the board go over?"

"What board?"

"You know, the detergent board I did for you. The big rush job. How'd it go?"

"Oh, that. It got killed."

"Everything gets killed," Morganstern complained to Ariel. "I don't understand why they bother showing so many different story-boards if they're just going to end up getting killed."

"It gives them something to talk about at meetings."

"But those damn things take a long time to do. They're a pain in the ass. There's eight to ten frames to each board, and each one has to be hand-drawn and hand-colored."

"You've got to stop thinking of it as artwork. You can't get too attached to what you do. Learn to disassociate yourself from your work."

"That makes everything kind of pointless, doesn't it?"

"Well, I never said advertising made sense."

Morganstern learned not to wince when some art director destroyed one of his boards. He learned not to care when a week's work would get thrown in the garbage. He just kept drawing, slowly but surely. Too slowly for some and too surely for others.

The only thing he enjoyed about his job was the paycheck. It was a wonderful feeling getting paid every two weeks, come rain or shine. His biweekly take-home was $429.35. If he had to work overtime, he got time-and-a-half, and if he had to work on the weekends, he got double time. He had never made so much money, so much steady incoming money, in his life.

On the first payday he went to the nearest bank to open a checking and savings account. Since Ariel had always written all the checks, he had never had any use for his own checking account. He had merely deposited and withdrawn savings as he needed them. He had never even owned a credit card. Metrobank was having a special month-long promotion: "The Metro Goes Swiss." The tellers wore Tyrolean hats, the bank guard sported a pair of leather lederhosen. Muzak piped in Swiss yodeling tunes, and there were signs offering free gifts: five pounds of Swiss chocolates for deposits under $5,000; for deposits over $10,000, a Swiss watch. As part of the Swiss promotion, Metrobank was offering a new type of savings account: "Swiss Savings, your own numbered account, right here in the USA. Minimum Deposit: $20,000."

Opening a checking account proved to be a little more complicated than Morganstern had thought. He studied the various brochures. There was Checking Plus, Checking Now, Privileged Checking, Ready Checking, and Basic Checking. The savings accounts were equally varied.

A pretty redheaded girl dressed as a Swiss maid walked up to him. Hooked over her arm was a milk bucket filled with application forms.

"Are you opening a new account?" she asked him. The tightly laced vest pushed up her breasts so that they spilled over and out of the white peasant blouse.

"Yeah, I'm a little confused. All I want is a regular old checking account and a savings account."

"Oh, that should be simple enough," she said, steering him over to an empty desk. She took an application form out of her bucket and wrote down the information as Morganstern gave it to her.

"How much are you depositing today?" she asked.

"I want to put most of my paycheck into the checking account, with just a little to open the savings." He handed her the check.

"Is this all?" she asked, studying the check. Disappointment clouded her pretty face.

"That's it," Morganstern said.

"Wouldn't you know?" She sighed. "The cute ones never have any money. Where do you work?"

"Bander and Biltmore, advertising."

"Oh, an advertising agency," she said, visibly brightening. "Then you should be making more money in no time. When you get your first raise, you come and ask me about our easy-access C.D.'s. My name's Miranda. See you next payday," she said. She escorted him over to the customer line and left him there.

There was one long line for check cashing, savings deposit, foreign currency, customer service, and tax assistance. People stood in a zigzag formation in between two blue velvet ropes. It was like waiting in line for a ski lift. A digital display panel flashed the number of the next available teller. The system apparently hadn't caught on. People forgot to keep their eyes peeled to the panel. After the number flashed silently several times, the next available teller screamed, "Next!" The first person in line got elbowed and shoved in the direction of the waiting teller by the people behind him.

Before leaving the bank, Morganstern applied for a MasterCard, which he received two days later with a letter welcoming him to "the world's most exclusive club of discerning shoppers." The letter included offers for MasterCard insurance, discounts on MasterCard luggage, MasterCard card-carrying case, a set of MasterCard fine china, and a new member's special credit line of $1500.

After the first month the newness of the job wore off and the everyday nine-to-fiveness stayed. He hated the feeling that someone else owned his time. The worst part was the way his work at the agency affected his painting.

"Christ, will you just look at this," he screamed one night. Ariel ran into his studio.

"What's the matter?"

"I've finally learned to loosen up. I'm painting fucking storyboards now."

Ariel looked at the painting. It was definitely a whole new style for Morganstern. It lacked his usual subtlety. It verged on being cartoony.

Morganstern took a palette knife and thrust it through the canvas.

"What are you doing?"

"They can kill storyboards. I can kill a painting," he said between blows.

"Quit the stupid job. It's not worth it."

"It is to me. I like being able to support myself."

"You're just being righteous," she said.

"I'd rather be righteous than wrongteous. There, I feel better," he said, throwing the mangled canvas in a closet. "We don't have the opportunity for artistic temperament in the bull pen."

"Matthew, if this is going to affect your painting, you have to quit. You can't do both."

"If Pollock could do it, so can I."

"Pollock held down two jobs?"

"Sure, he designed packages for a soap company while he painted."

"He did not."

"Oh, yes. He even won advertising awards. His family destroyed all his commercial work after he died, which is a shame. It was probably the most brilliant detergent packaging ever done."

"How can you joke about a thing like this?"

"I'm not joking. I'm suffering. This job is providing me with the opportunity to suffer, a dimension hitherto absent from my uneventful life. You'll see," he said, smiling down at her, "my art will ultimately benefit." Ariel looked at him skeptically. "Come on, give me a little Mona Lisa," he prodded. Eventually she smiled back.

5

Morganstern was now putting all his energy into household money matters. He was not about to be caught unaware again. He was watching, or trying to watch, every penny Ariel spent. He kept track of what he owed her, whether he was able to pay her then or not.

"How much was the Con Ed bill this month?" he asked one evening.

"Oh, about seventy dollars," Ariel mumbled.

"I don't mean about. I mean how much exactly."

"To the penny?" she asked, annoyed.

"Ariel, I want to know what our expenses are."

"Okay, okay." She glanced through her checkbook. "It was one-eleven-oh-three."

"One hundred and eleven dollars is not anywhere around seventy dollars," he said as he jotted the figure down in a little book he was keeping.

"You really know how to take the fun out of things," she said.

"The fun out of a Con Ed bill?" he asked, looking at her. Now that he was paying more attention to money, he was appalled not only at the price of things but also at Ariel's exorbitant spending habits. One day she had brought home six hand-quilted, hand-appliquéd throw pillows from a little boutique called the Gazebo.

"Do you like them?" she asked, scattering the pillows on the couch.

"They're nice. How much?"

"They were one thousand dollars each."

"You're kidding," he gasped.

"See, I can't even joke about it. You're so uptight about money."

He glanced at the price tag on one of the pillows. "Fifty dollars," he gasped.

"Now, why are you complaining? I just saved nine hundred and fifty dollars. Besides, you wouldn't deny me my little luxuries, would you?" Ariel asked, leaning into him.

"God forbid," he sighed, "a girl's got to have her throw pillows."

Morganstern realized that ultimately he had no say-so over her spending. Because of her greater earning power, she had controlling interest in their little partnership. She could do what she wanted with her money. But that didn't mean he had to like it.

As for Ariel, she hated being audited all the time. She didn't know how to get him off his preoccupation with their living expenses. Finally she arrived at a plan: if he insisted on a penny-by-penny accounting, she would give it to him, but good.

One night after dinner at one of their favorite Italian restaurants Ariel studied the check.

"Let's see, I had the veal piccata and the zabaglione and white wine. You had the chicken parmigiana, the salad, and no wine. Your share comes to eleven-twenty, plus tip, which would be one-seventy, making it twelve-ninety you owe me."

Ariel was doing the figuring on a new gadget she had recently acquired. It was a combination compact and pocket calculator. It allowed you to powder your nose and compound interest all at the same time.

"Why don't we just split it down the middle?" Morganstern said.

"Why should we split it down the middle? Mine's more than yours. It's just as easy to figure it out exactly. And that's the fairest way."

She put her share of the bill on the table. Morganstern handed her thirteen dollars. She took ten cents out of her bag and placed it on the table next to his plate. He had a tremendous desire to slap her hand. Instead he pocketed the dime, got up, and pulled her chair back for her.

"You're making a parody of this whole money thing," he said to her when they got home.

She looked at him innocently. "I thought you wanted to know exactly what your share of everything was."

"There is such a thing as going to ridiculous extremes," he said.

"I suppose there is." She smiled.

But it didn't stop with the Italian dinner. Morganstern set up a whole new system of household bookkeeping, so that each paid proportionately, according to his own share and ability. He still could not afford to cover half of the rent or half of most things that went into their very stylish life-style. With his system, they fractionally apportioned amounts from his check to every major household item. For instance, for the rent, she paid $625, Morganstern paid

$125. His idea was that he should feel like he was contributing something to everything. But by splitting it up in little pieces, his contribution appeared appallingly small. He couldn't stop complaining about the cost of things.

"Do you need all this light?" he asked her one night as she sat reading in the living room.

"Only if I want to see what I'm reading."

"I mention it because the Con Ed bill came today. It was ninety-three dollars."

Ariel didn't respond.

"I read that fluorescent bulbs use up less electricity."

"So do candles."

"Okay, forget it. I was just trying to economize a little."

She would combat his bouts of penny-pinching with acts of almost defiant extravagance.

Morganstern came home from work one night to find a big gift-wrapped box from Bloomingdale's sitting on the couch.

"What's this?" he asked.

"Happy Valentine's Day," Ariel said, giving him a kiss.

"It's not Valentine's Day."

"It's always Valentine's Day, heart of my heart. I saw this and it had your name on it. I just couldn't resist."

Morganstern opened the box. It was a beautiful paisley bathrobe. It didn't have his name on it, but it still carried the price tag. Two hundred dollars.

"Ariel, this is ridiculous."

She slid the robe over his shoulders. "Help. I think I'm going to swoon. You look so fabulous in it," she said, dramatically grabbing on to the doorway for balance.

"You'll have to return it," he said, taking off the bathrobe.

"I can't."

"Don't tell me it was on sale. Not for two hundred dollars!"

She nodded, her eyes twinkling with delight.

Then there was the maid. They discussed it like two adults. "I think we should have a maid. Neither of us has the time to clean the house. We both work hard all day, and who wants to come home to a dirty apartment?" she said.

"The apartment takes a half-hour to clean. I enjoy cleaning. It's relaxing. A maid is an unnecessary expense."

Early one morning the doorbell rang.

"Ariel, there's a woman at the door. She says she's the new maid."

"Don't worry, I'll pay for her," Ariel whispered to him in the bedroom.

55

"That's not the point," he whispered back. "I thought we agreed."

"You agreed. I didn't. Oh, please, Matthew, be nice. Indulge me."

"I don't have to indulge you. You already do a great job indulging yourself. Shit, Ariel, I don't even know how to talk to a maid."

"Leave her to me. We always had maids."

But nobody ever had a maid like Charitee.

Charitee was a recovered alcoholic and a born-again Christian. She was also a very smart businesswoman. She insisted on being paid in cash.

"Ah don't want no records," she explained. "What Ah earns is between me'n the good Lord." What she earned was forty-five dollars plus carfare. Carfare meant taxi fare, which was another ten dollars.

"Ah ain't ridin' no subway with cash money in my pocket," she explained. "It ain't safe."

Had Charitee broadened her horizons and taken up something other than housecleaning, she undoubtedly would have been a very wealthy woman.

"Yore vacuum ain't suckin' up. Y'all needs a new one. My brother sells 'em. I can get y'all a good deal." The good deal was a new Hoover canister which ended up costing them about fifty dollars more than the recommended retail price.

She also provided the cleaning supplies: obscure brands of cleansers, furniture polish, and detergent which turned out to be another little business her brother was in. A can of Home Pride Cleanser sold for $2.50.

Morganstern couldn't argue with the fact that she did a beautiful job on the apartment. He did have a problem with the prayer meetings, however. Neither he nor Ariel could leave for work without Charitee asking them to join hands in prayer.

"Lawd, bless this house and help keep it clean, and bless them that abides herein. Lawd, grant us peace and prosperity in the comin' economic crisis. Keep us safe from the tax people and protect our humble investments, in thy name and in the name of thy son, Jesus Christ. A-men."

Morganstern hadn't talked to Ivan since he started the job. He heard that Ivan was on a "shoot," which he learned early on was not a hunting expedition but the production of a commercial. One day he passed him in the hallway.

"Hi, man, how's it goin'?" Ivan said without breaking his stride.

"Fine, fine," Morganstern said.

"Let's have lunch," Ivan called over his shoulder.

"What time?" Morganstern yelled after him.

This happened several more times before Morganstern realized that "Let's have lunch" was in the same category as "Hi, how's it goin'?" It didn't require an answer and it didn't mean anything. The lunch didn't matter to Morganstern anyway, as he now brought his from home to save money. But he did wonder if Ivan was avoiding him.

After almost three months on the job, Ivan telephoned him. "Let's have lunch," he said.

"Right, let's have lunch," Morganstern agreed, and hung up.

Ivan called him back. "I mean let's have lunch tomorrow, twelve-thirty, Le Madrigal."

Le Madrigal was the fanciest restaurant in the area. Morganstern wore the blue blazer Ariel had given him. Ivan was dressed in jeans and a turtleneck.

"I have a proposition," Ivan said. "It's going to cause a lot of hard feelings in the bull pen, but there are always a lot of hard feelings in the bull pen, so that's no problem."

"What are you talking about?"

"I'm going to move you up to art director. You'll be assigned to the dandruff account. The client really sparked to what you did with the dandruff-fighters board."

"I thought that board got killed."

"It doesn't matter. Everything gets killed. But not everything gets sparked to. You'll be making twenty-five thousand a year to start."

"Ivan, I don't want the job."

"What do you mean, you don't want the job? Do you realize that any guy in the bull pen would give his right thumb for that job? I grant you it's not the most exciting account in the shop, but it's a beginning."

"I'm happy in the bull pen."

"You're happy earning twelve thousand a year?"

"Plus overtime."

"Where's your future? Are you going to be a fucking sketch man all your life?"

"There is too much responsibility involved, too much time. It would take away from my painting."

"But you're putting in the time anyway, why not get paid the money?"

"I appreciate what you're trying to do, Ivan. I'm just not up to an art director's job."

"Why? It doesn't require any special talent, believe me."

"That's just it. As an art director, I wouldn't even get to draw."

"You're saving yourself like some forty-year-old virgin. You think success is just around the corner. There's nothing around the corner. The art world is no different from advertising. You've got to get what you can get while you can get it. At least, in this business, you've got a way up. You know how? On my fucking back, that's your way up. Don't be so quick to say no. Think about it."

Morganstern did think about it. He told Ariel about Ivan's offer. "You know, he does have a point. As long as I'm there, why not get paid for it?"

"Are you crazy? You're an artist! Working in the bull pen is bad enough. But at least that's just a harmless, mindless job. You don't have to use your brain or waste your creativity. But being an art director is a career. It'll just suck you up. You've already got a career. Painting!"

"Some career. I've never even sold a painting, and I probably never will."

"Don't say that. You have to keep at it. I really can't believe you'd even consider an art director's job."

"Okay, okay. It was just a thought. And probably a dumb one at that."

Ariel wasn't done. "You didn't spend years slaving over an easel to become an ace advertising man, did you?"

"All right. All right. Don't get so upset."

But she was angry. The first day he punched in at the agency, he broke a contract in her mind. In taking that mundane job, he had let her down. She, who had so readily abandoned her dream to be a novelist, looked to him to preserve and pursue a loftier sort of life. What she had cherished in Morganstern were the qualities that she herself had given up or perhaps never possessed in the first place: his lack of desire for material things, his disinterest in money and gain, his single-minded pursuit of art for art's sake. These were things she admired and would have preserved at any cost.

They were on their way to meet Marcy and Bill Conrad for dinner. The Conrads worked at the same agency as Ariel. He was an art director and she was a copywriter. Morganstern had never met them before.

They were an attractive couple in their late twenties. Both wore tweed sports jackets, slacks, and silk shirts. Marcy Conrad wore a tie; Bill had an open collar. Their hair was cut in almost identical styles.

"Ariel says you work at Bander and Biltmore," Marcy said.

"That's a hot little shop," Bill interjected. "You're an art director, right?"

"No, I work in the bull pen."

"He's only been there a couple of months and they already offered to promote him to art director," Ariel interjected. Morganstern shot her a look. What the hell was she doing talking about a promotion that she herself had convinced him not to take?

"That's great. What accounts are you going to be working on?"

58

"I'm not taking the job."

"Attaboy," Bill Conrad said, slapping him on the shoulder. "Hold out for as much as you can get. They'll come back with an even better offer."

"Matthew's not really interested in being an art director. His primary interest is painting. He's just doing this temporarily."

"Painting? But hell, you can do that on weekends," Bill said.

"Take us," Marcy put in, "we're tennis freaks. I mean *real* tennis freaks. We devote our entire weekends to nothing but tennis. And at least once a year we manage to get away to a good tennis camp."

"I don't really know of any good painting camps," Morganstern said sourly.

"Well," said Marcy, changing the subject, "we had a really good meeting at the accountant's today. Guess what we're doing? It's so exciting. We're incorporating."

"Are you really?" Ariel said, her face suddenly animated.

"Oh, with our combined incomes, we have to," Bill Conrad said, taking the last sip of his wine spritzer.

"But it works out beautifully," Marcy added. "The free-lance income we make justifies the expense of setting up the corporation. We'll be able to take off part of the apartment as an office, all of the telephone, the cable TV. But the big plus is that we can take off Lindsay as a business deduction." Lindsay was their three-year-old daughter.

"Lindsay, as an employee of the corporation, will get her professionally related education courses written off when she starts private school next year."

"What exactly will your daughter's job in the corporation be?" Morganstern asked.

"She's the treasurer." Marcy giggled. "Isn't that great? Bill's secretary. And I'm the president."

"Do you know how much our tax bill was last year?" Bill Conrad asked between clenched teeth. "Do you have any idea?"

"You two are probably feeling the bite," Marcy said. "Oh, but I forgot, you're not married. That's smart. They really penalize us poor old married folks."

The discussion went on to tax planning, and Morganstern faded out of the conversation completely.

"You didn't like them," Ariel said on the way home.

"How could you tell?"

"Oh, I think the first clue was when you stopped talking fifteen minutes into the evening. The second clue, the real giveaway, was the fact that you spent thirty minutes in the men's room."

"Actually, I thought they were super people. They seem to have the perfect merger there."

"You could've participated a little in the conversation."

"What would you have me talk about—tax incentives or child-labor laws?"

"Well, you could've talked about business. We're all in the same business, after all."

"Sure, I could've asked Bill Conrad what his favorite color Magic Marker was. Or if he sees storyboards going up to fifteen frames in our lifetime. Oh, Ariel, come on. I've got about as much in common with those people as you have with Charitee's vacuum-salesman brother. I take that back. Actually, you probably have a lot in common with him."

"You're a snob. A real snob."

"Who's the snob? Who was trying to pass me off as an up-and-coming art director?"

"I was not, I merely mentioned that you got an offer for a promotion."

"Still, you had to slip it in. Not that I blame you. The Conrads probably wonder what the hell you're doing living with a lowly sketch man."

"I don't want to fight. I'm sorry. I guess they're just not your type of people."

"How can you say that? I don't think I've ever met a nicer pair of corporate executives."

They didn't talk for the rest of the ride home. Nor did they say anything as they got ready for bed.

"'Night," said Ariel, giving Morganstern a peck on the ear.

"'Night. Sleep well."

They lay there taut and rigid. He could feel the tension between the Bill Blass sheets. Then someone made a move.

There was an accidental brushing of foot against foot; one thigh touched another. Somehow Ariel's right breast found its way from her side of the bed to his, and lay trembling underneath Morganstern's hand. And then, as if pulled by magnets, their bodies moved together and they made love. Silent, frantic love.

It happened like this a lot. In the midst of the dickering and bickering, the tension and resentment, the hard looks and mean feelings, there would suddenly be a closeness, a warmth, a burst of the old, familiar happy love. And then they could talk.

It was as if his penis was a switchboard jack; when inserted into the proper outlet, it made the miracle of communication possible. Only after making love could they share their hard feelings, their bitterness and resentment.

"There are times," Ariel said, tears seeping from between the thick fringe of her close-shuttered lashes, "when I feel like I don't love you at all."

"I know," he said, his arms around her, his hand stroking the smooth, long line of her hip. "I feel the same way sometimes."

60

"I get so mad at you," Ariel said, nuzzling her nose into his neck. "But the worst part isn't the anger. It's this horrible feeling of cold dislike. It scares me."

"Sometimes I could kill you. And sometimes I feel like I don't even care enough to bother," he said, kissing the outer edge of her ear.

"Tonight I felt like I didn't know you and I didn't want to know you."

"Oh, yeah, I know." Morganstern sighed.

And having told each other in the most intimate, open terms how much they hated each other, they would fall in love all over again.

6

About a week after Ivan's job offer, Morganstern received another offer, probably the most exciting of his lifetime. A letter from a Sidney Shallot, owner of the Great Works Gallery, invited him to present his work for a month-long one-man show. Morganstern had never heard of the gallery before, but that didn't mean anything. There were thousands of galleries he had never heard of. One thing he was certain about: a one-man show could be a golden opportunity for him, a way to get his work seen, his name established, and maybe even some of his paintings sold.

He called Shallot and made an appointment to see him after work. The Great Works Gallery was located on the top floor of an abandoned knitting factory on West Broadway in lower Manhattan. The fact that the street contained nothing but old warehouses and plumbing-fixture companies didn't concern Morganstern. Everyone knew that these ugly, industrial, litter-strewn streets were New York's answer to the Left Bank.

Morganstern walked through to the rear of the gallery, where a closed door was marked "Office." He knocked lightly.

"Enter here, the timeless fellowship of the human spirit," a voice called out. Morganstern opened the door. Sidney Shallot sat behind a desk flipping through a recent issue of *Art in America*. He looked up and smiled. "You are the picture. I am the frame./ I am the gallery. You are the name," he recited. He was a small man in his early sixties, dressed in a beautiful pair of Chinese silk pajamas and a black beret. He sported a Salvador Dali-style mustache. Clenched between his teeth was a long ebony cigarette holder which held an even longer dark brown cigarette. He held the cigarette holder at such an angle that he seemed in danger of setting fire to an eyebrow.

"Matthew Morganstern," he said, getting up and extending his small hand. "I am a great admirer of your work."

"That brings me to my first question," Morganstern said, shaking Shallot's hand. "I wondered how it was you knew about me."

"Didn't you exhibit at the Village Art Show?"

"Sure, me and about six thousand others. Besides, that was over three years ago and it was just one painting."

"It was one painting that did not go unnoticed. Sit down," he said, pointing to a white silk couch. His cigarette dropped out of the holder, rolled across the desk, and fell onto the floor. Morganstern bent down, picked it up, and handed it back to Shallot, who took it and reinserted it into his cigarette holder.

"You ask me how I know of you, let me ask you what you know of me. And don't be afraid. I can take flattery as well as the next man."

"Actually, I don't know anything about you. I've never been to your gallery until tonight."

"Spoken like a true artist. It takes a thousand fools to come up with a lie . . . it takes but one artist to truly paint a sky," Shallot intoned. He waited for Morganstern to react.

"Yours?" Morganstern finally asked.

Shallot nodded, pleased. "They come to me unbidden and always in perfect rhyme. I never have to change a syllable. Now, then, to explain myself. What I am trying to do with my gallery is to intersperse shows between known and unknown artists so that artists who have yet to be discovered have an opportunity for some exposure and a chance to develop a following."

"Well, I certainly qualify in the unknown category," Morganstern said.

"Good, then let's get down to business." He took an appointment book from the top drawer of his desk and scrutinized it for several minutes. "Your show will have to be the next one. After next month my calendar is booked up through to the end of the year. Can you be ready in four weeks?"

"I guess so. Sure. I have the paintings."

"Fine. All that remains is the expenses."

"The expenses?"

"For the show. It's going to run you about three thousand dollars."

"You mean I have to pay you three thousand dollars to have a show here?"

"Apparently you are not familiar with the business of launching oneself into the world of art. The money goes for invitations, the

62

mailing list, the hanging fee, the refreshments, and so on. It's all itemized. All perfectly standard, I assure you."

"That's a hell of a lot of money."

"*Au contraire.* Three thousand dollars is not a lot of money. The sale of two or three paintings will more than cover the cost of the show."

"Let's just say I do happen to be lucky enough to sell some, how do you know how much my work will go for?"

"Rule of thumb, dear Morganstern." He took a little index card out of his pocket and read from it. "A two-by-three canvas, five hundred dollars. A three-by-five, seven-fifty. Five-by-seven, fifteen-hundred. Seven-by-ten, twenty-five hundred. And if you have anything over ten feet, we can charge a great deal more."

"But I'm not even a known name."

"That's exactly why we're having the one-man show, to get you known."

"Well, I'm going to have to think about it and let you know."

"Fine. Fine. But decide within the next few days. It is one thing for a car to search for a parking place . . . but quite another for an artist to be without a space."

Morganstern called his friend Zero to check up on the gallery and Shallot. Zero was one of the few artists he had kept in touch with from his art-school days. And since he had known him, Zero had run the gamut as far as artistic expression went. From impressionism to surrealism to superrealism to primitive "just following the market trends wherever they take me," as he explained. The last time Morganstern had talked to him, he was into performance art. His show at the O.K. Gallery, "Man with Toenails, Hair, and Newspaper Clippings Under Grow Light" (in which he sat in a chair underneath a grow light with a pile of toenail and hair clippings at his feet while he read aloud old news items from the New York *Times*), closed after one week, to no reviews.

Morganstern told him about Shallot's proposition. "The gallery is perfectly legit," Zero assured him. "You always have to pay for your own show when you're an unknown. But, personally, I think it's a waste of time."

"Why do you say that?"

"You should be thinking on a much bigger scale. Otherwise, you're never going to make any money in this racket. You figure it out: a three-by-five painting sells for seven-fifty. That means you're making about fifty dollars per square foot."

"Without wanting to offend your sensibilities by appearing crass and commercial, that sounds like a hell of a lot of money to this poor artist," Morganstern said.

"Oh, no, man, that's nothing. That's peanuts. You know what

I'm into now? Environmental art. I mean, we're talking square miles here, not square feet. If Christo could do it, why can't I?"

"Christo happens to be a genius. Besides, he financed most of his projects himself."

"And you call that genius?" Zero scoffed. "I've got a project that makes Christo's stuff look puny. Listen to this: 'Trashing Yosemite National Park.' The proposed budget is five million dollars. My only overhead is six hundred thousand rolls of toilet paper, which I can get at cost. Then I hire a few drones to wrap it around four hundred square miles of trees. What's left over, plus the money for the reprints of the sketches and the photographs, goes right into my pocket."

"That's a disgusting idea, Zero."

"I know. Think of the press coverage I'll get. Your one-man show is safe, it's traditional, but it's strictly small potatoes."

"Coming from you, I consider that an excellent recommendation for doing it."

That left Morganstern with the problem of the money. He didn't have $3,000. Since starting his bull-pen job he hadn't been able to save a penny. He asked at the agency about getting an advance on his salary, but they looked at him as though he were mad.

Ariel was thrilled about the one-man show. "Oh, Matthew, this is your big chance."

"I don't know how big a chance it is. The problem is, the show costs a lot of money."

"I thought they paid *you.*"

"No, they take a percentage of the paintings I sell. But I have to cover the initial expenses."

"How much is it going to cost?"

"Three thousand dollars. I'm going to hold off on doing it for now. I'm sure I can get Shallot to schedule something for next year."

"Don't wait. Do it now. I'll give you the money."

"I don't want you to give me the money," he snapped.

Ariel put her arms around him. "It's just a loan. You can pay me back out of the sales. Come on, sweetheart. This is a chance in a lifetime. Are you going to be silly about a few thousand dollars?"

"It's not silly. I've been dependent on you and your income long enough. If I'm going to do this, I want to do it myself."

"God, you are stubborn. You're going to wait a whole year until you can scrape together enough money? That's the most self-defeating thing I've ever heard."

They argued about it for hours, and then Morganstern finally agreed to the loan. He wanted this show more than anything else in the world. He had to set aside his pride on this one.

He also let Ariel talk him into getting some of his work framed.

"You have to give people at least some indication of how your work looks framed. It's one of the principles of good packaging."

The framing bill came to $2,700. Morganstern tried not to worry about the money. If everything Shallot said was true, all he had to do was sell ten paintings and he was way ahead of the game.

He picked up the mailing list and the printed invitations and gave Shallot a check. The list included everyone who was anyone in the world of art. He and Ariel worked every night for a week addressing the invitations.

"Look at this," Morganstern said, pointing to a name on the list. "Mrs. Grace Chase. I've read about her. She's the biggest collector of modern art in the country. Do you think she'll actually come?"

"Of course she'll come. Who would want to miss Matthew Morganstern's first one-man show?" Ariel assured him. "I just love the fact that all these people have to come to us now."

"Ariel, honey, they don't have to come."

"They better come," she said, narrowing her eyes. "If they don't, we will simply refuse to sell them any of your work."

"Whew! You really drive a hard bargain."

"Well, I've waited for this for a long time," she said. "They'll have to get down on their knees to buy one of your paintings."

Not since the days when they had sneaked into Broadway shows together had they functioned so much as a team.

"This is like addressing wedding invitations," he said, reaching for another envelope.

Ariel looked up and studied him for a long time. "Well, as long as we're on the subject, I'd love to get your views," she said.

"My views on what?" he asked, still writing.

"On wedding invitations, weddings, marriage, connubial bliss, the state of matrimony. Do you realize it's something we've never discussed?"

"We haven't?"

"You know damn well we haven't." She laughed.

He put down his pen. "Well, to tell you the truth, I've always thought of marriage as something other people did."

"Other people?"

"You know, settled types. Planned parents. People with china patterns and cemetery plots all picked out."

"Are you trying to tell me that you don't have your cemetery plot picked out?" Ariel's eyes widened in mock astonishment.

"Ever since I was a kid I've always had this embroidered image in my mind about marriage: 'Dad at the office, Mom at home, Kids in the tree house, Dog's got a bone.'"

"I hate to tell you, but there are a lot of married people who cannot plan beyond their next cemetery plots, let alone think of tree houses," Ariel said.

Morganstern grinned.

"For a highly creative person you have a very unimaginative view of the whole institution."

"Maybe so. I just think that it's the kind of thing that happens when the time is right."

"I'm the last person to push this conversation beyond its comfortable limits, but what exactly constitutes the right time in your mind?"

Morganstern shrugged his shoulders.

"Does it have anything to do with Dad making more money than Mom?"

"I didn't say that."

"You don't have to. Anybody who holds to embroidered images of marriage lays himself wide open to simple-minded interpretations."

"Okay, so I'm old-fashioned."

"And ultraconservative. And chauvinistic. And scared."

"That's the real me," he said. "The me you love."

She smiled and went back to addressing invitations.

She was right, Morganstern thought. It was a question of money. In the beginning, they had been too poor, and then suddenly Ariel was making too much money to fit in with his paradigm of the perfect marriage. He realized he had been waiting for something to happen. He needed to catch up with her, and this show could be his big chance. Marriage, a subject he had previously avoided, now became a very real possibility in Morganstern's mind. It's so real I'm afraid to talk about it, he thought.

The opening was scheduled for a Monday night. The Sunday before, Morganstern borrowed Zero's van and he and Ariel worked around the clock getting the paintings hung. They shifted the pictures around the gallery like two people who loved moving furniture.

"These two paintings look fabulous hanging next to each other. Maybe you should sell them as a pair," Ariel said.

"I'll be happy to sell them one at a time."

"You know, Matthew," Ariel said, standing back and scrutinizing one wall, "I think everything's way underpriced. Let's raise the prices."

"Let's not get greedy," he said, putting his arm around her.

"You don't understand. People are going to grab these up and then they'll be gone and we'll never see them again."

"If worse comes to worst, I'll just have to whip up a few more," he said.

She brought her face up toward his. "Kiss me, you mad, about-to-be-famous artist."

66

He leaned down and gave her a long soft kiss.

"Ah, love does come when least we know/ Surprising us in midtown and even SoHo."

Shallot stood at the entrance to the gallery, smiling fondly at Morganstern and Ariel. He looked around at the paintings, flourished his hand, and took a deep bow. "Morganstern, the master." His cigarette fell out of the holder and onto his foot. *"Merde,"* he said, stamping it out on the floor.

Before they left, Morganstern took one last look around. The gallery had enough space to accommodate his entire body of work. The idea of exhibiting all his paintings at one time in one place was both exciting and frightening to him. He saw his work as if for the first time, and he knew as he had never known before that he was good, he was damn good.

Morganstern left the agency early the day of the show, went home, showered, and changed into his blue blazer. Ariel arrived at the apartment just as Zero buzzed them from downstairs.

It was raining heavily. "I hope this weather doesn't keep people away," Morganstern worried. "Maybe we should have left earlier. This traffic is murder."

"Take it easy, man. We'll get there," Zero said. He was dressed in his opening-night finery: a multilayered, multicolored parachute top over tight, bright pink leather pants. His high-heeled leather boots matched the pants perfectly. He wore his shoulder-length hair in a tight sideways ponytail. In his left nostril was a brass nail.

"Doesn't that hurt?" Morganstern asked, pointing to Zero's nose.

"Beauty always hurts," Zero assured him.

Ariel looked painlessly beautiful in a melon-colored ankle-length silk dress. Morganstern wiped his hands dry on his gray flannel slacks. He was incredibly nervous.

A fire chief's car blocked the entrance to the street and they had to park a few blocks away. As they hurried through the rain, they passed two fire trucks. The whirling red lights cast an eerie, carnaval-like atmosphere onto the hulking gray buildings.

Halfway down the block they came to a cordoned-off area. Morganstern stepped out from underneath his umbrella and looked up. There was a fire. It was in the same building as the Great Works Gallery. Flames were shooting out of the windows.

"What's happening?" Ariel asked one of the firemen.

"A fire," he said, leering at her.

"I can see that. But what happened?"

"Some asshole that runs the gallery up there left a cigarette burning. Apparently there were a lot of paintings, and the whole place went up like a match."

67

"There can't be a fire. I'm supposed to have my opening up there," Morganstern said to the fireman.

"Oh, there'll be an opening, all right," the fireman said. "We'll have to gut the whole top floor."

Ariel screamed and covered her eyes with her hands.

Zero was walking around in circles, wringing his hands. "Oh, Jesus, man. Oh, Jesus, Jesus, Jesus. Oh, Christ, what a fucking, fucking waste," he moaned.

"Are you Matthew Morganstern?" Morganstern glanced down at a small woman dressed in a huge chinchilla coat. She had copper-colored hair and her lips were smeared in a thick magenta lipstick. A uniformed chauffeur stood at her side holding a big striped golf umbrella over her.

Morganstern nodded his head. He was unable to speak.

"I'm Grace Chase," the woman said. "Mr. Shallot tells me that was your work up there," she said, pointing to the blazing top floor. "I must say, it's the most exciting thing I've seen since Kolinski's Mud Slide at the Graham Gallery. In fact, I really don't know of anyone who's working in this particular medium."

Morganstern stared at the old woman a long time before speaking. "The fire isn't my show," he whispered.

"It's not?"

"No, it's just a fire. I had paintings up there." He spoke slowly. Each word had to be forced out.

"Oh. Oh. I'm so sorry," she said, patting him softly on the sleeve. "Well, you know, some of the great art of this century has been accidental. I would certainly give some serious thought to picking up on this if I were you." Morganstern turned his back on the old woman.

"Do give me a call when you schedule your next show," Mrs. Chase said as her chauffeur escorted her away.

"Fire art!" Zero exclaimed. "I don't believe it! She must be crazy."

Ariel was sobbing. Morganstern stood silently, his mouth slightly ajar. He was unable to tear his eyes away from the smoking, blazing building. The rain poured down onto his face as he watched his life's work going up in flames.

He refused to talk about the fire either that night or in the days that followed. Whenever Ariel tried to bring up the subject, he walked out of the room. Finally one night in bed she said to him, "Matthew, you have to talk about it. You can't just keep it all bottled up inside you."

He turned away from her. "I don't have to talk about it. You have to talk about it. I'm sure you think you've thought up the right things to say to make it all better. But there's nothing to say. So save your breath and spare me the words."

She began to cry. Morganstern grabbed his pillow and went into the living room. He spent the night on the couch. Since the night of the fire, Ariel had cried easily and often. But Morganstern was without tears. He was consumed by an anger so intense he felt he could easily kill someone. Who? he wondered. Shallot was certainly a prime candidate. But Ariel was a much better target. She was so incessantly solicitous and sympathetic, and she was so conveniently there.

"How was your day?" Ariel asked him one evening.

"Fine, terrific," Morganstern said. He was watching TV. He had never watched TV. "My storyboards are getting better and better. I think they are beginning to really reflect the inner me."

"Stop it!" Ariel shouted. "Stop talking like that. You lost your whole life's work and you walk around as if nothing had happened. Why are you so afraid to show your feelings?"

"These *are* my feelings," he said, getting up to switch channels.

The next night she brought home a fine sable brush and served it to him in a tall glass as he sat in front of the TV.

"Nice," he said. "What's it for?"

"The man at the art store assured me it works beautifully as a paintbrush." She sat down next to him on the couch. "Oh, Matthew, when are you going to start working again?"

"In case you haven't noticed," he said, his lips turned up in a thin cold smile, "I am working. Every day. Nine to five."

"I'm talking about painting."

"Painting? Nobody paints anymore. You should have gotten me a set of Magic Markers. Painters are out, art directors are in, according to recent market trends."

"You may have lost all your paintings, but you didn't lose your talent," Ariel said angrily. "It'll just take time."

Morganstern sprang from the couch. "Time? I don't have any time!" he exploded. "I have to be at work in the morning. I've got commercials to sketch. I don't have the time to waste on anything as frivolous and flammable as painting."

"Quit the job. Why are you so worried about a stupid job? You don't have to work," she screamed.

"You're right. I can stay home and have my sweetheart support me in the grand style to which I have become accustomed. I can live in our seven-fifty-a-month apartment and have our fifty-dollar-a-day maid come in and dust around me and gorge myself on our hand-delivered groceries. Shit. I could even get into enjoying these fucking fifteen-hundred-dollar drapes," he said, yanking at the drapes so hard that one entire section came unhooked.

"You could stay home and paint," Ariel said evenly.

"Or I could stay home and not paint. I'm becoming very adept at that. And why should I bother painting? Don't I already have everything any reasonable artist would ever want, without even having to lift a paintbrush?"

"It's not my fault there was a fire," she said between her teeth.

"That's true," he said, smiling, "but if it hadn't been for your unending generosity, I would have had to wait a year to have my one-man show and I might have missed the whole glorious spectacle."

"I don't believe it. You really are blaming me," she said, her eyes widening. "You're just upset. You can't really mean it."

"First you bug me because I'm not expressing my feelings, and then when I do, you tell me I'm not getting them right. Will you just get off my back?" He walked over to the closet and yanked his coat off a hanger.

"Where are you going?"

"I don't know. I just have to get out of here."

Morganstern walked downtown. He longed for the cold comfort of a dark, dingy hotel room. Being with Ariel in the apartment had made suffering and mourning all but impossible. On Thirty-third and Eighth Avenue he tried to check into the Hotel Columbus, only to discover that he had left his billfold at home. He went through his pockets. He didn't even have a subway token. It had started to rain.

He arrived home miserable and soaking wet. On the coffee table was a note from Ariel.

Dear Matthew,
I know you need some time to yourself. And at this point, so do I. I'll give you a call in a few days.

It wasn't signed "Love." It wasn't even signed. And she had neglected to mention where she had gone.

He was furious. Why couldn't she stay and fight it out like a man? he thought. She had probably booked a fucking hundred-dollar-a-night room at the Plaza. He found his billfold. There was six dollars in it. He couldn't even afford to take a taxi ride anywhere. How ironic it was that he, without a penny to his name, was trapped in this $750-a-month, wall-to-wall-carpeted, cleaned, and catered existence. While she was free to play the part of the homeless waif.

He picked the drapes up off the floor, started to rehang them, thought better of it, and kicked them under the couch. He called the Plaza. They had no one by the name of Ariel Hellerman registered. Where the fuck was she? Did she expect him to call every hotel in the city to find her? He realized that the next day was

Saturday. She wouldn't be at the office. He had no way of reaching her.

He was still angry, but the anger was no good without Ariel. It began to lose its edge. Part of him felt that she was to blame for the fire, for the loss of his paintings, for the fact that he was holding down a job he couldn't stand. But another part of him recognized that as irrational, unreasonable, and irresponsible. Morganstern was forced to spend the whole weekend listening to these two parts battle it out.

7

By Monday morning he was still mourning the loss of his paintings, but now added to that agony was the fear that he had done irreparable damage to his relationship with Ariel.

Why did he have to push her away like that? What was he punishing her for? The fire had been an accident. But he had been a mean, miserable son of a bitch on purpose. Before he left the apartment he rehung the drapes.

He faced work for the first time that day not as something to do between brush strokes, but as the only thing he had going for him. He wondered if he would ever pick up a paintbrush again. Could he ever get Ariel to forgive him? Could things ever be worse than they were right now?

And then, during the short subway ride to work, something happened to him. Pictures flashed through his head, ideas for a painting, for a whole new series of paintings, came to him for the first time since taking the job.

By the time he got to the agency he was filled with a sense of manic purpose. It was going to take a long time to create enough work for another one-man show, but he could do it. He knew he could. In the meantime, he needed to make more money. He needed to be able to pay Ariel back for the money she lost on the show, he needed it for himself, for the life they had to live together. He decided to tell Ivan he would take the art director's job. Ivan was right. As long as he was putting in the time, why not get paid for it?

Hell, if he could survive the loss of his work in a fire, he could damn well do anything. Hold down a tough job during the day and paint at night. He felt strong and confident and full of determination. He made an appointment to see Ivan at noon.

"I've been wanting to tell you for weeks how sorry I was about the fire. I couldn't fucking believe it. Are you okay?" Ivan asked, laying his arm across Morganstern's shoulders.

Morganstern moved out of his reach. "I don't want to talk about that, Ivan. I'm here about the art director's job."

"What art director's job?"

"The one you offered me, remember?"

"You told me you weren't interested."

"I changed my mind. I want it. I need the money."

"The money! You lost your entire life's work, and you're talking about money! Jesus, man, where is your fucking head?"

"My fucking head is into making a fucking decent living," Morganstern said, pacing back and forth.

Ivan sat down behind his desk and put his head in his hands. "It's all my fault. Well, I got you into this, and I'm going to get you out."

Morganstern stopped and turned to face him. "What the hell are you talking about?"

"I am not going to let you fall into the same trap as the rest of us hacks. No, sir. I'm going to do right by you if it kills me."

"Ivan, you're not making sense and it's driving me crazy. Is the art director's spot still available or not?"

Ivan took a deep breath. "Not for you, buddy boy. You're fired."

"I'm what?" Morganstern leaned across the desk. "I know you're kidding me. Because if I thought for one minute you were serious, I don't think I could control myself."

"Don't you see? I owe it to you. I owe it to your art. The easiest thing in the world would be for me to give you that art director's spot, to let you go on working here. But I'm tired of taking the easy way out. Your check will be ready by two. And don't expect severance pay. It's against agency policy. Which is good, because severance pay is just another trap."

"I just lost control," Morganstern shouted as he slammed his fist down hard on Ivan's desk. "You can't do this to me! If the art director's job isn't open, I'll stay in the bull pen."

"Do you understand obligation? Do you even remotely fathom the word 'friendship'? Do you know how hard this is for me? You're fired. Now, go home and paint."

"You bastard. How do you expect me to live?"

"Live off Ariel, for Chrissakes, that's what she's there for. I'll tell you what else I'm going to do. I've never done it before, but I'm going to give you a bad reference just in case you're tempted to try to get a job at some other agency."

Morganstern moved around the desk toward Ivan. "And I'll tell you what I'm going to do that I've never done before: I'm going to break your fucking head apart."

"Be careful of your hands, you fool," Ivan said, ducking away from Morganstern's fist and shoving his desk chair between them.

Morganstern glanced wildly about the office for something to throw. His eyes hit upon an advertising award, a bronze statuette. He picked it up and threw it against the plate-glass window. It bounced off. He picked it up again, and holding one end, he smashed it repeatedly against the glass until a fine cobweb pattern appeared on the window.

"As one friend to another," he yelled between blows, "I think you'll understand the significance of what I'm doing here."

"I understand. I understand," Ivan said from behind the desk chair. "It's good. It's good. Get it all out. Go on. You're the artist. You have a right."

Morganstern turned and flung the statuette in the direction of Ivan's voice.

Ivan stood up, pale and shaking. "Someday you'll thank me for this," he said.

Morganstern slammed Ivan's door so hard he heard it crack. He thought a minute, then went back and slammed it again. This time it actually splintered.

At two sharp he picked up his last paycheck, took it immediately to his bank, and cashed it. He was afraid if he didn't, Ivan, out of the goodness of his heart, would find a way to stop payment.

He had planned to call Ariel with the news that he had a brand-new high-paying position and had already started work on a new set of paintings. But now talking to her was out of the question. He was not only a painter without paintings, he was a man without a job.

As he unlocked the apartment door, he heard noises coming from inside. Ariel was home, he thought. But it wasn't Ariel, it was the maid. He had forgotten that it was her day. Now was no time for a maid. Particularly not for Charitee.

Charitee was responding aloud to a religious program on the radio as she scrubbed the kitchen floor.

"What you doin' home this time a day?" she asked him suspiciously.

"I lost my job. I'm afraid I'm going to have to let you go," he said. He didn't know if he was firing her out of practicality, or because he got fired, or just for the sheer fun of it. It had been something he had been dying to do for months. And he got tremendous pleasure out of it.

"I 'spect to get paid for my day's work," she said. She was taking it in stride. Apparently she had been fired before. "And I 'spect my two weeks' severance pay."

"Severance pay?"

"All God-fearin' folks gives severance pay. It's in the Bible. When Isaac tole Rachel: 'I cast you away from me, go forth onto the desert and reap what thee shall find, but go ye not without a fortnight of bread and grain and the fruit of the grape.' A fortnight is two weeks. That's where severance pay comes from in case you didn't know."

Morganstern was not about to dish out two weeks' pay that he could ill afford. "I'm sorry. We don't mix religion and remuneration. It's against our policy."

"Whose policy?" Charitee asked.

"Mine and God's. And God wants you to go now," he said in a thunderous voice.

He spent the rest of the day frantically phoning old painting clients trying to drum up some business. One of the people he called was a big-time television executive whose ten-room apartment he had painted almost four years before.

"I was wondering if you'd be interested in a paint job?" Morganstern asked.

"Well, yes, as a matter of fact, I just might be. How much does it pay?"

There was a long silence. Finally Morganstern said, "I don't think you understand. I'm talking about me painting your apartment."

"Oh, I thought maybe you had some extra work. No, I'm not in the market to have my apartment painted right now. I don't think my unemployment check would cover that."

Unemployment. He hadn't even thought of that. "How do you collect unemployment?" he asked the television executive.

"By being unemployed," the man answered. "Call the New York State Division of Labor. They'll give you all the information. And don't mention my name."

Morganstern called immediately. They gave him the address of his nearest unemployment office. It was too late to go that day, but he felt better. At least this was something to fall back on until he lined up some regular work.

He forgot all about his new paintings. All he could think about was where his next paycheck was coming from.

The phone rang. It was Ariel.

"Where have you been?" he asked.

"I've been staying at the Conrads'."

"The Conrads'?"

"Marcy and Bill."

"Oh, yes, the corporation. When are you coming home?"

"That's just it," she said. "I think what we could use right now is a little trial separation."

"How can we have a trial separation? We aren't even married."

74

"Will you please stop with your marriage-manual rules."

A separation without the benefit of marriage is like walking a high wire without the benefit of a net, thought Morganstern. "A separation happens to be a legal term that most married people take very seriously," he said. He was trying to stay calm.

"I take it seriously too. I think we need it."

"Are you trying to say you think our relationship will be better for it?"

"It can't get worse. We simply are not communicating. Not in the way we should. The fact that there was nothing I could do or say about the fire that could reach you, that really hit me."

"I'm sorry. I was a prick."

"Sorry has nothing to do with it. I just think it's a very big problem. The whole thing should have brought us closer together, and it didn't. It did just the opposite."

"If you don't mind, Ariel, I'd rather not have to go through fires just to prove our closeness."

"Speaking of fires—"

"And I'd just as soon not speak of them."

"Speaking of fires, I called Shallot to find out about his insurance. He wasn't covered."

"Great, what good news. Well, maybe you can take it off as a tax deduction."

"I'm not worried about my money, you asshole. I was hoping your paintings might be covered."

"Well, it's pretty hard to place a value on the work of an artist who's never sold a fucking painting in his life."

"You're having a great time feeling sorry for yourself, aren't you?"

"As a matter of fact, yes."

"Well, all the more reason why we should spend some time apart. I wouldn't want to spoil your fun."

"Fine. I'll have my stuff out of here in an hour."

"You don't have to leave the apartment. The Conrads are going to Europe for a month. They've asked me to apartment-sit while they're gone."

"Are they taking their little treasurer with them?"

"You know, another problem we have in the communication category is we don't know how to fight."

"I thought we were doing one hell of a good job."

"No, we don't know how to fight, and that's why you don't know how to apologize."

"I'm sorry," he shouted. "I'm sorry the Conrads are only going for a month."

Ariel hung up. Two minutes later the phone rang. "The rent is due, and you'll have to pay Charitee. I'll put a check in the mail."

Morganstern gritted his teeth. Until he lined up some work or collected on his unemployment, he needed her money and he hated her for it.

"You don't have to worry about Charitee. I fired her."

"You did what? How could you do that without consulting me?"

"We prayed to God for guidance and decided it was the best thing."

Ariel hung up again.

Why couldn't he talk to her? Why hadn't he apologized and begged her to come home? Why couldn't he tell her that he had lost his job and was frightened and lonely and needed her desperately? He answered his own question. It was because he was suddenly so totally dependent on her that he couldn't tell her.

But she shouldn't have left, he thought. By leaving, she had stepped out of the fray and changed the whole format. He only hoped it wasn't forever.

He tried to sketch out some ideas for a painting. But he couldn't concentrate. He was filled with a sense of urgency, of limited time. He knew he had to face the problem of a livelihood in the morning, of how to keep a very expensive roof over his head, how to get Ariel back. Painting would just have to wait. So would sleep. Morganstern paced the apartment for most of the night.

Morning came. Morning without Ariel and without the security of a job. He felt utterly lost, without a sense of direction. He spent almost thirty minutes literally walking around in circles. What should he do? Where should he go? Then he remembered the unemployment office.

He reached the office just as it opened at eight A.M. There were about seventy-five people already standing outside.

There was a large sign over one wall which read "Information About Claims." Underneath the sign were cards which divided up the alphabet A to L and M to Z. Morganstern got in the M-to-Z line.

In the adjacent line stood a man in his early forties, spiffily dressed in a three-piece pinstriped suit and carrying a handsome leather portfolio under his arm. He was reading *The Wall Street Journal*. He smiled at Morganstern. "Saxon Oil is down eight points," he said. "I told them it would go into a slump, but of course nobody listened to me. I hope they're happy now. Do you follow the market?"

"No, not really."

"Let me give you a piece of advice, *gratis*. Stay away, stay clear away from the oil exploratives. You don't have to quote me on that, just stay away from them. Stick with high-tech, you're safe there for now."

76

The line was not moving at all. The man in the pinstriped suit kept checking his watch. "Have you been here before?"

"No," Morganstern said, "this is my first time."

"I was just wondering if you knew how long it takes before you start collecting."

"No, I'm sorry, I don't," Morganstern said.

"You don't have any idea how much one gets a week?"

"Nope."

"Well, I for one think the whole thing is degrading." Morganstern didn't say anything. "Why don't they just mail us the checks so we don't have to go through all this?"

Morganstern shrugged his shoulders. The man whipped through the pages of his paper one more time, folded it up, and shoved it in his portfolio. He looked at his watch again.

"How much longer is this going to take?" he yelled up to the woman who was handling the A-to-L line. She looked up briefly and then went back to talking to the person at the head of the line.

"Petty bureaucrats," the man said to Morganstern. "Petty bureaucrats!" he then bellowed to the woman. "I'm not going through this. I refuse to give them the satisfaction! Come on," he said to Morganstern, "let's get out of here."

"That's okay," Morganstern said, "I'll wait my turn."

The man walked out.

It took Morganstern another forty-five minutes to reach the head of the line.

"What was the name of your former employer?" the woman asked without looking up.

"Bander and Biltmore," Morganstern said, giving her the address as well.

"And how long were you employed there?"

"About three months."

"No approximations. Give me the exact date of employment and of termination."

Morganstern thought a minute and then gave her the dates.

"And prior to that?"

"Well, before that I just sort of picked up odd painting jobs."

"Sorry, you don't qualify for unemployment. Come back when you've worked twenty weeks."

"What?" Morganstern said.

"You have to have been employed for twenty weeks in the past year in order to collect. Your employer should have explained that to you. Maybe they'll give you another month."

"Are you telling me to go back to the agency and work another month, so that they can fire me, so I can qualify for unemployment?" he said angrily.

77

"It's worth a try. Next, please."

He felt almost relieved. The man he had spoken to in line was right. It was degrading. He didn't like the idea of being supported by the state. He certainly didn't relish coming to this dull, dirty-green office once a week. He could manage on his own. It wasn't as if he didn't have a penny to his name. He still had $240 in his pocket left over from his paycheck. And he'd get more.

Morganstern paused for a moment outside the unemployment office, trying to decide whether to take the bus, the subway, or to walk. He felt something sharp stick him in the ribs. He looked down. It was a very elegant silver letter opener held by a well-manicured hand. He glanced up. The man in the three-piece pinstriped suit put his other arm around Morganstern's shoulders. They stood close together as if they were two old classmates.

"Your money or your negotiables," the man said under his breath.

"You're kidding," Morganstern said.

"Do I even remotely resemble a man who is playing a prank?" he said, giving a sharp jab with the letter opener.

"I don't have any negotiables," Morganstern said.

"Then your money will have to do."

"I don't have all that much."

"I may be desperate, but I'm not proud. Hand it over."

Morganstern reached for his billfold.

"Fold the money in half and place it in my right breast pocket," the man said. Morganstern did as he was told. The man gave him one last jab in the ribs. Morganstern winced.

"Don't forget what I said about the oil exploratives," he called back over his shoulder. "Stick to high-tech. And you might look into the health-care area." Morganstern stood there dazed.

The nearest police precinct was only three blocks away. There was the same sort of setup as there had been at the unemployment office, with cards to indicate where people should stand in line. Instead of letters of the alphabet, the headings were "Robbery-Mugging," "Assault with Deadly Weapon," "Rape-Murder."

He got in the end of the Robbery-Mugging line. There were about fifteen people in front of him.

A little old lady with a torn coat standing in front of him called out to a passing policeman, "Officer, I don't understand the difference between robbery and mugging."

The policeman explained: "A robbery is when money changes hands. A mugging is when money changes hands and they hit you." The woman nodded her head and got back in line.

The cop at the head of the Robbery-Mugging line took down the information from Morganstern, transcribing it directly onto a computer terminal.

78

"Where did it happen? What time of day? How much money was involved? Okay. Thanks for your cooperation," he said, signaling for the next person to sit down.

"Wait a second," Morganstern said, not getting up from his chair. "Is that it?"

"That's it."

"What do you do with that report?"

"We include it in our crime-report figures."

"Great. How do I go about getting my money back?"

The cop looked at him. "You've been robbed, fellah. There's no refunds with robbery. It's a cold, cruel, crime-ridden world out there. Don't you read the papers?"

Morganstern had read the papers. He had seen the crime figures. But it had never occurred to him that all those statistics represented actual individuals, real people like him who never, ever got their money back. He wanted to shout "It's not fair!" but he looked around at the long line of still-to-be-reported robbery victims and realized how hopeless the whole thing was. Shaking his head, he walked out of the police station.

He had three dollars in change in his pocket, plus six subway tokens. The subway tokens could always be cashed in for money, so he walked home. The phone was ringing as he opened the apartment door.

"I called you at work today. You weren't there," Ariel said without saying hello.

"I was forced to take early retirement," Morganstern answered, wondering why he was being so sarcastic. He was glad to hear her voice. "Ivan thought it was for the best."

"Ivan's always been a pal. What does he expect you to live on?"

"Oh, didn't I ever tell you?" he said, annoyed at the direction the conversation was taking. "I have a trust fund. All I have to do is notify the family lawyer to sell a few stocks."

"I'm sorry the jerk fired you. But it's not as if you lost the best job you ever had."

"No, just the only job I ever had," he said bitterly.

"I put a check in the mail yesterday for two thousand dollars. That should cover the rent and any bills that have come in, plus give you something to tide you over. I'm going out of town on a five-state store check. I won't be back for two weeks."

"I don't want your money," he said, relieved and resentful.

"And I don't want the landlord to evict us," she said, hanging up. Evict *us*. There was hope yet. She still thought of it as their apartment.

How had he gotten himself into this mess? He felt ashamed and impotent. He also felt thankful that Ariel at least cared enough to send a check.

He decided to devote the rest of the day to calling the house-painting clients he hadn't reached yet. He telephoned Mrs. Kibble, the woman who had canceled out on him, on the off-chance that her husband's financial situation had improved. Or maybe she had gotten fed up and divorced the guy.

"I've got a special going this week only, Mrs. Kibble. Twenty-five percent off my regular prices."

"Oh, you rascal you. You know how difficult it is for a woman to resist a sale. Maybe you could just do the bedroom for now and later on we can talk about having the rest of the apartment painted."

One room was better than none, and Morganstern agreed to start work the next day.

Early the next morning he got his drop cloths, paintbrushes, rollers, and rolling pans out of the storage room in the basement. He could borrow a ladder from Mrs. Kibble. He changed into his painting overalls, and before leaving, checked the mailbox downstairs. Nothing but a letter for him from MasterCard. He had paid the last balance in full but apparently it had arrived late, because he had incurred a service charge of sixty-three cents. Instead of the usual form there was a short note: "Did you forget? Your account is now seriously overdue. If remittance is not made immediately, we will turn the matter over to a collection agency." He wadded up the letter and stuck it in his pocket.

Julio was on duty as he left. "The password of the day is 'co-jones.' Know what that means?"

"No, what does it mean?" Morganstern asked.

"It means schmuck in Spanish," he said, laughing.

"Know what this means in Spanish?" Morganstern asked, shoving his middle finger under Julio's nose.

Mrs. Kibble lived in one of the older co-op buildings on Park Avenue and Ninetieth Street. Her apartment was many-roomed and elaborately molded in wood and plaster. It was not an easy place to paint and Morganstern had enjoyed working on it for that reason.

Mrs. Kibble answered the door wearing a frilly rose-colored peignoir set with furry little mules to match. She was a woman in her fifties, although it was difficult to tell which one of the fifties she was in. Her hair was dyed a brilliant, unrelieved ebony and was cut in the original Farrah Fawcett style. She had one of those amazing shelflike bosoms that seemed capable of holding a pair of candlesticks without any problems of balance.

She showed Morganstern to the bedroom. "This isn't too bad," he said, surveying the walls. "It shouldn't take me more than a day and a half." He negotiated the cost of the job, taking off, as promised, the 25 percent. They agreed upon a price of $150. It wasn't much, but it would help.

"You do such beautiful work," Mrs. Kibble sighed, watching him applying the last of the peach latex on the second morning. "Such nice, long, smooth strokes."

"Thank you, Mrs. Kibble," he said, not turning around.

When the job was completed, she said, "I hope you don't mind helping me move the furniture back."

"Don't you want to give it time to dry?"

"No, that's all right, we'll just keep everything away from the walls."

Helping her with the furniture amounted to pushing it all back himself while she directed its placement.

"I'm a little short of cash, Mrs. Kibble. I wonder if you could give me a check now for what you owe me," he said, after having moved the last piece of furniture into the finally decided-upon perfect spot.

"You know my husband always says that bartering is a beautiful system of exchange and people should use it more often."

"Bartering?"

"Instead of just a plain old check, what if you accepted payment in another form?" She lay down on the bed, her arm flung behind her head, her bosom majestically shifting with the change in gravity.

"You mean cash instead of a check?" Morganstern asked, knowing with certain dread that was not what she meant at all.

"To be perfectly honest," Mrs. Kibble said through softly parted lips, "my check wouldn't be any good, whereas I, I can assure you, would be very good indeed."

Morganstern gathered up his equipment quickly. "Just put the check in the mail," he said, knowing he would never see it.

When he got home, he counted his money again. He still had three dollars in change, but now he had only two subway tokens, having spent four to get to and from Mrs. Kibble's. They were fast becoming as precious to him as antique spoons. Should he cash them in now, or would their value increase over time? Should he spend the three dollars on food, or should he hold off until tomorrow? By tomorrow the price of a cup of coffee might be beyond his means. He went to bed. A sleeping man doesn't need food, he reasoned.

The next morning he went down to check the mail, hoping Ariel's check had arrived.

"Hope you weren't expecting anything too important," Julio yelled from the doorway. Morganstern ignored him. "Because your mailbox has been mugged," Julio added.

What the hell was he talking about? Morganstern wondered. He went into the little anteroom where all the mailboxes were. His mailbox door was pried off its hinges. There was nothing inside. Several others had been pried open as well.

"Where the fuck were you when this happened?" Morganstern asked Julio.

"Hey, I can't watch everything every minute. I was taking a pee. The super says he'll have your box fixed this afternoon."

Morganstern went back upstairs to phone Ariel about stopping the check.

"She's out of town," her secretary said.

"I know she is, but she sent a check and my mailbox got robbed this morning and I wanted her to be sure to call the bank to stop the check." The secretary said she would take care of it. And hour later there was a knock on the door. It was the landlord. All 250 pounds of him. "Everything okay?" the landlord asked. Morganstern suddenly remembered that tomorrow was rent day, and the landlord, probably sensing something amiss, like the fact that his rent check had been ripped off and the lady who paid the bills had temporarily relocated to another dwelling, was not taking any chances.

"Your mailbox is all fixed. Have any other repairs you want to tell me about?"

"No, everything's just fine."

"Heat okay?"

"Heat is just toasty."

"Neighbors giving you any trouble?"

"No, not at all."

"Pipes working?"

"Just fine."

"Never got a chance to see if you were all settled in."

"We've been living here almost two years," Morganstern said.

"That long, huh? Well, see you tomorrow, I guess."

"Tomorrow?"

"Rent day. I'll be around personally," he said.

"Don't you usually just slip the bill under the door?"

"Like I said, I'll be around personally."

He remembered the story now. The people next door had told him all about it. How the landlord, furious at a previous tenant for being late with his rent, had physically assaulted him, putting him in the hospital for two weeks. For some reason, charges were never pressed. The landlord apparently had friends in high places. Namely the district attorney, who lived in one of the penthouse apartments.

Morganstern went out and got the New York *Times*. He scoured the want ads. There was a whole section on career opportunities: director of engineering, metallurgical engineer, marketing manager, senior physicist—all things he couldn't begin to qualify for. He began phoning the jobs that he thought he could handle. Most of them were in the area of dishwasher or domestic. The lines were all busy.

Morganstern realized he was famished. He opened the refrigerator. An onion, a clove of garlic, a can of smoked oysters. When was the last time they had a Gristede's delivery? he wondered. The cupboards were equally bare. Tea bags and bouillon cubes. He made himself a cup of bouillon and dropped a few oysters in it to give it body. After one taste he threw it in the sink.

How long does it take a man to starve to death? he wondered. He remembered once reading that a healthy human can go for over a month without food. How long would it take a man to starve to death who's been severely beaten by an irate landlord? Pain most likely dulls the appetite, he thought.

He searched the apartment for money. He looked under the sofa and chair cushions for spare change and found none. Charitee was too thorough. He came across an old coin collection left over from his time in Italy and France. He knew the coins were worth only a few cents.

He considered his options. He could stay in the apartment until the landlord broke the door down. He could sneak out in the middle of the night, taking his possessions with him. What possessions? He would take Ariel's things and hock them first thing in the morning. When was Ariel due back? He could meet her at the airport and tell her he loved her and missed her, to please come home and bring her checkbook with her. But he didn't have enough money to get to the airport. He could call his parents and ask them for a loan. They could mortgage off the notions store and go on welfare. That would please them to no end. Then he remembered the notions store was already mortgaged to the hilt.

Morganstern knew he was at the end of his rope. Could he find it in his heart to mug someone? What would he use as a weapon? The only sharp instrument he was adept at using was a palette knife. He understood now why money was foremost on everyone's mind.

One simply and surely couldn't live without it.

He tried to reach Zero on the phone. Zero had money. The answering machine informed Morganstern that Zero was on an extended trip to Yosemite National Park. Morganstern left his name and number, hoping he didn't sound too frantic.

He was frantic. He spent the night again pacing the apartment. The next morning he dragged himself downstairs to check the mail. He wasn't really expecting anything. He knew, without a doubt, that Ariel's check would not be there. But checking the mail seemed like a perfectly appropriate activity for a man who was grasping at straws.

You never know, he said to himself. There could be a whole batch of free coupons.

There was a bill from Gristede's, the telephone and Con Edison bills, and a catalog from Lord & Taylor. All addressed to Ariel.

There was one letter for him. He opened it. It was from Publishers Clearing House. Ever since ordering the three money magazines, he had received a steady stream of correspondence from them. Special magazine offers, exciting news about the sweepstakes, opportunities to begin a fifty-two-volume collection of home-improvement books, and limited-time-only health- and life-insurance deals.

He always opened the letters because he got a kick out of the efforts they went to make them seem personal:

> Dear <u>Matthew Morganstern</u>:
> Think how your neighbors at <u>300 East 51st Street</u> in <u>New York City</u> will feel when they see you installing your brand-new barbecue/patio/gazebo right there in your own backyard. You'll be the envy of the <u>Coopers,</u> the <u>Meyers,</u> the <u>Gradys,</u> all those folks living there on <u>East 51st Street</u> in the city of Manhattan. Just think of it, <u>Matthew Morganstern</u>. . .

He opened the letter.

> Dear Mr. Morganstern:
> We are pleased to inform you that you are the grand-prize winner in the Publishers Clearing House Sweepstakes. Your check for $250,000 will arrive by registered mail within one week of this notification. Or, should you elect to take the option of $1,000 a month for life, or the equivalent in gold bullion, or the year-round vacation dream home, you may do so by contacting this office.

He had seen the commercials on TV. Mr. Edgar Brook of Bay Shore, Long Island. Mr. and Mrs. Tim Curran of the Bronx, Mr. and Mrs. Leonard Nedlin of New Jersey. Happy, smiling people standing in front of their new houses or new cars or new barbecue/patio/gazebos holding up letters of notification or checks, and he had believed it all. After all, they were identified by name, they were obviously real people and not actors, and they were telling the television audience that they had never thought they would win any-thing, and here they were with fabulous prizes and cash beyond their wildest dreams.

Had Morganstern seen himself on TV, he might have believed it too. But this wasn't television. This was Matthew Morganstern standing in the foyer of his apartment building on 300 East Fifty-first Street holding a letter that said he had just won $250,000. There was no announcer speaking to him. There was no camera aimed at him.

He examined the letter carefully. His fingers ran across the back of the page. He could feel the braillelike indentations. Someone had taken the trouble to type it.

He took a deep breath in an effort to slow the pumping of his heart. The air got trapped in his throat. He could not fill his lungs. For the first time, he understood fainting.

There is no reason to be afraid, he told himself. He had had dreams like this before. They had all seemed just as real at the time. Getting stuck in quicksand, being chased by Nazis, falling from tall buildings and watching the ground zoom up to meet him. He remembered then, what he always remembered to tell himself in those dreams: "Relax, relax. This is just a dream. Nothing will happen. You won't get hurt."

He read the letter again. He folded it carefully, and picking up Ariel's mail, he went back upstairs in order to be in his own apartment when he woke up.

On the way up in the elevator he kept repeating to himself: "Relax. Nothing will happen. You won't get hurt. This is just a dream."

II

Sudden Riches

Perhaps you will say a man is not young. I answer, he is rich; he is not genteel, handsome, witty, brave, good-humored, but he is rich, rich, rich, rich—that one word contradicts everything you can say against him.
            —Henry F. Fielding, *The Miser*

I

Apparently it was not a dream. A Mr. Gordon Fuller, director of contests for the Publishers Clearing House, verified by telephone that Matthew Morganstern of 300 East Fifty-first Street in Manhattan was indeed the winner of the Sweepstakes Superprize of $250,000 and that a check made out for that amount would be sent to him via registered mail.

It could have been a recorded message for all the excitement expressed by Mr. Fuller. He asked if Morganstern would be available for a publicity picture and if he would be agreeable to having his name and picture included in the "Real People Win Real Money—Lots and Lots of It" section of the next sweepstakes mailing.

"And you understand that neither you nor any member of your family is eligible to enter any future sweepstakes sponsored by this company?"

"I understand," Morganstern said, responding just as tonelessly.

No, it was not a dream, Morganstern thought. It was an elaborate joke. He was ninety percent sure of that. It was that ninety percent that kept him playing it straight. He was damned if he was going to make an ass out of himself. But then, there was that remaining ten percent: the suspicion that it wasn't a joke at all. That it might, in fact, be true. That, too, caused him to play it straight, just in case what was happening was really happening. He struck what he felt was the perfect tone with Mr. Fuller: straight, blank, wooden, sincere, and cautious. It exactly expressed his emotional state at the moment.

For two full days he did nothing. He didn't leave the apartment. He didn't get on the phone. He didn't pick up a paintbrush. He didn't eat. He didn't answer the door when the landlord knocked the first day, and he hid in the closet when he used his passkey on the second. For two full days, until the check arrived by registered mail, he was in a state of suspended animation.

And then it came. Just as he hoped it would. Just as he feared it would. Just as he never dreamed it would. He stared at the long white envelope for many minutes. His name was typed in official--looking black letters. Or at least a name that looked like his name. It was spelled the same exact way.

After what seemed like hours, he carefully opened the flap of the envelope. He could always reseal it if there was a mistake. The check inside was as long as the envelope. It was printed on a thick, cardlike paper, similar to a computer card. His name, or the name that was spelled exactly like his, was typed in the space that said: "Pay to the order of." The amount was imprinted by machine: one two, one five, and four zeros. And then the amount in script letters: "two hundred and fifty thousand dollars and no cents." That was when he freaked.

His first reaction was a sudden, intense, overwhelming, unspecified fear.

It was this fear that caused him to pick up the phone and dial his parents in Omaha. Long-distance telephone calls were something they frowned on because of the expense. They preferred letters or, better, postcards. His mother still wrote long, miniaturized notes to him on the backs and fronts of mail forwarded from his alma maters and various art organizations. They reacted to his phone call like parents react to telegrams during wartime.

"Matthew, what is it?"

"Nothing. I just thought I'd call to see how you were." He was immediately relieved to find out that they were both alive, not hospitalized, and apparently enjoying their "golden years" in good spirits. He refrained from telling them about the prize money. He also resisted the urge to tell them to lock all the doors and windows and not go out or drive the car unless they absolutely had to. After a rather staccato conversation, and well within the three-minute time limit, he said good-bye.

The next thing he did was check himself all over for lumps, tumors, and any or all of the seven cancer danger signs he had seen listed in one of Ariel's old *Vogue*s. He wasn't sure if the same seven signs applied to men as well as women, but they were all he had to go by. He ran in place three hundred times and then held his wrist against his heart so that he could monitor his pulse rate and heartbeat at the same time, listening carefully for any fibrillations. He seemed to be in excellent health. But this knowledge did nothing to reassure him or alleviate a growing sense of panic.

He looked at the check. It looked real enough. But he had no way of verifying it. All the banks were closed. He felt a tremendous need to put something to the test. The check, his life, the fates, his courage, reality, he wasn't sure what.

He knew he had to get out of the apartment. Had to walk it off. Whatever "it" was. He folded the check in half, put it in his shirt pocket, and buttoned the flap over it.

He began walking south on Third Avenue. He was acutely aware of the check. It lay over his right nipple like lead. He searched people's faces for a sign. Nobody even looked at him. Nobody eyed his shirt pocket. He kept walking, maneuvering through dogs on leashes, people walking in the opposite direction. At the corner of Thirty-fourth and Third Avenue he waited for several minutes for the light to change. He felt people moving past him, but somehow he couldn't synchronize his crossing with the "Walk" light flashing. He kept missing his cue. A taxi cut sharply around the corner. Morganstern saw the yellow out of the corner of his eye and he knew what was going to happen next. He knew it just as sure as the "Don't Walk" always follows the "Walk."

Morganstern felt his body being hurled through the air and he was surprised at the lack of pain, considering the formidable impact of taxi body against human flesh. Then he did feel the pain. His head smashing against the hard pavement, his breath exploding out of him, his blood slowly seeping onto the gritty gray sidewalk. He lifted his head slowly, painfully, high enough to see the taxi backing up to finish the job.

The light changed to "Walk." He took a deep breath and crossed to the other side of Thirty-fourth Street. He picked up a paper at the corner newsstand and tried to read and walk at the same time. At the next corner he threw the paper into a trash basket and turned right on Thirtieth Street. It was almost 6:30 now and the rush-hour pedestrians were thinning out. Morganstern walked quickly, looking neither to the left nor to the right.

At the entrance to Washington Square Park he looked up. A tall black man holding a paper bag, probably with a bottle in it, stood teetering on the curb. He was illuminated by the spotlights coming off Washington Square arch.

The black man lifted his bottle high above him. Morganstern turned just before impact. The bottle slipped off his head and hit him on the cheekbone, where it shattered against his face. Morganstern felt a quick sharp pain as the jagged glass cut through to the bone. There was a warm wetness as the blood poured down the side of his face and into his shirt collar. He turned to face the black man. He reached into his breast pocket and removed the check.

"Do you have a pen?" he asked the black man. "I'll have to endorse this."

"Do Ah looks like Ah carry a pen?" the black man snarled. He thrust the jagged end of the bottle forward into Morganstern's belly and twisted it. Morganstern's guts turned in his stomach, reacting to the pain. He doubled

over, clutching at his belly. The man still had hold of the
neck of the bottle. He continued to twist it slowly.

"Ah never won shit in mah life. In mah whole life no-
body never gave me nothin' but a hard time. Every
fuckin' day Ah buy a lottery ticket and every fuckin' day
Ah get shit. You, you motherfucker, you score first time
out."

The black man stepped off the curb to meet Morganstern in the middle of the street. Drool was running from his mouth. In his hand he held a dirty rag which he waved toward Morganstern. "Wash you' windshield fo' a quarter," he said.

"I don't have a car," Morganstern explained.

The black man looked bewildered. "Oh, right," he mumbled, lurching off in the direction of a taxi waiting for the light.

Morganstern walked by a building under construction on the corner of Bleecker and Broadway. The sun was just going down. He glanced up.

Something had been flung from the top of the fifty-floor
steel structure. It was a man, falling very slowly, his arms
and legs reaching out to get a handhold on thin air. Mor-
ganstern saw that it was he himself falling from the build-
ing. As he watched from the sidewalk directly underneath,
he landed on himself. He felt the awful whammy of hitting
and being hit. The pain of smashing into and being
smashed, the shock and surprise of falling from a great
height and being hit from a great height.

The piece of tarpaulin landed at his feet, curled against his ankles, and blew away into the gutter. Morganstern took his first deep breath. His lungs began to relax, his stomach to unfold. He shook the knots out of his hands and continued walking.

He had been walking for almost two and a half hours through crazy killers, crumbling buildings, falling bodies, and kamikaze taxi drivers. He had had enough. He began to reject the role of the featured fall guy, the cartoon character who stands at the crossroads waiting for the roadrunner, who at that moment is high above him, tilting a huge boulder off the edge of a cliff, directly over his head. He began to feel better, more relaxed, less afraid, and more able to see things in a calm, realistic light. He calmly realized he was just being hysterical.

At the intersection of Spring Street and Green Street, a charcoal-gray limousine, cutting the corner very close and very quickly, came within two inches of amputating Morganstern's outstretched left leg. He leaped back. The limousine pulled around the corner and came to a stop in front of the Oh So Ho Restaurant. The chauffeur, dressed in a matching charcoal-gray uniform, got out and opened the door for the occupants. A man around Morganstern's age, dressed much the same way Morganstern was, in Levi's and a blue workshirt, helped his woman companion out of the backseat. She was an electrically beautiful blond encased in an impossibly tight silver Spandex jumpsuit.

She swept an arm around the man's shoulders. He grabbed her playfully around the waist and lifted her several inches off the sidewalk. They exchanged a silly, loudspeaker sort of kiss and then zigzagged their way into the restaurant. They didn't appear drunk to Morganstern, just in high, rich spirits. The chauffeur got back into the limo, opened a paper, and began to read.

Morganstern had never seen anybody so happy. They certainly had money and they seemed to be having a lot of fun with it. Had they had it for a long time or did they just get it? It didn't seem to matter. He couldn't picture anything bad ever happening to them. If there were a terrorist bomb in the restaurant, it would miss them and kill one of the waiters. And not even their waiter. If everyone got ptomaine poisoning and died from the moo shoo pork they would survive without even a trace of acid indigestion. If their limo were in a head-on collision on the way home, it would be the chauffeur who would get it on the head, not them, he reasoned.

He started his trek back uptown. By nine o'clock he had reached Gramercy Park. Lights blazed from the elegant houses that lined the square. Nobody cutting down on Con Ed bills here. Many of the spacious town houses were one-family dwellings. This was millionaire's row. He caught glimpses of people sitting in wing-backed armchairs, legs carefully crossed, sipping cocktails, smiling, happy, unharmed. They were loaded, they were serene, they were safe. Nobody and nothing was threatening them. There was not a gash or a smashed head among them. Everything was okeydokey here in the lap of luxury, Morganstern said to himself.

He wondered if these people were protected by their wealth or if they were wealthy because they had managed to come this far through life without getting creamed by falling bodies. He assumed the former. He imagined it must be very much like a smallpox inoculation. Rich kids were exposed to money at a very early age; consequently they grew up inoculated against the dangers of a sudden windfall.

A windfall. That's what had happened to him, and that's what was bothering him. The term had an out-of-control, possibly disastrous sound to it. As soon as he got home, he looked up "windfall" in Ariel's dictionary.

A windfall is (1) a piece of unexpected good fortune, especially a sudden and substantial financial profit. This seemed to fit, but there was more. A windfall is (2) a tract of land on which trees have been felled by the wind; also the trees so felled. And (3) something, as ripening fruit, brought down by the wind.

Taking the definition in its entirety, he could begin to understand the elements of danger involved in being the recipient of a windfall. The problem of not knowing what the wind might bring down on your unsuspecting head—a check, a tree, or a bunch of ripened coconuts. Not knowing for certain whether that wind was an ill one or not until you examined the booty.

He thought about the rich and happy people he had observed on his walk home. If they were the recipients of windfalls, they seemed to have survived nicely. He had always considered himself a fairly happy person. Now he was wealthy. Could he still be happy? He could try. If the rich could learn to live with it, why couldn't he? He realized that this windfall, this check, this one little piece of paper, could change his whole life. Maybe it was that change he was afraid of. He made a conscious decision: he was going to be a rich and happy man, if it killed him.

He sat at Ariel's desk. He thought about her. He couldn't wait till she heard the news. Then he studied the check. Two hundred and fifty thousand. How much was that? He could not begin to grasp the amount. So many zeros. He had been making about $250 a week at the advertising agency. He took out a small sketchpad and did some calculations. If he had worked one thousand weeks he would have earned $250,000. A thousand weeks figured out to be nineteen years. Nineteen years of drawing dandruff and revising detergent commercials equaled $250,000. If he continued to work, say, another nineteen years, the figure would have been $500,000. If he slaved away until he was ninety-two years old, he would have earned $750,000 minus expenses like pacemakers, Seeing Eye dogs.

He doodled around with the zeros some more. Odd, he thought, how zeros by themselves meant nothing, and yet in the company of other digits could mean so much. He counted the zeros and changed the commas, and suddenly it struck him. Two hundred and fifty thousand was a quarter of a million dollars! "Holy God," he said out loud. He started to feel the fear working again from his stomach upward.

He gripped his charcoal pencil tightly, and in an effort to stave off his growing anxiety, began dividing up the figure, paring it down, getting control of it.

"Let's see," he said to himself. The rent was $750. He subtracted that sum from the $250,000 and was still left with a figure that threatened to jump off the page. He started chopping away at it in larger chunks, as if he were a sculptor working against a deadline on an enormous piece of marble.

He'd send his parents a check for twenty thousand dollars to pay

94

off the mortgage on their half of the two-family house in Omaha. He'd pay off all his bills, all the money he owed Ariel. That would leave him with about $225,000. He'd take her on a tour of the world's major art museums. Figure $10,000. No, make it $20,000. They'd take a year and go first class. He was left with $205,000.

Now what? Ah, yes, his dream. A place in the country. The re-converted barn with a large sunny studio for him and a nice book-lined den for Ariel. That would run no more than $50,000, he guessed. He still had $160,000 left over. How much could living in the country cost? Couldn't be much. Make it $10,000 a year at the most. Ten into $160,000 meant sixteen years of uninterrupted paint-ing. To be on the safe side, he cut that down to fourteen years, taking into consideration art supplies and unexpected expenses. Fourteen years of full-time, problem-free painting. By then he would have enough paintings for twenty one-man shows. In fact, given just two years of that kind of life, he would be ready for his next big show. And then he could certainly afford to have it in a nice fireproof gallery.

The more he figured it out, earmarked it, and divided it up, the wealthier he felt. There seemed to be no end to the money and the things he could do with it. There was no way to subtract from his feeling of plentitude.

He slept well that night for the first time in a week. He dreamed again of falling from a tall building, only this time he landed as light as a feather and took off again with just the slightest effort and the smallest intake of breath.

The next day he took the check to Metrobank. He had trouble filling out the deposit slip because he didn't leave enough room for all the zeros. By the third try he managed to squeeze them all in. Four squashed little circles.

Metrobank was promoting its Fast Track Account ("Get free monthly checking and 5.25% interest, compounded daily, just by keeping an average monthly balance of $5,000 or more.") They had adopted a railroad theme. All the tellers, bank managers, and guards wore striped engineer's caps, red kerchiefs, and overalls. There was a small electric train engineered by a bank guard. It car-ried three pretty girls who handed out brochures to people as they jumped clear of its metal wheels.

Morganstern looked for Miranda among the girls, but didn't see her. The sound effects of a much larger train and whistle were am-plified throughout the bank. Every few minutes a booming voice announced: "All aboard for the Fast Track Express, your first-class ticket to faster banking and interest on all your Metrobank ac-counts. All aboard, please."

The small train rammed into the back of one of the customers and there was a piercing scream.

Morganstern got in the checking-and-deposit line, which had thinned out considerably. The little train was low enough to make it underneath the blue velvet ropes and had discouraged many people from waiting in line.

"Next," someone shouted. At the same time, Morganstern was shoved in the direction of teller number ten. He was surprised to see Miranda, dressed in the required overalls, cap, and kerchief, now working as a teller.

"Hi, how are you today?" she said, giving him a hurried, semi-dimpled smile.

"Just fine," he said, passing over the check with his deposit slip. She glanced at the check, started to put it through the date machine, and then pulled it quickly back.

"Are you interested in opening a new account?" she asked in a low, slow voice.

"You mean a Fast Track Account?" he asked.

"No, I'm talking about a special privileged account."

"How does it work?"

"Here's all the information," she said, slipping him a small card. He read the card: "Miranda Martin, 555-5067, 24-hour deposits and withdrawals."

"Oh." He smiled.

She handed him back his copy of the deposit slip. "Congratulations." She smiled. "You've just made Metrobank's Preferred Customer List. Don't be a stranger, now."

Morganstern left the bank feeling like a million bucks. Like a quarter of a million bucks, he corrected.

He was a man with assets, with places to go, people to know, money to burn, mountains to climb, gifts to buy, promises to keep, pictures to paint, cities to conquer, dreams to dream, Ariel to see, things to do, things to do, things to do.

"Watch out, world, here I come," he whispered happily.

2

He spent the next few days in a continued state of agitation. Up and down and up and down. He had gone from nothing to something far too quickly. Now he had the bends. He knew that if he had been able to ease into his quarter of a million dollars he would've felt calmer and more in control.

Most people spent years planning, saving, and preparing for that momentous day when they would have more money in the bank than they had bills outstanding, he thought. If you stopped the average man in the street and asked him what he would do if he suddenly came into a quarter of a million dollars, he wouldn't hesitate for a second:

"I'd buy me a trailer and an acre of land in Sarasota, Florida, so I wouldn't have to drive all over the fuckin' country."

"I'd get a video tape deck, a video beam projector, and a video camera."

"I'd pay off my mortgage."

"I'd have the house insulated and install solar heating."

"I'd buy me an outboard motor and build a nice little cabin on Lake Placid."

"I'd buy gold."

"Shares in Sony."

"A home computer."

"A diesel-engine Mercedes."

"I'd invest in New York City bonds."

"I'd stake myself to a McDonald's franchise."

Morganstern knew that the average man would have his quarter of a million dollars spent before you could count to three. He had already earmarked the money in his head, but he had yet to spend a penny. He knew his plans were vague. They were really no more than dream plans. The trip around the world, the place in the country, were as surreal to him as the money.

He sat down and wrote a couple of checks just to get the feel of it. He wrote the rent check. Then he wrote a check out to his parents for $20,000. It was easy enough. But it still wasn't real. He made out a check to Ariel for $8,000. The money he figured he owed her for the past year, including what she put down for the one-man show.

He missed her. He desperately needed her to share the good news. What would her reaction be? he wondered. Would she want to leave for a trip around the world immediately, or start shopping for the reconverted barn? Undoubtedly she would have some good ideas on how to spend the money. He called Ariel's secretary and found out she was due back early the next evening. He had another whole long day ahead of him.

He tried to work on an idea for a painting, but he couldn't concentrate. He was too excited. His mind was unable to focus on anything but his new bank balance.

The next day he took his checkbook and went to Bloomingdale's to buy Ariel a welcome-home gift. He thought it was important to test out his new buying power directly. He spent three hours wandering through the store, getting lost in the various departments, literally going around in circles. There was so much to look at. There was too much to look at. He knew he could buy anything in the store he wanted, but he couldn't find anything he wanted to buy. Then he remembered the silk-blouse counter on the main floor and how much Ariel loved silk.

"I'd like to get a silk blouse for my girlfriend," he said to a rather elderly but determinately attractive woman.

"How much do you want to spend?" the woman asked him, biting the earpiece of her gold-framed spectacles.

Morganstern looked at the blouses hanging airlessly above the woman's head. "I really don't know. What do they cost?"

"It varies anywhere from seventy-five to two hundred dollars," the woman replied.

"Whatever you think would be best. It doesn't matter."

The woman was angry. "What do you mean, it doesn't matter? It most certainly does matter. I can't help you choose a blouse if you don't give me a price range."

Morganstern was stumped. "Can't we just pick it out by color?"

"Color has nothing to do with it," the woman snapped. "The same color can cost different prices." She called out to a younger woman at the end of the counter. "Ms. Atkins, this man refuses to give me a price range. And he expects me to help him pick out a blouse for his girlfriend."

"I don't know how much I'm supposed to spend," Morganstern explained to the younger saleswoman.

"You're supposed to spend what they cost," Ms. Atkins answered. "And if you have no idea what they cost, then you have no business buying a silk blouse."

"Okay, give me a two-hundred-dollar blouse," Morganstern said, thinking he was finally catching on to the world of fashion.

"What color?" the older saleswoman asked.

"Whatever color the two-hundred-dollar one comes in," he said.

"You can't go around buying blouses that way. You've got to pick the price and the color. Our salesgirls have only so much patience," Ms. Atkins lectured.

"Forget it," Morganstern snapped.

"I knew he wasn't going to buy anything," the elder saleswoman remarked as he walked away.

What was the matter with him? he asked himself. There he was, with all the money in the world, all the colors of the rainbow to choose from and he couldn't buy one lousy little silk blouse.

He was at JFK when Ariel's plane landed at six P.M. Her face lit up when she saw him. "What are you doing here?" she asked.

"Just cruising. Looking for a nice piece of ass," he said, hugging her.

"Well, will I do?"

"To tell you the truth, I really had my heart set on a stewardess. But, yeah, I guess you'll do."

"It's good to see you," Ariel said, squeezing his arm as they waited for her suitcase.

In the taxi on the way back to the city, Morganstern said, "I've got a little surprise for you."

"Did you get a job?"

"No."

"Oh." She thought a moment. "You did get the rent check, didn't you?" she asked, concerned.

"No, as a matter of fact, our mailbox got ripped off."

"You're kidding."

"It's okay. Your secretary called the bank and stopped the check."

"Then how did you manage to pay the rent?"

The conversation was not going the way Morganstern had envisioned it. Why was she dwelling on such trivia? A job. The rent.

"Take us to the World Trade Center," Morganstern told the taxi driver as they approached the city.

"The World Trade Center? Why there?" Ariel asked.

"It's part of the surprise."

When they arrived at the Twin Towers, Ariel started to reach into her purse to pay the driver. Morganstern quickly stopped her hand, then took out his billfold.

"But I'm on an expense account," she explained. "The company pays for it."

"The gentleman pays for it," Morganstern corrected, "and *je suis* the gentleman." He felt a slow acid burning in his stomach, but he refused to let his annoyance with her interfere with the evening.

"Tell me where we're going."

Morganstern pointed to the sky. "We're going to the top. To the summit. To the Windows on the World."

"Windows on the World? Why?"

"Because it's there, my dear, because it's there," he said, slipping into what he hoped was a fair imitation of Sir Edmund Hilary.

"We'll never get in without reservations," she said in the express elevator up.

"We do have reservations, darling. Some of us just have more reservations than others." He was still doing Sir Edmund Hilary. He felt the air get thinner and his ears plug up as the elevator sped toward the 108th floor and Windows on the World.

"The suspense is killing me. Come on, tell me what this is all about," Ariel said, giving him a gentle pinch in the ribs.

The maître d' approached them.

"Not in front of the help, dear," he said, putting a finger up to his lips.

"Your name, please, sir?"

"Morganstern."

The maître d' consulted his leather-bound reservations book and then nodded his head. "Morganstern, dinner for two. Very good, sir. This way, please."

He led them to a table by the windows. "Windows" was a misnomer, Morganstern noted. The entire restaurant was walled in glass. There was nothing between them and the air outside and the sidewalk one hundred and eight floors below but a three-inch plate of glass. He sat with his back to the view.

He couldn't contain himself any longer. "First things first," he said, and handed Ariel the check for eight thousand dollars.

"What's this?" She studied the check as though she were looking at an underdeveloped photograph.

"It's a check for eight thousand dollars. It's just an approximation of the money I owe you," he explained, grinning.

Ariel looked perplexed. "What money? You don't owe me any money." She put the check on the table and placed her hand over his. "Sweetheart, you shouldn't go around writing checks without having the money in the bank."

He handed her his checkbook. "Read that," he said. He couldn't stop grinning.

She laughed. "Why would I want to read your checkbook?"

"Go on, read it."

She opened up the checkbook and read aloud: "Check for cash, fifty dollars. Check for rent, seven hundred and fifty dollars. Check to Mr. and Mrs. Max Morganstern, twenty thousand dollars. Check to Ariel Hellerman, eight thousand dollars." She looked up. An expression of deep concern clouded her face. "Matthew, honey, this isn't funny. Checks aren't wishes."

"Read the deposit column."

She glanced down. "Two hundred and fifty thousand dollars." She forced a laugh. "I'm surprised it's not a million. Why are you being so stingy with yourself?"

"Because I only won two hundred and fifty thousand dollars," he said, his eyes gleaming.

Ariel sighed with exasperation. "Okay. I'll bite. How did you win two hundred fifty thousand dollars?"

"You are looking at the grand-prize winner of the Publishers Clearing House Super Sweepstakes. First prize, two hundred fifty thousand dollars."

Ariel's face went through a series of changes from impatience to disbelief, to a slow dawning, and finally shock. Her mouth fell open.

"Your mouth is open," he said with delight.

"Sweepstakes," she said in a daze. "When did you enter a sweepstakes?"

Morganstern noticed she was slipping right by the money and holding on to the little details for dear life.

"Well, I didn't realize I had entered myself," he said, laughing. "Remember when I ordered all those money magazines? Apparently part of the order was an entry blank for the contest."

Ariel sat forward in her chair. "You're not kidding? You're serious? This isn't a joke?"

"That's right," he said, leaning across the table to bring his face inches away from hers. "This is not a joke. This is for real. You are not dreaming. You can kiss me now." He gave her a kiss.

"Oh, my," Ariel said, pulling away from him and falling back into her chair as if struck. "Oh, my, my, my. That's amazing. I can't believe it." She looked at the entry in the checkbook again. "Oh, my. That's an awful lot of money," she whispered.

"I know," Morganstern exclaimed. "It is, isn't it?" He had hallucinated over it, been frightened by it, tried to make sense of it, been immobilized by it; now it was nice to finally get some outside verification. It *was* a lot of money.

"Isn't it incredible? Isn't it amazing? Huh? Isn't it?" he said in a rush.

Ariel shook her head as though trying to clear the cobwebs. "Wow," she finally said. "What are you going to do with it all?"

"Buy. Buy. Buy. Spend. Spend. Spend. Paint with it. Play with it. Live on it. Roll in it. Take a trip around the world with my one and only darling. Buy us a perfect place in the country. Buy you everything your little heart desires. Pay off old debts. Make new ones. Give to charity. Make political contributions. Go Christmas shopping. Buy smoked oysters. Buy lots of paint and fabulous sable brushes and silk blouses. Buy a small gallery. Paint big pictures. Buy a car. New drapes. Veal scallopini. A new maid . . ."

"Stop! You're going too fast."

"And," Morganstern said, not stopping for breath, "you can quit your job and go back to writing full-time. I'll be painting and you'll be writing, just me and you and you and me and oh how happy we will be," he sang.

"But I don't want to quit my job. Why would I want to quit my job?" Ariel cried.

"So I can take care of you, my little bird of paradise," Morganstern crooned.

"Stop it! Please. You're not making any sense."

Morganstern looked at her. She seemed on the verge of tears. She was twisting her napkin round and round her hand as if she were bandaging a cut.

The waiter handed them their menus. Ariel tore her gaze away from him and studied the menu, her eyes darting from right to left. She seemed much more interested in the food than she had in his checkbook entries, he thought.

"Chicken Kiev, twenty-two-fifty," she said. "That's outrageous."

"Forget about the prices," he exclaimed. "I just told you, I'm rich. We'll buy the restaurant and eat for free." He turned around and announced to the surrounding tables, "Order whatever you want, guys, it's on the house."

Ariel grabbed Morganstern's arm. "Matthew, please."

"Don't you understand?" he said gleefully. "There I was in the apartment wondering how I was going to pay the rent, wondering where my next meal was coming from, wondering how I was going to get the woman I loved to come back to me when I couldn't even afford to send her a lousy bunch of flowers. I was out of work, out of luck, and then this happens. It's like a miracle."

"This money is going to change your whole life," Ariel said somberly.

"Oh, I see what the trouble is. You're afraid it will spoil me. Turn me from a simple, easygoing man of modest means into a relentless, ruthless millionaire who will stop at nothing to gain his way." He reached under the table and ran his hand up her leg. "I promise you, darling, nothing will change the basic Morganstern. I will stay sweet and kind through it all, Howard Hughes be damned."

"You have to start thinking about what you're going to do with the money. I mean, think realistically."

"What are you so worried about? I'm going to have a good time with it. *We're* going to have a good time with it. Just think how happy Bloomingdale's will be."

"I just can't talk to you," Ariel said, shaking her head.

"Talk to me? Of course you can talk to me. What's the matter?"

"Honey, just because you won a little bit of money doesn't mean everything's going to be hunky-dory."

"A little bit of money?" Morganstern choked. "Boy, you really know how to hurt a sweepstakes winner."

"Please be serious. Just for a second."

"What in the world is there to be so serious about? Tell me."

Ariel took a deep shaky breath. "Money is a tremendous responsibility. You have to learn how to deal with it."

For the first time that evening, Morganstern stopped grinning. "Jesus, you act like I won a disease, not a contest."

"I'm just trying to be practical. It's not going to be all fun and games, and you have to know that."

"She's just trying to be practical," Morganstern mumbled to himself.

102

"And you have to talk to James," she said, "as soon as possible."

"James? Who's James?"

"You know, my accountant."

"What do I need with James? I can add and subtract. I'm not a complete fool," he said angrily.

"He can help. You've got to have a tax strategy."

"I don't understand you. This is supposed to be good news. A reason to celebrate. I just won two hundred and fifty thousand dollars. And you're talking about tax strategies, for Chrissakes."

"You have to have a plan. Otherwise they'll kill you," she said patiently.

"Kill me?" he snorted. "Who's going to kill me?"

"The IRS," she said. She pronounced the initials in such a way that it caused a chill to run up Morganstern's spine. The IRS. The letters sounded toxic, ominous, deadly. They fell into the same category as DDT, the FBI, the CIA, and the PLO.

"You don't have any real concept of money and finances," she continued. "That's what you need James for."

"Maybe James wants to go around the world with me," Morganstern snapped. "Waiter, check please."

"But you haven't ordered anything, sir," the waiter said.

"I don't give a shit. I want the check."

The waiter was confused. "I can't write out a check if there wasn't an order."

"All right. I'll take the filet mignon. How much is it?"

The waiter consulted the menu. "It's thirty-six dollars, sir."

"Fine." Morganstern handed him a fifty. "That should cover it. Keep the change. Come on," he said to Ariel, "let's get out of here."

"I can't believe how much it's changed you already," Ariel murmured in the elevator.

"Jesus Christ!" Morganstern yelled, slamming his hand into the elevator wall. "Changed me? Nothing's changed me. You know what your trouble is, you can't stand something good happening to me that you had nothing to do with."

"That's not true."

"Sure it is. This is one piece of bacon you didn't bring home."

"Now I'm getting mad," Ariel growled.

"Good," Morganstern said, folding his arms across his chest. "Join the crowd."

They glared at each other as the elevator continued its descent.

"You like me penniless and dependent. Then you can be the little sweetie who fulfills all my needs," he said.

"That is just so much bullshit," Ariel snapped.

"Then let me ask you, why are you so upset about me winning the money?"

The elevator doors opened on the first floor. A couple was waiting to enter.

"I'm not upset. I'm very happy for you!" Ariel screamed as she pushed her way past the couple and walked quickly toward the exit.

"Happy for me!" Morganstern bellowed in hot pursuit. "You know what I think? I think you prefer being unhappy for me. It makes you much more noble."

"Taxi!" Ariel yelled at a passing cab. The taxi screeched to a halt.

"You'd be much happier if I just tore up the check."

"Don't be stupid. Just call James. Or give it all to the IRS. I don't care. Taxi!" she screamed again.

"Here, lady. I'm right here," the waiting cabdriver said.

Morganstern grabbed her by the arm and turned her toward him. "When are you coming home?"

Ariel glared at him. "I don't know."

"Great." Morganstern addressed himself to the taxi driver, who had been deeply engrossed in their conversation. "I take her to a fancy restaurant and she won't even put out."

Ariel yanked her arm out of his grasp. "You bastard," she hissed, and got into the taxi, slamming the door.

He bent down and spoke through the open window. "I'm sorry," he said, lowering his voice. "I thought this was supposed to be a little separation. It's beginning to feel like a divorce."

Ariel stared straight ahead. "I need time, Matthew. I'm very mixed up right now," she said tonelessly. The taxi driver nodded his head in agreement.

Morganstern tried to cajole her. "Can't you be mixed up in the comfort of your own home?"

She didn't answer.

"Well, I hope you realize you're taking one hell of a chance with my relationship."

She turned toward him. "It's my relationship, too, remember?"

"I just hope you know what you're doing."

"So do I," Ariel said with a deep sigh. She wrote something down on a card. "Here."

"What's this?"

"James's number. Please give him a call." She leaned out the window and gave him a quick kiss.

He watched the taxi drive off. This was ridiculous, he thought. She loved him. He loved her. And he was furious with her. He had been so sure she would be thrilled about his big windfall. And she had acted as if he'd told her he met another woman. He was confused. But then, she was totally off the wall. Maybe he had hit upon something without realizing it. Maybe she did want him dependent on her. Maybe she was only happy if she could control the purse strings. Well, there was no way he would let something as stupid as money come between them. They would work it out somehow. Although at that moment, he wasn't quite sure how.

Fuck it, he said to himself. And fuck her accountant. And then he remembered her words. Not her words, her initials. The IRS. James will know what to do about the IRS, she had said. Morganstern had never had any dealings with the IRS other than filling out the short form on his tax returns. And in his case, the short form had been abbreviated. Ariel was right. He had better call James for an appointment.

The telephone woke him up in the middle of the night. "Matthew, this is your father, Max, speaking."

He sat up in bed. Oh, God, his mother had died.

"Don't worry, the rates are down, nothing's wrong," his father said, reading Morganstern's mind. "Hold on, your mother wants to talk to you." He heard his father yell, "Mother, it's your son, Matthew, on the phone." The next voice he heard was his mother's.

"Your father was very upset by your little joke."

"What little joke?"

"The check you sent us. I thought it was funny myself. I laughed. But you know how he is, he only likes his own little jokes."

"But, Mom, it wasn't a joke. It was for real. I won a big sweepstakes. A lot of money. The check is for you. Use it to pay off the mortgage. Or for anything you want. Buy a car. Get a new TV."

"Hold on, I better get your father."

There were unintelligible whispers and then his father: "I thought it was a joke."

"No, Dad, it's real."

"What kind of father do you take me for? Accepting money from my own son."

"You can pay off your mortgage."

"Oh. Very good, pay off the mortgage. And then what do I do? Curl up and die?"

Morganstern was getting mad. "I don't care what you do with the money. Just use it."

"Now, you listen to me, no-son-of-mine. Give it back to where you got it. Or give it away. Give it to the United Jewish Appeal. No, don't give it to them. They got enough already. Give it to Multiple Dystrophy."

"It's Muscular Dystrophy."

"I don't care who you give it to. Get rid of it before they find out."

"Dad, I didn't steal it. I won it. It's mine."

There was a moment of silence and then his father said, "Jews don't win money. They earn it or they go without."

"But, Dad—"

"I don't want to talk about it anymore. I'm tearing up this check and you had better do the same with the rest of it."

His mother got back on the phone. "He tore up the check."

"That's okay. I'm sending you another one."

"Don't. It would kill your father. After everything he's done for you, you pay him back like this. It's three minutes, I have to hang up, sweetheart. Take care. And listen to your father."

Why hadn't he realized it before? These two people, this dear sweet couple who had borne him and raised him, were crazy. He always knew they had trouble receiving gifts. His mother with her "Oh-nothing-for-me-dear-I-have-everything-a-mother-could-want—a-son's-love" routine. And his father. All the little presents, the sweaters, the earmuffs, the gloves, the books, all the things he had given him over the years had been put away, unused, later to be wrapped and presented back to him for birthdays, for good grades, for no reason at all.

He had given up buying them gifts or giving them anything while he was still in high school. It was Ariel's idea to send them the candlesticks from Tiffany's. He wondered what they had done with them. Probably he could expect them in the mail any day. Well, this was another matter. They had scrimped and saved, clothed him and fed him, helped him through art school; he was not going to give up. He was going to pay them back, whether they liked it or not.

As he tried to fall back asleep, he wondered why it was that the people he cared most about in the world—Ariel, his mother, his father—were giving him such a hard time about this tremendous piece of good luck.

One thing to be said for it, he was no longer being plagued by illusions of disaster. He had his own real-life miseries to contend with now. It was almost a relief. It was like worrying about a fatal disease and finding out from the doctor that you only had gall-stones, Morganstern reasoned. Gallstones are not good news, but they're a lot better than Hodgkin's disease. And for that they are greatly appreciated. They're real. They're measurable. They're even curable.

So his fears had finally found a home. His parents might never talk to him again. He and Ariel might be finished forever. Not good news. Not easy to live with. They were problems that he would have to contend with and overcome. But how much better, this alienation of loved ones, than a horrible murder at the hand of some unknown mugger. With that thought, Morganstern drifted off to a deep, dreamless sleep.

106

3

Just as Morganstern had once pictured James the accountant as a fat, balding man with a green eyeshade and black sleeve protectors, he had also envisioned his office as a dingy, windowless closet just large enough to accommodate an old metal desk, two chairs, and a large abacus.

The offices of James Gross, CPA, Ph.D., P.C., & Associates occupied almost one-third of a floor in a new building on Fiftieth and Second Avenue. Morganstern was asked by the pretty Korean receptionist to have a seat. A seat was whatever space one needed to take up of a wall-to-wall-to-wall built-in suede sectional couch.

"Dr. Gross will be with you in a few minutes."

"Doctor? I thought he was an accountant," Morganstern said with surprise.

"Dr. Gross is many things to many people." She smiled.

The waiting room was done all in earth tones. Beiges, taupes, sands, and rusts. There was a huge teak coffee table in the middle of the room which sported a Giacometti bronze sculpture. Above one section of the couch was a beautiful Georgia O'Keeffe print. Morganstern took a closer look. It wasn't a print at all. It was an original. The whole place smacked of calm, casual wealth.

After a twenty-minute wait he was ushered by another pretty Oriental secretary down a long beige hallway. The walls were covered in some sort of suedelike fabric. Morganstern sneaked a feel. It wasn't suedelike, it was suede. Hung at eye level on the walls were twenty-four signed photographs by Ansel Adams, framed in a bleached wood.

James Gross was as much of a surprise as his office. He was long, lanky, and lean, with sandy-colored, tightly curled hair and bright laser-blue eyes. Gary Cooper with a perm. He was dressed in the wealthy rancher style popularized by Ralph Lauren: a soft leather, possibly fawn-skin, jacket over a modified Western cream-colored shirt and beautifully tailored cavalry-twill pants. The shirt was unbuttoned far enough to reveal a chestful of sandy, springy hair. The only jewelry he wore was a Navajo silver-and-turquoise watchband. He got up from the desk slowly, measuring Morganstern with his eyes. A slow smile revealed the only un-toned-down thing about him: teeth so perfect they looked as though they had never been used.

He moved around the desk, extending his big flat hand toward Morganstern.

"It's a pleasure to finally make your acquaintance," he said in a low, deep voice with only the slightest trace of a New York accent.

"I've heard so much about you from Ariel. Have a seat," he said, indicating a comfortable armchair that seemed to be covered in pinto pony. "So you suddenly find yourself a quarter-of-a-millionaire," James said. "How do you feel about that?"

"Lucky, very lucky."

"According to Ariel, you won this money in a sweepstakes."

"That's right."

"Let's talk about that for a minute. Is there any guilt?"

"Guilt? About what?"

"About coming into the money so easily. Without actually earning it."

"I don't think so, no. I mean, it's not as though I did anything wrong. Why should I feel guilty?"

"Guilt is a funny thing, Matthew. It doesn't always conform to the tax laws. It's important that you get in touch with *all* your feelings. How do you feel about the fact that the mean per-capita income is four thousand dollars? Or that the average man would have to work sixty years to earn what you won? Or that it's enough to feed ten thousand children for twenty-five years? Or that it's equivalent to the same amount needed to pay the salaries of twenty-five schoolteachers until retirement?"

"I don't know, I guess I hadn't thought about it that way."

"Did your family have money?"

"No."

"You grew up poor?"

"Not poor. It's just they never had any money. I mean, anything more than what it took to pay the bills."

"Uh-hum. Okay, Matthew, when I say money, tell me the first thing that pops into your mind."

"Nothing. There's a blank."

"What about two hundred and fifty thousand dollars? What then?"

"Nothing. Nothing at all. Oh, I guess I see the check. The check I got from the sweepstakes. But that's it."

"Would you say you are enjoying, not enjoying, or indifferent to your newfound wealth?"

"I wouldn't say I was enjoying it. Not yet. But it's not as though I wasn't enjoying the idea of it. I'm certainly not indifferent to it, I can tell you that."

"Well, let's start enjoying it right now. Lie down on the couch, please," he said, pointing to a sort of chaise longue covered with a splendid Indian blanket.

"What? What for?"

"Before we can get into the dollars and cents of your financial situation, we have to get you to experience the satisfaction of it.

108

Too many people lose sight of just how beautiful money is. Please just follow my directions. Lie down on the couch."

Morganstern did what he was told. Having never met with an accountant before, he had no idea what was expected. Funny, he thought, he had always assumed they just did tax returns and gave financial advice.

James's voice took on a soft, soothing quality. "Close your eyes. That's it. Get into your space."

Morganstern opened his eyes. "I don't understand what you mean."

"I mean just relax, feel yourself relaxing, experience every part of your body, let your breath move in and out easily." Morganstern forced himself to relax. "Now, I want you to picture your money. What do you see?"

"I see the check again," Morganstern said, "made out to me for two hundred and fifty thousand dollars." He was surprised by the sound of his own voice. It sounded as if he were drugged.

"I want you to go beyond that, Matthew. Picture the money in actual currency."

Morganstern remembered the fifty-dollar bill Ivan had once shown him. He got the face of Grant clearly in his mind. He remembered the eyes and remembered Ivan saying: "There's a guy who knows something, who's been places, and who knows where he's going." Grant's eyes suddenly bugged out at him and then spun around in the engraved head. Morganstern flinched.

"Relax, Matthew. You're tensing up."

Morganstern made a concentrated effort. He took a deep breath and conjured up the fifty-dollar bill again.

"Okay, what do you have now?"

"A fifty-dollar bill."

"Good. Now, multiply that in your head until you get the total amount."

Morganstern began to create piles of fifties. Piles and piles and piles. "I don't know how many piles of fifties it would take."

"You don't have to be accurate, just get an overall sense of it."

Now Morganstern could see a field filled with stacks of fifty-dollar bills. They were wired together and piled up like bales of hay. Neat little piles of harvested money, stacked up as far as the eye could see. The sun was shining. The sky was brilliant blue. Morganstern felt a floating-back feeling as though the end of the lounger had tipped slightly. His head felt big and soft and far away from his feet. The floating sensation moved through his entire body. He felt terrific, warm and relaxed. He was going into a trance.

Then he was there, in the field, walking among the piles of money. He actually felt the warm sun beat down on his back. As he walked, he counted the bales: 101, 102, 103 . . . There seemed no end to the money, and yet he had no sense or concern about losing track of it. It was the most pleasurable pastime, walking and counting: 108, 109 . . .

"Now, once you get the money firmly in your space, I want you to visualize the things the money will buy you." James's voice sounded a million miles away.

Morganstern looked beyond the field toward the horizon. But there was no horizon. There was an enormous wall that reached from the ground to the top of the sky. The wall seemed to be filled with little squares, like oddly shaped windows. As he walked closer, he saw that they were paintings. Closer still, and he saw that they were his paintings. All beautifully framed and hung, perfectly lit by the sun.

He looked around and saw there were people standing and staring up at his paintings. He knew, without knowing, that they were art dealers, critics, collectors; he even recognized a few famous artists among the crowd. They were smiling and gesturing at his paintings. There was a sense of excitement as Morganstern moved among them. Some people had tears of joy in their eyes. One woman stood with her hands clasped together in front of her in a posture of sheer adulation. A few of the people, pulling their eyes away from the paintings, looked at Morganstern, undisguised admiration reflected in their faces.

"Okay, Matthew, the exercise is over. I want you to open your eyes." It took Morganstern a few minutes, but finally his eyes flickered open.

"How do you feel?" James asked.

"Great, rich, wealthy, loaded, famous, loved, terrific," Morganstern said, sitting up and stretching.

"Good. Did you bring your checkbook?"

"My checkbook? Yes, why?"

"Because now we have to write a check."

"Oh, sure," Morganstern said, sitting down at the other side of James's desk and taking the checkbook out of his pocket.

"Make it out to the Internal Revenue Service."

"Right," Morganstern said, opening the book to a blank check. "How much do I make it out for?"

"One hundred and seventy-five thousand dollars," James said.

Morganstern started to write the figure on the check. When he came to the first zero, he stopped. His hand was shaking. "What? You're kidding!"

"I haven't gotten to where I am today by making jokes about the IRS." James smiled.

"But why so much?"

Morganstern could feel a cramp move up from his hand toward

his elbow. Sweat was beginning to form under his arm. He felt dizzy.

"I'll explain. One hundred and seventy-five thousand represents seventy percent of the two hundred and fifty thousand dollars. Seventy percent is the tax bracket that getting that money puts you in. I'm rounding off, of course. It's actually fifty percent federal, eight percent city, and eight percent state, or sixty-six percent. Now, you can pay this off gradually over the year, but I think it's best to bite the bullet now, don't you?"

The expression never had more meaning to Morganstern. His teeth were literally set on edge. "But it's my money," he said. He was unable to control the tremor in his voice. "I won it."

"Only a part of it is yours," James said, talking to him very slowly, very patiently, as if he were a child. "The smaller part. The rest belongs to the government. The city gets a piece, and Uncle Sam gets a piece. You get what's left over." Morganstern almost expected him to end the sentence with "if you're a good boy," but he didn't. "How do you feel about that?" James answered his own question: "You're angry, aren't you?"

"Shit, yes," Morganstern said, "but then, I should have known it was too good to be true." He had a sudden flash of the field with the stacks of money. A cloud now covered the sun. In the distance he could see a tornado coming his way. The farthest pile of money shifted, separated, and was sucked up in the swirling wind. In his mind he tried to throw himself across as many piles as he could, but the tornado moved over him, curled around his body, snatched up the money, and blew it away.

Morganstern shook his head clear and went back to writing the check.

James reached out and stopped Morganstern's hand. "There are, however, certain things we can do to reduce your tax liability."

Morganstern tried to concentrate on getting the correct number of zeros. "If I have to pay, I have to pay. I don't want to do anything illegal."

James grabbed the pen out of his hand. "You're going to have to learn to trust me, Matthew. Everything I do is perfectly legal. Do you think I would ever do something that would jeopardize myself or my clients with the IRS? Look at me, Matthew."

Morganstern met James's intense blue gaze.

"Let me tell you a little something about myself. I think this will help you to see where I stand regarding the IRS. I believe in being perfectly candid and open and I expect my clients to be the same way with me." James leaned back in his chair, laced his fingers together, and turned to look out the window.

"I happen to have a Ph.D. in psychology. And yet my chosen career is that of a CPA. When I was still in graduate school getting my doctorate in psychology, my father was wrongly indicted for evasion of income taxes. On his way to his first court date, he suffered a heart attack and died. I felt I had failed my father. If only I had been there to help him with his tax returns, to stand up for him at the audit, it never would have happened. That's when I vowed to devote my life to helping people with their tax problems. I finished up with my Ph.D., then went back to school for my CPA. And here I am.

"Matthew, I have helped thousands of people. I can help you, too. But you have to make a decision to trust me. Do you or do you not trust me?"

Morganstern had no reason not to trust him. He was, after all, a certified public accountant. He nodded his head. "I trust you."

"Good. Now, first and foremost, and always remember this: the IRS is not on your side. The IRS has contempt for you. The IRS is out to destroy you if they can. And they will stop at nothing to accomplish this. My goal, my single goal in life, is to stick it to the IRS—on your behalf, and on behalf of the hundreds of taxpayers whom I am privileged to have as clients. I will do everything within my power to protect you from them. We're in this together, Matthew. You for your reasons. Me for mine." James reached both hands across the table, and Morganstern, greatly moved, exchanged a double crossover handshake with him. "Let's stick it to the IRS together."

James took a deep breath, removed a calculator from his top drawer, and put on a pair of wire-framed half-spectacles. "Now, down to business."

He began playing the buttons on the calculator with his long, thin fingers. As he played, he talked to himself. "The question is, how do we save Matthew Morganstern, recently moneyed and richly deserving, from exorbitant, inhuman taxes."

He played the calculator a few minutes more.

"How simple solutions are when one knows how to calculate." He smiled beatifically and leaned back in his suede desk chair.

"Here is what we do. First of all, we incorporate you. That way we can put twenty-five percent of your money into a corporate pension plan. Legal, simple, straightforward. The most direct way to put the money out of the government's filthy, slimy, grasping hands. A pension fund is *nontaxable.*" He pronounced the word "nontaxable" with the same relish that a compulsive eater would say "chocolate fudge."

"Incorporate? I don't understand."

"We make a corporation. Matthew Morganstern, Inc."

"But I don't know anything about corporations."

"You don't have to, Matthew. You're just an employee of the corporation. The corporation hires experts like me to tell you what to do. And my services"—this time he actually licked his lips before pronouncing the words—"are tax-deductible."

"Just what do I have to do as an employee of this corporation?"

"Ah, this is not just any corporation. This is *your* corporation. Set up by you, to serve you."

"But what do I do?" Morganstern said again, his mind jumping to long hours at a drawing table, producing piles of storyboards and tons of dandruff.

"You do what Ariel says you do so well. You paint."

"Paint?"

"Yes, you paint pictures. You cannot believe the business expenses an artist can take off," James said enthusiastically. "Art supplies, model fees, studio space, slide projectors, silk smocks, travel."

"Travel?"

"For research. Inspiration for your work. Absorption of local color. You know, ideas for landscapes. Sunsets on the Loire. The Taj Mahal by twilight. The bay of Hong Kong underneath a full moon. The Riviera at cocktail time. In order to paint landscapes, one needs to be able to work from the real thing."

"But I don't do landscapes per se."

James ignored him. "And then, of course, there are the operating expenses of the corporation itself: the stationery, the business cards, the office space, as distinguished from the studio space, the accounting and legal fees." He went back to his calculator. His fingers flew lightly and delicately over the keys. He played the machine with all the zeal of a synthesizer operator.

Morganstern watched him transfixed and then said, "I have trouble seeing myself as a corporation."

"Do you think Henry Ford saw himself as a corporation? Or Ralph Birdseye? Or Reverend Moon? The important thing to remember about you and the corporation is that you are two separate entities. You, the artist, are one thing. The corporation is something else. Always keep separate records, separate checkbooks, separate purposes. Your purpose, as the sole employee of the corporation, is to be happy, productive, and financially aboveboard. The purpose of the corporation is to stick it to the IRS. Keep all receipts—the more receipts, the better. We'll have to do separate tax returns, one corporate, one individual—"

"It sounds so complicated," Morganstern interrupted.

"Of course it's complicated." James flashed his flawless teeth. "You have to work twice as hard to keep your money as you did when you earned it in the first place."

"But I didn't earn the money. I won it."

"Ah, then you have to work even harder, don't you? You have to work very hard indeed."

It was all right with Morganstern. In degree of difficulty, nothing at the moment seemed harder than writing a check to the IRS for $175,000.

"Where was I? Oh, yes. As an employee of the corporation, you'll be paid a salary for painting."

"A salary for painting?" Morganstern repeated. He felt dizzy with pleasure.

"Let me explain the concept to you so you'll understand what we're doing. The whole idea is to move the money out of the corporation and into the individual account. The money in the individual account, the Matthew Morganstern-private-citizen-and-entitled-individual account, will go toward *tax-vantageous,* my word, investments."

"A salary for painting," Morganstern said again.

James got up from his chair and went over to stand behind Morganstern. "That's right, a salary to paint," he said. He began massaging Morganstern's shoulders as he spoke. "A salary to paint. A corporation to protect you. And an accountant to keep you safe from harm. By the end of the year," he said, speaking softly and slowly and massaging each word into Morganstern's shoulders, "the corporation will show zero profits and therefore will have no capital gains." Morganstern felt his eyelids getting heavy. "The income you receive as an individual will be aggressively invested."

"Invested," Morganstern crooned, his eyelids getting heavier.

"Twenty-five percent of the total annual income will have been safely vested into the pension plan."

"That's *nontaxable,*" Morganstern murmured.

"Very good," James said, patting him on the shoulder. He resumed his seat behind the desk. "And to cut down your tax liability even further, the remainder of the income you receive from Matthew Morganstern, Inc., will, minus the business expenses, which are tax-deductible, be *sheltered.*" Here James sprayed a light sprinkling of saliva when he said the word "sheltered."

"Sheltered." Morganstern sighed.

"But we'll talk about investments and shelters at our next session."

Sheltered, Morganstern thought. It sounded so safe, so snug, so cozy and caring.

"I'm afraid our time is about up," James said, consulting his beautiful watch. "By the way, did Ariel explain my fee schedule to you?"

"No, she didn't."

"It's simple enough. I get seventy-five dollars an hour for all session time and any time spent working on your books or preparing your tax plans. Your tax returns are, of course, a separate fee. And, as I said before, my fees are . . ."—he shot his finger out at Morganstern.

"Tax-deductible," Morganstern shot back on cue.

"Good, you're getting it. My secretary will set up the next appointment. Here's the name of a lawyer who'll take care of incorporating you. Now, let's go out there and do it."

They clasped four hands again and said in unison: "Stick it to the IRS!"

4

Minutes of the first meeting of the board of directors of Matthew Morganstern, Inc.:

Meeting was called to order on the 15th day of February, 1980, at the offices of Mansfield, Tucker, Rosen, Rosen & Sanchez at ten A.M. The following were present: Mr. Matthew Morganstern and Mr. Hudson Sanchez. It was resolved that the Corporation proceed to carry on the business for which it was incorporated as set forth in the following appended guidelines: to engage in the business of producing, creating, preparing, conceiving paintings, sketches, sculpture, and other visual or conceptual works of art for hanging, exhibiting, viewing, merchandising, and disposing of any such property in any manner including reproduction, leasing, or as collateral for purposes of private or public consumption; to invest and deal with the funds and assets of the Corporation in any manner and to acquire by purchase or otherwise interests in partnerships and joint ventures, the stocks, bonds, notes, debentures and other securities and obligations of any government, state, municipality, corporation, association, or partnership, domestic or foreign, and, while owner of such securities or obligations, to exercise all the rights, powers, and interests or privileges of ownership, including, among other things, the right to vote thereon for any and all purposes; to acquire by purchase or otherwise and to sell or otherwise dispose of any type of investment property, tangible or intangible, whether or not income-producing.

"Wow," said Morganstern.

"Sign here," Sanchez, the lawyer, said, indicating a line at the bottom of the minutes of the meeting. "Now, here are your corporate records." He handed Morganstern a big black notebook with his name emblazoned in gold-embossed letters along the binding. "Inside is your corporate seal, your stock certificates, and so on and so on."

"What do I do with all this stuff?" Morganstern asked.

"Use it as a doorstop. It's just part of the package."

"When do we have our next meeting?"

"That's it. One meeting is all you need to set up a corporation. Haven't you ever been incorporated before?"

"No, it's my first time."

"Well, there's nothing to it. Just call us up when you want to dissolve it."

"Why would I want to do that?"

"A corporation is no different from a marriage. When it no longer serves your purposes, you get out, right?"

"I wouldn't know, I've never been married."

"You've never been incorporated, never been married. I bet you've never even been sued."

"That's right."

"Well, your life is just beginning, isn't it?"

"What am I supposed to do next?" Morganstern asked Sanchez as he was ushered out of the office.

"Go home. Get rich. Get plenty of exercise. And pay our bill when it comes."

Morganstern took his corporate record book to the nearest coffee shop and studied it. Inside the book was a little plastic pouch. Inside the pouch was a heavy metal stamp. Morganstern tried it out on the paper place mat in front of him. In embossed letters he read: "Matthew Morganstern, Inc." The words formed a circle in the paper.

"What's that?" a waitress asked, pointing to the place mat.

"That's my corporate seal," he said, showing it to her. "I just got incorporated."

"Neat," she said, "just like Howard Hughes."

"I guess so." Morganstern laughed.

"Well, don't neglect your nails," she said. "Always keep your cuticles pushed back, that's important."

"Thanks," Morganstern said, "I'll remember that."

"So, what'll it be, sir?"

"Oh, I'll just have a cup of black coffee."

"Listen, you can have more than that. If you're a corporation, you should have the pecan pie. It's made on the premises."

"No, just coffee, thanks."

"Same thing happened to Hughes," she warned. "First he became a big corporation, then he stopped eating and let his nails grow. I'll never understand how you big-business guys think you can ignore your health."

Morganstern studied the book. It was divided into sections with little index tabs separating each one: Certificate of Incorporation, Bylaws, Certificates of Stock. There were one hundred actual stock certificates in the back of the book, representing two hundred common shares each. Each one was imprinted with the corporate name and engraved with an eagle against a backdrop of mountains, fir trees, clouds, and sky. In one claw the eagle carried four long arrows and in the other a branch of some unidentifiable foliage.

Morganstern wondered what the arrows and branch symbolized. Poverty and Wealth? Peace and War? Stocks and Bonds? It was the first stock certificate he had ever seen. And, lo and behold, it carried his name. He was very proud. He felt a strong kinship to Henry Ford, Thomas Edison, General Electric, to the great American dream. He felt at one with the noble eagle.

Morganstern called James from the coffee shop to tell him that he had been duly incorporated. "What do I do now?"

"Open up a corporate checking account and transfer the money from your personal account to that. Then we're in business."

All the way home from the bank, Morganstern kept singing to the tune of "Cheek to Cheek": "Business, I'm in business, and my stock is just as solid as a rock . . ."

On the corner of Third Avenue and Sixtieth he bumped into an old friend he hadn't seen in years. Stuey Schlossman was a professional social worker who had dedicated his life to helping the poor. Morganstern had first met him in Paris, where Stuey was hoping to practice social good in a fabulous foreign setting. He had run out of money fairly quickly and returned to the U.S.

"It's all bureaucratic bullshit," Stuey had explained. "Paperwork, justifying your time, and more paperwork. The system makes it impossible to really help the truly needy. Besides, the pay is an insult."

Morganstern had run into Stuey on 110th Street a few years later. He was selling Crock Pots from the back of a truck to raise money for a group he was involved with.

"FM, man, that's what it's all about. Financial Meditation. We study under Swami Budranktanak. He's a graduate of the Harvard Business School."

"How does it differ from Transcendental Meditation?"

"We meditate for money. That's where the bliss is. Swami gives

117

us mantras from the New York Stock Exchange. You want to know what my mantra is?"

"I thought you weren't supposed to tell."

"FM isn't like TM. We have full disclosure. Anyway, the mantra Swami Budranktanak gave me is DataGn. You know what that stands for?"

"I don't have the slightest."

"It stands for Data General. And do you know what Data General is selling for? Fifty and a half. It's up three-eighths of a point. Microcomputers, man. Explosive growth. I couldn't have asked for a better mantra."

"Sounds like a long way from social work, Stuey. What happened to the Public Good?"

"Haven't you heard? It's in the hands of the private sector. I haven't given up the battle. I'm just changing my game plan, that's all."

"Hey, it's the mad artist. What's new?" Stuey said. He was dressed, unusually for him, in a three-piece business suit.

"Well, I just got incorporated today."

"Great. How come?"

"It's a long story. Actually, it's a short story. I won a lot of money in a sweepstakes and my accountant suggested I do it for tax purposes." The words just rolled off Morganstern's tongue.

Stuey set down his attaché case. "No kidding? How much money?"

"Two hundred and fifty thousand dollars."

"You know, Matt, this is some coincidence. You just became a corporation, and just this morning I came up with a fantastic new corporate investment plan. I'm on my way now to California to present it to some very high-level investors. But, tell you what I'm going to do. I'll give you a call in a week or so and if it's not all spoken for, I might be able to let you in on the deal. I can't promise anything. But it would be great doing business with an old pal. Don't do anything till you talk to me."

Morganstern waved good-bye to Stuey and made his way to Central Park South and went into the park. As he walked he was aware of the huge skyscrapers that housed America's corporate giants. He felt that they were aware of him. He was warmed by their presence. The eyes of Exxon, Gulf & Western, and General Motors were upon him. He was the new guy in town.

He wanted to celebrate. It was no fun being a corporation if you couldn't throw an office party, he thought. He called Ariel at her agency. He hadn't talked to her in two days, since the night at Windows on the World. He had wanted to give them both time to get over the nastiness of the evening. But more than that he wanted a

118

chance to prove to her that he was capable of taking care of business before he spoke to her again.

"You are speaking to the chairman of the board of Matthew Morganstern, Inc. This being the first day of business for the aforesaid corporation, I am calling an emergency session tonight for the purposes of sipping champagne and conducting a very private celebration between interested parties. How do you vote? Yea or nay?"

"Oh, Matthew, I'm in the middle of a meeting," she said breathlessly. "Can I call you back?" He heard people talking heatedly in the background.

His face was burning with embarrassment. Why hadn't she told him she was in a meeting when she picked up the phone? Why had she picked up the phone in the first place if she couldn't talk?

"Sure, call me back. You'll probably be able to reach me at my corporate headquarters," he said testily.

By the time the phone rang a half-hour later, he had regained his good spirits. "Matthew Morganstern, Inc."

"So you got incorporated," Ariel said.

"Signed and sealed. Do you want to crack a bottle of champagne against America's newest corporate giant?"

"Hold on. . . . Tell them I'll be right there," he heard Ariel whisper to someone. "I'm sorry, Matthew. I've got to go back into the meeting. The client's waiting."

Morganstern was beginning to get miffed. "What about tonight? Can I see you?"

Ariel sighed. "I'm supposed to leave this afternoon for Fort Lauderdale. We have to reshoot some stupid orange-juice commercial because the orange juice didn't look pulpy enough. Can I take a rain check?"

A rain check? This woman who for three years had shared his bed, his dreams, his life, her fucking smoked oysters, was talking about rain checks?

"Sure, let's have lunch sometime," he said, and slammed down the phone.

Ariel burst into tears. Her preproduction meeting had to be delayed twenty minutes while she went to the ladies' room and wiped the Fabulash from underneath her eyes.

Meanwhile, Morganstern, feeling contrite, attempted to call her back. He was told by her secretary that she was in a meeting and couldn't be disturbed.

He stared furiously at the phone. He was damned if he was going to let her rain on his corporation. He was sick and tired of trying to figure out what was going on in her head. He was much more concerned at that moment with what was going on in his crotch.

Since getting incorporated that morning, he had been in a state of almost constant erection. In fact, ever since winning the money he had felt incredibly horny. At first he attributed this to Ariel's absence. Now he had the feeling there was some sort of strange connection between his newly acquired capital and his cock.

To hell with Ariel, he said to himself. He didn't need her. The city was filled with available, desirable women. There was nothing wrong with trying something or someone new, he reasoned. Just this once. After all, he and Ariel weren't married. They weren't even speaking. And they had never even promised one another to be faithful, whatever that meant.

He was a corporation now. He had to think of what was best for the company. He felt lonely, needy, and hornier than ever. Was this the price of financial power? he wondered. Was this the burden of the one-man corporation? The loneliness of the long-term investor? Not if he could help it. The chairman of the board needed a broad—it was as simple as that.

Morganstern had never been what could be termed a swinging bachelor. He had never really dated in the true sense of the word. He met women, one at a time, got involved with them on a singular, albeit short-term basis. He had never been to a singles bar, never "scored" in the Hamptons, never shared his fears and inadequacies at a Unitarian Church meeting for people on the make, never been invited to bring his own bottle and, if lucky, take home his own girl from one of the big private-apartment parties.

He looked around for his little black book and then remembered he had never had one. All he had was an old sketchbook which he had used for sketches and notes and the names and addresses of people he had long since lost touch with. He found the notebook and opened it. There were sketches of his feet and hands and other people's feet and hands. There was a onetime attempt at poetry when he was lonely and traveling in Europe between one unknown language and another.

He found a few numbers of women that predated Ariel and predated his memory. Names whose faces he could not now even conjure up. Then he remembered the girl from the bank.

He opened his billfold. There, folded up neatly, was his $250,000 deposit slip, and right next to it was the card with the number of the tantalizing little bank teller, Miranda Martin. "Don't be a stranger," she had said.

He dialed her number. While he waited for her to pick up, he rehearsed his opening: "Hi, I'll bet you'll never guess who this is . . ." "You probably don't remember me, but . . ."

"Hello." It was her. He wasn't ready.

"Hi, Miranda?"

"Yes."

"This is Matthew Morganstern."

Silence.

"Matthew Morganstern. We met at Metrobank. You said I could call."

"What's your account number?"

Morganstern glanced down at the deposit slip. "Zero-nine-nine-five-zero-zero-seven-dash-six-six-one-one."

"Oh, sure. Hi. How are you?" She suddenly sounded very happy to hear from him. He wondered what her reaction would have been if he had misread his account number.

"Um, I was wondering if you'd like to go out sometime."

"Well, I don't know about going out, but I would love to come over and talk to you."

"You would? When?"

"I could be there in about half an hour."

'Terrific. Do you know where I live?"

"Of course. Metrobank knows everything."

Morganstern raced for the bathroom. He took a long hot shower, followed by a short cold blast. He dried himself, and since he didn't own any cologne, he splashed on some of Ariel's old perfume. It was L'Air du Temps and it was a mistake. He took another quick shower to wash off the fragrance of lilies of the valley.

What to wear? What to wear? He put on a clean pair of Levi's and a silk kimono jacket Ariel had given him for Christmas one year. He changed his mind and put on a cotton turtleneck. Exactly thirty minutes after he hung up with Miranda the doorbell rang.

He opened the door and there she stood, wearing one huge pair of breasts, or so it seemed to Morganstern. The breasts were encaged in the kind of tight halter top that Morganstern thought dancers wore only in the privacy of their exercise classes. She was also wearing circulation-stopping designer jeans and high-heeled mules.

What tits, he said to himself. He could swear they entered the apartment a good three seconds before the rest of her. They had a life and a mind of their own, moving this way and that like some strange sightless animals. She crossed the living room and took a seat on the couch.

"You know, I was going to call you if you didn't call me," she said, curling her legs underneath her. Morganstern listened for the sound of her skintight jeans ripping. She smiled up at him and patted the spot next to her on the couch. Everything was moving so fast. He was beginning to miss the preliminaries. "And you picked tonight, of all nights. I'm celebrating my seventh anniversary tonight."

Oh, shit, Morganstern thought. She's married. Well, what did it matter? This was just to be a fling. A short excursion off the beaten track. "You're married?" he asked.

"Oh, no, I'm not married. It's seven years ago today that I started with Metrobank."

"No kidding?" Morganstern said, moving closer to her on the couch.

"It's a wonderful bank," she said. "You're so lucky to have your account with us. Did you know that Metrobank is New York's largest bank and that it employs more people and serves more customers than any other bank in the metropolitan area?"

"No, I didn't know." Morganstern casually draped his arm over the back of the couch.

"Metrobank pioneered electronic consumer banking. It was the first bank with twenty-four-hour banking and fully computerized teller services," she said, her chest swelling with pride, her breasts threatening to erupt out of her tight leotard. "As a result of that, we increased our share of the market by forty percent." She leaned toward him. "Imagine, one-point-nine-five transactions take place every second of every day. That's fifty-five million transactions a year. Just as we're sitting here hundreds of people are slipping their Metrocards into little Metroslots all over the city."

Morganstern was getting a hard-on. He put a hand on her thigh. She put her hand on his. "Do you remember the Metro television campaign, 'Your money is safe with us'?"

"Oh, sure," he said, massaging her thigh lightly. "Terrific campaign."

"Well, it's true. Metro really cares about people and their money. They want their customers to have faith in Metro's banking system. To know that everything we do at the bank is for them. Like the commercial says, 'Trust is a two-way street.'"

Jesus, Morganstern thought, what the hell was she talking about? Maybe she was just at a loss for conversation. She was probably as nervous as he was. "Would you care for a drink?"

"I don't drink. Alcohol destroys the brain cells, and Metrobank needs all my brain cells operating at their very best. You know, they trained me. They taught me everything I know. They took me fresh out of high school and gave me skills."

"That's wonderful," Morganstern murmured. He put his other hand on her shoulder. She didn't seem to mind. His erection showed no signs of flagging. He decided to get right to the point. "Would you like to go into the bedroom?"

"What for?"

"To lie down."

"Oh, I see. You want to have sex with me." She looked at him longingly and then shook her head. "I wish I could, but I just can't."

"Why not?"

"I gave up sex for Metrobank."

"What? Did they make you take a vow or something?"

"Oh, no, it was my own choice. You know, before I found Metrobank I used to sleep around a lot. I was very into drugs and sex. I was totally screwed up until Metrobank took me into their training program. They saved my life. That's why I came here tonight."

"I don't understand. I got the feeling you were interested."

"Oh, I am. I'm always interested in meeting people with new money. Metrobank needs people like you. Did you know that the bank spent ten million dollars changing their name and their logo and their deposit slips and everything just so customers would feel closer to them? And they do research all the time to find out how their depositors feel about the different services. And yet, with all that work, all that catering, all that love, people still take their money out and put it into the money market. Just because they get higher interest and more liquidity. Do you know how that makes Metrobank feel?"

"No, I don't." He sighed. At least his erection was gone.

"People don't realize that when they deposit their money in Metrobank, it's a commitment. Interest rates should have nothing to do with it. Here," she said, taking several pamphlets from her purse, "these explain all about our Free Access CD's, our three-month special certificates, and all sorts of other high-yield savings plans. Read them, and if you have any questions, call me, day or night."

"Do they pay you to work at night?" he asked, taking the pamphlets from her.

"Of course not. I don't need to be paid. The joy of knowing I'm doing good is reward enough. Metrobank wants you to find happiness in banking now and forevermore. Do you believe that?"

"I believe it." He sighed.

"Do you believe it's not the saving, but the being saved that counts?"

"Sure. Absolutely," Morganstern said. She got up and walked toward the door. He followed her, dazed.

"Money markets are the work of the devil. They are all that is avaricious and evil in the world. Remember that," she said.

"I will," he replied, opening the door for her.

"And remember this," she said, taking his chin in her soft little hand. "Metrobank loves you."

"Thank you," Morganstern said.

He watched her walk her breasts down the hallway toward the elevator. She turned and waved. He waved back. She must be the 80's version of the 60's flower child, he thought. From peace and love to savings and checkings. CD's instead of OD's. How things had changed. Or how things hadn't changed.

For the first time since he could remember, Morganstern slept late the next morning. It was almost eleven when he was woken up by the doorbell. He opened the door and was surprised to see Ivan Ludlam in his fur-lined trench coat and flashing teeth.

"I warned you but you wouldn't listen to me," Ivan said. "I told you to leave money and avarice to the rest of us, but oh no, you had to go and win a sweepstakes of all things, thereby compromising your artistic integrity. Well, we all make mistakes. It's not my place to judge. It is my place to offer assistance and guidance where needed, so I'm here to take you under my wing, old pal."

"I don't want any," Morganstern said, slamming the door in Ivan's face. Ivan leaned on the doorbell for a full minute before Morganstern answered it again.

"Ivan, I've gotten enough of your help to last me a lifetime."

"Don't mess with me, Morganstern," Ivan said, pushing past him. "I may be the best friend you've got. Who else would take time out of a busy schedule just to get you started on the right foot?"

"Started how?"

"Old Ivan is here to give you a few pointers on how to enjoy the fucking good life. Get dressed. You're coming with me."

"I'm not going anywhere with you."

"You know," Ivan said, throwing an arm around Morganstern's shoulders, "after all is said and done, you still remain one big asshole, that's what I love about ya. Come on, hurry up. I haven't got all day."

Despite himself, Morganstern was curious as to what Ivan had in mind.

"Where are we going?" he asked as they walked quickly down Madison Avenue.

"To Girabaldi's."

"What's Girabaldi's?"

"Have you ever heard of Tiffany's?"

"Yes."

"Well, Girabaldi's is to the rag business what Tiffany's is to the ring business. They sell men's clothes."

"I don't need any clothes, Ivan."

"I can't believe that you, who have devoted your life to the visualization of things, can be so fucking blind." Ivan stopped and turned Morganstern toward a store window. "Just look at yourself. You look like the tail end of a bread line. You can't expect people in the world of business and finance, which you so suddenly find yourself thrust into, to pay you any fucking heed, let alone respect, dressed the way you are. You need to look the part, my man."

Girabaldi's was a beautiful store occupying three floors of a converted brownstone on Twenty-seventh Street off Madison. It was all glass and chrome and tan leather. Inside, a tall, thin young man was aimlessly fondling the stacks of shirts and racks of ties. It was hard to tell if he was a salesman or a customer who was merely browsing. Ivan snapped his fingers at him.

"*Servicio*," he said, "*servicio, per favore.*"

The young man lifted his pretty upper lip in a snarl before turning away.

"These fags are the worst," Ivan said to Morganstern. "They'd rather stare at themselves in the mirror than be caught dead waiting on you."

An older man came down the stairs from the second floor. "Signor Ludlam!"

"Ah, Girabaldi, thank God you're here. My friend needs your help, as you can obviously see."

Ivan and Girabaldi spent an hour picking out shirts and ties, jackets and pants, even socks and shoes, and then made Morganstern try on everything. The jackets were all soft and unstructured, the pants slightly baggy with little pleats in front, the ties thin, barely covering the buttons on the soft cotton shirts. After switching shirts and jackets, replacing ties, they gave him a pair of shoes to put on. The leather was so soft, Morganstern could swear they were melting on his feet. They turned him around slowly, scrutinizing him from every angle.

"It's a beginning." Ivan sighed.

"Yes," agreed Girabaldi, "he has the body for it."

"Okay, take a look," Ivan said, unfolding the leather-backed three-way mirror on the wall.

Morganstern was amazed. He liked what he saw. He felt the sleeve of the jacket. "This is nice," he said. "What is it?"

"It's cashmere and wool, you fucking hick," Ivan said. "Okay," he said to Girabaldi, "we'll take the three jackets, the four slacks, the six shirts, the shoes, and the ties."

"I don't need all that stuff," Morganstern protested. "I'll just take what I'm wearing."

"Need!" Ivan shouted. "Need is not the point here. Have. That's the point. First you learn to have, and once you've got that down, then you worry about needing. That comes later."

"I don't give a shit. I'll take this, and that's it."

"Okay, okay," Ivan said to Girabaldi. "Give us the bad news."

"Signor?"

"The bill. What's it come to?"

Girabaldi took out a small calculator and tallied up the total. "Seven hundred and fifty dollars."

"So, what can you do for my friend on this?"

"I don't understand, signor."

"Deals. We're talking deals here. He'll pay in cash."

"That doesn't make any difference. Many of my clients pay in cash."

"I was going to write a check," Morganstern interjected.

Ivan took Morganstern aside. "Being a hebe from the Midwest, you wouldn't know about this. We call this jewin' em down. Keep out of it; leave it to me." They went back to Mr. Girabaldi. "How about if you send the stuff to New Jersey. It'll save us on city taxes."

"We don't send things."

"Okay, okay, my friend. You've got us where you want us. Here's what I'm going to do. I'm going to throw in a couple of concepts for your next advertising campaign. I've seen what you do in *The New Yorker* and it sucks. So for a couple of my prize-winning, sales-building thoughts and a check for three-seventy-five, I think we can call it a deal."

"I'm sorry, Mr. Ludlam, the price for the garments is seven-hundred-fifty."

"You got it." Ivan threw up his hands. "Write him a check, Morganstern."

Morganstern wrote the check.

"That's what I love about that store," Ivan said as they left. "They never come down on their prices. That's a real class operation."

"Why'd you bother trying to bargain with him if you knew that?"

"Are you kidding? If I didn't try, the man would have no respect for me. Nobody but a fool pays those prices without putting up a fight. Besides, it keeps me in shape." They stopped on the corner of Madison and Forty-first, outside Ivan's agency.

Ivan turned Morganstern around and looked at him. "So, how do you feel?"

"You know, you were right. The clothes feel great. I'm glad I bought them."

Ivan studied him for a long time. "And what are you going to do with the rest of your money?"

"Well, for one thing, I'm going to paint. For the first time in my life I can afford to paint without worrying about how I'm going to live."

Ivan grabbed Morganstern by his new cashmere-and-wool lapels. "Paint? You just think you're going to paint. You won't paint. You'll worry about money just like the rest of us. Yessir, money's going to become very, very important to you. Money, stocks, bonds, investments, tax shelters. But you can take it from me, it's all fucking nothing."

"Let go of my jacket, Ivan."

Ivan released the lapels. "I'll tell you what's important," he announced to Morganstern and to the people who had gathered around them, hoping for a street fight to liven up a dull lunch break. "Love. Love is what it's all about." The crowd grew larger. Ivan turned to address them. "This man had it all. He had it all and he blew it. He had poverty, simplicity, creativity, purity, a nice piece of ass whenever he wanted it. This man had love." He turned back to Morganstern. "And what did you do? You threw it in the garbage."

Morganstern wanted to get away from this crazy man, but not before he had a chance to hit him. He grabbed Ivan by the tie. "Have you been talking to Ariel?" he hissed.

"Talking to Ariel? I have been bleeding with Ariel, I have been crying with Ariel."

"When did you see her?"

"I don't need to see her. I know. I talk to Marcy Conrad all the time. She told me Ariel moved out. You are some prize asshole, my friend." Ivan turned back to the crowd, who were beginning to get restless and bored. "Take a look at a prize asshole. This asshole threw love in the garbage. A beautiful woman who gave up a career as a brilliant novelist to keep him in oil paints and turpentine. And as soon as he strikes it rich, what does he do? He drops her. He pissed on love. True love. Do you think those men would be homosexuals if they could find true love?" he said, pointing to two men Morganstern recognized as the president and senior vice-president of Ivan's agency.

"Do you think I would be such a driven, well-dressed, successful advertising executive if I could find true love?

"I worked hard, made it big, I am making so much money right now I don't know what to do with it, and I would trade it all, every penny, with the exception of some New York City bonds which haven't matured, for one thing and one thing only: love."

Morganstern had had enough. He took Ivan in his arms, bent him over backward and looked longingly in his eyes. "But I love you, Ivan," he said, planting a quick wet kiss on Ivan's mouth. He released his hold suddenly and Ivan fell backward on the sidewalk.

Ivan looked up at Morganstern and laughed. "You are the biggest asshole I know," he shouted as Morganstern strode down the street. "That's why I love ya, ya fucking crazola."

Morganstern wondered why the street scene with Ivan hadn't made him angrier. Was this an effect of his newfound fortune?

There was a sense of distance, of immunity from the craziness of people and the roughness of life in the city. It was as if he had been coated in Teflon. Traffic was just as loud, the streets just as dirty, and the people just as bizarre, but he felt as though he were protected from it all. Nothing could touch him. Not even Julio.

"Good morning, Mr. Morganstern," Julio said, tipping his hat to Morganstern, who was on his way to his second meeting with James the next morning.

Morganstern stopped in his tracks. "What did you say?"

"I said, good morning, Mr. Morganstern," Julio said, tipping his cap a second time.

"What's the password?" Morganstern asked.

"The password? It's 'Have a nice day.'"

"'Have a nice day'? That's it?"

"That's right. You want a taxi, Mr. Morganstern?"

"Sure. Call me a taxi," he said, amazed.

"Okay, señor. You're a taxi. Hee-hee-hee." Julio doubled over with laughter.

"And, you're a *cojón*," Morganstern said, walking past him into the street.

He found himself smiling. It was the smile of a Teflon-coated man.

5

"So, how do you feel about being incorporated?" James asked at the beginning of their second meeeting.

"Good."

"Come on, Matthew, you can do better than that."

Morganstern, anxious to move out of the emotional and into the financial, sensed the only way they would get there was if he gave James sufficient psychological fodder. "I feel powerful, strong, manly, big, invincible, all-American, potent, and protected."

"Good, very good." James smiled. "Now, let me ask you this: how do you feel about the breakup with Ariel?" That took Morganstern off guard.

"What do you know about Ariel and me?" he said angrily.

"You have to understand that Ariel and I have a very special relationship. I have a special relationship with all my clients. Well?"

"Well what?"

"Matthew, you have to be more open about your feelings. Otherwise, we'll never get anywhere."

"I don't see what my feelings about Ariel have to do with our business dealings," Morganstern snapped.

"Your state of mind and everything that affects it ultimately affect your ability to make sound financial decisions. Trust me, Matthew. Go on, give."

128

"Okay. I feel sad. Lonely. Scared that we'll never get back together. And pissed," he said impatiently.

"You're angry? Why?"

"Because of the whole way she's reacting to what I consider to be an incredible piece of good luck. Because everything seems to be a negative with her these days."

"I needn't tell you that money—either the lack of it or sometimes even the excess of it—is one of the major problems that most couples face in a relationship. You have to give it time. You have to give her time. Meanwhile, we can work to solidify your corporation, get your business running smoothly. Ariel will come around. She's a very caring woman. A very sensitive woman. A very lovely, very sensual woman."

"Cut it out," Morganstern yelled.

"Very good, Matthew. A quick gut response. Excellent. Now, shall we get down to business? Today we're going to write some checks. The first will be for the pension plan. Make it out to Matthew Morganstern, Employees Pension Plan, for"—he tapped on his calculator—"thirty-two thousand, two hundred and twenty-two dollars and forty-nine cents. I'll give you the name of a broker later. She'll open up a money-market account for you and advise you in stock purchases."

He took the check from Morganstern and stared at it. "It's so pure, so simple. They'll never get their hands on this, never.

"Now, then, let's give the bastards a little something, just to nibble on. Keep them off our trail, so to speak. Later, when we start getting into tax shelters, we'll cut them off completely. Make out a check to the IRS for $9,441.18," James said, gritting his teeth.

Morganstern made out the check and handed it to James.

James leaned back in his chair, holding his hands up above his head. "I won't touch it. You mail it to them. I simply will not be a part of it. Now, on to more pleasant things." He smiled. "The salary check. You'll be drawing a salary of . . ."—again he ran his fingers on the calculator—"$10,558.82 a month."

"I make it out to me, from me?"

"That's right. As I said, the money moves from the corporation into your personal account."

"That's a hell of a lot of money. What do I do with it?"

"What does anyone do with a salary? You live off it."

"But that's almost three thousand dollars a week."

"So? You're going to have a lot of expenses. If you find you don't need it all, you just invest what you don't need. That's why you have a stockbroker. Now, travel and entertainment money: you'll be drawing three hundred dollars a week, or twelve hundred a month cash for travel-and-entertainment expenses."

"Who am I supposed to entertain?"

"Anybody connected with your business."

"Business?" Morganstern had momentarily forgotten what his business was.

"The art business," James reminded him. "That means you take out art dealers, collectors, gallery owners, other artists, suppliers, potential models, so on and so forth."

"But I don't understand the difference between money I need to live on and travel-and-entertainment money."

"One is business and the other isn't. One is tax-deductible and the other isn't."

"Why is taking someone out to lunch a tax deduction?"

"Let me explain: you take an artist friend to the Four Seasons for lunch. He gives you a terrific tip on how you can get more stretch out of your canvas. You have met for the purposes of advancing or improving your career. You have partaken of food and drink. But it's like a business meeting. Just look at it this way: the corporation employs you to be an artist. An artist has to eat. It's what is commonly known as an expense-account lunch."

"Well, to tell you the truth, I don't usually eat lunch."

"Have dinner, then. Why are you being so resistant? What are you afraid of? Let's get in touch with that."

"It just seems like an awful lot of money to spend on meals. I don't know that many people in art. I don't even know that many restaurants. And it sounds like I'm putting one over on the government."

James stood up and leaned over the desk. "Don't flatter yourself. If you could put something over on the IRS, you wouldn't need someone like me. We always work within their rules.

"Just to review: your personal living expenses come from your salary. Your corporate expenses, the expenses of running the business, the travel-and-entertainment allowance, are deductible. Now, here's the name and number of a stockbroker." He handed Morganstern a card which read: "Getty Milford, Bartlett & Co." "She's bright, she's bold, she's a proven money-maker. She'll help you manage your pension plan, open up a money-market account, and advise you in aggressive short-term investments."

James got up, came around his desk, and clamped a hand down on Morganstern's shoulder. "I know you're confused. Confusion is good. It ultimately leads to the exposure of deeper feelings. You're a corporation now, Matthew, and you have to learn to act like a corporation: mature, responsible, aboveboard, and on guard. But always remember: the IRS would like nothing better than to have you behaving like a sniveling idiot." He gently pounded Morganstern's shoulder with his fist. "So let's stick it to 'em. Stick it to 'em. Stick it to 'em." He stopped pounding. "Our time's up. See you next week."

130

Morganstern called Ariel at her agency and was told that she was still on location and wouldn't be back in New York for two weeks. "Is there anywhere I can reach her?" "I'm afraid not. She's in the groves, waiting for the oranges to ripen."

According to James, the first thing on Morganstern's agenda was to open up a money-market account. He called the Bartlett number and asked for Getty Milford. She came to the phone immediately.

"Hi, Matthew." It was the warmest, softest, sexiest, soothingest voice Morganstern had ever heard. A tingle ran down the back of his neck.

"Hi, Miss Milford."

"Getty," she breathed.

"Getty. James Gross gave me your name. He said you could open up a money-market account for me and also act as my broker."

"Oh, I can. I will. It would give me great pleasure. I'll be happy to open anything you'd like."

Morganstern gave her all the information she needed.

"Now, you'll be wanting to set up a portfolio soon. I hate doing these things over the phone, so we'll get together for that. Meeting, talking, making contact, that's the best way to do business, don't you think?"

"Absolutely," Morganstern said.

"You'll be hearing from me soon, Matthew"—breath, sigh—"very soon. If you have any questions in the meantime, call me. I'm here to serve you in every way possible."

Morganstern couldn't wait to meet Getty Milford. If she looked anything like she sounded, he was in for a real treat. But then again, she might just be another kook like Miranda from Metrobank. Time would tell.

Morganstern thought about what James had said. He was right. He had to approach this new corporation in a mature, responsible way. No more childish naiveté. This was business.

He paid a visit to the art-supply store where he had purchased the tube of Cadmium Red. He felt like a different person with his corporate checks folded neatly into his billfold. He knew exactly what he wanted to buy. He had a long list in his head. There was a beautiful antique mahogany easel in the window.

"How much for the easel?" he asked the salesman. It was the same salesman who had waited on him before.

"There's not enough veal in Texas to pay for that."

"I'm paying with money today. How much?"

"Four hundred and fifty dollars."

"Fine, I'll take it." Morganstern selected ten new prestretched canvases and thirty tubes of paint. Then he walked to the back of the store to look at the sable brushes. "I'll take a number eleven, a number six, a number two, and a number four."

"How exactly are you going to pay for all this?" the salesman asked.

"Do you take checks?"

"Sure we take checks. We also prosecute for insufficient funds."

The bill came to $1,350. Morganstern wrote out a corporate check and the salesman called the bank.

"They say you got the money in your account," he said with amazement. "Listen, why don't you open up a charge with us? That way you only have to write a check once a month."

Morganstern was struck by the irony: in his poor days it was always cash on the line. But now that people found out he had the cash, they wouldn't let him spend it.

He spent several hours arranging and rearranging his purchases. He was well aware of the fact that he hadn't done any painting since he lost all his work in the fire. He was anxious to make up for lost time.

He took out one of the smaller canvases and placed it on the new easel. For almost half an hour he stared at it, admiring the whiteness, the cleanness, the blankness of it. Then he turned it around sideways, hoping the change from vertical to horizontal would spark some ideas. But his mind was as blank as the canvas. He looked down at the table next to him, where his palette, brushes, and new paints were neatly arranged. He had laid out the oils according to the color spectrum, with the reds, oranges, and yellows closest to him and the greens, blues, indigos and violets farthest away. He reversed the order, putting the darker colors closer. He examined his new sable brushes. He had placed them in a crystal vase. Then he decided that the vase was too deep, making it difficult to remove a few of the shorter-handled brushes. He rummaged through the apartment looking for something shallower and finally settled on an old plastic Tupperware orange-juice container.

He looked at the canvas again and then looked out the window. He had never noticed the fact that there was a narrow concrete ledge with a little steel barricade outside the window. It was the perfect place for a window box . . . .

At the neighborhood plant store, he purchased a green metal window box, ten pounds of potting soil, and six geranium plants. Two hours later he stepped back and admired his work. It was a nice touch, a little bit of nature against the gray rectangular background of the city. He returned to his easel. It had begun to grow dark. He switched on the extender lamp that he had attached to the top of the easel. He saw himself silhouetted against the canvas. He changed the angle of the lamp, but still there were shadows. The lighting was terrible. How had he ever managed to paint this way? He glanced down at his watch. It was almost six o'clock. Would the lighting store still be open?

At Jeff's Fixtures, he looked at the various track lighting. It was priced according to the number of spots and the length of the track. Installation wasn't included. He made arrangements with Jeff to install the lighting at the end of the week, and wrote a check for the full amount. All in all, he felt that his first full day as an operating business had been fairly successful.

Morganstern decided against trying to paint that night. Without the track lighting it would be a waste of time. He could get a fresh start in the morning. After all, he had the whole day free and clear with nothing else to do but paint. For some reason, that thought did not bring him the same pleasure it once would have.

After three days of staring at the blank canvas, he began to grow panicky and snow-blind. He called Zero, in a state of near-hysteria. "I've lost it. I've lost it."

"Lost what?" Zero asked.

"I can't paint anymore. I can't even think up any pictures. Nothing comes to me, nothing. "It's gone, all gone."

"Don't be ridiculous, man. You don't lose talent just like that. It takes years. It's obviously just a typical case of artistic block. Sit tight. I'll be right over."

"What are you talking about?" Zero said, walking over to the canvas Morganstern had left propped against the easel. "That's terrific. I particularly like the way you duplicated the original texture of the canvas. Very smart, too. You probably heard that minimal-art prices have skyrocketed." He took a catalog out of his pocket. "Johnson's *White on White* fetched sixty-five hundred."

"It's not minimal art," Morganstern said. "It's just untouched, uninspired canvas."

"Untouched canvas? Fabulous! You may have really hit upon something here: superminimal art. Think of the money you save on oils." Zero was pacing up and down. "Wait. I have an even better idea: no canvases."

"Oh, come on, Zero. You're not helping me. Let me ask you something. Have you ever drawn a complete blank?"

"No, man, when I run out of ideas, I just look at the catalogs, see what's selling, get a feel of where the market is going. That always gives me ideas. Think about money—it works every time."

"I think money is the problem," Morganstern said. He told Zero about the sweepstakes and about getting incorporated. "So here I am, with all the time and money in the world, all the materials I could ever need, and I can't paint a thing."

"Well, no wonder," Zero said. "Now it makes sense. Look at this place."

"What's wrong with it?"

"You can't expect to work in an environment like this. It isn't professional. Where's your corporate identity? Does IBM operate like this? No, of course they don't."

Zero dragged Morganstern to the Haskell Office Furniture Store.

"Come on, Zero, I'm a painter. What do I need office furniture for?" Morganstern protested.

"First and foremost, for the depreciation."

"What's that?"

"Ask your accountant, he'll explain it all to you."

"All this stuff is a business expense?"

"That's right."

"And that makes it tax-deductible?"

"Right again."

Morganstern still didn't understand how it worked. But he felt reassured by the words. Somehow it seemed important to accrue business expenses if one was a corporation, he thought.

Zero selected a wood-grained heavy-gauge steel desk, a typing chair, a matching three-drawer filing cabinet, and an IBM typewriter.

"This is crazy. What am I going to do with all this stuff?"

"It's not for you. It's for your secretary."

"What secretary?"

"Have you ever heard of a business without a secretary?"

"I don't have anything for a secretary to do."

"That's what you think. A secretary is going to free you up so you can get back to painting."

"Free me up from what?"

"From answering the phone, handling your mail."

"I don't get any phone calls or mail."

"That was before. Now that you're a corporation, it's a whole different story. There are mailings to do, letters to send, publicity releases to give out. Then there's the follow-up and detail work. How do you think Picasso got to be so big?"

"I always assumed it was because he was a brilliant and prolific artist," Morganstern said sarcastically.

"Yeah, but who cared? Who knew? He had to promote himself just like everyone else. Picasso understood the principles of business. He knew that it doesn't matter whether or not you had the product to sell, you still have to be able to reach the public. You have to position yourself, promote yourself, market and merchandise."

"I don't buy that."

"It's true. Ask yourself: why do so many artists, guys with the

134

most incredible talent, never make it? Why do they just fade off into obscurity, while others become big names? Think about it. You'll see I'm right."

Morganstern didn't know if Zero was right or not. He just knew that spending money was beginning to come very easy to him. Almost as easy as painting once had been. He wrote a check for the things Zero had picked out.

Zero glanced at his watch. "Hurry up, we have time to get over to the printers' before they close."

"Printer's? What for?"

"For your stationery. What's your secretary supposed to type on? Canvas?"

At the printers', Zero took out a little pad of paper and quickly sketched a design.

"What's that?" Morganstern asked, looking over his shoulder.

"Your logo. MM, Inc. Nice, clean, modern. Sans serif. Like it?"

"Sure, it's fine."

"Wait a second." Zero took back the pad, wrote something on it, and handed it back to Morganstern.

"'Artists working through art to achieve artistry,'" Morganstern read. "What the hell does that mean?"

"That's your corporate slogan. You've got to have a corporate slogan. You can't just have a logo hanging there with no explanation. Look at Exxon. Look at IT&T. You've got to reach out and touch someone. You've got to make a statement that is human, relevant, and ecological. You don't want people to just see you as another big business. You have to show you have a soul *and* a goal. Which is another reason why a secretary is mandatory. As a bona fide corporation, you have an obligation to the American economy to provide jobs. And, I've got the perfect person."

"Well, maybe I could try her out for a day or two."

"It's not a her, it's a him. All the big corporations are hiring male secretaries now. And this guy's terrific. He's an out-of-work actor named Cornwall. Also, he's English, which adds a nice touch of class. Come on, we can get the invitations another day," Zero said, pulling Morganstern out of the stationery store.

"What invitations?"

"To your party."

"But I don't have any paintings to show right now. What's the sense in having a party?"

"You don't have a party to show your work. That's gauche. You have a party to get people, the right people, in a receptive frame of mind for when you do have an opening. That way, all the folks who came to your first party and stuffed down the fresh shrimp and guzzled all the expensive imported champagne will feel obligated to attend your opening."

135

Ariel was right, Morganstern thought to himself on the way back to the apartment. The money was changing his life. But, hopefully, for the better. He wondered how she would react to the office furniture and the changes he had made in the apartment. Well, he couldn't worry about that. He was in the fast lane now, and he had to keep moving to stay ahead of things.

6

The next day Morganstern met Cornwall. He was a tall, alarmingly thin man in his late forties who wore his mahogany-brown hair combed up from the back and looped several times back and forth in a zigzag pattern across his balding crown. His eyebrows and mustache were dyed to match. He must have been wearing Pan-Cake makeup, Morganstern thought, because the color of his face differed radically from that of his neck. His face was an unrelieved tan, while his neck had the color and consistency of a plucked chicken wing.

"Is Cornwall your first name or your last name?" Morganstern asked.

"It's my stage name," Cornwall said proudly.

Morganstern was trying to assume the correct tone of the potential employer. "Can you type and take dictation?"

"I can do better, sir. I can take direction. I was trained at the Royal Academy. I gave up the theater, however, for the more lucrative opportunities available in commercial television. But until I get, as they say, my big break, I'm at your disposal."

"We should talk about salary. I was thinking that I probably won't need you for more than two days a week, if that. What do you think would be a fair salary?"

"Oh, sir, that's not for me to say. However, if we are speaking about fair recompense, how does one hundred dollars a day strike you?"

"It strikes me as expensive."

"Ah, but you know of course it's a business deduction." There they were again, those magic words. Everybody seemed to be in on it. "Okay, it's a deal," Morganstern said.

The phone rang. Cornwall walked over to it. "How shall I answer, sir?"

"I guess just say hello."

136

"What I mean is, what accent would you care for me to use? I do several: French, cockney, Irish, Italian, Indian, German. I can also do a few regional American speech types. My Deep South is very good, I think."

The phone continued ringing. "Why don't you just speak the way you normally would?"

"As you wish, sir." By the time he answered the phone, whoever it was had hung up. Morganstern wondered if it had been Ariel. He decided to try Cornwall out on a letter.

"Sure 'n' begorah," Cornwall said, screwing up his face in a cherubic smile and clasping his hands in front of him in a show of glee, "a letter is what you'll be wantin', and I'm the man to be doin' it for yer, Erin go bragh."

It wasn't so much the quick change of character, but the fact that it seemed to require a different reaction, a sort of supporting role, from Morganstern. He was finding it difficult to keep up with the actor.

"Can we drop the accents for a while, Cornwall?"

"As you wish." Cornwall sat down at the desk, found a pad of paper and waited, pencil poised.

"Whenever you're ready, sir."

Morganstern thought a minute and then began: "Uh . . . Dear Mom and Dad, um, enclosed please find two airline tickets, round-trip from Omaha to New York. The date is left open for whenever is convenient for you . . . If things aren't too busy at the store, I would really like very much—"

"Excuse me, sir," Cornwall said. "Could you spell Omaha."

Morganstern spelled it out.

"O-m-a-h-a," Cornwall repeated, writing laboriously. "What a strange name."

"Where were we?" Morganstern asked after a few minutes.

Cornwall glanced at his pad. "We were at Omaha. You know, sir, it might go better if you were to write it all down and then I could copy it off onto the typing machine."

Morganstern wrote the letter out in longhand and gave it to Cornwall to type.

Cornwall removed a piece of stationery and an envelope from the desk drawer. He studied the logo and read the slogan. "'Artists working through art to achieve artistry.' Very nice, sir, if you don't mind my saying so."

"Thank you, Cornwall."

Morganstern watched as Cornwall typed. He used his two index fingers, one at a time, stopping every few seconds to correct a letter with White-Out and blowing on each correction until it was completely dry. It took him almost forty-five minutes to finish the letter. Morganstern realized he had hired himself the world's worst secretary. He didn't have much use for a good secretary, for that matter, so what difference did it make? And Cornwall certainly seemed like he could use the job, judging by the way he dressed.

"Do you have any other correspondence, sir?"

Morganstern thought a moment. "I'm supposed to be sending out some sort of promotional letter, but I'm not quite sure what it is I want to say. I'll have to give it some thought."

"As you wish. Do you mind if I use the telephone while you're thinking?"

"Be my guest."

Morganstern went into the kitchen to do the dishes in order to give Cornwall some privacy while he made his call. The apartment being as small as it was, he couldn't help overhearing. Cornwall made a series of calls to what must have been casting agents or commercial directors. Each time he made a call he changed his accent. The conversations all took the same tack: Did they want to hear his voice tape? Did they want to see a composite picture? Were there any forthcoming commercials that might suit his particular talents?

When Morganstern overheard him speaking to his mother in England, he protested. "You're running up quite a phone bill there, Cornwall."

"Not to worry," Cornwall replied. "This is your business phone, isn't it? The calls are deductible."

Morganstern was beginning to understand the principles of tax deductions and business expenses. Tax-deductible obviously meant free, and business expenses meant no expense at all. No matter how much you spent or how high your business costs were, it really didn't matter. The government just paid you back. Taking it to the nth degree, if you spent enough on business-related items, the government would end up owing you. No wonder the rich got richer and little businesses grew into giant corporations. It was quite a system.

From that moment on, he stopped worrying about running out of money. And the minute he did, he experienced a strange phenomenon. Money seemed to attract money. Within one week, the following events took place:

1. He received a check from Mrs. Kibble for painting her apartment and a note of apology.

2. The man who robbed him outside the unemployment office rang the bell one afternoon. He returned the money he had stolen from Morganstern, explaining that he had landed a terrific new job and that he was now very "bullish on America." He knocked over a small coffee table as he left the apartment.

3. Mr. Shallot called Morganstern to tell him he had a check for him from his share of the fire.

"I don't understand. All my paintings went up in smoke."

"Mrs. Grace Chase bought the entire building. She plans to keep it intact as a memorial to artists who perished in the Mt. St. Helens eruption."

"I wasn't aware that any artists were killed by the volcano."

"Her point exactly: 'How soon we forget.' Those were her words, and this is her way of paying them homage. She insisted on you getting your share because she said you inspired the idea. It comes to five thousand dollars."

4. On the sidewalk in front of his building he found a dollar. He took it to the nearest newsstand and purchased a New York State lottery ticket. He won $23.50. He wasn't even surprised.

5. Marcy Conrad of Bill-and-Marcy, Ariel's advertising friends, called him up. She said she wanted to buy a painting. He explained he had no paintings to sell.

"Oh, that works out perfectly. We're in the middle of redecorating our apartment and we couldn't hang anything right now anyway. How much are you charging for your paintings?"

The figure $5,000 stuck in Morganstern's head. He told her his price.

"Terrific. I'll put a check in the mail so we can have dibbies on the next one you do."

"What happens if you don't like the painting?"

"Don't be silly," she assured him. "How could anyone not like a five-thousand-dollar painting?" "Have you heard from Ariel?" Morganstern asked. "No, we haven't," Marcy replied.

So in one week, without lifting a finger, Morganstern made $11,898.50, plus whatever it was the government owed him for business expenses.

He tried to think of a subject for the painting that Marcy Conrad had commissioned but his mind was as blank as the canvas. He spent several hours trying to rough out a promotional letter to art dealers and galleries and then realized there was no way he could put into words paintings he had yet to commit to canvas.

After calling his friend in Australia, agents in New York, Chicago, and L.A., Cornwall seemed to be getting bored and restless. Morganstern was worried he would quit. He realized that he liked having him around. He didn't even mind all the quick changes in character.

It was strange, all the years he had spent painting, he had never felt the need for company. Whenever he was involved with a picture, he had taken little notice of anyone or anything around him. He not only enjoyed but also needed the feeling of companionship that Cornwall provided. He had always known that painting was a lonely pursuit. But now he realized it was not half as lonely as *not* painting.

He wondered how to keep Cornwall occupied. The man seemed to have an excess of nervous energy.

Cornwall came up with the perfect solution. "When does your maid come in?" he asked.

"I don't have a maid. We used to have one, but I had to let her go."

Cornwall suggested that they cut down the office work to one day a week and he would serve as maid, valet, cook, and domestic consultant for three days a week. "With the appropriate adjustment in salary," he added.

"That's four hundred dollars a week?"

"That's right. Of course, you know that the cleaning and care of office space is deductible?"

"Of course," Morganstern said.

Cornwall opened charge accounts at various East Side houseware stores, where he purchased hundreds of dollars' worth of imported furniture oils, polishes, chamois cloths, and the uniforms appropriate for his new duties. Morganstern found him to be a terrific housekeeper and cook. And Cornwall seemed to enjoy it tremendously. He had plans to redecorate the apartment, and after cleaning, shopping, and taking care of the laundry, he busied himself making sketches, collecting swatches, and interviewing decorators.

Morganstern called Ariel's office each day, and each time was told that she was still on location. He continued trying to paint. He found that one little interruption, one little distraction or errand, would throw him off for the whole day. Before, he had been able to steal away an hour here and an hour there, in between house-painting jobs or after work at the advertising agency, but now he needed his time to be totally free and clear in order to even think about painting. A little thing, like reading the New York *Times* at breakfast, could ruin the day's work for him. Breakfast itself was a delaying tactic, he decided. He made up his mind: on Cornwall's day off, he would finally get down to it. No breakfast. No newspaper. Just the quiet apartment and the day stretching out before him. He lay in bed that morning trying to fight off the dread. Finally he forced himself up, got dressed, and stood in front of his easel.

Minutes dragged into hours. The longer he stood there, the more anxious he felt. He couldn't remember how he had ever begun a painting before. Where had the ideas come from? How had he transcribed them onto that vast Antarctica of canvas?

Finally, unable to bear it any longer, he left the apartment and spent the rest of the day at the Metropolitan Museum of Art.

He decided he was going through a transitional period, perhaps moving on to a new level of his work. The thing to do, he told himself, was to relax, not to worry about it, let this be a time of introspection and incubation. The pictures would come to him when they were ready. He couldn't force them.

He returned from the museum and let himself into the apartment. Ariel was sitting on the living-room couch with two suitcases at her feet. She had her coat on.

"Well, hi. What a surprise. How are you?" Morganstern stood in the doorway, nervously slapping his hands together.

"I'm fine, just fine," Ariel said smiling. "How are you?"

"Just great. Couldn't be better." He took off his coat and hung it in the closet, where it promptly fell off the hanger. "So, when did you get back from Florida?"

"Oh, a couple of days ago."

"And you didn't call?" he asked, annoyed. "I must have left one hundred messages with your secretary."

"I don't trust the phone. Not since our last wonderful conversation."

"Oh, right." He sat down on the couch next to her. He felt inexplicably on edge, as if he were an intruder in someone else's home. "Well. How did your orange-juice commercial go?"

"Nice and pulpy," she said, staring at him.

"And the weather? How was the weather?" He was unable to take his eyes off her beautiful mouth.

"Warm, very warm," Ariel said, her eyes glowing.

"Humid?" he asked, leaning closer, as if she were about to give him a piece of top-secret information.

"It's always very humid in Florida." She sounded short of breath. "Everything is warm and damp."

Morganstern was amazed at the ability of those soft lips to do something as difficult as form words.

"Humidity makes you feel the heat more," he said. Their faces were separated now by only inches.

"Yes, yes," she breathed. "It does."

Their mouths moved across the remaining space in slow motion and they kissed. He sighed. She moaned. They kissed again. Her arms went around his neck. He reached inside her coat and ran his hand up her slender side to the warm damp spot underneath her arm and then moved it across to rest lightly upon the astounding softness of her breast.

There was no time for the long hot trip into the bedroom. They were on the floor. Their clothes scattered on the couch. Ariel lay underneath him. He hovered over her like a big bird. Her hard nipplenubs tickled his bare chest, her soft strong arms clung to his neck. He felt the warm welcome of her well-exercised thighs hugging his back and the wetslick pull of her pussy pulling him in and holding him. They made love without speaking.

141

Afterwards Ariel called out from the bathroom, "I hope you didn't mind me letting myself in while you weren't here."

"Ariel, for heaven's sake, this is your apartment, too," Morganstern said, getting off the floor and putting on his shorts.

There was a long pause, and then: "It doesn't look like my apartment." She emerged from the bathroom wrapped in a mauve towel, one of Cornwall's latest purchases. "Where'd you get the Bill Blass shower curtain?"

"Oh, that's Cornwall. He's changed a few things."

"Who's Cornwall?" She stepped into her beige lace panties.

"A guy that works for me a couple of days a week. A sort of secretary-maid."

"Oh, so you're an employer now?"

"Why are you being so sarcastic?" he asked, watching her as she struggled with her panty hose. One leg was turned inside out. Her fingernails jammed into the toe, tearing a hole.

"I guess because I'm feeling sarcastic," she said. "It just feels very odd walking into what used to be my home and seeing the most putrid-color towels hanging in the bathroom." She stood in the doorway of his studio, buttoning her blouse. "I see you got a new easel. It's very handsome. How's the painting going?"

"Fine. Fine." Why did he suddenly feel like they were two not very good friends trapped on a long train ride together?

"I didn't see any work around."

"I'm working in my head at the moment," he said testily.

Morganstern picked up the two suitcases and began to carry them into the bedroom.

"Where are you taking those?"

"Into the bedroom."

"Oh, I'm not staying. I'm taking those with me."

"You're what?" Morganstern dropped the suitcases. "I saw these, and naturally I assumed you were moving back in."

"I came by to pick up some of my things. I'm apartment-sitting for the Conrads' next-door neighbors."

"You mean you came by just to pick up some stuff? That's it?"

"That, and I guess I wanted to see how I felt."

"And how, may I ask, do you feel?"

"Foreign, strange, faraway, detached, alienated," she said sadly.

"You must have just come from a session with James," he snapped.

"And I hate track lighting," she murmured.

"Sorry you weren't here to be consulted." He took a deep breath. "Ariel, I hate to sound trite, but we can't go on this way. You've got to make up your mind whether you want to be together or apart."

142

"I guess I'm not sure I'd fit into your new corporate structure," she said, fiddling with the luggage tag on one of her suitcases.

"Goddammit, if I'd known the money was going to be this big a problem, I'd have opted for the fucking year-round vacation dream house instead of cash."

The downstairs buzzer rang. Ariel sprang up. "Oh, God, that's James. I told him to pick me up here."

"Are you having an affair with James?" He spoke through tightly clenched teeth.

"Don't be silly. He's my accountant," she said, as if "accountant" were synonymous with "aged grandfather." "He's taking me to a Merrill Lynch seminar on investments for women."

"Great," Morganstern said. "I hope you have a very profitable time. I suppose you want me to help you with the suitcases."

"No, that's okay. They're only half-full," she said, picking them up.

"What did you really come by for? To see if we could still fight or if we could fuck?"

"Both, I guess," she said, her eyes filling.

"Well, you sure got your money's worth." Morganstern yanked the door open for her.

Was that it? Morganstern wondered. Was that the end of it? She had her clothes, she had an apartment to sit, she had a job, she had another life. Would he ever see her again? He walked into the bedroom and looked in the closet. It was still more than three-quarters filled with her things. The two suitcases had barely made a dent.

God, love was so sick, he thought. Funny, how it had once seemed so very simple to him. Maybe what he felt for Ariel wasn't love at all. Maybe it was just dependence. Habit. Obsession. Maybe his relationship with her had been some sort of basic training for the real thing. He wished he had something other than Ariel to worry about. Then he remembered he did. He had his painting block. That was certainly a concern. Perhaps it was the trouble with Ariel that was interfering with his ability to paint. It made a lot more sense to him than the idea that his newfound fortune had robbed him of his creative drive.

One thing for sure. He needed something to get his mind off Ariel. He called his stockbroker to find out how the money market was doing.

"The time has come," Getty Milford said in her husky whiskey voice, "for us to have a meeting of the minds. Are you free for lunch tomorrow?" She picked the time and the place. One o'clock at the Four Seasons. She would meet him at the bar.

At one-fifteen, every man at the rectangular-shaped bar turned to watch the tall, beautiful brunette walk up the stairs, one long leg at a time. She paused at the top step. She was dressed all in white—a tight nubby V-neck sweater over a skirt which was tailored in design but incredibly sexy in execution with a slit that went halfway up her long, firm flank. Her leg was bent, poised, perfectly positioned so that he could see through to the inside of the other thigh. She wore high, sexy sandals. Her full dark hair was combed back from her forehead and fell just to her shoulders in a tumble of casual curls. Her eyes slanted up slightly at the corners. Her mouth was full and painted an amazing apple red, matching exactly the fingernail she had placed quizzically at the edge of her lower lip. She spoke to the maître d', who pointed in Morganstern's direction.

Was this Getty Milford? Could this be my stockbroker? he thought. No, it couldn't be. Where was her pinstripe suit? Where was her attaché case? Where did she keep her calculator? And where was her bra?

She sat down next to him on the banquette, crossed one sleek leg over the other, and touched his hand lightly with her long apple-red fingernails. He was almost overwhelmed by the scent of gardenias she gave off.

"I'm sorry I'm late," she said. "I had to come all the way up from Wall Street. It was hard to tear myself away. The trading was sooooo heavy today. God, I love it when it's like that." She reached her arms over her head and stretched with satisfaction. Morganstern was hit with another waft of gardenia.

There was a sort of soft focus to her, as if she was getting ready to film, or had just finished filming, an X-rated movie scene. Her skin glowed, her mouth glistened, even her eyelids glistened. Morganstern shot a look at her breasts. The nipples looked as if they might at any moment break through the soft material of her sweater.

"Have you ever played the market before?" she asked.

"No, never. This will be my first time."

Her eyes lit up with pleasure. She leaned very close to him, her breast pressing into his arm. "Oh, I'm in luck," she said. "A veritable virgin."

"Yeah, I guess I am," he said. He felt his face getting warm and his penis getting hard.

"Well, then, I want you to put yourself completely in my hands. I want you to be able to trust me. We're going to take it very slow at first. But before long you're going to love it as much as I do. I promise you."

The waiter came over to take their drink order. Morganstern ordered a glass of red wine. Getty ordered a Clamato cocktail. "Clams are an aphrodisiac," she said matter-of-factly.

She took a copy of the New York *Times* out of her bag and opened it to the financial section. "See," she said, going slowly

144

through the pages, "there's the New York Stock Exchange, the American Stock Exchange, and my personal favorite, Over-the-Counter."

Morganstern's eye scanned the endless columns of barely decipherable type. "How do you know which stocks to buy? There's so many."

"Well, everyone has their own system. Mine is sort of an instinctive approach. All I have to do is see the name, and I know. I get a little spasm that tells me it's going to be the hot stock.

"Now, the important thing in playing the market is not the specific stocks or companies, it's understanding the four major rules, which are as follows: Diversity. Liquidity. Longevity. And stamina," she said, ticking them off on her pretty fingers.

"Diversity is not putting all your eggs in one basket. You wouldn't want to invest everything in energy stocks, for instance. Just as you wouldn't always want to sleep with the same woman or have sex in the same way. Right?"

Morganstern nodded his head. The veins in his face felt like hot tea was being pumped through them.

"Liquidity is important. It's being able to get your money out fast, especially in economically shaky times. Investing in a new company that has good short-term growth is just like a quickie; you get all the satisfaction and none of the hassle.

"The opposite of that, longevity, is sticking with a stock for the long haul. Going with it through all the ups and downs and the ins and outs. Resist the temptation to pull out too soon, and the rewards can be very, very satisfying."

As she spoke, she made movements with her hands which could only be construed as sexually explicit gestures.

"And stamina. Stamina is staying on top of it, whether your investment is a quickie or a long-term commitment. It's staying hard when the market goes soft, staying strong when the economy looks weak; it's having the ability to ride the market through every hump and every slump."

He looked around to see if they were attracting attention from any of the surrounding tables. Getty took his chin and turned his face back toward her. Her breathing was growing heavy and there was a light sheen of perspiration on her upper lip.

"So again," she said, staring into his eyes and breathing the words at him slowly, softly, and with a certain urgency, "Diversity, Liquidity, Longevity, and Stamina. Are you following me?" she asked, touching the corner of his mouth lightly with her forefinger.

"I think so, yes."

"Oh, we're going to have a wonderful time, you'll see. There's nothing quite as beautiful as the stock market, especially the first time. Come on, let's go," she said, getting up, "I want to show you something."

Getty took him to the nearest Bartlett's office. It was a large, pleasant, wood-paneled room off Fifth Avenue. Over two dozen brokers worked quietly at their desks. In one corner of the room was a lounge area where comfortable leather couches were arranged around a huge screen. Numbers and letters passed across the screen from right to left. Two men sat on one couch watching the screen and taking notes. Did she actually work in this place? Morganstern wondered.

"This is our customer-information area," Getty explained. "You can come here anytime and watch the day's returns." She sat down on one of the deep leather couches and pulled him down next to her.

"I don't understand what all the letters stand for," Morganstern said, staring at the screen.

"I'll translate," she whispered. "Oh, good, we're at the F's. They're my favorite. Faberge, 26⅛, up 1⅛. That's one-eighth of a dollar. Feders is selling low at seven, down one-eighth . . . oh, oh, Federal Express is up 1⅞." She grabbed his hand and held it in his lap. "Federal Standard up ½ . . . Firestone down ⅜ . . . Foote Cone and Belding up 1½ . . ."

She moved her hand underneath his so that it was lying directly on his crotch. Morganstern glanced at the two men. They were totally engrossed in the stock returns, their eyes moving rapidly from right to left.

"Oh my, Foxborough is up 2½, oh, good, good," she moaned with pleasure. "Frigidaire, down a half . . . Forelinger, Inc., up one, Fugua up one, selling 15¾ . . . and I bought at eight . . . Oh . . . oh. . ." She moved her hand lightly over his now-erect penis. "Flag, down a half . . . Fla Rck up a half . . . Fluke J. up a quarter . . . Frantz up an eighth . . . Friona up 2½ . . . Frischs up 3½ . . . oh, my God . . . fuck me," she whispered, not taking her eyes off the screen.

"What?" Morganstern said, not quite believing his ears, but instinctively trusting the hand signals. She turned to him, her eyes glowing, her lips parted and moist. "Fuck me," she said again.

Morganstern looked around the Bartlett's office. No one was paying them, or her busy hand, any attention. She couldn't possibly mean here, in front of all these brokers, he thought. Getty pulled him up.

"Come on, let's get out of here before I get crazy," she said. *Before* she gets crazy? he wondered. He could barely walk. They hailed a taxi outside the office, and Morganstern gave his address to the driver.

146

"Don't you love it?" she said, caressing his leg and breathing softly against his neck.

"What?" he moaned.

"The stock market."

"Oh, yeah, it's damned exciting," he murmured.

"Hurry," Getty said as soon as they got into the apartment. "Let's do over-the-counter."

Oh, no, he thought. He'd been duped again. She was another business-crazed woman like Miranda from Metrobank. Over-the-counter was just a kind of stock. The only thing that turned her on was the market.

But he was wrong. Getty had something else in mind.

She led him into the kitchen and leaned against the butcher-block counter.

"Over-the-counter," she sighed, pressing her entire body against him and slowly rotating her hips from side to side. "It's my favorite position." She kissed him deeply, her tongue tickling the inside of his mouth.

And that's how he had her, over-the-counter, her long, strong legs holding him to her, her back arched, her dark hair tumbling down. She cried out several times: "Up an eighth, up a half, up, up!" He plunged deep inside her and felt her moving, moving, tightening, loosening. He heard her moan: "Up three-quarters," and he thrust himself into her even deeper than before. It was exquisite, exciting sex.

They took a shower together and made love again. "Now, down to business," she said. She sat on the bed, cross-legged, wearing one of his old shirts only half-buttoned.

He wanted her again. But she was all business now.

As Morganstern was soon to discover, nobody did business the way Getty did.

"For your pension plan, I suggest we go with Mutual Funds. They're secure, they have a high rate of return, and they're liquid, in case you later decide to invest your money in other things, like real estate. Now, for your own personal investments, I think we can put together a nice portfolio of diversified stock that will give you a taste of the market without committing too much of your capital at this time. I think about twenty thousand dollars to be spread over a group of ten different stocks would do. We'll select a mix, some long-term, some short-term, a combination of guaranteed returns, plus good fast growth. Am I going too quickly for you?" she asked, smiling at him sweetly.

"I'm just having a little trouble making the transition," he said.

"Oh, you mean from sex to stocks? There's really no difference," she explained. "Sex and money are totally connected. The only dif-

147

ference is that with sex you ultimately reach a satiation point, whereas with money you never do. You know, a lot of the other brokers at Bartlett's think I use sex to an unfair advantage. I've won the top sales trophy six times in the past six years. But I make it a rule never to mix business with pleasure."

"You did with me, didn't you?"

"No siree. First we had sex, and now we're doing business. They may overlap a little, but I never really mix them. Shall we pick your stocks now?"

"Sure. I'm game."

"The initial twenty thousand is not going to make you a millionaire," she explained, "but it'll give you an idea of what it's like to diddle in the market."

She handed him the financial section of the paper. "Okay," she said, "I want you to read to me. Start with the B's on the New York Stock Exchange."

"Should I read the numbers?"

"No, just the names."

She lay back on the bed while he stumbled through the long list of names: "Bnk Am . . . Bnk Tr . . . Bausch . . . Bay StG . . . Beker . . . Belch . . . Belco P . . . Bendix . . ." She groaned and stretched languorously. He began to get a hard-on.

"Keep reading," she crooned. He tore his eyes away from her and tried to concentrate on the column of B's.

"Benef . . . Berkey . . . Best Pd . . . Borden . . . Borg . . ."

"Faster," she whispered.

"Brist M . . . Brnsk . . . Brose . . . Bucy . . . er . . . Budg pf . . . Bundy . . ."

"Bundy, say it again," she moaned.

"Bundy," he said.

"More."

"Bundy . . . Bundy . . . BundyBundyBundyBundy." He threw down the paper and fell over her.

"Oooooh. Aaaaaaah. Bundy," she sighed. "Buy Bundy. That'll be the first."

They selected ten stocks this way: by whichever name struck her fancy.

"But I don't know anything about these companies," he said, looking at the list of stocks later.

"Neither do I. But they do feel good, don't they?"

"Yes, they feel great."

"As I said, the only thing to remember is Diversity, Liquidity, Longevity . . . and Stamina." She pulled him down into her arms. They fell asleep, the pages of the New York *Times*'s financial section scattered around them.

Morganstern awoke to find Getty gone. She had left him a note:

"That's the biggest rise the market has seen in a long time. Love and kisses and send me a check for $20,000. Getty."

Morganstern was in a great mood. He had a broker, a stock portfolio, a secretary/valet/maid/cook/decorator, money in the bank, more on the way, and even a commission for a painting if he ever came up with an idea for it. And he had the prospect of seeing Getty Milford again. Hell, maybe he'd invest another $20,000 in the market. It was well worth it. What a great way to make money.

He thought of Ariel, and for the first time since she walked out, he didn't feel needy, horny, moody, and angry. If she wanted to make things impossible, then let her. Let her spend all her time at investments-for-women seminars; he had his own way of taking care of business.

He stretched and groaned. Every muscle in his body ached, ever so slightly. He felt terrific.

If this is what they meant by the good life, well, it was okay with him.

III

The Good Life

Money is honey, my little sonny,
And a rich man's joke is always funny.
    —Thomas Edward Brown, *The Doctor*

Morganstern learned that there were certain responsibilities that went along with the good life. At the top of the list was the ability to give a great party. The idea for the party had originally been Zero's, but Cornwall got behind the project and soon the planning and preparation for Morganstern's first big social affair became a full-time job.

At first, Morganstern had problems justifying a party. He had always looked at parties as occasions with a specific purpose: an anniversary, a graduation, a birthday, the coming of the new year. He had never understood the New York habit of having a party just to have a party.

Cornwall patiently explained: "It's a business party. An opportunity to meet and mingle with people who can further you in your career and your social standing. The important thing is to get access to a good mailing list."

"Well, I do have the mailing list left over from my ill-fated art show," Morganstern said. He found the list and gave it to Cornwall. "How many people do you think we should invite?"

"Two hundred is a good round number," Cornwall said.

"Two hundred people? Are you kidding? I couldn't possibly fit them all in this place. Unless they came in shifts."

"First of all, they won't all accept. Second, one doesn't have a party in one's own home. It has to be someplace novel and alluring, otherwise people have no reason to come. Not to worry, I'll find the perfect spot."

Cornwall spent several days and about $350 in taxi fares canvassing all of New York for the most novel, alluring place in which to throw a party. At the week's end, he returned triumphant.

"I think this will do splendidly," he said, handing Morganstern a brochure.

Morganstern read the first page: "The SS *Magic Carpet:* 125 feet in length, carrying 3,400 square feet of sail. Full crew. Special midnight cruises around Manhattan."

"But this isn't a restaurant. It's a boat."

"To be more precise, it's not a boat, it's a sloop," Cornwall said. "The food will be catered by Chez Nicole's, who do a lovely seafood buffet. They'll provide everything: the bar, barmen, waitresses, and so forth. We can go over the menu in more detail later. But first we have to get the invitations out."

They went to the same printers that had done Morganstern's business stationery. "I should have preferred Tiffany's, but they take a good six weeks," Cornwall said.

They ordered 200 embossed invitations on mauve paper. They had to pay an extra $150 because it was a rush order.

"Matthew Morganstern, Inc., cordially invites you to a buffet supper the evening of May 15 aboard the SS *Magic Carpet,* departing at nine P.M. from Dock 11, South Street."

Cornwall hired a small punk-rock band called Bankrupt to play background music. They narrowed the mailing list of 500 down to 200 of the most influential, or as Cornwall referred to them, "the most interesting," people, and Morganstern threw in a few names of his own: Ariel, James, Stuey Schlossman, Zero, and his parents. He began addressing invitations while Cornwall attended to other details of the party.

"Who are these people?" Cornwall asked, picking up one of the envelopes Morganstern had just addressed.

"Oh, those are my parents."

"You've invited your parents?" He scrutinized the envelope. "From Omaha?"

"They won't come," Morganstern said. "It's just a gesture."

The invitations went out two weeks before the party. Some of them had to be hand-delivered because, according to Cornwall, there were some people who opened their mail only at the end of each quarter.

There were ten acceptances, twenty-three refusals, and 167 no-replies.

"How can we tell the caterer how much stuff to bring?" Morganstern asked. He knew Chez Nicole's was charging him by the head, and even though the party was a write-off, it seemed to him a shame to waste so much food.

"We'll just have to approximate," Cornwall said. "Better there be too much than not enough." He approximated on the high side for the food and the liquor and the little silver-sailboat charms which were to be given as party souvenirs to all the ladies.

The food (including hot and cold buffet, clam bar, hot and cold hors d'oeuvres), the wine and the liquor, the 200 engraved invitations, the cost of postage and/or hand delivery, one chartered boat with crew, four waitresses, three barmen, the silver charms, and the band came to $20,000. The figure had absolutely no meaning to Morganstern.

Morganstern arrived at the dock at 8:30, a half-hour before the party was scheduled to begin. No one was there except the captain,

154

his crew, the caterers, waitresses, and waiters. He paced the dock nervously. Quarter to nine. Still no one. He had a $20,000 party to launch and no guests.

At nine sharp they came en masse. Arriving by taxis, limos, cars, and on foot. They surged past him, almost edging him off the dock. There was not one face he recognized in the entire crowd. But everyone seemed to know each other. It was as if they had attended the same parties all their lives. Morganstern was the last to board the boat. He spotted Zero, who reintroduced him to Mrs. Grace Chase. He thanked her for the $5,000 check.

"Don't mention it, my dear boy. Your work that night was an inspiration. I'd like you to meet my dear friend Mrs. Carlyle Lord, who is also an avid collector."

Mrs. Lord, a frail little old woman, offered a wrinkled, clawlike hand to the air next to Morganstern's left hip. He suddenly realized she was blind.

"Blinky, this is the young artist I told you about who does such exciting work with fire," Mrs. Chase shouted in her friend's ear. Mrs. Chase turned back to Morganstern, and as if reading his mind, explained her friend's ability to collect art without the benefit of sight: "Blinky has managed to put together the most wonderful collection, and she does it all just with her sense of touch. The thicker the paint, the better she likes it. Isn't that right, Blinky dear?" she screamed in the little old lady's ear.

Mrs. Lord continued to smile, not saying anything. Apparently she was deaf as well. She ran her hand along the varnished trim of the boat. "Skimpy, modern stuff," Blinky said, her small face screwed up in disdain.

Stuey Schlossman brought over his date, an extremely tall, very black, powerfully built woman who wore dark sunglasses and army fatigues. She looked around her, staking out the ship and each of the guests. She kept her right hand deep in her pocket, as if she were carrying a gun. Stuey didn't introduce her but took Morganstern aside and in a low voice said, "What do you think of my date?"

"She seems very nice," Morganstern answered politely.

"Don't you know who she is? That's Dorothea Williams, the famous radical. She's been in hiding for the past fifteen years, ever since the Dow Chemical Building got blown up."

"What's she doing here?" Morganstern asked nervously.

"She's trying to raise venture capital for a fried-chitlin food chain. Isn't that the wildest? She went into hiding as a revolutionary and came out a capitalist. And, get this: she still carries a gun."

Waitresses dressed in short silk maid's uniforms, wearing high spike heels, carried trays of miniature sausages en croute, stuffed mussels, terrine of pork, and huge fresh shrimp with green sauce. Waiters made endless trips back and forth from the two bars to the thirsty throng of guests. The band never showed up. Cornwall had paid them in cash, in advance.

The boat pulled smoothly away from the dock, powered by its engine. It was a beautiful night with only the gentlest southwest breeze. Morganstern saw Cornwall put on a life jacket. His face was pasty underneath the Pan-Cake makeup.

"What's the matter? You look ill."

"It's only fear, sir. I never learned to swim, you see. I'll be down below if you need anything."

"Oh, hey," Zero whispered in his ear, "you've really struck it rich. The Van Dams are here." He pointed to a couple who were both almost six feet tall. They were dressed more casually than the other guests, she in a Lilly Pulitzer dress of bright pink and apple green and he in yellow slacks and a blue blazer. Their hair was an identical, immaculate silver gray. "The William Van Dams are money, real Southampton money," Zero explained. Someone must have pointed Morganstern out as their host, because the Van Dams made their way over to him and introduced themselves.

"So very nice of you to have us," Mr. Van Dam said.

"What a charming evening," Mrs. Van Dam offered. Both spoke without moving their lower jaws.

"She has lovely lines, hasn't she?" Mr. Van Dam said. Morganstern thought he was talking about his wife. "Reminds me very much of my *Sea Foam,* which, as you know, I sold last year."

He realized then that Van Dam was talking about the boat and assumed that Morganstern not only owned the *Magic Carpet* but kept up with the comings and goings of other yacht owners.

"My crew found these wood hulls the devil to keep up. I'm afraid they convinced me to go modern. They tell me fiberglass is the only thing. With a touch of teak and mahogany for color, of course," he said, chuckling. He still hadn't moved his jaw.

"Of course." Morganstern chuckled back.

"At any rate," Van Dam continued, "Kiki and I can't stay long, what with the Princess in town and that terribly tedious fund-raiser at the Met. But we wouldn't have missed this for anything, isn't that right, Kiki?"

"We wouldn't have missed it for the world," Mrs. Van Dam concurred. "I told him we couldn't manage both tonight, but Wimmie does so love a bit of sail."

"It's a shame we'll have to leave so soon."

Where did they think they were going? Morganstern wondered. They were in the middle of the fucking East River.

"Oh, look," Mrs. Van Dam said to her husband. "The Burnsides are here."

"Darling, the Burnsides are everywhere," he replied. A short red-faced man wearing a yachting cap and his two-foot taller wife waved from the bow of the ship.

"Halloo, Benty . . . Halloo, Sissy," Mr. Van Dam called out. "That old crook," he said to Morganstern, "I must ask him how his company is weathering the labor strikes. Do excuse us, Morgie."

Morganstern felt like an artichoke leaf: tasted, relished, and discarded all in one swift closemouthed motion. He watched as the Van Dams and the Burnsides greeted each other with all the warmth of people on opposite sides of a sticky litigation.

Strange people, he thought. They had spoken to him as though they had known him for years, as though they had all been members of the same exclusive kids' club: Wimmie and Kiki, Benty and Sissy, Blinky and Morgie, sitting around the old yacht club comparing sails.

As they circled the Statue of Liberty, the wind picked up a little, giving a gentle slope to the sloop. The Conrads caught his eye. He had invited them because they were friends of Ariel's and he thought she would appreciate it. They were dressed in identical British naval middies. Hers had epaulets.

"Have you seen Ariel?" Morganstern asked.

"No. But I know she was planning on coming," Marcy Conrad said. "How's our painting going?"

"Fine, just fine," Morganstern mumbled. He turned his back on the Conrads and bumped headlong into Ivan. He hadn't invited Ivan. Apparently the Conrads had.

"Big boat, big expensive party, fancy hors d'oeuvres, fresh jumbo shrimp, twelve dollars a pound, fancy schmancy guests, goddamn stars and moon are out, nice little fucking breeze, a fucking romantic evening, and you don't even have a date, do you?" Ivan said, grinning. "Couldn't even get yourself fixed up, am I right? Fucking-A I'm right," Ivan yelled after him as he rushed off for another drink.

He didn't know if the boat was heeling more or he was feeling the effects of four vodkas. He was cornered by an Iranian named Tehmet Ali Agnet, who introduced himself as an international art dealer and handed him his business card. It wasn't so much a card as a fold-out flier. Morganstern tried to focus on it. In large letters followed by exclamation points were the following words: "Agnet & Sons, Inc., International Art Dealers, Announce a Prevention-of-Bankruptcy Sale! Discounts on Original Oils!" Underneath a picture of a painting of a deer standing in a forest was the caption: "Never Before, Never Again, will you be able to get this Beautiful Sofa-Size Painting at Budget-Size Prices! Also available from our inventory: Hall-Size Paintings, Paintings Suitable for Bathroom and Kitchen, Paintings Designed to Match any Decor! And, for a limited time only, buy a Collection (minimum of three paintings, your choice of sizes and frames) and get one Painting Free!"

The party had been in progress only about thirty minutes when Morganstern heard the captain shout: "Ready about." The boat turned back toward the harbor.

"What's going on?" Morganstern asked one of the crew members.

"We have to go back to the dock."

"What for? Is our time up?"

"No, some couple wants to be dropped off. They've got another party to go to, or something."

The Van Dams stood at midships ready to disembark. They waved merrily to Morganstern. "Great fun, Morgie. Thanks ever for having us."

As they drew nearer to the dock, Morganstern saw what must be the Van Dams' limousine waiting at the pier.

There was a couple standing at the end of the dock. Latecomers to the party, he thought. As they tied up to the pilings, Morganstern saw that it was James and Ariel. They boarded the ship and squeezed their way to the bow. Because of the crush of the crowd, Morganstern was unable to get over to them. He wasn't sure he wanted to anyway. What the hell was Ariel doing with James? This wasn't a bloody seminar. He took another drink off a passing tray and gulped it down.

The sails were rehoisted. The wind had picked up considerably. The boat heeled over and Morganstern had to grab on to the rail for balance. He was feeling slightly queasy.

He saw Getty Milford and waved. She looked beautiful. She was, as usual, dressed all in white, a gauzy draped affair that gave the effect of being far more revealing than if she were walking around the ship stark naked. She swirled her way toward him, her arms outstretched.

"Oh, God," she breathed, leaning into him as if she had just finished a five-mile run, "I just heard about a stock that's going to give you the biggest hard-on. It's a brand-new company that's going public. The best part is that they're right in your field. It's called Cop-Art."

"What do they do?"

"It's a syndicate that's been formed to sell shares in some of the world's most fabulous art. For instance, they just bought Rembrandt's *Homer Contemplating the Bust of Plato* for three million dollars. What they do then is sell shares to members. Each member has the right to hang the painting in his home for a certain period of time. Or, if a member chooses, he can sell his time share to another art lover, usually at a profit. The whole point is to take great art out of

158

the museums and put it back in people's living rooms, where it belongs. With the prices of art skyrocketing these days, I think this is going to be a very hot issue," she said. "Oh, look who's there. Benton Burnside. I'll see you a little later, lover." She kissed him wetly.

"Hell of a good party, excellent deduction." Morganstern looked up. James and Ariel were standing at his side. "You've really shown a lot of progress, Matt. I'm proud of you," James said, clasping Morganstern strongly by the hand. James moved off to talk to another group of people.

"Nice party," Ariel said.

"Nice of you to come."

"Who's the woman in white?" Ariel asked with a studied casualness.

"Oh, her. She's just my stockbroker."

"Some broker," Ariel mumbled.

"Are you and James between seminars tonight?"

"James was kind enough to escort me," Ariel said haughtily.

James called to Ariel. She bestowed a bright brittle smile on Morganstern and then joined the group that James was talking to.

The boat seemed to be picking up speed. People were huddled along the windward side, holding on to the rail with one hand and their drinks with the other. The food was largely being ignored. Plates of shrimp slid across the deck; stuffed mushrooms and lobster puffs rolled off their trays.

The wind was blowing steady and strong and the sails were hauled in tight. The boat was tilted over almost on its side. Morganstern made his way back to the stern to talk to the captain. He was steering the boat with his knees on the wheel while he held on to a large tumbler of whiskey with both hands. He had a strange but happy gleam in his eye.

"Aren't we going a little fast?" Morganstern asked. The moment the question was out of his mouth he heard a loud crash. One of the heated serving dishes had fallen off the gimballed table onto the deck. Chicken livers and water chestnuts wrapped in bacon rolled across the teak deck, following the path of the stuffed mushrooms and lobster puffs.

"We go with the wind, matey. If you wanted controlled speed, you should've chartered a ferry. Ready about," the captain shouted.

"Ready about," a crew member screamed back.

"Hard alee."

The boat came about quickly and then heeled way over on the opposite tack. A chafing dish flew off and landed upside down on the deck. The insides of the cheese-and-crabmeat crepes oozed out from underneath the heavy silver dish and were mixed with the salt water washing over the floorboards.

"Batten down the bar," the captain yelled.

"Aye, aye, sir," came the answer, almost drowned out by the wind.

The guests seemed to be enjoying themselves. There was much shrieking and shouting, waving and laughing.

Getty was holding on to one of the shrouds, her white filmy dress blowing straight away from her body like a flag. Water continued pouring in. This just seemed to increase the gaiety of the crowd, many of whom were barefoot and soaked through.

Morganstern didn't know how they managed, but the waiters staggered from one guest to another, handing out drinks as fast as people could down them.

He hadn't seen Cornwall since they first left the dock. Suddenly he appeared from below, his face green, his eyes wild with fright. He crawled up the deck to the windward side of the boat, where he promptly got sick all over himself.

The wind died down almost as quickly as it had come up. The rest of the party went "swimmingly," as someone—Morganstern couldn't remember who—said when they finally returned to the pier. All he knew was he had been drinking like a fish.

The *Magic Carpet* tied up at the dock. It stood as still and as flat as a bathtub, and yet Morganstern could barely maintain an upright position.

He looked around for James and Ariel but they had disappeared. The crowd surged off the boat, obviously in great spirits. Morganstern was the last to leave. He heard shouts of "Thank you," "Nice evening," "Let's do it again sometime," but he was too drunk to care. So much for Morganstern, giver of great parties, he thought.

When he arrived home, Julio told him there were two people waiting for him in the lobby. Morganstern squinted through the glass door. There was an elderly couple camped out on the lobby sofa. They looked strangely like his parents. It was his parents.

"Mom! Dad! What are you doing here?"

"You invited us to your party, didn't you?" his father said. He was wearing a rumpled old suit, vintage 1945. His mother was dressed in what must have been her best housedress with matching babushka. There were three Woolworth shopping bags at her feet.

"What a surprise," he said, trying to act as sober as possible. He hugged one and then the other. "Why didn't you tell me you were coming? I'm really glad you're here. When did you get here, anyway?" he said all in one breath.

He helped his mother with the shopping bags. "Be careful," she cautioned, "there's a brisket in there."

Brisket. Why had his mother brought brisket all the way from Omaha?

160

"Well, so. How was your flight?" He was desperately trying to make conversation with his own parents.

"We didn't fly," his father said. "We took the bus."

"The bus? Why didn't you take the plane? I sent you tickets."

"The bus is sixty-five dollars round trip. Greyhound has a special excursion fare. Three days, six major U.S. cities. We leave tomorrow for Albany."

In the kitchen, Morganstern's mother unpacked her brisket, a smoked tongue, stuffed derma, and two Tupperware containers filled with celery stuffed with Cheeze Whiz. There was also an olive loaf which had been cored out at the center and filled with cream cheese and pimiento.

"I brought this for the party," she explained, "but we got here too late."

"It's time for bed," his father announced. "We'll talk in the morning."

Morganstern got his parents settled in the bedroom and then he collapsed on the couch and fell into a drunken sleep. He awoke late the next morning to the smell of brisket and onions. He dragged himself into the kitchen. His father was sitting at the kitchen table clipping food coupons out of the *Daily News*. His mother was at the stove stirring something in a big pot. Morganstern's head was spinning. He grabbed hold of the empty kitchen chair and lowered himself slowly into it. The smell of brisket was overpowering.

"Here's your son, Mr. Rise-and-Shine, all ready to start the day," his father said, not looking up from his coupon clipping. "Fix him one of your tuna-fish omelets, Mother."

Morganstern gagged. "I don't want anything, thanks, Mom. I'm not hungry."

"Of course you're not hungry. Alcohol eats away your stomach lining. It's all here in *The Reader's Digest,*" his father said, handing him a clipping from a file of clippings he carried with him everywhere. "Your mother is cooking. You'll eat."

"Please, not a tuna-fish omelet," he begged. It was too late. She was already opening a can of Chicken of the Sea and spooning it out into a bowl. The odor of tuna combined with the brisket and onions sent him running to the bathroom.

When he returned to the kitchen, his omelet was waiting for him. And so was his father. He stood by the kitchen table, his arms folded across his chest. His mother busied herself rearranging his spice rack.

"Sit. I'll talk while you eat," his father directed.

Morganstern sat down. His head was still pounding. His stomach was heeling to windward.

"Our bus leaves in an hour," his father said.

"Why don't you stay a few days, as long as you're here?"

"If we miss the bus, we lose our excursion fare. To you that's nothing. To us it's like wasting good food," he said, indicating the disgusting concoction on Morganstern's plate. "Let me say a few words," he said, as if until that moment he had been silent. "Matthew, we've always given you everything you ever wanted."

"I know, Dad. Thank you."

"You don't have to thank us. We're your parents. We love you. But maybe we went too far. Maybe we spoiled you. You could have gone into business with me, but I never insisted. I know notions aren't what they used to be. You wanted to paint. Painting is a good field to be in. It's creative. It's colorful. It makes people happy. A person certainly doesn't go into it to make money.

"But I don't see any pictures here. No painting. No creating. All I see is money. Maybe you're too old to listen to your father. But listen to Einstein at least."

"Einstein? What does he have to do with anything?"

"When he was a young man, Einstein was perfectly happy futzing around with his formulas. And then suddenly he got too smart for his own good. One day he had a simple little theory of relativity and the next day he's Mr. Big Business. The money starts pouring in. They're buying up his atomic bombs right and left."

"Dad, I don't think they paid Einstein to make atomic bombs. As a matter of fact—"

"Don't interrupt your father while he's talking," his mother said quietly.

"And now," his father continued, "who do you think they blame for killing the Japanese? A Jew, that's who. A Jew who should have stuck to his p's and q's. That's the shame of it. It could have been anybody. But it had to be an Einstein."

His father took a deep breath. "There's a lot of hate out there, Matthew. A lot of prejudice. We've always tried to protect you from it. But you're old enough to understand: Jews have been persecuted throughout the ages, and do you know why?"

Morganstern forced himself to participate. "I guess because of their religious beliefs."

"No. It's because of their bank accounts, that's why. When God first created the idea of money, he meant for there to be enough to go around. Some for everybody. Even-Steven. A lot of people weren't happy with that. A lot of people wanted more than their share. Now, some of those people happened to be Jews. We're only human, after all."

It hit Morganstern. His winning the sweepstakes had affected them much more than he realized. They had always been strange on the subject of money, but having it come into the family so suddenly had finally pushed them over the edge.

162

"You know what they call gentiles with a lot of money? They call them rich. Wealthy. Well-to-do. Aristocratic. But Jews, that's another story. A Jew with money is a money-grubber. Or a moneylender. Or money-hungry. Or a goniff. And, in a sense, it's true. Something happens when Jews get mixed up with too much money. They get a little crazy. Look what it's done to you. Just look at you. You used to have a nice personality. What happened to your personality?

"You also used to have a girlfriend. I'd like to know what you did with her!"

"Don't ask," Morganstern's mother said. "It's none of our business." Which, translated, meant she was dying to know. His mother had never met Ariel in person but had talked to her on the telephone. Her fondest dream was for Morganstern to be married to Ariel, or to a reasonable facsimile.

"I never even got to meet her," his mother said to the empty, greasy frying pan.

"You'll meet her, Mom."

His mother turned around, and her eyes lit up. "When?" she asked.

"I don't know," Morganstern said, shaking his head.

"How can you know anything when your mind is filled with money? I tell you, it's a disease, Matthew. An addiction. Jews should stay away from it. Leave the loot to the goyim, to the Vanderbilts and the Rothschilds."

Morganstern had let the Einstein comment pass, but he had to clear up the case of the Rothschilds. His headache just wasn't getting any better.

"Dad, the Rothschilds are Jewish."

"Sure, they converted. They want to get on our good side. They're not dummies. Come on, Mother, we'll miss our bus."

Morganstern's mother kissed him quickly on the cheek. "The brisket could use another hour," she said.

His father took one last look around as he stood in the doorway, and then he turned to Morganstern and said:

"You've always made us very proud, Matthew. Ever since you were a little boy. But I never thought I'd live to see the day when a son of mine had a filing cabinet in his living room. We're going now. So kiss your father good-bye."

Morganstern gave the old man a kiss and a hug.

"And don't forget what I said."

Morganstern was filled with all sorts of conflicting emotions. He was glad they were leaving and yet he was sorry to see them go. On one hand he felt very close to them, and on the other it was as if two people from another planet had just spent the night in his apartment. He was thankful to be alone, and he was terribly lonely. He

163

realized that he was still high from the night before and knew that he was in for a hangover that would last the rest of the day.

He left his tuna-fish omelet coagulating on the kitchen table and dragged himself back to bed.

2

Morganstern simply could not get Ariel out of his mind. Just because they couldn't live together didn't mean they couldn't be friends, he reasoned. And, it followed, if they could be friends, they could be anything, maybe even lovers again. He dialed her number.

"She's at her accountant's for the rest of the afternoon," Ariel's secretary said. Morganstern left word for her to call him.

She was spending an awful lot of time with James, he thought. Was there anything going on between them? He didn't think so. But he couldn't be sure. After all, who would have ever dreamed he would end up sleeping with his stockbroker?

Meanwhile, Ariel was having a very difficult session with James.

She was thinking about Morganstern. What was he doing? Was he missing her? Was he as miserable as she was? His party made her realize how well he was doing without her. Why had she ever left him? It made going back so difficult.

"You're not listening." James sighed in exasperation.

"I'm sorry," Ariel said, snapping to attention. "What were you saying?"

"I was saying that this latest raise in salary puts you in a very vulnerable tax situation. An IRA isn't sufficient. You've got to make some decisions on more income-protecting shelters."

"Whatever you say."

"If you're going to be making this kind of money, you just can't be so passive about it. What happened to the Ariel I used to know?"

"I just don't care anymore. I'm tired of finances and tax planning. I'm just tired of the whole thing. The more money they pay me, the less it means."

"Ariel, Ariel, Ariel. What am I going to do with you?"

"It's true. The money is just a trap. The more I make, the more I need, and the more I need, it seems like the less I have. And the less I have, the more I'm tied to a job I can't stand."

"That's a huge rationalization. Your disenchantment with your

164

job is simply a way of not facing your fear of success. You've done so well up until now. Let's try to push through this resistance of yours."

"And I'm tired of all the psychology," Ariel said, bursting into tears. James got up from the desk and came to stand behind her chair.

"My dear girl," he said, placing his hands on her shoulders. "Don't you see how conflicted you are?" He massaged her shoulders lightly. "Of course it's difficult for a woman as beautiful and sensual as you are to be making a big man-sized salary. But we can work it out. You've just got to trust me."

"I do trust you," Ariel said, her shoulders stiffening beneath his fingers. And she had. His tax returns, though highly creative, were mathematically correct and always filed on time. His advice had always been sound. His manner always kind and caring.

"You can't go through life closed up and afraid, depressed every time you receive another ten-thousand-dollar raise." He continued massaging, his long fingers extended down over her collarbone, inches away from the beginnings of the tops of her breasts.

She stopped crying. "I'm not depressed."

"Oh, yes you are. You think your executive position and salary are forever robbing you of your femininity and desirability. But I can show you it's not true. I want you to give yourself over to me completely. Open up to me. Don't hold back."

"Don't hold back what?" Ariel asked, turning in her chair to look at him. He took her chin in his hands.

"I think the time has come for us to consummate our relationship."

"What do you mean, consummate? What relationship?" Ariel said, startled.

"You'll see," James crooned, caressing her neck. "Once we make love, you'll begin to get over your foolish fear of money."

Ariel bolted from her chair. "James, that's absurd! I can't make love with you."

"I know, you think of it as too incestual." He chuckled.

"No," Ariel snapped, "it's too unappealing."

"You're still fixated on Matthew. You should try to get over him. He's absolutely the worst type of man for you."

"And you think you're the right type for me?"

"I've done your tax returns for the past three years. I've been involved with you intimately on every itemized deduction. Who could know you better and know what's best for you than me?"

Ariel backed toward the door as James moved closer. When he reached out to grab her, she fled.

She was annoyed. Now she had to find herself a new accountant, preferably one who didn't have a Ph.D. in psychology and could keep his hands in his pockets.

When she returned to her office, she was delighted to find the message from Morganstern. She was tempted to tell him about James, but decided against it. After all, James was still his accountant. She had recommended him in the first place. And he was an excellent CPA, although, she thought, probably a terrible lay. All that fake macho Western gear made her highly suspicious. Hopefully, Morganstern wouldn't have to concern himself with that part.

She returned Morganstern's call.

"Are you free for a nice friendly dinner?" he asked.

"I can't think of anything nicer or friendlier," Ariel replied.

Cornwall had suggested Inn on the Glen as the most romantic restaurant in the city. Morganstern told Ariel to meet him there at eight o'clock.

Inn on the Glen was like something out of a fairy tale, situated just inside Central Park, almost hidden by huge trees which had been strung with tiny, twinkly white lights.

As Morganstern waited outside, he felt as if he were standing in the middle of an enchanted forest, a magical place filled with strange and fantastic creatures—white unicorns, gazelles, little elves and fairies, winged deer and snorting centaurs.

He looked down at his elegant Italian-shod feet and imagined that they had turned to hooves. He felt randy and wild, like a centaur on his first date with a fairy princess. He tested the ground gingerly, pawing the soft grass. He pictured his cock growing and swelling beneath his powerful flanks. When Ariel arrived, he would have at her, right there on the grassy knoll while the gentle little forest creatures looked on with warm Disney eyes and the tiny elves clapped their pudgy hands with delight.

It was that kind of night. It was spring.

Ariel arrived in a taxi at 8:15. He had never seen her look lovelier. She was dressed in a simple beige suit which was softened by a white silk shirt that fell partly open with only the slightest prodding from her breasts. Her hair was caught up in a tousled topknot, curly wisps of hair framing her face.

"You look fabulous," he said, his nostrils flaring with desire.

"You don't look so bad yourself." She smiled up at him, touching the lapel of his jacket. He felt that this was not just going to be another dinner. It was a new beginning, a fresh start. They were entering the springtime of their love. He was excited, happy, intent on everything going well. Tonight he was really going to be on his hooves, avoiding the usual trouble spots and areas of disagreement.

Ariel had a wonderful sense of quiet about her, as if upon entering the park she too had experienced the same magical spell.

They were shown to a room that looked out onto the jeweled

166

park. It was crowded, but the other diners served only as a muted background to their table. Leaning slightly forward in their chairs, they stared at each other, a reflection of candles and some other more magical light in their eyes. Conversation didn't seem necessary. Words were a part of another world beyond the enchanted forest.

"Our specials for the evening are as follows . . ."

How long had the waiter been standing there? Morganstern had no idea. They slowly came out of their reverie and turned their attention toward him.

"Roast boar with truffle sauce, roast hare with wild rice, venison stew, and broiled ram chops."

Morganstern and Ariel exchanged a look and burst out laughing. "Do you have something a little more domesticated, like a steak, or maybe chicken?" he asked the waiter.

"We're all out of steak and chicken," the waiter said. Another waiter carried a flaming platter to the adjoining table. Morganstern had to lean away to avoid being singed.

"What are you going to have?" he asked Ariel.

"The broiled ram chops sound like the tamest thing on the menu."

"Make that two," Morganstern said, "and we'd like to see the wine list, please."

The waiter brought the wine list. "What goes with ram chops?" Morganstern asked Ariel.

"I think probably a rosé." Ariel chuckled.

They were both having a wonderful laugh about the superchicness of the place, these two people who had once shoplifted Gristede's together.

Morganstern took Ariel's hand in his, brought it to his lips, and gently bit the soft flesh of her palm just beneath the thumb.

"You could have had an appetizer," she said, giggling.

"My appetite is already stimulated enough as it is." Ariel glowed.

Things were going so smoothly, so effortlessly, so magically. It was hard to remember that this was the first good time they'd had in months, Morganstern thought.

"That was quite a party," Ariel said.

"Did you have a good time?"

"Oh, very nice."

"James got you home all right?"

"I got home by myself," she said pointedly.

"Oh, good," Morganstern said, unable to conceal his satisfaction. He wanted to avoid the subjects he knew would be troublesome: When was she moving back in with him? Did she realize she had made a disastrous mistake in moving out in the first place? Had she seen any good men lately? In avoiding the stickier areas, he settled on what he thought was a good safe topic: her job.

"So, how's work?" he asked.

She stopped smiling and made a face. "Awful, I hate it. They put me on a new product, a feminine-hygiene product. Do you know what that is?"

"Some sort of douche or something."

"You're in the right general area. This happens to be a new belt-less pad called Heavy Nights." Ariel's voice took on a tired sarcasm that Morganstern had never heard before. "New Heavy Nights is unlike any other maxi pad because it has not three but five adhesive strips. So it stays in place better. Plus, and here's the real product advantage, it has thirty extra-absorbent layers which trap wetness in millions of tiny little pockets. So there are no middle-of-the-night emergencies, no embarrassing stains on sheets and nighties."

Morganstern suddenly had a vision of innocent little Disney-eyed creatures covering their ears with their soft furry paws.

"Well, there must be a need for this kind of product, otherwise why would they make it?"

"Oh, there's a need, all right. They've discovered this awful gap in the marketplace. See, you got your Light Days mini pads, you got your panty shields, you got your maxi pads with 'new improved protection,' and now you've got these tourniquets for hemophiliacs. Do you realize how many trees it takes to make one Heavy Night maxi pad?"

The waiter brought the ram chops. The conversation was not in keeping with Morganstern's idea of a romantic dinner. But he could see that Ariel was sincerely distressed and he wanted to hear her out. He looked down at his chops. They were a little too rare. Ariel was still going strong.

"And do you know how they come up with these wonderful new feminine-hygiene products? A bunch of men in a lab slave over something they call an artificial vagina. I kid you not. It's a real triumph of twenty-first-century technology: computer curse."

She took a deep breath. "I'm sorry. This isn't very attractive dinner conversation."

"That's okay," he said, taking one of her hands in both of his.

The waiter came and without comment removed their untouched food. Apparently uneaten meals were not unusual at Inn on the Glen.

"Dessert?" the waiter asked.

"Nothing for me," Ariel said.

Morganstern was famished. He glanced at the menu. The desserts seemed fairly domesticated. "I'll have the chocolate mousse," he said, "and hold the honeysuckle garnish. And I guess you might as well bring the check, too." He handed the waiter his American Express card.

The waiter returned with the dessert. There was a plastic butterfly perched on the peak of the mousse. Morganstern carefully removed it and set it aside. The waiter returned Morganstern's American Express card along with the charge slip. Morganstern added a tip, tallied up the total, and signed his name. He tore off the bottom copy, turned it over, and began to fill out the form on the back.

"What are you doing?" Ariel asked.

"I like to take care of this at the time, otherwise I forget."

"Forget what?"

"You know, all this stuff." He read off the expense record: "'Type of entertainment, number of persons, business purpose.'"

"What do you need it for?" she asked.

"My expense records."

"You're taking this dinner off as a business expense?" She looked hurt, but Morganstern didn't notice. He was still writing.

"I take off all my dinners as business expenses," he explained. "James said I need all the deductions I can get." Suddenly Morganstern smelled the unmistakable scent of gardenias. Simultaneously he heard the swish-swish of bare skin moving underneath raw silk. Without even turning around, he knew the silk was white and the bare skin underneath it belonged to none other than Getty Milford. The look on Ariel's face confirmed his suspicions. She was staring right past him; a frown apostrophied her normally smooth brow. The next thing Morganstern knew, two warm, soft arms slipped around his neck from behind, and two warmer and softer breasts pushed against his back. A kiss was gently placed in the oversensitive center of his ear.

"Guess who?" Getty whispered softly. Morganstern wondered: if he guessed wrong, would she go away? If he ignored her, would she go away? Getty's long dark hair fell in front of his eyes. Her chin was resting on the top of his head. There was no escape. He glanced up and smiled.

"Ariel, I uh . . . don't think you met Getty Milford, my stockbroker. This is Ariel Hellerman."

Morganstern glanced at Ariel. She was smiling, but her smile looked as if it had been spray-painted on.

Getty pulled up a chair and placed it next to his, ignoring Ariel completely. "Did you catch the stock report today?" she asked, running her index finger lightly along his earlobe.

"No, no, I didn't. Getty's a stockbroker," he said to Ariel.

"So you said." Ariel had stopped smiling.

"Bundy went up seven points today," Getty whispered in his ear.

"Who's Bundy?" Morganstern asked, flustered. Getty laughed

delicately and ran her fingers through his hair. "One of your stocks, silly. Remember, we picked it out *our first night.*" She underlined the words in such a way that the meaning could not possibly be misconstrued. Morganstern realized he was blushing, which caused him to blush even more.

"Rumor has it that it's going to split two-to-one."

"What does 'split' mean?" He was trying to keep everything on a strictly business level, a safe question-and-answer format.

"It means that for every one share you held before, you get two shares. And if it continues to keep going up as it has"—she brought her face to within an inch of his—"well, I'll leave that to your very fertile imagination. God, I love a good split," she breathed, staring into his eyes.

She kissed him lightly on the lips. "We've got to get together and plan our strategy. I'll call you tomorrow. Or tonight. Will you be home tonight?" Morganstern shook his head emphatically. "Well, then, tomorrow," Getty said, and giving him one last lingering caress on the cheek, she returned to her table.

"You have a very conscientious broker," Ariel said coldly.

"She really knows her stuff," he explained lamely.

"Yes, I'm sure she does. You seem to be very bullish on her."

"Oh, come on, Ariel," he said feebly.

"Did you sleep with her?"

"Did I what?" Morganstern exclaimed, trying to project in his reaction a sense of outraged innocence. It didn't work.

Ariel reached over and picked up the American Express receipt. She tore it into tiny little pieces, and then, holding them above his mousse, she let them sprinkle down like a coconut garnish.

"There's your write-off, you jerk-off," she hissed. Then she got up from the table and strode quickly out of the restaurant.

Morganstern was furious. How many times was she going to walk out on him? How long did she think she could keep him dangling? It wasn't his fault he had slept with another woman. And he wasn't sorry he had. Ariel was turning out to be the only sour note in his otherwise sweet existence. He was determined not to let her ruin his life. His new, moneyed, magical, profitable life. He was going to set his priorities and stick to them. Priority number one: his peace of mind; number two: his painting; number three . . . number three . . . number three . . . He racked his brains for a number three and finally settled at two.

He arrived home with a tremendous desire to work on a painting. It was the only way he could get his mind off the disastrous evening, and off Ariel. It was the only way he could lose himself completely.

He took a clean canvas out of the closet and put it up on the easel. He stared at it for a long time, trying to empty his mind of everything. He let his thoughts float. Two for one. Two for one. He

170

remembered he had bought 2,000 shares of Bundy, Inc., at $10 each. It had gone up seven points. That meant it was $17 a share. He had made $14,000. No, that couldn't be right. He refigured it. Seven times two thousand was $14,000. Unbelievable. And in such a short time.

Now, if the stock split, that meant he would own 4,000 shares. Would they be worth $17 each or would the value get cut in half? He had forgotten to ask Getty that. But, let's just say the value was cut in half. Let's say the stock dropped down to $8.50 a share, it would still mean he'd have $34,000 worth of stock. Jesus Christ, that meant he would have almost doubled his investment. Now, that's what he called aggressive investing.

Suddenly he looked at the canvas. It was no longer blank. It was filled with figures and notations in charcoal. All his projected profits filled the space.

He took the piece of charcoal and scribbled furiously all over his calculations. Then he grabbed the canvas from the easel and threw it on the floor. He picked it up again, ran his foot through the middle of it, and then flung the mangled canvas into the closet.

3

Stuey Schlossman called Morganstern and asked him to meet for lunch at a new restaurant located in an old abandoned Salvation Army building a few blocks off the Bowery. The place was called the Welfare Roll and was very popular with people who worked in the Wall Street area.

As soon as Morganstern arrived, Stuey got right to the point. "I have the investment idea to end all investment ideas. Sit back. This is going to knock your head off. Are you ready?"

"I'm ready," Morganstern said, putting aside the menu.

Stuey took a deep breath. "Do you know why poor people are poor?"

"Because they have no money?" Morganstern guessed.

"Don't be a smart-ass. It's because society labels them and deals with them that way. Underneath every poor person is a potential millionaire."

Morganstern couldn't argue with that.

"Think of the expression 'making money.' They don't say 'finding money' or 'getting money', it's *making* money.' It's one of your basic productive skills. Are you following me so far?"

"I think so, yes."

"Now, the government has always been tremendously unimaginative in their approach to the needy. All they can think about is getting them off welfare and off the taxpayer's back. My idea is bigger than that. I'll make the poor rich. That's what my whole venture is about. Look at these." From his attaché case he removed a series of pamphlets. They were still in the very rough stages with penciled-in headlines and pictures indicated by little squares: *Success and Profit for the Underprivileged; How to Start Your Own Successful Business While You're Still on Welfare; 36 Hours to Getting Rich: A Crash Course in Capitalism for the Illegal Alien,* with the subhead "Wetback Today, Greenbacks Tomorrow" (in English and Spanish).

He handed Morganstern a card which read: "S.U.E., Director of Operations, Stuart Schlossman."

"What's S.U.E.?"

"Society for Underprivileged Entrepreneurs. That's the parent company of my organization. The goal of my organization is to teach poor people to move beyond fear and poverty toward achievement and success. Instead of teaching them how to hold down a job, I show them how to hold a company. 'Think management level, not poverty level'—that's my message.

"Now, in order to get government backing I need funds to make a formal presentation, to get the brochures printed, etc. How's the old cash flow, my good man?"

Morganstern looked into his billfold and counted the money. "I've got about seventy-five dollars."

Stuey was insulted. "I'm talking about seed money, not coffee money. Do you have your checkbook with you?"

"No, I don't."

"That's okay. We can stop by your apartment and pick it up. I think fifty thousand should cover the initial printing costs, costs of skeletal staffing, etc."

"Fifty thousand? I'm sorry, Stuey, I really should talk to my accountant before making an investment that big."

"Let me talk to your accountant. If I like what he has to say, I might let him handle my books once the operation is set up."

Morganstern paid the bill and they walked out of the restaurant. Stuey was still talking.

"I know you don't care about the capital-gains part of this, but your accountant might be interested in the fact that it has all the makings of a great tax shelter. I can practically guarantee you returns of five to one. So get back to me as soon as you can. I want to keep my investors down to a minimum."

172

It was spring. To Morganstern, once a season of renewals, of pigeons wooing in the park, of tender city greenery, of promises of love. Now, it seemed, spring was a time of unlimited investment opportunities, seed money, start-up money, nest eggs for the future. Stuey wasn't the only one to approach Morganstern about new ventures. His money was attracting people like the proverbial honeypot. The possibilities for aggressive investments were coming at him fast and furious.

Zero talked to him about collectibles. "You know, of course, that art is the ultimate collectible, the connoisseur's hedge against inflation. And doesn't it make good sense to collect in an area that you yourself are already involved in and knowledgeable about?" It did make good sense, Morganstern thought. "What I am talking about here is a collection of work that offers you a guarantee you won't get with any other artist. Namely, the guarantee that it will not be duplicated, reproduced, or ripped off in any fashion. The longer you hold on to these pieces, the greater the demand and the greater the value. If you have a bad year, say, in five years, and have a cash-flow problem, you simply sell one of the paintings, which by that time will have increased in value manyfold."

He had a look at the art Zero was trying to get him to invest in. It turned out to be some of Zero's very earliest work. "I did these when I was eight years old," he said, showing each canvas to Morganstern with undisguised pride. "Eight years old! Even then I had a feeling for the avant-garde."

What Morganstern was looking at was a series of paint-by-number pictures: a profile of a horse's head, a full figure of a horse grazing, an Indian chief, an Indian chief on a pony, a collie, and most familiar of all, a deer standing in the woods.

"See, I saved the original directions for authentication. They show how I took the numbers that were called for and reversed them. If it was the lowest odd-number color, I made it the lowest even-number color. I call it Code Painting. What do you think?"

Morganstern thought that the pictures, though oddly colored, were very neatly done. "How much are you asking?"

"I think five thousand would be fair."

He didn't want to hurt Zero's feelings, but he thought five thousand dollars was awfully steep, even if Zero ever became a big-name artist. "Five thousand for all ten?"

"No, no. Five thousand each."

"But that's fifty thousand dollars." Why was everyone hitting upon the same exact figure? he wondered.

Zero threw an arm around Morganstern's shoulder. "Listen, I can understand you may have problems investing in a fellow artist's work. There is a natural professional jealousy going on here, which we shouldn't ignore. But it would be a shame to let a little petty· competitiveness get in the way of a good healthy hedge against inflation."

"Let me talk to my accountant on this."

"Okay. But hurry. They're going to go like hotcakes," Zero said, carefully stacking the ten small paintings in a pile and locking them in a cabinet.

Bill Conrad approached him about a movie deal. He planned to produce it independently and then sell it to one of the "majors."

"It's an epic tragedy dealing with enlightenment, homosexuality, feminism, the need for balance, death of the family, and a meatless society," he explained.

"That sounds like a terrible idea for a film," Morganstern said.

"That's the point," Bill Conrad interjected. "We make the film. It loses money. We take a tax loss. What do you want? *Star Wars* and capital gains? Where is your head, fellah?"

Morganstern again pleaded his accountant and told Bill he would get back to him.

Everyone was after him for an answer. Morganstern was experiencing a strange queasiness in his gut. It seemed to occur now whenever people brought up the subject of money. His money. He feared that he was developing something his father had always warned him about: a nervous stomach. The result of talking about money, especially during mealtimes.

He was getting phone calls from complete strangers. A Mr. Bresner of the Wall Street Hotline called.

"We're a twenty-four-hour service that will contact you in any part of the continental United States with the slightest fluctuation of any ten stocks you choose to put on our hotline monitor. Plus, we have a special Rise and Shine service which will wake you up with that day's opening Dow-Jones average. Plus, we offer our subscribers a special investment-screening service to evaluate all investment proposals, cut out all riffraff . . ."

A man called to talk about death insurance. "We can insure your Keogh Plan, your IRA, your stock holdings. We protect your estate from killer estate taxes. Can you afford to say no? Can you afford to let your loved ones and/or beneficiaries go unprotected?"

Someone selling a handsome leather-bound wallet-size budget and tax diary: "Are you prepared to meet your auditor? This easy-to-carry record book records expenses, mileage, entertainment, features tax-savings hints and attractive illustrations of the fifty state birds."

Stuey, Zero, and Bill Conrad called him repeatedly. For the first time Cornwall was kept busy answering the phone, taking messages, and generally putting people off.

The mailbox was stuffed with offers from banks, investment companies, insurance companies, invitations to business-management seminars, brochures offering investment-opportunities-of-a-lifetime. There was a special introductory offer for *The Winslow Reader*.

"A weekly financial report from America's leading financial forecaster. My predictions, judgments, focuses, and bottom-line inside tips. People in the know and in the dough don't make a move without Winslow. First year special subscription rate, $17,500."

There was an interesting letter from a man who signed himself the Minnesota Millionaire. It was written by hand on yellow legal paper: ". . . So, there I was, down and out, fired from my job for drinking and delinquency, my wife had left me and taken the kids, they had repossessed my car and were about to foreclose on my house, and it seemed like there wasn't any farther that I could fall when I MADE THE INVESTMENT DISCOVERY OF THE DECADE. I am willing to share the wealth with you. It's all there in my book, *The Drinking Man's Way to Riches in These Sober Times.*"

In addition to the phone calls and mail, people actually came to the door.

A well-dressed young man got Morganstern out of bed early one morning.

"Are you for or against the war?" he asked.

"What war?" Morganstern said with alarm.

"Any war."

"I'm against war," Morganstern replied, and started to shut the door.

"Good, then you'll be interested in our investors group: Citizens for Strategic Metals. Why should the warmongers rake in all the profits? Look at the budget: one-point-five trillion dollars for defense. And what does that mean to you and to me? It means strategic metals. It means stockpiling. I'm talking Tungsten, Magnesium, Germanium, Chromium, Titanium, Molybdenum. For a fifty-thousand-dollar minimum investment you can get a piece of the action, profit from huge defense spending, further the cause of peace in this fiscal year . . ."

Morganstern shut the door in the middle of his spiel. But he could still hear the man talking: "Manganese, Gallium, Tantalum, Indium, Rhodium, Cobalt . . ."

Even Cornwall was after him to make an investment. After the apartment was completely redecorated in peach pink and apple greens ("Our Spring Look," as Cornwall explained), his interests turned to business. One day he cornered Morganstern, who was on his way out to make yet another tour of the Madison Avenue art galleries in desperate search of some sort of inspiration.

175

"The Xerox 8200," said Cornwall.

"What?"

"I never have been much for machinery, but I think we must have it." He had been in deep conference with a very young, very good-looking salesman the day before. Morganstern had assumed it was someone who worked for the decorator.

"What is a Xerox 8200?"

"It's a duplicator that gives you XL-10-quality copies at the rate of seventy per minute. It automatically feeds originals, makes two-sided copies, automatically reduces, collates, and staples. We can lease it or buy it."

"I don't really see the need, Cornwall."

"Then what about the Xerox Display Writer system? It's a word processor that checks spelling in six different languages, retailing for $7,895."

"We hardly use the office equipment we have," Morganstern said. "I mean, it's not as if I were a writer or anything."

"Actually, I was thinking that writing could be just the thing for you, sir. You might find it comes a lot easier than painting. It's only a matter of coming up with the right words."

It was the first time Cornwall had said anything about Morganstern's profession. He was clearly let down by his employer's lack of productivity.

"I don't want a word processor," Morganstern snapped. "And I'm not interested in changing art forms."

"Just as you say, sir. One other thing, before you go. I talked to our insurance man."

"Our insurance man?"

"If something should happen to either one of us, it could be disastrous," Cornwall said. "Do you know what hospital costs are these days? Without insurance, I can't afford to be sick. I took the liberty of contacting New York Life. We don't qualify for a group plan, but I did get a very nice policy, I think. Blue Cross/Blue Shield and a hundred-thousand-dollar major-medical for each of us." He handed Morganstern some forms. "You have to sign these and return them to the company."

Morganstern had never thought about insurance before. The only time he had been covered was when he worked at Ivan's agency. He knew he was Cornwall's only source of income and that made him feel responsible, protective, and slightly paranoid. What would Cornwall do without him?

And what would he do without Cornwall? He enjoyed having him around, not because he waited on him hand and foot but because he was constantly dreaming up new projects that gave Morganstern a sense of industry and accomplishment. In fact, Cornwall's salary was one of the few corporate expenses that he still felt good about. He sprang for the insurance for both of them.

Getty was after him to put yet more money in the stock market. He had already invested $40,000—$20,000 in the initial stock buy followed by another $20,000 for Cop Art. The stocks were doing incredibly well. He was making a lot of money. Still, it made him feel queasy.

"Let's get together tonight," Getty said, "strictly business."

She arrived at his place at ten P.M. wearing a trench coat and carrying the New York *Times*. She took off her coat. She was wearing nothing underneath. "My business suit," she explained.

"Your way of doing business seems to be a little on the unconventional side," Morganstern gasped, unable to tear his eyes away from her beautiful body.

"Lie down on your stomach," she directed. "I want you to get in touch with a few important investment principles." She took a bottle of eucalyptus oil from the pocket of her coat, rubbed some on her hands, and straddling his back, proceeded to massage his neck, his back, his arms, his buttocks, and the backs of his thighs and calves in slow, strong, sensuous motions. His erection felt like a hydraulic lift capable of elevating his entire body a foot off the bed.

As he moaned and groaned, Getty intoned: "The secret of successful stock investing is finding your own pleasure and pressure points. At what point is the pleasure of the gamble overcome by the pressure, the fear of losing? The stocks you choose must offer a balance," she said, slipping his legs apart and applying oil to the insides of his thighs. "There are, I have discovered, certain erogenous stocks that can combine the danger of risk with the thrill of increased earnings. These speculative and exciting short-term gains create an intense need for quick release. Then, there are those sustained pleasures of the long-term investment—the blue-chip, guaranteed dividends. Every investor needs to discover in himself what constitutes that perfect symbiotic portfolio so that he can experience the joy, the coming together of stocks and stockholder, the simultaneous orgasm of investor and investment."

Morganstern groaned aloud as Getty reached between his legs and gently stroked his balls. He turned over and grabbed for her, but she resisted him, reaching for more oil.

She massaged his feet, working her way slowly up the front of his body. "A lot of people are afraid of the market. It's a fear of loss of control. They have to learn to open up to the movement, the trading, the selling, the ups and downs, the sensuous undulation of a vigorous Dow Jones." She was, by this time, working in an excruciatingly circular fashion around (so close to and yet so far from) his genitals. "So many investors just dabble in the market without ever knowing satisfaction or complete fulfillment."

It was too much. Morganstern pulled her down on top of his oil-coated body. "I'll do it. I'll do it," he cried.

"I'm recommending a company called Genuine Parts," she whispered in his ear. "Third-quarter earnings: 370 million in sales, 48.6 million in profits. Twelve months' earning per share: $2.40."

"I'll take it," he said, rolling over and entering her quickly, slickly; investing himself with everything he had.

When they were finished, or when he was finished, because she seemed never to be, she smiled and said, "At our next meeting we'll discuss stocks and bondage."

After Getty left, Morganstern began to worry again. He worried about the fact that he had just invested another $5,000 in something called Genuine Parts and he didn't even know what the hell it was. He knew Getty had a point: he needed to find the perfect symbiotic portfolio. But he wondered if he was investing too much money in the stock market. What about all the other kinds of deals people had been talking to him about? How did you know if you were doing the right thing? He couldn't get to sleep. He spent most of the night tossing and turning, weighing and deliberating, counting and calculating. Finally he was able to close his eyes just as the sun was coming up.

4

Morganstern almost overslept for his appointment with James that morning.

"You seem agitated," James said, leaning back in his Barco-lounger and fixing Morganstern with his oh-so-steady gaze.

Morganstern was continually amazed at the man's ability to read him. "I guess the world of high finance takes some getting used to," he said.

"Go on," urged James.

"Well, I've been talking to some of my friends about investments, and I just can't seem to figure out what to do with my money."

"Did you commit yourself to anything?" James leaned forward, a look of concern on his face.

"No, I told everyone I had to talk to my accountant." He was using the terms "my accountant" and "my money" with an easy relish, in much the same way a new bride in the first throes of newly wedded bliss will say "my husband" and "my home," never dreaming that the day would come when "my husband" and "my home" would turn into "my marriage" and "my house." As in: *"My marriage* is on the rocks" and "He's not getting his hands on *my house."*

"What kind of investments have your friends been talking about?"

Morganstern briefly outlined the various proposals from Stuey, Zero, and the Conrads. When he had finished, James said, "Let me explain a couple of principles of investment to you: first, as I've told you before, you need to invest aggressively. You have to be assured of a return on your money that keeps up with and exceeds the rate of inflation and, in your case, because of your irregular income"—what income? Morganstern wondered—"it has to go beyond that. If you invest well, you should be able to live off the interest of your investments and never have to touch the capital. So, rule number one is: good returns. Rule number two is: never, never invest with your friends."

"Why not my friends?" Morganstern asked.

"Let's do a little psychodrama to illustrate my point," James said, standing up and walking around the desk. "Say I'm your old pal Stuey. You give me fifty thousand dollars to invest in a new company. I'm very grateful, of course. I say: 'Thanks, Matthew, you're really a friend. I'll never forget you for this!' Now, I take the fifty thousand dollars and I blow it. Either I blow it because I am a rotten businessman with a lousy idea or I blow it the easy way: I skip the country, rent a villa in Cap D'Antibes, throw parties every night, and spend my days buying gifts for my girlfriends. You don't hear a word from me. Not even a postcard about your 'investment.' A year later you run into me on the street. I try to avoid you, but you catch up with me. What do you say?"

Morganstern jumped right into the game: "How's it going, Stuey?"

"That's what you say? After I take fifty thousand dollars of your money without even the courtesy of a financial report?"

Morganstern rethought it: "Hi, Stuey. Where's my fifty thousand dollars?" he said cheerily.

James began pacing around the room, cracking his knuckles, pulling his hair, and grabbing nervously at his crotch. It was amazing. He had Stuey's mannerisms down pat, and he'd never, as far as Morganstern knew, met the man. "God, Matthew, I was going to call you, I really was. I really feel punk about this, man, but the money's gone. All gone. Every penny. Yours, mine, everybody's. I've lost everything. I'm a ruined man."

"No shit," Morganstern said, dazzled by James's performance.

179

James reverted to form. "See what I mean? Your best friend just told you he screwed you out of fifty thousand dollars, and all you can say is 'No shit.' You can't get mad. You can't hit him. It wasn't his fault you were stupid enough to hand over the money in the first place. That's why you never lend money to friends. Because if friends don't pay you back, all you can do is terminate the friendship. Scout's honor, cross-my-heart-and-hope-to-die, is not collateral for a loan. You've got to learn to say no. You see a friend coming toward you with an outstretched hand, a look of pleasant expectancy on his face, you have a big capital-N No all ready for him."

"Okay, okay, I get the point."

"I hope you do," James said, resuming his seat at the desk. "Just because you've won some money doesn't mean you have to conduct a giveaway for all your good old pals."

"Well, they were just trying to give me some investment tips," Morganstern said loyally.

"You want to know about investments, you ask me. I'm not your friend. I'm your accountant. I'm the only person you can trust. I'm the only person who has your best interests at heart. You want to know about stocks, you ask Getty. She's your broker. By the way, how are your stocks doing?"

"Fine. Terrific."

"How much have you put in the market?"

"Forty-five thousand."

"No, I don't mean how much did you make. How much did you invest?"

"Forty-five thousand," Morganstern repeated.

"What! I distinctly told her no more than twenty thousand was to be invested," James said, pounding the desk. "That woman is insatiable."

"Wait a second. You yourself told me to buy stocks through her."

"That's right. I didn't think it was necessary for me to also tell you to use your head. Forty-five thousand is one-fifth of your capital. You never want to put that much in the market at one time. You have heard of the crash of twenty-nine, I assume." James took a deep breath. "Well, what's done is done. I just hope the market continues doing well."

Morganstern felt his stomach lurch.

"Matthew, I'm not going to be able to monitor everything you do. You've got to learn to stand on your own two feet. I am not your father."

"Speaking of my father, I was wondering if there was some sort of annuity or trust fund I could set up for my parents. You know, so they could receive money, but in a sort of indirect way."

"Rule number three is the same as rule number two: never invest in your family."

"I'm not talking about investing. I wanted to pay off the mortgage on their house, but they wouldn't hear of it. So I'd like to arrange something so that for once in their lives they'd have something to fall back on."

"You mean you want to make a gift to them."

"Yes, a gift."

"Do you realize that you can't make a gift of any real value without paying a gift tax? That's how the IRS takes care of spontaneous acts of generosity. And beyond that, do you know what Freud had to say about the need to give parents money?"

"No, I don't."

"It symbolizes the infantile bowel movement."

"What?"

"When you were a baby, did you ever play with your own feces?"

"No, of course not. Not that I remember."

James ignored his denial. "Giving money to your parents is the same thing. Mommy says make poo-poo and the good little baby makes poo-poo to satisfy his mommy, and he's so proud of what he's done he smears it all over his crib. It's a special production, a wonderful gift. That's how an infant views it. It's a stage you should have passed through some time ago, Matthew. Both you and Ariel," he added.

Morganstern was annoyed. James might be a brilliant accountant, but he found his psychological interpretations totally off the wall. And why was he bringing Ariel into it?

"What about Ariel?" he barked.

"I'm not at liberty to discuss my other clients' financial situations. It would be a breach of confidentiality. I will say this about Ariel, however: stay away from her. She's poison. She's no good to any man at this point in her life."

"Why do you say that?"

"She's got an unnatural attachment to her father."

"I don't think that's true. I don't even think they're that close."

"Always suspect the not-too-close relationship between father and daughter. Her problems with her father are at the bottom of everything that is going wrong with her personal life, her career, and most of all, her finances. It's so clear. She's trying to get her father's approval, and at the same time she's afraid of the love she feels for him. She wants to free herself from him and his values. Ergo, she is successful in her career and a failure in her financial dealings. If the two of you could only learn to break your infantile patterns, your dependency on your parents, you'd both be rich, I assure you."

The guy was a little crazy, Morganstern thought. It was probably what made him so good at what he did. Morganstern still held to the paradigm of mad geniuses. But he hated hearing the accountant talk about Ariel as if he knew her better than Morganstern did. He felt a tremendous sense of distance, a painful longing. He missed her terribly.

"Did you bring your checkbook, as I asked you to?"

He nodded and placed his big blue corporate checkbook on the desk in front of James.

James turned the pages slowly, shaking his head back and forth as if he were looking at the X rays of a man with terminal stomach cancer. "That party really cost you a bundle," he said after several minutes had passed.

"It was a business expense," Morganstern said defensively.

James continued to peruse the checkbook. "Who is Cornwall?"

"My secretary/maid. He cleans my apartment/office."

"Uh-hum. And who is Andre of Second Avenue?"

"That's the interior decorator that Cornwall hired to redecorate the office."

"Art Beek-O. Those are art suppliers?"

"That's right."

"And, of course, we all know who American Express is." James closed the book and sighed deeply. "You're spending money like it's growing on trees."

"It's mostly on business expenses," Morganstern protested.

"Perhaps I didn't explain about business expenses. Business expenses don't mean you get it free. It just means that a certain percentage of what you spend can be deducted, that's all. Think of it this way: every dollar you spend is a dollar spent, every dollar you earn is a dollar earned. Do you follow me?"

Morganstern nodded.

"At the present time, you are earning no money. But you're doing one hell of a job spending it. At this rate, you'll be broke by the end of the year," he said calmly, handing the checkbook back to Morganstern.

"Broke?"

"Well"—James smiled—"maybe not broke, but hurting, which of course will be nothing compared to the pain you'll experience when the IRS gets done with you."

Morganstern was already in pain. His belly clenched in a spasm. As James had directed in the beginning, Morganstern had successfully separated himself from his corporation. ("You are one thing. The corporation is something else.") Consequently, he hadn't thought of the money he had been blowing as his own. It belonged to the corporation. The corporation might as well have been General Motors. It never occurred to him that he had been ripping himself off.

182

"This is serious, Matthew, very serious. You've got to get into a shelter, and you've got to do it now."

"I thought my pension plan was a shelter."

"The pension plan is a nice, legal, minimal shelter. I'm talking about a shelter that involves somewhat more of a risk and offers far greater rewards. I'm talking about keeping the IRS's grubby, grimy, grasping hands off your money." James's face was red with emphasis. "Because if you don't get into a good three-to-one or five-to-one shelter soon, you're going to lose it all. Internal Revenue is just waiting, hatchet in hand, to tax your balls off. You've got to protect yourself. And the only way to do that is with a good shelter."

Shelter. Shelter. In Morganstern's mind there appeared a vision of a snug little cabin nestled at the edge of a woods. Smoke was pouring out of the chimney. It was such an appealing, cozy, secure picture, he had difficulty pulling himself away from it.

"Maybe I can explain it this way," James said, noticing the faraway look in Morganstern's eyes. "Did you ever play pinball as a child?"

"I was probably too busy playing with my feces."

James ignored the sarcasm. "Think of a tax shelter as a pinball game. The ball represents your capital; the holes, the IRS. If you don't play well, the ball drops into one of the holes and the game is over. But if you can get good with the flippers and buttons, you can keep the ball in play. The longer you keep it in play, the more points you rack up. The longer you keep your capital away from the IRS, the greater your chances are of making money off your money.

"Now, here's an excellent shelter I want you to consider," James said, handing him a thick folder. On the cover Morganstern read the name "G. Gross, Inc." Gross was James's last name.

"Is this any relation?" he asked.

"My mother." James smiled.

"Your mother?"

"After my father's death, my mother became a brilliant tax lawyer specializing in tax-shelter packages."

"How much money do I have to put in?"

"Say, fifty thousand altogether."

Fifty thousand was everybody's lucky number, Morganstern thought.

"And where does all that money go?"

"What do you mean?" For the first time, James looked slightly confused.

"I mean, what does it get invested in?"

"Well, this particular shelter is an investment in a five-year tortoiseshell expedition in South America."

"Tortoiseshell?"

"Tortoiseshell," James said, tapping a picture frame that sat on his desk. "The world's tortoiseshell supply is very limited, as you probably know. What's the matter? You look perturbed."

"What happens if they don't find any tortoises in South America? What happens if they end up after five years with nothing to shell? It sounds a little risky to me."

"Of course it's a risk. Any worthwhile shelter is going to be. You don't make money by playing it safe. Besides, the specific enterprise isn't important, it's the numbers that count, and how they look on paper. Maybe this particular shelter is a little too exotic for you. Here," he said, handing Morganstern another, even thicker folder. "This one will be more to your liking. My mother recommends it highly. Study it. But make up your mind soon. These are limited partnerships and there are only a few left."

Morganstern took the folder and his checkbook and started toward the door.

"Matthew."

He turned.

"I don't care if you trust me or not," James said, again reading Morganstern's mind, "but trust this: there comes a time in every man's life when he has the choice—it's either sink or shelter. It's entirely up to you."

5

Morganstern stayed up all night reading the preliminary offering James had given him. If the tortoiseshell shelter had been exotic, this one at least had the advantage of seeming more down-to-earth. It was an investment in an apartment development. That much he could make out. He still couldn't understand what all the figures meant and whether or not "the project," as it was called, was a good one or not. Here is what the prospectus said:

> Rainbow Paradise Valley Estates, Inc., is a limited partnership formed for the purpose of constructing, leasing, and operating a 150-unit multifamily dwelling known as Rainbow Valley Villas.
>
> The subject, a 9.2-acre site, is conveniently located on the southeast corner of Interstate 5 and Garden of the Gods Highway. North of the site is the proposed Dow Chemical Amusement Park and Botanical Garden, and

south, currently under construction, is the Garden of the Gods Chemical/Industrial Park Annex and Small Business Center and the future site of the Colonel Sanders Recreational Vehicle Museum.

The villas have been designed to blend in beautifully with the nearby Garden of the Gods and the surrounding famously scenic Rocky Mountains. This previously arid and beautifully desert-foliaged area is to be one of the first recipients to benefit from the proposed Colorado Emergency Water Act of 1982. . . .

The idea of investing in a project that provided people with a place to live, in a scenic and up-and-coming community, appealed to Morganstern. He had read enough to know that real estate was a good thing to be into. But he was very bothered by the fact that he couldn't see the project with his own eyes. Fifty thousand dollars might be just a drop in the bucket to the general partners, but it was a lot of money to him. He wanted to know if the doors shut snugly, if the windows raised and lowered, if the roof kept out the rain and the basement kept out the runoff. If there was any annual precipitation at all. He wasn't an expert on construction and he wasn't sure he would know a good building if he saw one, but the tax-shelter report that James had given him did nothing to assuage his doubts.

The tax-shelter project was 150 units in two twenty-story buildings. A lot could go wrong in twenty stories. Without realizing it, Morganstern was beginning to develop one of the essential qualities of an investor: an underlying, unshakable sense of suspicion and distrust. He read everything he could about tax shelters. He found they shared one commonality: they all involved large amounts of money, and anybody could join. Nonetheless, shelters seemed to be the accepted way in which the rich stayed rich and the average middle-income person could ward off the debilitating effects of inflation.

And inflation. That was another thing. He needed time to decide on a tax shelter, but now he discovered that there was no time. There was a fucking war going on. The War on Inflation. The headlines filled him with a sense of helpless dread: "INFLATION ERODING ASSETS"; HYPERINFLATION AND FINANCIAL COLLAPSE"; "MAJOR BANKRUPTCIES"; RUNAWAY PRICES"; A DRASTIC DROP IN THE AMERICAN STANDARD OF LIVING"; "INCREASING NATIONAL ANXIETY."

The chairman of the Federal Reserve Board, a calm, reasonable-sounding organization, made the statement that "The greatest *risk* facing us is accelerating inflation." *Time* magazine said, "It is a *frightening* economic problem and rapidly becoming [the President's] most *dangerous* political liability as well."

And what the hell was it? Was this what he had experienced that day in Gristede's many months before? Probably so. But the concept of inflation had been limited in his mind then to the high price of veal scallopini. Now he saw it for what it was: a nationwide epidemic, something for which there was no known cure, that threatened the well-being of every American citizen, the President on down.

What had caused it? What would eradicate it? And what about credit curbs, skyrocketing interest rates, back-to-back double digits? What did it all mean? Why was inflation such a difficult concept for him to grasp?

He had always understood the Depression, and he hadn't even lived through that. His father's descriptions had been very graphic.

The Depression was standing in line to get a bowl of soup; it was no job, no money, no gas for the car, and no car. It was tailcoated bankers falling from the tops of tall buildings, miraculously missing the people who were selling apples for five cents apiece or three for a dime on the sidewalks below. It was all quite clear. Depression was being poor.

The term "inflation" had always sounded to Morganstern like the opposite of "depression." That meant there should be a plenitude of jobs, of money, of food. But according to the papers, the politicians, and the people who called themselves economists, inflation was worse. It was more insidious and certainly more complicated. And if inflation was so bad, then what the hell was a recession? He couldn't even begin to think about that one.

The more he read, the less he understood; and the less he understood, the more frightened he became. Now the shelter decision was far more than just an interesting investment opportunity, it was a matter of very grave concern.

And it was a decision he had to make alone. Without Ariel. Whose fault was that? he wondered. As much as he missed her and needed her, he was unable to make contact. He felt as if he had been sent off to the big war and that she was the girl he left behind. Would she wait for him? If he were killed, would she find someone else? His need for her was so great at that moment, he simply could not allow himself to give in to it. Mixing business with pain was not getting him anywhere. He forced his mind back to the matters at hand.

He didn't sleep for three days straight. His eyes burned from reading books on inflation and investment in inflationary times, not to mention back issues of *Fortune, Business Week,* and all the money magazines that he had ordered and never looked at. The more he read, the less he understood. One piece of information emerged very clearly, however. Many of the magazines reported on victims of tax-shelter scams, people who lost all their investment money *and* their tax-shelter write-offs. Morganstern took note of this. Just because it looks like a shelter doesn't mean it's safe, he said to himself. He couldn't just take the first tax shelter James offered him. He'd have to keep looking around.

And he'd have to start watching his money. Each of the shelters Morganstern read about involved anywhere from $50,000 to $250,000. He remembered what James had said at their last meeting: "At the rate you're spending money, you'll be broke by the end of the year." The word "broke" brought to mind a vision of multiple fractures, a body lying mangled at the foot of a tall building. He was filled with a sense of his own financial mortality.

He noticed that the bills were piling up. When he had first opened his corporate checking account, he had enjoyed writing the checks. The impressively thick book of clean white checks added to his sense of unlimited funds. The amounts never mattered and the checks somehow never represented actual money to him. It was like giving out autographs: they had great value to other people but meant little to him. The slight dent paying bills made on his bank balance was hardly noticeable.

Now he found that he was procrastinating when it came time to pay his bills. He didn't even want to write his monthly salary and travel/entertainment-expense checks. What did he need all that money for? Once he wrote the checks and deposited them in his personal account, the money was as good as gone, frittered away on things that he couldn't even remember.

No wonder his capital was going so fast. His expense check was huge. His salary check was ridiculous. His continuing inability to make a shelter decision made him feel terribly fearful and financially vulnerable. He wanted to gather his money about him and sit on it like a mother hen.

He telephoned James. "Why do I need to draw so much salary?" he asked.

"Your salary is calculated to account for the twenty-five percent allocated to the pension plan. You have to earn that much in order to have invested that amount in a pension plan."

"But do I have to spend every penny?"

"No, I never said that. What many people do, especially with expense money, is cash the check, take what they don't need, and put it away in a safe-deposit box. The IRS has no way to trace that. There's no record of deposit, therefore you can't be taxed on it. However, this could be construed as a minor evasion of taxes. As your accountant, I can't advise you to do it, especially over the telephone. Do you get my meaning?"

"Yes, I think so. Yes, I do. Thanks, James."

"And, Matthew, without wishing to alarm you, the tax shelters I

187

mentioned to you are filling up fast. You've got to move quickly, Matthew. Remember, he who hesitates is taxed."

Morganstern made a trip to the bank. He deposited his salary check and cashed his expense check. He took $1,200 downstairs to the safe-deposit department, which was on the lower level of the bank.

Sitting at a desk, working over a long drawer filled with cards, was Miranda Martin, the Metrobank cultist. Her breasts gently grazed the tops of the index tabs as she inserted the cards in their proper place. Morganstern pushed the buzzer at the edge of the metal gate. She looked up. Her face broke into a wide, warm smile. "Well, hi. I haven't seen you in such a long time. I was worried that you weren't still with us."

"What are you doing here?" Morganstern asked after she buzzed him in.

"Metrobank felt I was getting too committed. They put me down here so I could get in touch with my inner core. Metrobank loves me," she explained, "and they know what's best for me. Did you want to rent a safe-deposit box?"

"As a matter of fact, yes."

"We have all sizes," she said, leading him over to the vault area and pointing to the different boxes. "We have big ones, little teeny ones, and medium-size ones. For all depositors, great and small."

"I think a small one would be fine for now," Morganstern said, unable to meet her glowing gaze. One of her breasts nudged him back in the direction of her desk. She gave him an application card to fill out. Someone buzzed at the metal gate.

"Oh, Mr. Ronkley, come on in," Miranda said as she buzzed the gate open. Mr. Ronkley, a distinguished-looking gentleman in his late forties, handed Miranda his safe-deposit key. She entered the vault and returned a few seconds later carrying the largest of the boxes. He followed her into one of the viewing rooms, where she carefully placed the box on a built-in table. The room was no bigger than a closet and it contained, in addition to the table, a chair, an ashtray, a calendar, and a waste basket.

Morganstern saw the man lift up the lid of the box and remove a bottle of red wine, a chunk of cheese wrapped in plastic, a Zip-Loc bag of Wheat Thins, and a small blue towel. He took off his gray pinstripe suit jacket and pulled a silk smoking jacket from the box. He put the jacket on, sat down on the chair, opened *The Wall Street Journal,* and began to read. Morganstern watched all this, fascinated, while Miranda processed his application form. A few seconds later an attractive woman in her thirties, dressed in a simple tailored dress, buzzed at the gate.

"Hi, Mrs. Bryant. Mr. Ronkley's already here," Miranda said as she let the woman in.

Morganstern watched as the woman rushed into the small viewing room. Mr. Ronkley and Mrs. Bryant fell into each other's arms. The door was kicked shut. From behind the closed door Morganstern could hear the sounds of soft moaning and groaning.

Miranda handed Morganstern a copy of his application and two safe-deposit keys. Then she disappeared into the vault and returned carrying a small box. "This is box number two-thirty-three," she said. "I hope you like it."

"It looks fine," Morganstern said, following her into the room adjacent to the one occupied by the mysterious couple. The moaning and groaning continued; the volume had increased.

"What are they doing in there?" he asked Miranda.

"They're having an extramarital affair," she said, smiling. "I get a lot of those, what with hotel rates the way they are. Metrobank loves lovers," she said, her eyes sparkling. She seemed to be waiting for something. Meanwhile, the $1,200 was burning a hole in his pocket. "Do you want me to stay with you? It can get lonely in here." The weight of her breasts caused her to list slightly toward him.

"No, that's okay, I'll be all right," he said, flustered. Once alone, he quickly took the thick wad of bills out of his wallet and placed them in the box. He wanted to count it to make sure the teller had given him the right amount. He also had an irresistible urge to run his fingers through the money. But he didn't want Miranda or anyone else to hear the riffling of new bills. He knew he was doing something illegal. He could feel the sweat forming on his forehead. From the room next door came the high-pitched sound of a woman building to or achieving an orgasm. Relax, he said to himself. If people could safely carry on an illicit relationship in the bowels of the bank, then certainly no one would pay any attention to something as trivial as socking away a little petty cash. Still, he was nervous. He wondered if there were any hidden cameras.

He closed the lid, opened the door, and gave the box back to Miranda. He hurried out of the bank and hailed a taxi going uptown. When he reached his apartment he got out of the cab and removed his billfold to pay the driver. It was then that he realized that he had no money. Not a dollar. He had put all his cash in the safe-deposit box so the government couldn't get their hands on it and he had neglected to keep any for himself.

He looked around for Julio, the doorman, who was nowhere in sight. He asked the driver if he would mind waiting a minute and went inside to buzz his apartment on the intercom. Luckily, it was one of Cornwall's working days.

"Morganstern, Incorporated," Cornwall answered.

"Cornwall, it's Matthew. I'm downstairs. Do you have any cash on you?"

There was a long pause. "Why?" Cornwall asked suspiciously.

"This is going to sound stupid, but I've got a taxi waiting here and no money to pay him."

"Why did you take a taxi if you didn't have any money?"

"Please, Cornwall, the meter is running."

There was a sigh. "I shall be down presently."

Presently he was, carefully removing a folded-up ten-dollar bill from a small leather coin purse and handing it to Morganstern. There was a stern look of disapproval on his face. "I don't think we should make a habit of this," he said, "an employee lending money to his employer is rather bad form, don't you agree?"

"Don't worry. I'll pay you back as soon as I go to the bank."

"I thought you already went to the bank."

"I did. But I forgot to get any money."

"Yes, I see," Cornwall said. He stood and watched as Morganstern got back in the taxi and drove off.

Back at the bank, Morganstern wrote a check for a hundred dollars and got in the check-cashing line. As luck would have it, he got the same teller he'd had before. Stop being so paranoid, Morganstern told himself, he'll never remember.

The teller didn't look up as he ran the check through the machine and then placed it in the stack of canceled checks at his elbow. "Do you want this in small bills, or are you stashing it away with the other?" the teller asked.

Morganstern fled with his money.

He was feeling worried, watchful, and more wretched by the day. His stomach was continually acting up. He thought he was getting an ulcer and made an appointment with an internist Zero recommended. He had no ulcer. He was in perfect health. The doctor recommended Gelusil and T. bills. His nurse insisted he pay before leaving. "We're trying to cut down on bookkeeping costs," she explained.

He was obsessed with the financial pages of the New York *Times.* He studied them for hours, as if the words would suddenly rearrange themselves and reveal the secret, the simple explanation of how the world of money really worked. He was watching his stocks now with all the interest and attention of the lifetime investor. Who was this Dow Jones? he wondered. His stocks seemed to be doing all right. But there were too many little movements that disturbed him. Up a point, down a point, up an eighth, down a quarter. Every time the market dipped, so did his stomach. And the Gelusil didn't help. He thought about what James had said about investing too much in the market. He called Getty.

"I think you should sell some of my stocks."

"When they're doing so beautifully?" she said. "That's crazy. If I were you, I'd buy more."

"James said it's too big a chunk of my overall capital to have invested in the market at one time."

"James is a premature ejaculator," she said mildly. "The best thing for you to do is forget about the market altogether. Stocks have a way of behaving poorly when they're watched too closely. It's like having sex in front of an audience. It may be fun for a moment but the performance will invariably suffer."

Morganstern was not reassured. He couldn't go to a movie, a museum, pick up a magazine or a paper, take a walk, or eat a meal without thinking about diminishing returns, inflation, taxes, tax deductions, tax bites, tax credits, prime rate, long term, short term, and shelters, shelters, shelters. He didn't seem to be enjoying life anymore. He certainly wasn't enjoying his money. With the exception of his mandatory expenses he had all but stopped spending it.

Everyone was after him to make an investment decision. The phone never stopped ringing. He no longer even looked at the messages Cornwall left. When he was forced to answer the phone himself he took to lying: I've already gone into a shelter. My money's all tied up. I gave at the office. I save at the bank. My accountant's on sabbatical.

He felt he was losing control of his life. He experienced a strange, heavy, colorless feeling, unlike anything he had ever felt before. Gloomy days made him feel bad. Bright and sunny days made him feel worse. He finally realized what it was: he was unhappy, terribly, totally unhappy. He had heard the cliché but it never meant anything to him until now: money didn't buy happiness. But he knew what did. A good shelter—that was the answer, that was the key to man's contentment and peace of mind.

He couldn't even think about painting, and when he thought about Ariel he was alarmed by the realization of how much time had gone by since he saw her last. Oh, my God, he thought, I really am losing her. He would be struck during those moments by an intense pain and longing. He remembered other days and another life when the very thought of Ariel made him feel in love, happy, and alive.

For the hundredth time he vowed he would call Ariel and he would get back to his painting. Just as soon as I get my affairs in order, he said to himself, sounding, to his dismay, like David Niven about to embark on a trip around the world.

6

Zero called him one morning. "Are you going to the party tonight?"

"What party?"

"What party! *The* party. Grace Chase's annual bash. Didn't you get an invitation?"

He probably had gotten an invitation. It was undoubtedly with all the bills that lay unopened on his desk. "What kind of party is it?" he asked, not really caring.

"Every year she throws a benefit in honor of some long-forgotten, long-dead artist. This year it's Arshile Gorky. I assume you've heard of him."

Morganstern had. There wasn't an artist in the world who hadn't lain awake on a bad night fearing Gorky's fate might also be his. Gorky had a real genius for tragedy. It wasn't enough that he lost all his work in a fire, discovered he had cancer, and then broke his neck in a car crash. Oh, no, he managed to survive all that. But then he found his right arm, his painting arm, was paralyzed, and while he struggled desperately to learn to draw with his left arm, his wife packed up the kids and left him. Left him standing there, unable even to lift his poor numb right arm to wave good-bye. Which was when he took the only wise and creative action left to him: he hung himself in the woodshed.

"A party for Gorky doesn't sound all that festive," Morganstern said, thinking of the circumstances of Gorky's life and death and remembering, for the first time in a long time, his own charred work.

"Oh, don't pay any attention to the theme, she just needs to justify the expense, that's all. And her parties are extravagant. Jumbo shrimp, fresh lobster tails, bluepoint oysters," Zero said, as if the mere mention of crustaceans made it all worthwhile.

"I don't know if I feel like it." Morganstern knew he sounded like some tired old fogy.

"Come on, man, you can't miss it. Do you know how much scalpers are getting per ticket?"

"She sells tickets?"

"Of course. I told you, it's a benefit. They'll use the money to erect a statue of Gorky in some parking lot or something. Anyway, it's well worth the price of admission."

Morganstern certainly had nothing better to do, and upon opening the invitation he found that a ticket to Grace Chase's *Hommage à Gorky* was only $25, and tax-deductible.

What the hell, he thought to himself, a little diversion from financial matters might do him some good.

The party was held in Grace Chase's Fifth Avenue duplex, an apartment of huge proportions with ceiling-to-floor windows overlooking Central Park. There were hundreds of people: beautiful people, bizarre-looking people, people dressed as if for a costume party, famous people and people who looked as if they wanted to be famous. Many of the same guests that had attended Morganstern's party were there.

Grace Chase greeted Morganstern just as he was reaching for his first drink. "Thank God, a bona fide artist. Blinky, look who's here," she said over her shoulder. Behind her stood Mrs. Carlyle "Blinky" Lord, the blind art collector.

"Who is it?" Blinky asked, looking in the wrong direction.

"It's that very talented Mr. Morganstern," Mrs. Chase said.

"I don't recall," said Blinky.

"I must take you around and introduce you," Mrs. Chase said to Morganstern, whereupon she took Blinky by the hand and left him standing there.

Morganstern sipped his drink. Next to him, two men in dinner jackets listened to a tall chinless woman.

"I can't for the life of me get this gold thing sorted out," she was saying. "For instance, that terrible situation in Poland . . . does that make it a good time to buy gold or a bad time?" One man shook his head; the second man nodded his.

Morganstern finished his drink, picked up another, and moved through the room listening to various conversations. The Van Dams (Wimmie and Kiki) were talking to another, almost identical couple. Mrs. Van Dam flicked her cigarette ashes on the carpet and then carefully rubbed them in with her foot, as though they would blend into the royal-blue rug.

"I'm writing a letter of protest to Senator Moynihan about this space-shuttle program," Mrs. Van Dam was saying. "They spend so much of our tax money and yet they insist on using the same old spaceship each time . . ."

Morganstern spotted Stuey Schlossman and Dorothea Williams, the black revolutionary-turned-capitalist. They were in a deep conversation with a man who looked like David Rockefeller. Dorothea was wearing a parachutist's jumpsuit cinched in at the waist with a cartridge belt. There were several cartridges missing. Morganstern watched as the man took out his checkbook, wrote a check, and handed it to her.

Two men who looked like they could be brothers were talking intently, ignoring their wives, who stood beside them looking terminally bored.

"How's the government to know? You say you rent the house to me, you even have my rent checks to prove it. So you have your little house in the country and you get to take it off as a rental property with all the deductions."

"What do I do with your rent checks?"

"You cash them and just slip the money back to me under the table."

193

"But I would have to declare the rent," the second man said.

"Of course. That's how you prove it's a rental property."

"Dummy," the second man shouted. "I'd be declaring money that I never even made."

The first man pondered this a moment. "Oh, I see your point," he said.

A short, stout man was holding court with a group of six other men. "I'm telling you," he said, "if I hadn't sheltered when I did, I would have been a dead man."

Morganstern joined the group. "What kind of shelter did you go into?" he asked politely. The fat man stopped talking, and every man in the group turned to stare at him. After several seconds of silence, Morganstern, his face red with embarrassment, excused himself and walked away. As soon as his back was turned, he heard them talking again, this time in muffled whispers.

Why were people so free with their advice about how he should invest his money and so closemouthed when it came to talking about what they did with theirs? he wondered. A good shelter was obviously the best-kept secret in town.

Reproductions of Gorky's work and photographs of the artist hung on the walls in one room. But nobody was paying the slightest attention to them.

James was there. Morganstern was happy to see that Ariel wasn't with him. "Found anything in the way of a shelter yet?" James asked.

"No, I haven't," Morganstern said.

"You're cutting it awfully close on this thing, Matthew." Morganstern felt his stomach drop. "I hate like hell to see you get penalized. We'll talk about it tomorrow. Don't forget to bring your checkbook," James said, moving off in the crowd.

"I heard you talking about shelters." A thin little man with glasses cornered him against the wall. "Can you give me a tip . . . anything?" he asked, grabbing Morganstern by the lapels. "I'll pay handsomely for it. The government's going to get me, but good."

"I'm sorry, I'm in the same position you are," Morganstern said, trying to free himself from the man's perspiring grasp.

"You fucking selfish bastard," the man screamed after him.

Morganstern wondered what the hell he was doing here. He had nothing in common with these crazy people. Or did he? Hadn't he been circulating through the crowd eavesdropping on conversations in the hopes of picking up a good tip on a great tax shelter? He was sick of it all. Sick of the people, their never-ending talk of money, and his own preoccupation with the same thing.

He was just about to leave when somebody embraced him from behind, pressing her obviously female body against him.

"Heavy trading leads to heavy petting, which leads to you-know-what." It was Getty, looking gorgeous in a tight white satin dress. "Shall we say *adieu* to all these charming people and adjourn to your place?"

She put the words right into his mouth. It turned out to be their only successful exchange that evening.

Only once in his life had he ever lost his hard-on, and that had been with Ariel when she was going through problems about her newly acquired success. But this time it wasn't a matter of losing his erection. He couldn't find it in the first place.

"What's the matter?" Getty finally asked after what seemed to be hours of trying. He didn't really know. He hadn't had that much to drink. He was tired, but nobody could be that tired. "If you're worried about the market slump, don't. It'll rally."

"What slump?" he asked, sitting up in bed.

"Oh, Dow Jones closed a little down today, that's all."

"How much money did I lose?" he asked, his heart pounding.

"I don't know that you did lose any money. Besides, it's only a loss on paper. It doesn't mean anything."

Morganstern wondered why profits in the stock market had always counted as money, losses were only "on paper."

"Just relax," she said, pushing him back down on the bed. But he couldn't relax. And as hard as he tried, he couldn't get enough tension together to produce a half-decent erection. He felt miserable, frustrated, and panicky.

"Don't worry," Getty said as she was leaving, "the market will go up again."

But will I, he wondered, will I?

He lay in bed staring at the ceiling. How had he gotten himself into this: this meaningless, joyless, loveless, hopeless existence? Since winning the sweepstakes he seemed to have lost everything of any value. His ability to paint, his ability to enjoy life, and at the top of the list, Ariel. He missed her terribly. He wanted to call her, but he was no more able to pick up the phone than he had been able to make love to Getty. What would he say to her? What did he have to offer her? Not security. Not happiness. Not peace of mind. Not even, it appeared, a decent roll in the hay.

He was desperately tired and yet he dreaded falling asleep. He felt alone and frightened. What would tomorrow bring? Or worse, what would it take away?

When he finally drifted off, his sleep was punctuated by a series of dreams; it was like a film festival of nightmares, each one more terrifying than the next. He was woken up early the next morning by the sound of his own screaming.

It was a Morganstern very much worse for wear who hurried to James's office for his scheduled appointment.

James surprised him by getting right down to business without any of the usual psychological warm-up: "We've got to write quite a few checks this morning. Social security, employee withholding, state, city and federal taxes, your corporate taxes, and so on. So get out your checkbook and let's get to it," he said heartily.

Morganstern opened his checkbook and picked up a pen. "Make the first one to employee withholding for six thousand dollars."

His hand stiffened and trembled. He couldn't move the pen across the check.

"What's the matter?" James asked.

"I can't move my hand. It feels like it's paralyzed."

"Great Scott," James said, jumping up. He examined Morganstern's hand closely. "Any other symptoms?" he asked with interest.

"What do you mean?" Morganstern said, drawing back.

"I mean have you noticed any other dysfunctions. For instance, anything of a sexual nature?"

"What exactly are you driving at?" Morganstern said angrily.

"This seems to me to be a classic case of hysterical paralysis. You didn't make a shelter decision when I advised you to, and now you're so paralyzed with fear, you can't make any move at all. You can't even write a simple check," James explained enthusiastically.

"Well, I'm ready now. I'll go into any shelter you have."

"But I don't have anything."

"What are you talking about?" asked Morganstern, his voice rising.

"These things come and go very quickly. I told you that."

"I've got to have something." Morganstern sounded as if he were pleading for a fix.

"I'm sorry, old man. I can't help you out right now. I'll have more things coming in around the end of the year."

Something in Morganstern snapped. He sprang from his chair and leaned over James's desk. "What do you mean you can't help me out? What the hell am I paying you for? First you tell me: shelter, shelter, shelter. Then you tell me you don't have anything. You and your goddamn interpretive accounting. You've been fucking me around from the very beginning."

"Now, calm down, Matthew."

"Calm down, my ass!" Morganstern slammed the hand—paralyzed only moments before—down on James's desk. "I quit! No! What am I saying? I don't quit. You're fired!"

James went on calmly, as if nothing had happened. "Don't you see what you're doing? Just as you're about to make a real break-through, you want to quit. It's a typical anxiety reaction to progress. . . ."

James was still talking as Morganstern stormed out of his office.

*   *   *

The phone was ringing when Morganstern let himself into the apartment. "I just wanted to reassure you about your stocks," said Getty. "You'll be happy to know that I checked them all over and they haven't been affected in the slightest by the little slump I mentioned. Matter of fact, overall, you're doing very well. As of today, you're almost seventy-five thousand dollars ahead of the game."

"That's fantastic!" Morganstern said.

"I thought that would be a nice little boost."

That clinched it. James had cautioned him about putting too much money in the market, and look how well he was doing. From now on he was going to take things into his own hands. If he had to have a shelter, he'd find one on his own. If there were financial decisions to be made, he'd make them. He didn't need a goddamn CPA to tell him how to live. He was going to live his life the way he wanted to and with whom he wanted to. He was going to get back to basics. He was going to trust his instincts. Money could take care of itself. He had more important things to concern himself with.

He quickly glanced through the day's mail. Something caught his eye. A flier from a company called Tax Haven on Earth, Inc.: "Tax and Real Estate Consultants, specializing in farm properties, country estates, and breeding operations. Free one-day junkets available by appointment." The cover of the brochure featured a beautiful photograph of a small red farmhouse with a barn and silo situated on the crest of a rolling green meadow. Fat black-and-white holsteins grazed in the foreground.

Morganstern was off in his fantasy; he was sitting with Ariel on the front porch of the little farmhouse, smelling the grass, listening to the birds, watching the sun set, sucking on a stalk of wheat.

In his mind, the tall silo held all of his money safe and sound while Ariel held his hand in her warm soft lap. There it was, all laid out: a haven for him and Ariel, a home in the country, peace of mind, a shelter from any impending storm.

He called the office of Tax Haven on Earth, Inc. He was in luck. There was a junket scheduled to leave the very next morning and they had an opening available.

"Could I bring a friend?" Morganstern asked.

"Bring a friend. Bring the whole family. And bring a blank check while you're at it," the man said. "We've got some upstate listings that are not to be believed. Especially if you're in the market to shelter some capital."

At last, he had a plan. He had hope. He had a reason to call Ariel.

"Are you working tomorrow?"

"Tomorrow's Saturday," Ariel said.

"Good, then you're free to take a trip to the country."

"What for?"

"I'm making a little excursion to upstate New York to look at some country properties. I want you to come with me." He was his old assertive, decisive, optimistic self.

"You're not planning on moving, are you?" Ariel asked, her voice quavering slightly.

"I am seriously considering packing the wagon, hitching up the horses, and heading out West."

"Upstate is north, not west."

"Whatever. At any rate, I'd like to have your opinion."

There was a pause. "Oh, well. It would be nice to get out of the city for a day," she said noncommittally. "I'd be happy to come. But, just to look." She was using the same cautionary note one would use on a six-year-old who was about to be taken to view a fresh litter of puppies.

"Sure, sure. Just to look," Morganstern echoed happily.

7

Early the next morning Ariel and Morganstern were driven upstate in a Chevy van by a Mr. Calhoun, the real-estate broker from Tax Haven on Earth, Inc.

Calhoun had a strange, baked look to him, as if he had been left sitting in the sun too long. He wore a safari jacket with matching pants and a thick gold chain around his tanned crepy neck. There was a one-eighth-inch gap between his blond brush-cut toupee and his gray sideburns.

Morganstern sat in the front seat next to Calhoun, while Ariel sat in the back quietly enjoying the scenery along the Taconic Parkway.

"I came out here from the Coast about a year ago," the broker explained, moving his mouth around an empty Aqua filter. "The Arabs have come in and ruined California. Real-estate values are all shot to hell. It's gotten so nobody can afford anything. You know how much a little two-bedroom in Venice goes for now? It would break your heart if I told you." Morganstern showed no inclination to guess. Calhoun whispered the price: "$175,000, maybe $180,000. Two bedrooms, mind you. Ten minutes from the beach. So I decided to pack it in and follow the crest of rising property values." He switched the filter from one side of his mouth to the other as if it were a toothpick. "You may not know it, but New York State is still relatively virgin turf."

They continued along the curving Taconic for about two and a half hours until they reached the exit for Chatham, New York. Calhoun turned off and drove along Route 66 for another hour. From the backseat came the sounds of Ariel oohing and ahing every time they passed a reasonably attractive house or farm. "I feel like I've been released from prison," she said at one point. She was like a kid out on holiday.

"Now, this area here is primo-prime," Calhoun was saying. "Of course, you don't have the ocean, but you've got something a lot better: poor farmers dying to unload their places for peanuts. It's far enough from the city so you don't pay commuter prices and it's close enough to civilization so you don't go bonkers." He made short stubby gestures with his hands, which were adorned with gold rings, on what seemed to Morganstern to be all the wrong fingers. "I'm going to give you kind of a smorgasbord today so you can get the lay of the land and I can get an idea of the kind of investment you folks want to get involved in."

Morganstern wished the guy would shut up. He was spoiling the beautiful day with his yammering. He turned around in his seat to look at Ariel. She seemed unbothered by Calhoun's nonstop conversation. She was deeply immersed in a book entitled *Upper New York State: Its Charms and Its Farms.*

It was a perfect day. The countryside was green and lush. Not far off, he could see the soft mounds of the Berkshire Mountains, and in the distance, the blue peaks of the Adirondacks. The contours of land were gentle, soft, and giving, like a woman.

The first properties they saw were not very enticing. Ariel didn't even bother getting out of the car. She continued reading her book.

The first stop was Caesar's of Sleepy Hollow, a forty-unit motel that must have been built in the fifties. The small casino, convention room, and swimming pool were added on later.

"They were banking on the casino law to be passed, but then they couldn't hold out. It would still make kind of a cute motel, though."

The rooms were done in desert pastels. The "Magic Finger" beds were covered in fake Navajo-blanket bedspreads. In the courtyard was a fountain with a huge plaster-of-paris statue of the Headless Horseman in the center. From the spot where the head would have been was a small eruption of bubbling water. The motel was on the market for $190,000, all fixtures included. Morganstern shook his head.

Next came a huge egg farm, complete with egg-laying factory, packing facilities, barns, house, and abandoned general store, for $210,000.

"That building over there houses twenty thousand layers," the owner said, pointing to a building that was as large as a 747 hangar. "They work their asses off, averaging over sixteen hundred cartons of eggs a day. It's totally automated so you don't have to lay a finger on 'em." Morganstern shook his head. He had never realized how bad chickens could smell.

About a mile up the road they stopped at Averill Harriman Mobile Homes Estates, which was on the market for $175,000. It consisted of twenty almost-new trailers arranged in an Indian attack formation around a natural mineral-spring pool. "This is the owner's home," Calhoun said, pointing to a turquoise-and-silver mobile home resting slightly askew on stacks of cinder blocks. The trailer was enclosed by a six-inch picket fence. Inside the fence, on freshly planted grass, a plastic Dutch boy and girl held a sign which read: "Casa Proprietor." In addition to the Dutch pair there was a big white plastic mushroom with red polka dots, a green plastic frog, two white plastic ducks, and a very realistic-looking plaster deer with fawn. The creatures were all arranged in a crèchelike fashion around the steps to the trailer, their painted eyes staring off in different directions, as if they were guarding the entrance. Again Morganstern shook his head.

"Don't underestimate the mobile-home area," Calhoun said. "What you give up in picturesqueness you can make up for in quick profits."

They drove by a sleek, manicured 400-acre horse-breeding farm which was selling, according to Calhoun, for a "cool six mill." Ariel and Morganstern rolled their eyes at each other.

"I've been saving the best for last," Calhoun said toward late afternoon. He stopped at the foot of a long dirt road. "There she is."

At the end of the road, on the crest of a small hill, stood a pretty white colonial farmhouse. Behind it was a big white barn, and behind that were several other, smaller buildings painted a rustic country red.

"Two-hundred-year-old, charming colonial in good condition, ninety-five acres, gracious lawns, wooded hills, prime pastureland, streams, ponds, barns, outbuildings, all equipment and livestock included. This farmette is yours for the asking, for, and this I don't believe," he said, peering closely at the card, "a hundred and ten thousand. Terms: cash down, which is good, with interest rates what they are these days."

"Oh, Matthew, look," Ariel said, pointing to a small pond midway up the hill. "Real ducks."

As they drove by the pond, the ducks watched them pass, making a 180-degree turn with their heads, their fat little white bodies remaining motionless in the grass.

"Now, this farmette could be a very smart investment for the right party," Calhoun said as he maneuvered the van up the slightly rocky road. "You know what this acreage would go for in L.A.? Eighteen, maybe twenty million. An easy twenty." Morganstern didn't feel it was necessary to point out that L.A. was a good three thousand miles away.

"Oh, look, Matthew, sheep," Ariel exclaimed, pointing to a herd of animals grazing in a far pasture.

"Goats are one of the mainstays of this potentially profitable little tax shelter," Calhoun remarked as if he were reading cue cards for a late-night TV commercial. "You see, instead of paying taxes to the IRS on your capital gains and your income, the money goes right into this place. The government considers losses on a farm as write-offs. They end up helping you pay for it. You can take off practically everything that has to do with agriculture: your fuel, your feed, your feed supplements, your electricity, depreciation on your livestock, your machinery, and so forth."

A couple stood framed picturesquely in the colonial doorway. The man must have been in his early sixties. He was tall, strong-looking, had a ruddy, healthy complexion and white flyaway hair. The woman standing next to him came only to his shoulder. She was pleasantly chubby, with round, shiny cheeks and hair even whiter than his, which she wore back in a loose, fat bun. They both smiled broadly.

"These folks are the owners, the Kinderhoffs," Calhoun said.

"Folks call me Senior," the man said, stretching his big red hand toward Morganstern.

"I'm Matthew Morganstern and this is Ariel Hellerman."

Senior Kinderhoff turned to Calhoun. "If Mr. Morganstern wants, I can show him the lay of the land."

Morganstern was more than happy to have the farmer show him around. He had had enough of the fast-talking, figure-quoting salesman. He liked the looks of Kinderhoff. Obviously he was a simple man of the earth.

"Maybe your missus would like to have Mrs. Kinderhoff show her the ropes," the farmer said kindly.

"I'd love it, thank you," Ariel said, beaming like a new bride.

"Come on, dear, let's leave the menfolk to their boring business talk," Mrs. Kinderhoff said. Morganstern couldn't believe it. Ariel Hellerman, high-powered advertising executive, followed right after Mrs. Kinderhoff, her eyes demurely downcast, a sweet smile painted on her face, as if she had just been nominated for county 4-H queen. "I'll show you where I put up my pickles and such."

"Oh, good," Ariel gushed.

The farmer led Morganstern away from the house. Calhoun followed behind. "Now, let's take a look at the meat of the place," Senior said. He showed them into the big white barn. "This here's the milking barn." There were two long lines of stalls, thirty-six on each side of the barn. In one room off the main barn was a huge metal vat out of which ran thousands of feet of tubing. The tubing connected to individual machines in each of the stalls.

"Now, this here's your Mini-Orbit Surge," the farmer said, picking up one of the metal-and-tubing contraptions. "Gives good milking action, no breakdown, it's as good as the day I bought it. Now, you see, you got your four nipple attachments"—he pointed to four black nozzles. "That's designed for cows, originally. With your goats, all you got is just the two nipples. The advantage being that you can use one milker for two animals, get through the milking twice as fast."

"What do you do with the milk?" Morganstern asked.

"Oh, goat milk's in great demand," the farmer answered. "See, it's got a higher digestibility than cow's milk. It's good for people who have allergies and such. It's considered a real delicacy in these parts. Then, of course, you got your goat cheese—"

"You know how much they get for goat cheese at Zabar's?" Mr. Calhoun interjected. "Almost six dollars a pound." Zabar's was an expensive, and consequently extremely popular, delicatessen on Manhattan's West Side.

"Course, the main reason I switched over from cows to goats is that I prefer the animal. They got a lot more sense and they're a lot nicer to deal with."

Morganstern liked that. Here was a man who was not solely guided by the profit motive.

"Out back there you see your herd, prime brood does. Some people call 'em nanny goats, but the correct term is does. Does and bucks and kids."

"Does and bucks and kids," Morganstern dutifully repeated.

"Those are top production goats, good udders, they milk ten months on, two months off. The good ones produce almost two thousand pounds of milk a year."

"You're kidding," Morganstern said.

"Nope. That's about one thousand quarts, or ten times their body weight. But you don't care about all these figures. All you need to know is they're good producers.

"Here's something that'll interest you, I think," Senior said as they climbed up to the crest of the hill behind the farmhouse. "See that swampy part?" He pointed down to the other side of the hill. Morganstern nodded. "Haven't done anything with it myself, but that could be a real money-maker."

"What is it?" Morganstern asked.

"Peat moss. It's filled with a couple of hundred tons of peat moss."

"Do you know how much they get for peat moss at Zabar's?" Calhoun asked excitedly.

"I'm not even sure what peat moss is," Morganstern said.

"It's the stuff they use for house plants and for those little gardens they put inside glasses."

"Terrariums?"

"Yeah, that's them." Senior nodded. "Well, anyway, I never got around to doing anything with it, as I said, but I bet it could fetch a pretty mean price."

"No kidding? How much?" Morganstern asked despite himself.

"Oh, can't say for sure. But I do know that if you let the stuff sit and stew for a while you end up with coal."

"Coal!" Morganstern exclaimed.

"Mother just didn't want all that machinery comin' in, and can't say as I blame her," the farmer remarked.

Kinderhoff took Morganstern and Calhoun through the toolsheds. Morganstern didn't know any of the equipment. Inside the tractor shed was a huge old John Deere tractor. The farmer patted the sides of the rusty metal. "Sound as a dollar. Wouldn't trade this beauty for anything. They don't make 'em like they used to, I can tell you that. Your new John Deeres are all painted tin and plastic knobs.

"That's your acreage over there for corn, alfalfa, rye—whatever you have a mind to put in, she'll grow." He bent down, scooped up a handful of dirt, and held it up for Morganstern's inspection. To Morganstern it looked like ordinary red dirt. Senior let the dry soil sift through his fingers. "Top-grade," he said fondly. "Nice, isn't it?"

"Yes," Morganstern agreed, "it's very nice."

"A fellah doesn't need to lift a finger and he's got everything he needs here. You got your chickens for fresh eggs, all the goat milk you can drink, and you got the hogs over there," he said, pointing to a small penned-off area where Morganstern could see three large pink mounds lying half-covered with mud. "They'll be ready in a couple of months."

"Bacon and eggs. Do you know how much they get for bacon and eggs—"

The farmer interrupted Calhoun. "It's a nice little spread," he said modestly, "if you got a taste for the country life."

"How come you're selling?" Morganstern asked.

"Well, to tell you the truth, we'd hold on to it for another two hundred years if we could, but I got a little problem with my heart. I can't manage it anymore," he said, tapping his hard-as-wood chest.

"Aren't any of your kids interested in taking over the farm?"

"Oh, no." He chuckled. "My boys all got careers of their own. The old ways just don't appeal to them. Well, and I guess I can understand that, too," he said sadly.

Morganstern wanted to embrace the big old man. He wanted to tell him he would carry on the tradition, that the farm would be safe and would prosper in his hands.

Meanwhile, Mrs. Kinderhoff was taking Ariel on her own tour. The farmhouse was rather ramshackle on the inside, the furniture a cheap pine colonial reproduction. But Ariel could see through it all to a vision of her own perfectly decorated, beautifully remodeled home. And Mrs. Kinderhoff seemed to be sharing Ariel's exact view. The woman was definitely not a country bumpkin, Ariel decided.

"You could knock down that wall over there between the dining room and the kitchen and have a nice open airy eating space. Been meaning to have this old kitchen redone for years. But never seemed to get around to it. 'Course, everything needs a coat of paint, and the bathrooms are a disgrace, but seems like as soon as the kids got grown and moved out, there was never that much need to do anything.

"Look at the wide plank floors. You don't see much of that anymore.

"This house is over two hundred years old, so it's got its charms. You just have to dig for 'em, is all."

Ariel could see the charms. The small-paned, old glass windows (the frames needed replacing), the sloped ceilings (a little plaster, some nice wallpaper), the old brick fireplaces (which, for some reason, were sealed with concrete), the wainscoting (which was broken and missing in many places). The furniture would have to go, as would the curtains and rugs, but all in all, the house had tremendous potential.

Mrs. Kinderhoff led Ariel out the back door and down the side of the hill. "There's my garden, or there's where my garden goes when I'm feeling up to it," she said, pointing to a small plot of land fenced in by a white picket fence. Inside the fence were weeds in every variety. "Here's where the tomatoes usually go, the lettuce here, zucchini there, and next to that the eggplant. And over there, the asparagus."

"Oh, you've got asparagus?"

"Big as a man's leg."

In Ariel's mind the garden of weeds transformed itself into neat little rows of picture-perfect vegetables, beautiful crisp salads, and fat green asparagus.

"Smell this," Mrs. Kinderhoff said, picking a delicate white flower from the weeds and holding it to Ariel's nose. It had the subtle, quick-fading fragrance of a famous-name perfume.

"Ooooh, heavenly," Ariel sighed. "What is it?"

204

"That's your Queen Anne's lace. Grows wild."

"And what's that?" Ariel asked, pointing to a long, slender purple flower growing from a fuzzy green stalk.

"That's just weeds."

"You mean these things grow all by themselves?" Ariel asked, pointing to the vast field of wildflowers and weeds.

"Oh, yes." Mrs. Kinderhoff laughed. "They don't need the slightest bit of encouragement. Come on, I'll show you my favorite part." She took Ariel over to one of the little barns. "This here's the nursery," she explained. Inside the barn, were ten baby goats. They clamored around Ariel, trying to suck her fingers. She squealed with delight. A brown-and-white kitten squeezed between her legs and a huge mixed-breed dog tried to hump her as she bent over to pick up the kitten.

As they left the barn Ariel glanced over to where Morganstern stood with the other men. At the same moment he looked up. Their eyes met across the field crowded with wildflowers and beautiful weeds. Everything was washed over with the warm gold of the setting sun.

While Ariel was having her ears filled with fabled gardens and her fingers licked by wet barnyard tongues, Morganstern was talking turkey with Senior Kinderhoff and the broker Calhoun.

He felt that he had been handling the whole thing in a very intelligent manner, asking the right questions at the right times. The past months had taught him something: there's nothing wrong with talking dollars and cents. People expect it and you're a fool if you don't ask the price of things.

"What's the price again?" Morganstern asked, hoping it had gone down.

"Hundred and ten thousand, everything you see included." Senior took Morganstern aside and said in a lowered voice, "Now, I'm not supposed to say this, but I got another offer from a fella yesterday. A real pushy sort. I'm not so all-fired quick to sell that I'm going to grab the first check that's waved in my face.

"Anyway, young man, the important thing is that you shouldn't feel pressured. That would be a mistake." He gave Morganstern a big strong slap on the shoulder.

"Excuse me a second, will you?" Morganstern said. He rushed across the field to where Ariel stood. She was still holding and stroking the little kitten. "What do you think?"

"Oh, Matthew, it's a wonderful farm. Did you see the baby goats?"

"I'm going to buy it," he said, "but only if you're part of the package."

"You mean, quit my job and move up here?"

"You can always get another job. But I don't think we'll get another chance," he said pointedly.

Ariel was all aflutter. "Aren't you being a little impulsive? Shouldn't you look at other places? Maybe you should give James a call. Make sure it's a good deal."

"James doesn't know any more about farms than I do. I'm through letting him run my life. It's my money. I'm going to spend it the way I want to. And the Kinderhoffs already have another offer. I don't want to lose this place. What do you say?"

"But, Matthew, can you afford it?"

Morganstern had already done a quick calculating in his head. He had more than enough money to pay for the farm, and that wasn't even counting all the money he'd made in the stock market.

"Aside from my vast fortune, I've made a killing in the market."

Ariel stopped smiling. "I suppose you're still dealing with the same hooker, I mean broker?" she said icily.

"Oh, no, I got rid of her," Morganstern said. "I've got myself a nice little guy with a pinstriped suit." A look of relief passed over Ariel's face. "We'll eat health food, get up with the sun, go to bed with the goats, plant vegetables. Just a quiet simple life. No more rat race, no crowds, no cranks, no corporations, no banks, no business meals, no accountants, what do you say?" he asked, resting his hands on her shoulders.

"Well . . . I've always wanted to live in the country."

"We could be so happy . . . I know we could," Matthew added.

"If I quit my job, I'll get about ten thousand dollars in profit sharing, if that's any help," said Ariel, always the practical one.

"I told you, money is no problem. In fact, money won't even be an issue," he vowed. "Don't you see the beauty of it? We don't ever have to argue about money again. We just put it in the land and watch it grow. Say you'll do it. Come on, Ariel. Say you'll at least give it a try."

Ariel threw herself in his arms. "I'll try anything as long as we're together," she cried happily.

"Mr. Kinderhoff," he shouted, "wrap it up. We'll take it."

Morganstern wrote the check. Strange how one moment it seemed like an incredible amount of money and the next moment it seemed like nothing. Just a piece of paper with a lot of zeros.

"Now, you young people don't want to go rushing into anything you're not sure of," Senior said, taking the check. "You sure you don't want to think about it?" Morganstern shook his head. The fact that the farmer was giving him such an easy out only strengthened his resolve to go through with the deal.

"Just give me a day or two to transfer the money into my account, and then you can deposit the check."

As they drove off, the Kinderhoffs stood on the front porch of the

206

farmhouse, their arms around each other, their free hands waving good-bye. The farm was left in a rosy afterglow as the last of the sun slipped behind the big white barn.

Ariel snuggled happily against Morganstern's chest. She felt peaceful and content. She could see their lives stretched out before them now: she in the kitchen canning asparagus, he in the barn milking the goats; she collecting delicate wildflowers from the field, he putting a new coat of paint on the house; she and he taking a walk at sundown, the little baby goats gamboling after them. She saw them getting up early in the morning, doing pleasant little farm chores till noon, and then they would stop for a picnic lunch in the grass. Afterward they would make love under the open sky. Then he would be off to his easel, she to her domestic chores. Their days would be blessed with peace and productivity, harmony and simplicity, fresh air and home-grown vegetables.

She was so proud of Morganstern. He seemed to really know what he was doing as far as the farm was concerned. Winning all that money had taught him a lot about finances and wise investments.

Morganstern felt alive and happier than he had in a long time. He knew he had made the right decision. Ariel seemed so happy. How could they go wrong? This was the kind of life they needed to make everything good between them again. And beyond that, it was a damn smart investment. The goat milk, the peat moss, just the sheer value of the land, not to mention Uncle Sam's help, made it all even more positive. There was no question about it, he had found the farm shelter of his dreams. And he had done it without anyone's help.

Oh, it was a little scary, of course, putting all his eggs in one basket like that. But it had the benefit of simplifying everything so beautifully. No more weekly meetings with James. No more fussing over finances. No more searching for the perfect shelter. He had found it with this farm. Now his capital, his mind, and most of all his heart were totally committed to a life that was simple, down-to-earth, and financially secure.

Cuddled in the backseat of the van, they savored their separate but equal fantasies. Matthew and Ariel. Ariel and Matthew. Just a couple of city kids finding shelter in the virgin turf of upper New York State.

IV

Give Me Shelter

Vile money! True. Let's have enough to save our
thinking of such stuff.
      —William Allingham, *Blackberries*

It took them a week to pack it all in. It was a week of frenzied activity and undiminished high spirits. They each went about their own errands with a sense of mission, with the purposefulness of two pilgrims setting off for the promised land.

Ariel quit her job in the face of her agency's pleadings and promises of more money. She found another apartment-sitter to apartment-sit in her place. And she gave all her clothes to the Good Will.

"I don't need a fancy New York wardrobe for a simple life in the country," she explained to Morganstern.

"What are you going to wear, then, work shoes and overalls?"

"Oh, I'll throw something together." She laughed.

Morganstern had much to do. First on his list was to cover the check he had written to Senior Kinderhoff. He sat down and figured out his finances.

He had started out four months ago with $250,000. Since that time $40,000 had gone for salary and expenses, $30,000 was paid out in taxes—a total of $70,000, gone just like that, with little, if anything, to show for it. Of the $180,000 left over, $100,000 was still sitting in the Barlett Moneymart account earning interest. But that was not quite enough to cover the check to Kinderhoff. Then there was the $35,000 in his pension plan, and the $45,000 he had invested in the stock market, which according to Getty's last reports had grown to over $120,000. He had $255,000 in total assets. That meant he had $5,000 more than what he won in the sweepstakes. Not bad for a rookie capitalist.

He was going to be fine, just fine. He had to see James to take care of any loose ends and settle accounts with the IRS. He realized that this was the first time he had made any kind of major move without the accountant advising him. And he worried, just for a moment, that he might have been premature in firing James. But then he remembered that he had already made his move. He had signed his name and given his word. He was a landowner now, a grower of crops, a tiller of the soil, a man with responsibilities to shoulder and rewards to reap. He had promises to keep and, he sang to himself, "goats to milk before I sleep."

He was at a new stage in his life. A two-fisted, firm-footed, clear-eyed stage that did not allow for wavering and worrying. He decided he would call James only after everything was in order, only after he had taken all the right steps to expedite the move. And then it wouldn't be to get his advice or approval, but to rid himself of all the trappings of his unhappy urban existence. He would cash in on his pension plan. He didn't need the tax shelter anymore, and the whole idea of a pension plan seemed ludicrous. A pension was for someone old, enfeebled, about to retire.

He telephoned Getty. "I'm so glad you called," she breathed. "I was just thinking about you. A terrific new issue is coming out tomorrow and—"

Morganstern interrupted her. "I'm not buying, I'm selling." He told her he wanted all his Moneymarket funds transferred over to his checking account at Metrobank and that he wanted to liquidate his stocks.

"I'll be happy to transfer your money, darling, but you don't want to sell your stocks right now."

"Why not?"

"They're doing so well, I would hate to see you cash in early and miss a continuing upward climb."

Morganstern thought it over. It would be nice to have his investment in the market working for him. He told Getty to liquidate just $20,000 worth of stock.

"So why the coitus interruptus?" she asked.

"What?"

"Why the sudden pull-out from the money market?"

"I bought a goat farm upstate and I'm putting all my money into that." Just saying it made him feel sure and strong.

"Upstate New York. Where on earth is that? Don't tell me, that must be that horrible green area outside of Manhattan!" Morganstern laughed. "But, darling, that's so boring. What in the world are you going to do for fun?"

"Don't worry, I'll manage to keep myself amused," he assured her.

"If you want, I could come up for a weekend. I've never been to the jungle before."

"I don't think so, Getty," he said quickly. "I'm really going to have my hands full."

"You rascal you. I bet the area is overrun with farmers' daughters." Morganstern laughed again and hung up.

The $100,000 plus the $20,000 he got from the sale of some of his stocks left him with $10,000 after Kinderhoff's check cleared. He remembered the $1,200 he had stashed away in his safe-deposit box. He wanted to get his hands on every available penny.

Metrobank was having one of its special promotions: "Metrobank

Friendship Week. Bring in a friend as a new Metrobank depositer and win up to $1,000 in free prizes."

"It's exactly the same as your piggy bank, honey," a woman was saying to a small boy whose face was red with crying. "Don't you want Mommy to have a nice new toaster-oven?"

In the safe-deposit department, Miranda Martin was sitting behind a desk piled high with clean folded towels.

"Hi, Matthew, you'll have to wait for a few minutes, all the rooms are occupied." She got his safe-deposit box out of the vault while he waited. Finally two young men, their faces flushed, their jackets flung casually over their arms, emerged from one of the rooms.

Inside the vacated room, he took the $1,200 out of the box and counted it. He had a fantasy that the money had somehow magically multiplied inside the metal box. But it hadn't. He put the $1,200 in his billfold.

"I won't be needing this anymore," he said, handing the box back to Miranda. Her mouth fell open.

"What do you mean?" Her voice was tense and high.

"I'm closing up my account here," he said, moving toward the door.

"Oh, no, you can't do that. You just can't," she cried, throwing herself on him. "Please, think what you're doing."

He gently extricated himself from her rather strong grasp. "I'm sorry, Miranda, but I'm moving out of the city."

"But we have twenty Metrobank branches throughout the greater New York area," she called after him.

Morganstern didn't want Cornwall to feel as if he were being abandoned. He made him an offer: he could move out to the country with them and help out on the farm. He would have to take a cut in pay, but he would get free room and board and all the goat milk he could drink.

Cornwall's lip curled. "Many thanks for your kind offer, sir. But I can't afford to be that far away from Madison Avenue."

Morganstern saw a '76 Dodge Ram Charger advertised in the New York *Times*. He offered the owner of the "fully air-conditioned, two-tone van, with tinted glass and stereo tape deck" $2,000 cash, $500 less than what he was asking. The guy jumped for it. To Morganstern, it was further evidence of his business prowess and another asset to be notched in his belt. He was a man of property, of substance, and now, a man with wheels. He knew that these last few months he had been hoarding his money, protecting it and shielding it as if it were under attack. Once he began spending it, and spending it on the right things like the farm, he felt strong, tough, invincible.

213

Why hadn't he ever realized it before? He really was a take-charge kind of guy. He had to give Ariel some credit, too. Without her, he never would have had the nerve to set out on this venture in the first place.

He got mixed reactions from the people whom he told about the move. His parents were delighted. They knew nothing about farming, but to them it sounded as if Matthew had returned to his senses, to his basic good-boy nature. The fact that Ariel was going along with him added to their pleasure.

Zero, who had managed to unload his series of code paintings on some eccentric collector and who was off for an extended stay in Europe, scoffed at the whole idea. "Gauguin did Tahiti, Van Gogh did the south of France, but upstate New York? The only guy who's ever had any success with that rural crap is Wyeth, and, I mean, how many deserted barns can you paint?"

Ariel's friends the Conrads were enthusiastic. They had just come into a great deal of money from Marcy's mother and were thinking of going into farming too. "Who knows," Marcy told Ariel, "maybe we'll end up neighbors. We could get together and have a dough-raising or whatever they call them."

When Julio the doorman heard about their leaving, he stopped Morganstern to ask for his Christmas tip six months early. Morganstern took great pleasure in stiffing him.

Finally he called James. "I thought my services were no longer required," James said coldly.

"I need to talk to you about a couple of things."

"Well, of course you do," James said, noticeably warming. "That's nothing to be ashamed about. It takes a lot of courage to reach out for help, to admit you've made a mistake."

They made an appointment for that afternoon.

"You did what?" James said after hearing about the farm deal. "This is something you dreamed, right?"

"No, no. It's real. I bought the farm. It's beautiful. We're moving up there tomorrow."

"We?"

"Ariel and I."

"Ariel is going with you?" James asked, his eyes narrowing. "To live on a farm? With goats?" he sputtered. "She talked you into this, didn't she? It's not enough that she's committed financial suicide, oh no. She's got to make sure she takes you along with her. I warned you about Ariel."

"Leave Ariel out of this," Morganstern said calmly. "It's a good farm. A proven money-maker. And it'll make a damn good tax shelter."

"Perhaps I neglected to explain fully the principles of sheltering. My apologies. In order to make a tax shelter work, you've got to

214

have the income coming in. I mean by this, an excess of steady income above and beyond what you require to maintain your life-style. Are you planning on winning another sweepstakes in the near future? Or are you trying to tell me that the farm is going to bring in that much money?"

"It could very easily," Morganstern said confidently.

"Uh-hum." James nodded his head. "Well, I grant you that a farm shelter can take care of your taxes for the rest of the year. You won't have to pay the IRS anything. You can pour any money you have or might possibly make right in with the sheep dip."

"Goats," Morganstern corrected.

James held up his hand. "Let me just say this: if you know as much about farming as you do about basic finance, you are in deep, deep shit, I don't care what kind of dip you call it."

Morganstern ignored the accountant's ominous tone. "I want to dissolve my corporation and cash in my pension plan."

James chuckled, his teeth held tightly together, as if epoxied in place. "Your pension plan, is it? No problem. We'll liquidate it right here and now." He quickly filled out a form. "There you are, all liquidated, thereby nullifying all tax benefits. You get the money. All you have to do is hand over half to the IRS."

Morganstern felt like punching the accountant right in the middle of his tight teeth. But he held his temper. He had no interest in a fight at this time. He had to save his energy for the work ahead. He was glad to be rid of the pension plan, the corporation, anything that had to do with James.

"Might as well write the check to the IRS now," James said, grinning madly.

Morganstern made out a check for half of the pension plan and postdated it.

"Another little detail—my bill."

"I've already written you a check," Morganstern said, handing it to him. James studied the check as though doubting its authenticity. "And that includes today," Morganstern added.

"Well, I guess that concludes our business," James said.

"Not quite," Morganstern said, glancing at his watch. "We still have a few minutes left in the hour. Let's talk about your feelings, shall we? I notice you seem to be having difficulty in making this break. I wonder if perhaps it might have something to do with feelings of impotence—"

"Get out," James roared.

Morganstern smiled and got up.

"You never did get it, did you?" James said.

"Get what?" Morganstern asked, turning at the door.

"You never understood, you fool: money is not your friend."

But it was, Morganstern mused on the walk home from James's

office. Even if the market took a bad turn, even if his stocks went down, which according to their past performance was highly unlikely, he still had a fabulous $110,000 farm. Money was certainly his friend; it was just a matter of knowing how to handle it.

Their last night in New York was like the night before a wedding. They slept in their separate apartments. Ariel had to hand over the keys to the new subleaser bright and early the next morning. At six A.M. Morganstern awoke, packed up his art supplies and a few clothes, and was at Ariel's at 6:45.

"Come on up," she said, "I've got a few things to carry."

"A few things?" he said. The living room was filled with cartons and shopping bags.

The few things included her new country wardrobe, which consisted of a half-dozen chamois shirts from Kreeger & Son, a fancy sporting-goods shop; a sheepskin jacket from AntArtex; five Laura Ashley cotton shifts and nightgowns; and several pairs of new boots.

"It's not all for me," she said. For him there were several Northwood shirts, a pair of British trousers "for outdoorsmen," and a down jacket. There were bolts and bolts of Liberty of London cotton. "For the curtains," she explained.

"I didn't know you sewed."

"You don't have to know how to sew to make curtains. And look what else I bought for the house." There were two hand-wrought copper wastebaskets with Irish setters at point imprinted on them, also a pair of in-flight copper mallards that graced the top of a wrought-iron weather vane. There was a squirrel-resistant bird feeder of high-impact acrylic, a cordless electronic flood alarm ("I really don't think they have a flood problem up there, Ariel." "Well, it doesn't hurt to be on the safe side"), an ultrasonic rodent eliminator ("Drives out rats and mice with extremely high-frequency sound," she read from the tag), a homeowner's thirty-two-piece toolchest, an easy-to-assemble Rotocrop compost bin, a portable hydraulic log splitter, a leather log carrier, an electric asparagus steamer, two rope hammocks, a Weber grill, and last but not least, a monogrammed doormat with the initials A&M in yellow against a royal-blue background.

"I never realized that Hammacher-Schlemmer carried so many farm things," Ariel said happily. "I guess a lot of this stuff seems silly, but I was so excited, I figured, what the hell."

It took them almost an hour to pack Ariel's purchases into the van, and by eight o'clock they were on their way. The morning smog was just settling in over the Hudson River as they drove up the West Side Highway. It gave Morganstern enormous satisfaction to see that most of the traffic was headed in the opposite direction, toward Manhattan. He leaned out the window and at the top of his lungs shouted: "Good-bye, big gray buildings!"

216

Ariel joined in: "Good-bye garbage in the streets!"

"Good-bye, muggers and junkies!"

"Good-bye, noise and dirt!"

"Good-bye, high rents and lowlifes!"

"Good-bye, transit strikes!"

"Good-bye, clogged pores!"

"Good-bye, roaches and rats!"

"Good-bye, crazy accountants!"

"Good-bye, Heavy Nights Maxi Pads!"

Around Peekskill, the houses thinned and the trees thickened as the Taconic wound its way through the green hills which looked to Morganstern like soft fat nudes lying in repose. You could almost OD on the greens alone, he thought. Apple green, mint green, forest green, kelly green, grass green, blue green, spruce green, olive green, leaf green, and every-green-in-the-world green colored the high woods and rolling meadows of the Hudson Valley.

"Good-bye, New York City!" Morganstern yelled.

"And hello, heaven," Ariel shouted.

2

Mr. and Mrs. Kinderhoff were waiting when they arrived at the farm. With them was their eldest son, Karl, a huge husky man who appeared to Morganstern to be done entirely in comic-book colors: sunny yellow hair, sky-blue eyes, and pink glowing skin. "Karl here is the family genius," his father said. "Best damn dairyman in the state."

"My folks do tend to brag on," Karl said modestly. He extended a hand toward Morganstern that was as big and pink and meaty as the side of a hog.

"We just wanted to make sure you folks got settled in." Mrs. Kinderhoff handed Ariel a mason jar tied with a red gingham ribbon. "Thought you might like some of my pickled-corn relish."

"Oh, how nice," Ariel exclaimed, holding the jar to her chest as if it were filled with cultured pearls from Cartier.

"We get two kinds of farmers up here," Senior said. "We get your city people who are just playing at it. They move up here, plant a couple of rows of radishes, and come fall, they harvest their radishes and hand 'em out to all their friends in the city, sayin', 'See! We're farmers.' Then there's the people who are serious, who work at it, who take this land and their God-given ability and make the most of it. That's the kind of folks this goat farm and this country need. Why else would Uncle Sam give so many farm credits, tax credits, write-offs, and such to the American farmer? The government sure don't do that for people who make all their money on Wall Street and grow radishes for fun. End of speech."

"Come on, Senior, these children have some unpacking to do."

"If you're interested in doin' some serious dairy farming, Karl here can start you off on the right foot. He's the local farm-extension agent. And he don't charge a penny for his services. Ain't that right, Karl?" Senior said, slapping his son's big fleshy shoulder.

"That's right, Dad. The farm extension is a free service provided by the government, available to all the farmers in the area. You want to talk dairy, you just give me a call," Karl said, handing Morganstern his card.

"We got to scoot on home," Mrs. Kinderhoff said. "They're putting new carpeting down in our trailer this morning."

"You're going to be living in a trailer?" Ariel asked, clearly appalled.

"Oh, we've got the cutest little two-bedroom down at Averill Harriman. It's got everything built in, all modern appliances, and no darn stairs," Mrs. Kinderhoff enthused.

"You folks come by for a visit when you get a chance," Senior added.

Morganstern felt a pang of pity for these good, warm farm people. How sad it was that old age and poor health had forced them to give up a farm they loved and land that had probably been in their family for generations, to go and live within the tin confines of a trailer for the rest of their days.

"Well, I guess we got the old keep-'em-down-on-the-farm pep talk," Ariel said, putting her arm around Morganstern.

"I guess we did," he said, watching the Kinderhoffs drive down the long, dirt driveway.

Morganstern unpacked the van while Ariel stood on a ladder going through the top cupboards of the kitchen, removing old dusty canning jars. The phone rang. "Honey, can you get that?" Ariel called.

"Oh, God, I can hardly control myself." It was Getty, breathing hard.

Morganstern glanced at Ariel. "Who is it?" she asked.

"It's, uh . . . Bernie, my stockbroker," Morganstern whispered.

"Oh, baby, baby, baby, this is it," Getty was moaning. "This is like nothing I've ever felt before. Oh, it's so good, so good. Sugar, soybeans, cotton, fresh eggs, cocoa, wheat, and . . . oh, God, hog bellies."

218

"I, um, I'm not following you," Morganstern said, keeping his back to Ariel and his voice on an even level.

"Commodities, commodities, com-mod-i-ties. Oh, Jesus, I'm coming." There was an explosive gasp and then Getty was back whispering huskily, "Did you come too? Oh, you will, you will, it'll be so good for both of us. I just finished a course in commodities trading. I'm transferring over to that department. Trading on futures makes the stock market seem like dry humping now. A friend of mine increased his earnings by one thousand percent within one month."

"How does this affect me?" Morganstern said.

"I want to sell off your stock and open up a discretionary account in commodities for you."

"What's that?"

"A discretionary account gives me the freedom to trade on your sweet sexy behalf."

"Well, yes, it sounds interesting," Morganstern said, anxious to get off the phone. Ariel was standing at his side.

"Oh, you're going to be sooo rich, rich beyond your wildest wet dreams. Oh, God, I think I'm coming again. Give me the word, darling, yes or no?"

"Yes, sure, go ahead."

"Aaaaaaaaaaaaaah," Getty gasped. "Oh, you're so good."

Morganstern hung up. His face was burning, and to his dismay, he had a slight erection.

"What did he want?" Ariel asked.

"Oh, he's getting me into some new stock. Nothing exciting," Morganstern said, pressing himself against the kitchen sink.

"It must be somewhat of a letdown, dealing with a man, after your other stockbroker."

"Oh, not at all," Morganstern said. "This fellow is all buttoned up."

Ariel leaned against him as he leaned against the sink. "You hungry?"

"Famished," he groaned.

"I'll just take a run into town and pick us up a little something," she said, patting him on the fanny.

"Maybe we can bypass lunch." Morganstern turned and grabbed her.

"Uh-uh, we need our strength."

Morganstern thought about calling Getty back when Ariel went into town, but then decided against it. The less contact with her, the better. Ariel would blow her stack if she knew that Getty was still his stockbroker. A discretionary account, she had said. Good. Discretion was certainly called for in this instance. Getty had done very well for him in the past, and he trusted her judgment now.

The idea of investing in things like hog bellies and soybeans made sense. They were real, solid, genuine things of the earth. He would let her handle everything. He felt that the less he worried about money at this stage in his life, the more he could make.

Ariel returned with the van loaded to the bursting point. "You'll never guess what they have in town," she said. "The neatest little shops and discount stores. Can you imagine, all the way up here."

There were designer sheets and towels, bedspreads, shower curtains, throw pillows, cloth napkins, wineglasses, stoneware, Danish canister sets, salt and pepper shakers. "And look at this," Ariel said, holding up a large wicker basket. "It's a real English country picnic basket. Isn't it fabulous?"

Morganstern nodded his head.

"I guess I went a little bit overboard," Ariel added guiltily.

"Don't worry about it," Morganstern said.

"It's all paid for out of my profit-sharing money."

"Oh? Do you have any left?"

"About twenty-seven cents," Ariel said. Morganstern throttled her playfully. "Just kidding, just kidding," Ariel gurgled. "Seriously, I'm really going to watch my spending from now on. I have to remember I'm not on a salary anymore. Hey, before we get into plowing the back forty, let's have a picnic."

She changed from her morning outfit, which had been a little Laura Ashley cotton sundress, into Pierre Cardin overalls. They carried the English picnic basket and an old quilt she had picked up for "practically nothing" to the top of the hill behind the house. From there they could survey the entire property, the barns, the outbuildings, and the sloping pastures.

She unpacked the food. Cold chicken curry, marinated mushrooms, stuffed artichokes, a cold pasta, a loaf of French bread, and a ripe Brie.

"Where did you get all this?"

"Oh, there's the greatest little country store in town. Ye Olde L'Epicure. Everything is homemade. They even do catering." She took out a cold bottle of Pouilly Fuissé and a little antique crystal vase which she filled with wildflowers.

"Isn't this perfect?" She smiled, surveying the spread.

"You're perfect," he said, pushing her back on the grass. His hand reached underneath the bib of her soft denim overalls. "Wait a second," she breathed. She got up, took off her overalls and her hand-embroidered peasant shirt and lay down on the quilt. Morganstern's hand went to her warm breast, the other slipping into her Christian Dior lace panties. Her wetness ran to meet his fingers; her nipple rose to his lips. "Ohhh, God, Ariel."

220

"Ohh, Matthew, come inside me, please."

Suddenly he was inside, strong and hard inside her. The sun warmed his back, the grass tickled his legs, and she pillowed his body with her soft-buoyant breasts and her warm, tight thighs.

And she came and then he came, and quickly and surprisingly she came again before he softened and smalled and finally slipped out of her.

They lay on their backs, letting the warm sun soak into them. "I feel like we've come home," he sighed.

"Me, too," Ariel said, taking his hand in hers. "Oh, Matthew, it's going to be so wonderful."

"I don't want to be another radish farmer," Morganstern said. "I'm going to put my money back into the land. I'm really going to make this place pay off. I'll be the best damn goat farmer in the county."

"And I'm going to be the best girl any goat farmer ever had," Ariel said happily.

"I'll get Karl Kinderhoff over here tomorrow morning to explain everything."

"Good. You handle the farm and I'll handle the home front. I'll make goat cheese and yogurt, I'll can peas." She sat up and looked around. "And, Matthew, what a perfect place for you to paint."

"I know. Can you believe that only a week ago we were running around New York City like two chickens with their heads cut off?"

"Do chickens really run around with their heads off?" Ariel asked worriedly.

"I don't know. I'll get Karl to give me a chicken briefing." He sat up and surveyed his land. The day had been saturated in rich colors and painted in perfect shapes. The many greens of the countryside. The unbelievable clean blue of the sky. The black smudges of the goats grazing in the pasture below. The sharp square lines of the outbuildings and barn set against the soft contours of the hill.

It was as if a shade had been drawn up. Suddenly he could see again. Pictures, partially and fully visualized, flowed through his mind. Colors came to him full force, undiluted. Compositions laid themselves out in a simple, symmetrical logic.

He had been living between the pages of a ledger all these months. He had not been able to see beyond the long columns of figures. His life had been limited by black and white and gray numbers, by pluses and minuses, profits and losses. Now he could see again with the clear accurate eyes of an artist. It was as it had been before the money came into the picture. His head was manufacturing images so quickly he felt he would never have enough time to translate them to canvas. He was filled with a wonderful sense of redemption. He couldn't wait until he got the farm under control so he could get back to his painting again.

3

"When I get done with you, you're going to know as much about dairy farming as any man in the area," Karl Kinderhoff said the next morning as he helped Morganstern carry the hydraulic log splitter out to the back of the farmhouse.

"I got the feeling from your father that none of his sons were interested in farming anymore."

"Oh, no, farming's in our blood," Karl explained. "We're all into it one way or another. It's just that we ended up specializing. After I graduated from Cornell I knew that working one farm would be too limiting. I became an agent because there's a real challenge and a whole lot of satisfaction in helping other folks make their farms pay off." Karl got a clipboard out of his car. Morganstern couldn't help noticing that he was driving a Mercedes. The farm-extension business must be pretty good, he thought.

They walked over to the milking barn. "My dad explained about the conversion over to goats, did he?"

"That's something I was meaning to ask about. I noticed yesterday on the way up here that most of the farms in the area have cows. I didn't see any goats at all."

"My dad's always been a free thinker," Karl said. "Now, then, how much milking have you done?"

"None, really. In fact, I've never even been on a farm before."

"That's good. Because when you start fresh like you're doing, you don't pick up any bad habits or outdated practices. You get it right the first time.

"Milking is a matter of good conditions, good stock, good feed, good machinery, and good management. Good management is what you got me for. Good stock you got out there," he said, pointing to the 150 goats grazing in the fields. "That leaves good machinery, good feed, and good conditions. Let's take a look at your machinery and see what you got." He looked around the barn as if he had never seen it before. "Well, you got top-quality cow-milking machinery here. This is the claw," he said, picking up the four-nozzled attachment.

"One claw can milk two goats," Morganstern recited.

"Good, you're a quick learner." Karl traced down the hoses to the pipes to a room off the main milking room. "This is your milk-control room. You got your Surge Electrobrain automatic pipeline, your Surge Pacemaker that controls the pacing of the milking, and you got your milk pump receiver panel, he said, pointing to a wall of switches and knobs.

"Course, your vat has got to go."

222

"Vat?"

"That glass container over there. Doesn't meet state regulations. See, the state has got requirements for all dairies. You don't meet 'em, you can't sell your milk." He jotted something down on the clipboard list. "What you need here is a thousand-pound stainless-steel vat."

"You mean I've got to buy a whole new vat?" Morganstern asked. Even with the sense of unlimited money, Morganstern felt it was wise to be cautious about his spending.

"Don't worry about that. We'll get into the buying part later. Besides, my brother Kaddy runs the local farm- and milk-machinery place. He'll take care of you. He ain't about to rip off one of the family," Karl said, throwing a big, brotherly, twenty-pound arm over Morganstern's shoulders.

"Okey-dokey, moving right along." He led Morganstern out of the control room into a smaller room next door. He kicked a squat red metal motor that lay covered by cobwebs in the corner of the dimly lit room.

"I think you'll be wanting the new five-power Alamo Surge."

"What's wrong with this one?"

"It don't work. Don't give consistent vacuum action. And that's the key to this whole milking setup."

"What's a new Alamo Surge going to run?"

"Aw, hell, I don't know. Not much. Kaddy'll be able to give you exact figures on that. Now, let's take a look at what building needs doing in the main milking barn. Dad started the conversion, but when his heart thing came up, it just sapped the strength right out of him.

"Okay, finishing the rest of these platforms is a real simple job. It's a matter of having the platforms right so's the goats will be at an easy milking level and the equipment don't drop in the dirt. Mayhew'll be able to handle that for you."

"Mayhew?"

"My brother. One of the best contractor-builders in the whole county. He loves a problem like this. You remember what I said about good conditions?" Morganstern nodded. "Well, here is where it applies," Karl said, gesturing around him. "The principle being, the more controlled the conditions, the better milk output you get. It's no different than people working in offices. You give 'em good light, good desks, and good pay, and they'll produce. With goats, the pay is the food. But Kenny'll cover the food department with you. He's a whiz at that."

"Another brother?"

"Yeah, he should be here any minute. He's a dairy-feed consultant. Okay, now, come winter, you'll want to keep the temperature at a steady forty-five to fifty degrees, and of course, keep the humidity way up. Kaddy's got a terrific new climate-control unit you might look into. I'd also check out one of those Pioneer Daireo-Stereo systems."

"Music?"

"That's right. We got studies to prove that classical music can account for a ten-, maybe even a twenty-percent increase in milk production. Well, you'll talk to Kaddy about that.

"Now, I imagine you'll want to keep your payroll down to a minimum?"

"I'd like to keep everything down to a minimum until I get the hang of things," Morganstern said.

"Well, you should look into the cow-flow trainer. People swear by 'em. Works fine with goats. It's a kind of automatic gate that herds 'em, teaches 'em to respond as a group." He jotted that down, too.

"This seems to be getting very involved," Morganstern said.

"Naw, it just seems that way." Karl laughed. "That's 'cause you're new at all this. Let's go outside, then, and look at your feed situation. That's going to be your most important item. Oh, here's Kenny now." Karl introduced Morganstern to a tall, blond, pink-and-blue replica of himself.

Kenny Kinderhoff had a strand of wheat sticking between a small gap in his two front teeth. "Pleastameetcha," he said, smothering Morganstern's hand with his own.

"Kenny here has his degree in feed science, so he knows what he's talking about."

"Has this guy been treating you all right?" Kenny asked Morganstern as he took his brother's head under his arm and attempted to squash it flat. Karl responded with a hefty jab to Kenny's ribs.

"Fine." Morganstern smiled, warmed by the friendly horsing around.

"You watch out for Kenny here," Karl said in a muffled voice. "He'll have you spoon-feeding those goats chopped apples and sweet oats morning and night."

Kenny came down on the back of Karl's neck with a hand chop that was strong enough to do the work of the hydraulic log splitter, but Karl just shook it off with a shrug. The two men separated themselves with a final exchange of shoulder slugs.

Kenny took over the meeting. "Did Karl explain to you that the more you feed 'em, the more they milk, and the better you feed 'em, the higher the butterfat content? Butterfat is where the money is, of course. Now, feed is all very scientifically worked out according to the type of herd, available crops, and so forth." He spoke very rapidly. Morganstern wondered if he should be taking notes. As if reading his mind, Karl said, "Don't worry about remembering

224

all this stuff, either me or Kenny will always be available to answer any questions that come up."

"Yeah, this guy here could talk dairying till the cows come home and leave again for parts unknown. He'll bore the pants right off you, if you don't watch out."

That prompted a new round of arm socks and head squeezes. There was such a good feeling of playfulness and brotherly high spirits that Morganstern was tempted to join in.

"Okay, now, let's get serious," Karl said. "This man needs to get down to business."

Kenny nodded and continued. "Your Nubians is very good eaters."

"Nubians?"

"That's the kind of goat you got. They're right up there with the top butterfat producers. But they're tricky. They got their own particular tastes. It's just a matter of knowing what they like, and you'll have 'em eating like hogs."

"What kind of mix do you think he'll need, Kenny?"

"I'm a firm believer in Pro-Right, all the way," Kenny said to his brother.

Karl took that under advisement for a moment. "Pro-Right, yeah, they make a good mix, I'll grant you that."

"What's Pro-Right?" Morganstern asked, feeling he should take a minimal part in the conversation.

"That's a supplemental feeding program of corn silage, haylage, green chop alfalfa, home-ground grain with equal parts of shelled corn and oats, and then your thirty-percent dairy supplement, which utilizes a regulated protein-solubility concept," Kenny spun off.

"Boy, Dad sure got his money's worth when he sent you to school," Karl said, slapping his brother in the ear.

Kenny answered with a quick slug to the stomach. The two brothers walked around to the equipment barn. Morganstern followed.

"What about a Schwartz mixer?" Karl asked Kenny.

Morganstern's ears perked up. Jewish farm equipment? he wondered. "What's a Schwartz mixer?" he asked.

"That's your top-of-the-line automatic feed mixer. Can't exactly use spoons on a couple of tons of feed," Kenny answered.

Karl elaborated. "The point being that the more automated you are, the more efficient you are and the more profitable your farm is. And the more profitable it is, the more time you have to spend with your pretty little missus."

"Has he got a pretty little missus?" Kenny asked his brother.

"You can say that again," Karl said.

"Has he got a pretty little—"

225

Karl thwonked his brother in the shoulder. "C'mon, let's take a look at the silo situation."

There was a tall concrete structure bound together with heavy steel wire that stood at the entrance to the barn. The three men looked up at it for a long time.

"Whatdaya think, Ken?" Karl asked, deferring to the feed expert.

"Oh, it's gotta go. No question about that. I was just trying to figure if he would be better off with a sixty-foot Blue Angel or a ninety-footer."

"I think the sixty-footer. Why should he spend unnecessary money?"

Morganstern was heartened by this concern for his finances. And without even having to be asked, Kenny Kinderhoff explained about the Blue Angel. "Blue Angels are those big blue Harvestores. They're the best silos on the market today. See, these old concrete numbers cause seepage," he said, kicking the side of the silo and chipping off a good three inches with his heavy work boots. "The advantage of having a good silo system is that you can grow and store your own feed for long periods of time. It'll save you thousands a month. No sense spoiling good forage with bad storage, is my motto."

"What's forage?" Morganstern asked, feeling stupid.

"That's your silage and haylage. It's just a fancy name for what they eat."

Silage, haylage, storage, spoilage. Morganstern's head was spinning.

"He'll be wanting the Butler, too," Karl reminded his brother.

"Oh, sure." Kenny turned to Morganstern to explain. "The Butler is a small silo for grain pellets which are a vitamin supplement to the forage."

"We should take a look at the John Deere." John Deere, as Morganstern already knew, was the name of the tractor.

There was much tire-kicking and fender-pounding directed at the big red tractor. "I think Kad's got a good rebuilt one down at the garage."

"Your dad said this one's in good condition," Morganstern said.

"Well, Dad can be funny about old machinery. Gets attached to it like it was a pet or something. You talk to Kaddy, he won't steer you wrong."

"Now, all this's going to take a while to set up. In the meantime, you're going to need an extra pair of hands. You still got to milk your goats, you know. Cowpie's going to work for you until you get fully automated. Cowpie!" Karl yelled across the field, where the goats had gathered in groups of ten and fifteen. Morganstern could

226

see nothing but goats, and then, slowly rising from the center of one group, was the biggest man he ever saw.

"His name is Cowpie?"

"That's what we call him 'cause that's what he kept falling into when he was a kid. Cowpie! C'mon up here. Right now."

The huge figure lumbered up the slope toward them. "He's our baby brother and he's special," Kenny said fondly. Morganstern could see he was special even from that distance. Cowpie must have been twice the size of either of his brothers.

"He's a little slow, but he's a heck of a good worker. And he does love his goats."

"Yeah"—Kenny guffawed—"that he does."

Cowpie stood, hands hanging loosely at his sides, a huge grin splitting his round face. He had the same Kinderhoff coloring, but more of it. Morganstern hoped he didn't have the Kinderhoff proclivity for horsing around. A noogie from him was likely to cripple a man for life, he thought.

"You pay him four dollars an hour. He'll be happy to have it, wontcha, Cowpie?"

Cowpie held up a huge hand, spreading his sausagelike fingers out wide. "Five dollars," he said, grinning and drooling.

"Listen to that, will ya? He's been working on his figures," Karl exclaimed. "Good boy, Cowpie." He threw an arm around his brother and gave him a kiss on the cheek. "Dad'll be real proud. Didja hear that, Kenny?" Both brothers beamed at Cowpie.

"Hneh, hneh, hneh," chortled Cowpie.

"Okay," Karl said, going back to his checklist, "here's how it rounds out as I see it. We need the Alamo Surge, a new gutter cleaner—"

"A new gutter cleaner?" Morganstern interrupted.

"Oh, yeah. The one you got now is shot. You've got to maintain a sanitary milking operation, otherwise you won't be able to give your milk away. And you sure as hell don't want to clean up after those guys by hand, do you?"

"No, I guess you're right."

Karl went back to his list. "The sixty-foot Harvestore, the Butler, both of which pay out, is that right, Kenny?"

"Right, Karl, no problem with the pay-out program."

"Okay, the John Deere—hopefully Kaddy still has that rebuilt one—the new milk vat, the conversion from flat to parlor barn—"

"All this sounds like it's going to cost a fortune," Morganstern said. "My money's sort of tied up right now . . ."

"If you have a money problem, talk to Uncle Kruger. He's farm credit in this area. He'll take care of you," Karl said.

"Money's the last thing you have to worry about," Kenny added. "Seepage and spoilage, that's your big concern."

"This Uncle Kruger is just going to give me some money just like that?" Morganstern asked skeptically. He had lived in New York City long enough to know that you never got something for nothing.

"Oh, no." Karl laughed. "He doesn't give it away. It's a loan. But the terms are so good, it might just as well be a gift."

"How much do you figure I'm going to need?"

"Well, Uncle Kruger'll talk to Mayhew and Kaddy and get estimates on building and machinery, and then he'll best be able to tell you how much you're going to want. Hell, you'll have it paid back by the first couple of milkings, at any rate."

"Tell him about Carnation Ormsby," Kenny said.

"Is that another brother?"

Kenny and Karl burst out laughing. Karl explained, "Carnation Ormsby Madcap Fayne was a famous cow from Wisconsin. In fact, they got a statue of her up there in Madison or someplace. Anyway, she produced her own weight in butter in a single year. I don't need to tell you what butter goes for."

Kenny took up where Karl left off. "Now, your Nubians, if fed right, give fifty percent butterfat. That's over four times as much as any of your average cows. A good goat will average two thousand pounds of milk a year. There was one, bless her heart, who produced almost five thousand pounds, that's twenty-five hundred quarts."

"You figure anywhere on the modest side and you won't be talking money worries, you'll be talking new cars and color TV's," said Karl. "Ain't that right, Cowpie?" he said, slapping his brother on the back.

"Five dollars," Cowpie said again.

"Okay, we'll leave the kid with you. He knows everything there is to know about milking goats. He'll show you how it's done. And we'll have Uncle Kruger give you a call. The sooner you make your improvements, the sooner the farm starts running itself."

"How long do you think it will take to make all these changes?" Morganstern asked.

"Figure three months at the most, and that's to do the job right."

"Well, I really appreciate all the help."

"Don't you mention it. Like I said before, the better you do, the better we all do. You be good, now, Cowpie."

"Hneh, hneh, hneh," came the expected reply.

Morganstern found Ariel in the bedroom putting away their clothes in an old mahogany wardrobe. He told her what Karl and Kenny said about making the farm a completely automated, totally efficient, high-production operation. From the direction of the milking barn came the cry: "Milk. Milk. Milk."

228

"What's that?" Ariel asked.

"That's our hired help, Cowpie. The youngest of the Kinderhoff boys. He's helping with the milking until we get automated."

"Milk. Milk. Milk," Cowpie called again.

"I guess it's milking time."

"Do you need any help?" Ariel asked.

"Hey, woman, us goat farmers don't need nothing from no one 'ceptin' a good meal, a warm bed, and a hot woman."

"Whatever you say, Pa."

Morganstern went to join Cowpie in the barn, while Ariel swept the house from top to bottom. When she was finished, she looked in the smoky mirror over the bathroom sink. Her cheeks glowed for the first time in years without the benefit of Estée Lauder Tender Blusher. She felt as if she had been reborn or just returned from a week at the Green Door beauty spa.

She went into the kitchen and opened all the cupboards and closets. She washed down the shelves and lined them with a pretty laminated paisley paper she had gotten in town. Then she stood back and admired her handiwork. She had never had so many shelves and drawers and little cubbyholes. She couldn't wait to start filling them.

She sat in the living room, thumbing through the L. L. Bean catalog and picking out their winter wardrobe. For him, some Timberline flannel shirts. For her, a hand-knit Icelandic sweater. A lined Baxter State parka for him. Bean's alpine knickers for her. And a dozen pair of cross-country ski sox to go with them. A pair of insulated overpants for him. A down mackinaw jacket for her. For both of them, some Norwegian long underwear. Then there were the Wellington boots, the wilderness jackets, cotton turtlenecks . . .

She studied the local paper and noticed there were a good many auctions and estate sales scheduled for the weekend. She wanted to pick up some nice old wicker for the front porch. Being way out there in the country, she figured she could probably get it for a song. She also reminded herself that no matter what Morganstern said about having enough money, she was going to keep a careful watch on her spending.

She felt serene and clean, newly born and newly in love. She walked over to the barn and from the doorway watched the two men working. She wondered if she should lend a hand with the milking. She thought not. There was probably a distinct separation of women's work and men's work here on the farm. That was fine with her. She had no desire to assert herself or compete in their area. She would tend to the hearth, cook the meals, warm the bed, nurture her man, and redecorate her home. She would provide the beauty, the harmony, the coordinated colors and imported fabrics. How much more satisfying it was than the life she had been leading.

No meetings, no clients, no storyboards, no struggling in the marketplace for the bigger job and the better salary. Humming a little tune to herself, she wandered back to the farmhouse, picking flowers along the way.

Morganstern and Cowpie took turns milking. The stanchions used to keep the animals in place were designed for cows, and so the goats had to be held by the neck by one person while the other one milked. They switched off every five goats. Morganstern got the hang of it pretty quickly. The washing of each teat, the squeeze-pull squeeze-pull of the milking, and then dipping the teat in a special solution to sterilize it and seal it off. It took about seven minutes per goat. Only 125 goats had to be milked, as some were too young and others had just given birth and it was too soon to milk them.

When a pail was full, Morganstern would take it and pour it into the glass vat. His hands cramped and his arms hurt. But it was good, satisfying work. The pulling of the teats, the filling of the bucket, the simple repetitious ritual of it was relaxing.

At one point while resting, mid-goat, he looked up at Cowpie and was surprised to see him press his mouth firmly against a goat's black shiny lips. Cowpie looked at Morganstern. "Hneh, hneh, hneh." He grinned and then leaned back down to kiss the goat tenderly on the eyelid.

Morganstern felt like a voyeur. He turned away embarrassed.

Endless hours later they were finished with the milking. He could see where raising the goats or lowering the floor made a hell of a lot of sense. His back ached, his arms ached, and he had difficulty moving his legs. But still, he felt terrific.

The barn had to be cleaned. Cowpie swept the little black pellets into the gutter and Morganstern hosed them through.

"Dollars," Cowpie said, holding out his massive hand.

"How about if I pay you all at once at the end of the week?"

"Dollars," Cowpie repeated, smiling.

"Okay, okay." Morganstern figured out the time and handed Cowpie thirty-five dollars. He wondered if he should keep a record of his wages. He was too tired to think about it.

As he started to walk toward the house, he heard the excited grunting of the pigs. He had forgotten about feeding them. The chickens probably needed feeding too. He located the bags of feed in the small shed next to the chicken coop.

"Honey, aren't you finished yet?" Ariel had changed her clothes again. She was now wearing a long-sleeved white cotton nightgown with a thick red shawl thrown over her shoulders. Her hair was done up in an old-fashioned topknot. She looked like the perfect picture of the pioneer bride. The kind the Indians used to swap muskrat tails for.

"Just about," he said, mixing the pig feed with a little water.

"Hard day at the office?" she asked, running her fingers through his hair.

"My back will never be the same," he groaned.

"Just because you're doing such a terrific job, you win one free Ariel Hellerman Special Country Back and Body Massage," she said, leading him to the house.

Early the next morning, while Morganstern slept, Ariel checked the chicken coop. She carried two dozen warm brown eggs back in the skirt of her Mary McFadden pinafore. She practiced making eggs over easy. It took her about ten to get the knack of turning them over and then flipping them back again without breaking the yolks.

Morganstern awakened to the sounds of squealing pigs, squawking chickens, and cracking eggshells. He stretched with pleasure.

Ariel brought him breakfast in bed on a wicker tray complete with bud vase and wildflowers. The eggs were delicious, the yellow-ocher yolks thick, yet runny. Morganstern had never known eggs could actually have flavor. The goat milk was tangy and the sprouted-wheat bread that Ariel had purchased in town, although priced exorbitantly at $4.50 a loaf, was unbelievably good.

"I'm going to learn how to make bread like this," she said. "They give bread-baking lessons every Monday night at the gourmet shop."

They put aside the breakfast tray and made love. From downstairs Morganstern heard Cowpie yell: "Milk. Milk. Milk." He smiled. His woman lay wet with love in the center of their soft double bed. His morning stretched out before him. His goats awaited him, his land beckoned him. Looking out the window, he could see that even the birds perched on the telephone wires had ruffled up their feathers in anticipation of another perfect day.

He felt like he had been born on this farm. The city, the stock market, the prime rate, James, Ivan, Miranda of Metrobank, the whole money-mad world seemed like a million lifetimes away. He stretched and got up.

As soon as he was finished with the chores and the milking, he promised himself, he would set up his easel and begin to paint again.

4

Uncle Kruger Kinderhoff of the Farm Credit Bureau dropped by that afternoon to welcome them. "Congratulations. I understand you're the proud new owner of the family estate." He chuckled, his Kinderhoff blue eyes twinkling in merriment. His white hair stuck out in cowlicks all over his head. His big round belly strained against a bright red plaid shirt. The line "It shook, when he laughed, like a bowlful of jelly" ran through Morganstern's mind. The warmth he exuded made the rest of the friendly Kinderhoff clan seem cold and remote by comparison.

"Never much into farming myself. What you're looking at is the big banker of the family." He chortled. "I'm the fella to see if you're in need of a little start-off money."

"Your nephews mentioned that to me," Morganstern said. "To tell you the truth, I'm not completely comfortable with the whole idea of borrowing. I do have money of my own."

"Listen, if you got your money working for you, then you don't want to touch a penny of that. Other people's money is the best way to go. 'Least that's what Aristotle Onassis always said."

"Well"—Morganstern smiled—"I'm not exactly Aristotle Onassis. I don't want to get in over my head."

Ariel came out onto the front porch. "And this must be your pretty little missus," Uncle Kruger said, beaming at Ariel. Ariel smiled.

He turned back to Morganstern. "I like your thinking, young man. Do you mind if I call you 'young man'?" Morganstern shook his head. "And you call me Uncle Kruger, like everyone else. Anyway, that's what I call smart thinking. 'Course you don't want to get in over your head. But let me explain something about farm loans. They're not like your regular buy-a-ranch-house get-a-new-car kind of loans. No sir.

"Farm Credit Bureau is a group of us local businessmen set up just to help you new farmers financially. And why? Why do we make it so easy to borrow money? Why do we give you a break on the interest—a good two percent less than prime? Why are we so loose with our terms?"

"Yes. Why?" Ariel interjected.

"Why? Because we need you, that's why," Uncle Kruger said, addressing himself exclusively to Morganstern.

"Listen, you don't have to be a genius to know that our young folks are leaving farms by the droves. Either they're branching out like my nephews or they're moving into the city to become business people. If it keeps on going like it has, who's going to grow the food this nation needs? Who's going to make sure everyone gets three squares a day? Take just milk. What would happen if there weren't enough fresh milk to go around? Kids all over America would be losing their teeth, right and left, uppers and lowers. A toothless country! That's a country that's wide open for takeover. You get

232

those chunky Ruskies coming in here, and they'll just gobble us up. Antiballistic missiles or no antiballistic missiles. Look at Iraq. Look at their dairy production and look at their teeth. No wonder they lost the war.

"This country was built by farmers. Farmers are what have kept us strong. You say you don't like the idea of borrowing money. You got to think beyond your own personal feelings. It's your responsibility to get this farm into good order. And it's our responsibility to make sure you got the money to do it. It's a matter of national supremacy. You don't become the strongest nation in the world on condensed milk and stale crackers.

"So you see, young man, the debt is not yours. It's ours. And it's not really ours. It's America's. This nation needs the farmer. He's the foot soldier of the future." Uncle Kruger placed his hand firmly on Morganstern's shoulder and looked him in the eye for a long moment before speaking again. "You come on down to Farm Credit and we'll fix you up with whatever you need."

Morganstern was very much moved by Uncle Kruger's speech. Ariel, however, was slightly skeptical. "Foot soldier of the future? I mean, really. I get the feeling he's selling you a bill of goods," she said after Uncle Kruger drove off.

"What he said was true. Everyone knows it's better to use someone else's capital instead of your own. Particularly if you can get a good deal on the interest."

"Why is he selling so hard, then?"

"He's not. He's just being friendly and helpful. You've been in the city too long, sweetheart. It's what's called doin' a good turn."

"Maybe you're right." She bent down to examine a wildflower. "Just so long as you don't borrow more than you can pay back."

"Oh, there's no danger in that," Morganstern assured her.

She picked the flower and held it to her nose, inhaling deeply. She sneezed violently three times and then pinned the goldenrod to her hair. "The last thing I want to do is get involved in anything that even remotely smacks of finances. I'm sure you know what you're doing," she said dreamily.

"You want to feed the chickens?" Morganstern asked.

"I'd love to. What do they eat?"

"Chicken feed," he said, kissing her on the ear.

"Ah, nature's wonderful scheme of things," she said. They both laughed.

While Ariel went off to feed the chickens, Morganstern sneaked in a call to Getty.

"I've got you all set up," she said breathlessly. "You own contracts on five thousand bushels of soybeans at four dollars a bushel. I've also put you in margins on powdered eggs, fresh eggs, wheat, and thirty-six thousand pounds of pork bellies. Can you imagine: pork bellies, round, pink, firm piggy tummies. And then we're into frozen orange juice, which my sources tell me is absolutely going to go through the roof—"

"Spare me the details. I just wanted to make sure everything is okay," Morganstern said. Through the window he could see Ariel stroll slowly back from the chicken coop. "I do have one question. I may be needing some cash. I don't know whether to take out a loan or sell some of my commodities."

"Old Mr. In-and-Out," Getty said, laughing. "I just got you into this. You don't want to sell off now. It's all carefully arranged according to weather and crop forecasts and international market developments. Don't worry, I'll keep you constantly posted."

"That's another thing," Morganstern said quickly. Ariel was walking up the front steps. "I know this sounds odd, but don't call me, I'll call you, okay?"

"Well, make sure you do, lover boy. It's important to keep in close, close touch."

"Who were you talking to?" Ariel asked.

"Oh, my broker."

"He's really good, huh?"

"As good as they come," Morganstern said.

Ariel laid a bunch of wildflowers and long grasses on the kitchen counter. "You know that sign down at the end of the driveway?"

"Which one?"

"The one that says 'Deer Crossing.' Now, this may sound stupid, but is that a sign to tell deer where they're supposed to cross the road or did someone once see a deer cross there and mark the spot with a sign?"

Morganstern realized he didn't know the answer either. "That's just one of the many things I'm going to have to find out," he said.

Morganstern paid a visit to the Farm Credit Bureau the next morning. It was a one-room office located on the third floor of the Grange Hall in the nearby town of Appleville.

"How much money do you think I'll need altogether?" he asked Uncle Kruger.

"I got a pretty rough breakdown right here," Uncle Kruger said, referring to a piece of paper on his desk. "I talked to Mayhew and Kaddy and they gave me estimates on the building and equipment you'll be needing." He handed Morganstern the piece of paper.

Blue Angel Harvestore—60 ft. $42,000
Schwartz mixer $15,000
Butler Pelleteer $12,000
Alamo Surge 5 h.p. $5,000

1,000-pound stainless-steel vat $10,000
Automatic gutter cleaner $2,500
Rebuilt John Deere tractor $20,000
Conversion of flat barn to parlor, including plans, labor
and materials $30,000
TOTAL $136,500

"Jesus! That's more than I paid for the whole damn farm."

"Well, you did get quite a deal on the place, I'll grant you that. Senior never did have a head for the almighty dollar."

"It's a hell of a lot of money," Morganstern said.

"Ho, ho, ho. This ain't a lot of money. This is nothing. What we're talking about here practically ain't worth doin' the paperwork on. If I were you, I'd round it out to an even two hundred thousand. It's always better to borrow more than you need."

"I'd rather stick with just what I need," Morganstern said, remembering Ariel's remark about borrowing too much.

"Well, let's take another look at this," Uncle Kruger said, looking at the estimate. "I do appreciate the fact you want to start off slow." He took a short nub of pencil out of his shirt pocket, licked the tip, and began figuring. Morganstern found the absence of a pocket calculator somehow reassuring.

"Okay, the Schwartz mixer you can wait on. You won't be needing that until after the Harvestore is in. The Butler you can hold off on, too. Automatic gutter cleaner? Well, that's a good thing to have. It'll save you a lot of work right now. But if you really want to watch your expenses . . ."

"It would be nice," Morganstern said, holding to his conservative line.

"Okay, off it goes. I don't know how, but Senior has kept that old John Deere running pretty good. What you do is talk to Kaddy. See if he can recommend a good mechanic to be on standby in case of any breakdowns.

"As far as the barn goes, I happen to know that Mayhew is planning on using it as a showpiece to drum up business, so I think if we're smart we can get him to take off five thousand dollars from that price. Let's see what we got here now." He tallied up the total. "Eighty-two thousand. Just saved you fifty-four thousand, young man. And I think this is a good handleable amount for a fellow starting out."

"How much does that come to a month?"

"Well, figure a five-year loan at twelve percent, that comes to . . ."—he calculated quickly—"$2,082 and change. Hell, you can practically pay that out of the missus' canning profits."

Morganstern thought about Ariel canning. And then he thought about Carnation Ormsby and all that butter. He could easily handle it and not even have to touch the bulk of his capital. He had about $28,000 on hand from his pension plan and his stock sale. And he had a conservative $110,000 in the commodities market. Probably much more if everything Getty predicted held true. Twenty-eight in his pocket and a minimum of $110,000 working for him in New York. Hell, he would be fine.

"One more question: what happens if, for some unknown reason, I can't make my payments?"

"You mean, if worse comes to worst?" Uncle Kruger chuckled. "We just take over the farm, put it up for auction, pay off the mortgage, and you keep the profit. That way a fella has a chance to get out without losing his shirt. Fair enough?"

"Sure, that sounds fair."

"But there ain't no way you're gonna go broke. In three months you'll be a fully operational dairy farm. Besides, you got your money working for you in the city, I imagine. It's making money, right?" Morganstern nodded. "The money your investments make go right into the farm instead of Uncle Sam's pocket. That little goat farm is one hell of a tax shelter."

Morganstern thought it a little odd that the same man who was preaching a nation of healthy teeth was talking tax shelters and money out of Uncle Sam's pocket. But he didn't dwell on it. He was too happy. He had his girl, his farm, the simple country life, and a tax shelter too. There really was a haven on earth, Morganstern said to himself.

"Now, later on, when you decide to put in your automatic gutter cleaner, your Pelleteer, your Daireo-Stereo, and what-have-you, you just come back and take out another little loan. See, your farm is your collateral. When you came in here this morning you had $110,000 worth of collateral. You put in $82,000 more and you're talking now about almost a $200,000 farm. I'd say that's pretty good for a day's work."

"It sure is," Morganstern agreed.

"Now, you know what old Francis Bacon said about money?" Morganstern shook his head. "Money is like horse manure. It's no good unless you spread it around."

He handed Morganstern the check for $82,000. "So go out there and start spreadin', young man. You want more where this came from, you just give Uncle Kruger a call."

"Thanks very much," Morganstern said, taking the check.

Uncle Kruger put an arm around his shoulder and ushered him to the door. "Don't thank me, young man, thank America."

Morganstern took Uncle Kruger's advice and started spreading the money around immediately. With one-half payment up front, the people from Harvestore began construction of the huge blue

236

silo. Mayhew Kinderhoff obligingly knocked $5,000 off his estimate, as Uncle Kruger had predicted, and he and a crew of five men began work on converting the barn.

The Alamo Surge motor was paid for and delivered, as was the stainless-steel vat. Kaddy Kinderhoff had already sold the rebuilt John Deere, but he recommended someone to help keep Morganstern's old tractor functioning.

"My cousin Tinker Kinderhoff is as good an all-round mechanic as you'll find in these parts. He can keep your old John Deere running if anyone can. If that don't work out, I got a beauty right here just raring to go," he said, pointing to a brand-new tractor.

"How much is it?"

"She lists for forty-five, but I can let you have her for forty with all the options."

"I think I'll give Tinker a try," Morganstern said. Just because he had no money worries didn't mean he shouldn't worry about buying unnecessary tractors, he reasoned.

Work on the barn was slowed up by a delayed lumber delivery. The five men sat around for three days.

"Are they being paid even though they aren't working?"

"'Course they are," Mayhew said. "They got to eat, don't they? But don't worry about it. If we run into overages, I'll let you know."

One day a truck pulled up with several hundred square feet of Astroturf.

"What's that for?" Morganstern asked Mayhew.

"The interior. That goes on top of the platforms."

Morganstern remembered what Karl had said about rubber matting for the goat's legs. The price of Astroturf had skyrocketed way beyond what Mayhew had estimated, as had the pine paneling for the walls of the milking parlor.

Kenny had arranged for him to buy feed from a local dealer. His prices seemed to go up every week.

"That's what happens when you're forced to deal with people who aren't family," Kenny complained. "But as soon as you get harvested and get your silo filled, we won't have to bother with him anymore."

"Harvested?" Morganstern asked.

"Yeah, over there," Kenny said, pointing to the far-off fields, where weeds and wildflowers grew in abundance. "Oh, shit! You ain't got your corn planted yet."

"Nobody told me."

"My fault," Kenny said graciously. "I'll handle it. Don't worry, it's only mid-June. You got time for at least one, maybe two cuttings on hay, and plenty of time for the corn, if we have a decent fall. I'll get a crew on it right away." He hired an emergency planting crew of three men at a cost of fifty dollars a day for each man. The old John Deere broke down on the second day of planting. Tinker was called in immediately. He spent another two days taking the entire tractor apart, piece by piece.

"I did my best," he finally said, shaking his head sadly, "but she's a goner."

"What should I do?" Morganstern asked.

"I think you better give Kaddy a call."

"Don't tell me I'm going to have to buy a whole new tractor!"

"You can't have a farm without a tractor. That's like having a limousine without a chauffeur." Morganstern thought the analogy rather strange coming from a plain-talking, down-home sort of guy like Tinker.

"You're in luck," Kaddy said on the phone. "I had to take back the rebuilt John Deere from the guy I sold it to."

"Why was that?"

"Oh, he couldn't keep up with his payments. So I can let you have it for twenty thousand dollars. No, wait. I'll give it to you for seventeen-five. But it's got to be cash."

Uncle Kruger's rough estimate of costs turned out not to be so rough after all. At the end of a month the money he had borrowed was gone. The machinery was paid for and labor and building costs were met as they were incurred. Mayhew was kind enough to delay his own personal fee until the work was completed. He said he felt bad about the overages.

The overages were now up to five thousand dollars, which was exactly what had been knocked off his original price.

Morganstern couldn't sell the goat milk to any big distributor because it hadn't been passed by the state inspectors and couldn't be until the barn was done. Karl Kinderhoff had found local buyers who were willing to take some of the milk off Morganstern's hands. The money he got selling it on the black market covered Cowpie's weekly salary.

"Wait till you get all hooked up," Karl said. "That's when you'll see the money come pouring in." Morganstern had less than two months to go until Dairy Day. Every few days or so, Karl or Kenny or Uncle Kruger would drop by and give him a pep talk. They complimented him on his effort, on the progress being made, and the general state of the farm. Morganstern felt greatly cheered after each visit. He felt he was part of a much bigger thing. No more the loneliness of the one-man corporation. They were working together to make a better, more profitable farm. They were brothers in the land. Comrades in arms.

The fact that every man on the farm was either salaried by him or profiting indirectly from the work being done didn't really faze him.

238

They were in this thing together. One for all. All for one. Foot soldiers of the future.

"Boy, those Kinderhoffs really have a regular consortium," Ariel remarked one day. "Do you realize that everyone working for you is related?"

"I know. It's like one big happy family," Morganstern said.

"They're going to be one big rich happy family, thanks to their cousin Matthew."

Morganstern was now down to eight thousand dollars in cash. But he wasn't worried. He knew that he was close to getting the farm into a real paying operation. Besides, he didn't have the time to worry. He was too busy working.

The only problem was his painting. Each morning, he would get up and say to himself: Today I'm going to spend at least one hour at the easel. He had set up a studio in the huge attic of the house. The light was good and it was more room than he had ever had before. And whether he was milking a goat or slopping the pigs, vivid pictures continued to flash through his head. But he never found a minute to paint.

The two-man milking operation was a pain. By the time they got done milking the last goat, they were ready to start all over again with the first. Morganstern hired two of Karl Kinderhoff's boys to help. They asked for the same five dollars an hour that Cowpie was getting. This prompted Cowpie to hold up five fingers and a thumb.

"Six dollars." He drooled. Morganstern wondered exactly how retarded the big man was.

Even with the extra help, Morganstern was still working his ass off. It never ended. If it wasn't the milking, it was the feeding; if it wasn't the feeding, it was cleaning up the shit. If it wasn't tending to the goats, it was caring for the chickens or trying to catch the hogs, who continually escaped from their rather shaky pen. Mayhew made him an estimate on a new pigpen, but Morganstern wanted to try his hand at it. He had, after all, a special interest in hogs because of his commodities deal. The pigs grew bigger by the day, and within a few weeks the pen he had built was no longer large enough.

"Honey, I think you're overfeeding them," Ariel said.

"You can't overfeed pigs," Morganstern argued. "The fatter, the better. Just look at those bellies. Have you ever seen a more beautiful bunch of pork bellies?"

"Never," Ariel agreed.

Morganstern liked the pigs, but he loved his goats. He took to referring to them as "the girls." They actually came when he called.

"You're getting as bad as Cowpie," Ariel observed one evening as Morganstern absentmindedly stroked the back of a big, sleek nanny.

"It's purely paternal." Morganstern laughed. "I think of them all as my daughters. They really are beautiful, aren't they?" he said, flipping back the nanny's broad drooping ear. "And they're such good producers. You girls are going to support me in my old age, aren't you?"

The nanny looked up at him. "And pretty soon your barn will be all finished. The best goat-milking barn money can buy. Nothing is too good for my girls."

"Next thing I know you'll be getting them all braces for their teeth," Ariel remarked. Morganstern laughed. Ariel put her arms around him. "You know something, honey? I am so proud of you. You're doing a terrific job. Who would ever believe you've never done this before?"

"Oh, the goats know," he said. "It's all in the hands."

Morganstern was pleased with the farm. There was a general feeling of productivity and progress. Things were getting done, improvements were being made, and his collateral was being secured and increased in value by the day. He paid his loan payments out of the money he had on hand, which was going fast. But, still, they were right on schedule. It was D Day minus sixty days. September 1 was slated as the official opening of Morganstern's Dairy and Goat Farm.

Morganstern wasn't the only one going through the cash. It was as if Ariel had to rid herself of the last vestiges of her former life. She went through her profit-sharing money in record time. There seemed to be no end to the things they needed, and the stores and auctions in the area were wonderful. She bought antique baskets, beautiful soft rag rugs and quilts, a genuine butter churn that no longer functioned as a butter churn but made a terrific umbrella stand. She bid for and got a fabulous set of copper pots and pans. She bought a Shaker-style corner cupboard for the kitchen, an old oak table and four slat-backed armchairs. She started a collection of pewter plates. She found a terrific Garland wood stove which she was able to pick up at the dealer's price. She bought hundreds of dollars' worth of flowering plants at the local nursery, planted them around the house, and hung them in baskets from the front porch.

She was just getting into wicker porch furniture when she ran out of money. It hit her in an odd way. She was about to write a check for the most charming wicker rocker at the Antique 'n' Things shop in Appleville when she realized she had no money left in her checking account. For a woman who had heretofore prided herself on her ability to be financially independent, she was strangely nonplussed.

For the next few days she took to getting money from Morganstern in dribs and drabs. "Honey, do you have a couple of dollars, I'm going in shopping." She would ask for the cash in a way that made it seem as if she herself had money, but only in very large bills.

Finally unable to bear the nickel-and-dime routine any longer, she confessed all to Morganstern. "It's gone. All my money's gone," she said tearfully. "I can't believe how frivolous I've been. I spent it all, and now I don't have a penny to my name."

"Don't worry, sweetheart. I've got plenty of money. How much do you need?"

"I want you to put me on an allowance. Really, I need that. It's high time I learned to economize. Just give me enough money for food every week."

"But, Ariel, you can't go around without any money in your pocket."

"A hundred dollars will do fine," said the woman who had once spent that much a week just on imported cheeses, sausages, and smoked oysters.

And so started a new phase in Ariel and Morganstern's relationship. The allowance period.

It gave her the nicest, warmest, cuddliest feeling. For the first time since she moved away from her parents, restraints had been placed on her. And they were warm, comforting, secure restraints, like the soft straps of a baby Snuggli. She no longer had to worry about money. About earning it, spending it, saving it, having too much of it. It was a wonderful relief. She felt like a little girl again.

Sitting on his lap that night, she put her arms around his neck and said, "As of here and now, I am putting myself on a budget. You'll see. I'll be the greatest little economizer going, I swear." Morganstern should have remembered that a vow from Ariel was invariably the first step on the road to compulsiveness.

In this case, she drew around her lovely shoulders the mantle of household drudge. While Morganstern became a slave to the farm, she became a slave to the household, the household budget, and to him.

She took to washing and ironing their clothes, which she had previously dropped off at the Wash 'n' Dry in town. It was no small feat, since the washing machine the Kinderhoffs had left was an old Bendix wringer-washer—only a few years older than the heavy upright Hoover that she had to use to vacuum the house. She scrubbed floors on her hands and knees and waxed them the same way.

Morganstern walked in one day while she was hand-buffing the living-room floor. She was singing an old Cole Porter song to herself.

. . . Farming is so charming, they all say . . .
Of our great celebrities doing it today . . .
The natives think it's utterly utter

241

"Honey, you don't have to do that," Morganstern said. "We can hire someone."

Ariel looked up and smiled. "Nobody can do my floors the way I can," she said, sitting back on her heels and knocking over an open can of Johnson Beautifloor buffing wax, which because of the slanted floors ran quickly across the room and disappeared under the floorboards.

Saving money became a mania with her. She read an article in *Family Circle* about how a woman saved $150 with coupons and special refund offers. She organized her shopping list accordingly.

The labels from four five-pound boxes of Aunt Jemima pancake mix, the tops of six packages of Old London toast, the front labels from two jars of Kraft jelly, six empty packages of Durkee's brown-gravy mix, nine labels from Armour Star potted meats, and six labels from Armour Vienna sausages brought her one dollar back for each, or six dollars in all.

And if it wasn't money back, she got other things. For a fifteen-ounce label from Cope's popcorn she got a free eight-ounce bottle of Cope's imitation butter. For five proof-of-purchase seals from Kellogg's Sugar Snaps cereal she received a set of two Manners and Safety place mats ("Don't eat with your knife, always chew before you swallow"), three proof-of-purchase seals from Kellogg's Rice and Rye cereal fetched her a set of multicolored measuring spoons, the quality seal from six boxes of Marcal thousand-count tissues entitled her to three free boxes of Marcal pocket-size hankies.

In *Woman's Day* magazine she read an article entitled: "106 Things to do with Turkey, All for Under $1.00 a Serving," and she did them. Over a two-week period they had turkey-squash stew with herb dumplings (.89 a serving), french-fried turkey croquettes with tartar sauce (.65 a serving), squash-stuffed turkey breast (.29 a serving; she had saved on a bushel of squash), poached turkey necks (.30 a serving), turkey hash, turkey parmigiana, turkey Stroganoff, and turkey enchiladas.

One night, while sipping his New England turkey chowder, Morganstern said, "I don't want to complain, but do you think we could have something else besides turkey tomorrow?"

"Honey, turkey's so economical and versatile," Ariel said, quoting directly from *Woman's Day.*

"Still, it's turkey. A change of pace might be nice. Do you need more food money, is that the problem?"

"Oh, no. I can manage perfectly well with what I have," Ariel said, rising to the challenge.

There followed a flurry of prizewinning money-saving recipes culled from every available magazine and local newspaper. Deviled-egg patties, macaroni and chick-peas, chicken-liver gumbo, potted-beef Wellington, tuna scallopini, blanquette de tongue, hash-brown deep-dish hamburger pie, creamed turnips and eggs on toast, sweet-'n'-sour Vienna sausages, and her special Saturday-night dinner, shrimp surprise.

"Why is it called shrimp surprise?" Morganstern asked, eyeing the steaming crusty casserole, which was covered with browned American cheese.

"The surprise is, it doesn't have shrimp. The recipe called for sea scallops, but they were too expensive, so I used catfish."

"So it's like a double surprise," Morganstern said, spooning a very small portion of the creamy, cheesy concoction onto his stack of Old London toast.

If Ariel needed something personal, either she didn't buy it or she bought it at the local dime store. Luckily, her Bendel's underwear was still in good shape, because the local dime store featured non-bikini panties made of thick cotton. One day she actually searched for Tampax on sale. She saved Morganstern the cost of a haircut by trimming his hair and his beard and, for the first time since leaving the city and Elizabeth Arden, she tweezed her own eyebrows and gave herself facials with generic mayonnaise.

She enjoyed the penny-pinching, the hard work, the making ends meet. It gave her a deep sense of satisfaction. It was a real challenge, staying within and sometimes well within the hundred-dollar-a-week allowance. Occasionally she would go over budget and then be tormented by feelings of failure and guilt. She would rack her brains for ways of making it up from her next week's allowance.

Morganstern felt good about the new setup. He was now the big provider and recognized as such. He enjoyed the role. He liked the fact that Ariel was going out of her way to keep him fed and happy and staying well within her means to do it.

D-Day minus fifty-five days. They were both working harder than they ever had in their lives. With the knowledge that things would eventually ease up, they put their shoulders to the wheel and their whole hearts into the effort.

Morganstern felt that they had successfully switched roles, changed patterns, made allowances and adjustments. They had gone through a lot together and come out for the better. How many couples could claim the same? He felt they were very fortunate indeed. They had their health, their farm, fresh air, fresh eggs and milk, good friends and supporters in the Kinderhoffs, and they had each other. What more could any two people ask for?

243

5

On the night of July 2 the phone rang. Ariel ran to get it.

"Guess who that was?" she said when she returned to the dining room several minutes later. "Marcy and Bill Conrad. They bought a farm about thirty miles away from us and they invited us down for this Saturday."

"I don't know if I can get away, honey. We've got less than two months before opening day."

"Oh, come on, Matthew. One day isn't going to kill us."

"I can't imagine the Conrads on a farm."

"Neither can I. But apparently they put all the money she inherited from her mother into this place."

"Don't tell me they gave up their corporate business for the farm life."

"No, they just come up on weekends."

"Oh, then it's not really a bona fide farm. It's probably just a little country place with a couple of apple trees or something."

The Conrads' little country place was two hundred acres of prime pastureland totally enclosed by a whitewashed split-rail fence. At the entrance to the private road that led to the house was a hand-carved sign with gilt letters which read "Swan Lake Farms."

As the name promised, there was a lake and there were swans. A dozen regal white birds floated on the glass-blue surface of a large pond, which also carried the reflection of a huge white Georgian mansion. The mansion stood on the edge of an immense freshly mowed lawn surrounded by majestic maples and grand old oaks.

Marcy and Bill Conrad waved a welcome from their Corinthian-columned porch. They were both dressed in artfully faded plaid shirts and presoftened denim pants. Ariel recognized their clothes as Ralph Lauren's new Rough Wear. She had drooled over the collection in a recent issue of *Vogue* at the Appleville drugstore. She wasn't able to buy the magazine, since it wasn't on her budget.

When Bill Conrad shouted, "Welcome to our little corner of the world," Morganstern knew it had been a mistake to come.

The Conrads showed them through the house. There was a large reception hall, a formal dining room, a formal living room, a solarium, a study, and what Marcy Conrad called a "gourmet kitchen," which was complete with every stainless-steel modern kitchen appliance imaginable, including both a microwave and a convection oven.

In the kitchen they were introduced to an older woman named Marlene who "helps us out with the cooking."

"What time is chow?" Bill Conrad asked Marlene, as if she were the driver of a chuck wagon and he were one of the hired hands.

"About seven, sir," Marlene replied.

"Good. I'm so hungry I could eat a hog."

"That's what we're having, sir."

"Atta girl." Bill laughed. Morganstern wondered if Marlene got paid extra for being Bill's straight man.

Upstairs were the six bedrooms and six and a half bathrooms. Every room was perfectly and completely decorated in Early American antiques. Ariel couldn't keep her hands off the Shaker benches, the polished four-poster beds, the incredible old quilts and needlepoint pillows. Her fingertips acted as calculator buttons. Exorbitant prices flashed through her mind in red digital numbers.

In one of the bedrooms they met Milly, who "helps out with the tidying up." Milly was down on her hands and knees polishing the hardwood floor with a chamois cloth. Morganstern noticed a strange look on Ariel's face.

"I hope you can stay the night," Marcy Conrad said.

"We'd love to—" Ariel said.

"We can't," Morganstern interrupted. "We can't leave the farm for that long."

"Won't your caretaker keep an eye on things?" Bill asked.

"We don't have a caretaker," Morganstern said. "We only have Cowpie, and I don't trust him alone with the goats for that long."

"Oh, you have goats? So do we."

"Those are goats?" Morganstern asked with amazement. He could see little resemblance between the long-horned, shaggy-haired creatures grazing in the lush fields and his own sleek black herd.

"These are Kashmiri goats. You know, from India," Bill explained.

"How often do they have to be milked?"

"They milk themselves," Bill said, pointing to the baby Kashmiris who trailed after their mothers. "We don't raise them for milk. We grow them for the hair."

"The hair?"

"That's what cashmere is made from. We get about sixty dollars an ounce."

"Cashmere goats!" Ariel exclaimed.

"They only have to be combed during the shedding season. That's Bert over there, he helps out with the combing. The guy he's talking to is Orly, he's our herdsman."

"I'm going to get Bill to buy me a loom and then I can knit my own sweaters," Marcy told Ariel.

They were introduced to Alan, the stableman, whose sole job seemed to be to take care of Lindsay's plump little pony. There were no other horses in the ten-horse stable.

"We're going to get a couple of horses as soon as Marcy and I learn to ride," Bill said.

Lindsay, the Conrads' three-and-a-half-year-old daughter, was away at camp.

"Isn't she a little young for camp?"

"It's a toddler camp," Marcy explained. "They teach the little ones wilderness skills."

"We've got fifty hogs and our own smokehouse. That means we can have bacon, sausage, spare ribs, or crown roast anytime we want. In fact, the ham we're eating tonight was born, raised, and smoked on these premises. Isn't that right, Otto?"

Otto, the swineherd, smiled and nodded.

"Have you got chickens?" Marcy asked Ariel.

"Oh, yes, we do," Ariel was happy to say. "They make wonderful eggs."

"Our chickens won a prize at the county fair this year. Ingrid helps us show them." Ingrid, Otto's wife, served as chicken keeper and swan feeder.

In the distance, on top of one of the higher hills, Morganstern spotted a huge white disk tilted up toward the sky. "What's that?"

"Oh, that's our little satellite TV receptor," said Bill. "If we didn't have that, we'd only get two channels up here. You know, when we first came out, Marcy and I tried to rough it. But we found we just couldn't do without HBO."

In addition to the satellite dish, the Conrads had their own emergency generator, two greenhouses (one for tropical fruits and the other for tropical flowers), and a huge outdoor flagstone fireplace/barbecue pit with a built-in rotisserie and toaster-oven. There was a caretaker's house, a gardener's house, and a guest house that "needs a little work." There was a huge heated swimming pool with a cabana fashioned in the shape of the main barn, and a "health hut" which contained a sauna, a steam room, a Jacuzzi, and a hot mineral tub. There was also a tennis court.

"We haven't gotten night lights yet," Bill Conrad apologized. "By the way, you didn't bring your rackets, did you?"

"No, sorry," Morganstern said.

"That's too bad. It's really hard to get a good doubles game going up here."

"Oh, Otto and Ingrid don't play?" Morganstern asked with thinly veiled sarcasm.

"As a matter of fact, Marcy thought of paying for lessons for them. That way, we'd always have a doubles game right here on the premises. Hey, Marcy," Bill called out. "Matt here had the same idea you did . . ."

Marcy showed Ariel through the greenhouses and introduced her

246

to Stan, the gardener, who was working on the last touches of an elaborate Japanese rock garden.

"I'm having a little trouble with the waterfall, Mrs. Conrad."

"Keep trying, Stan. We've got to have a waterfall," Marcy pleaded. "That's the most important part."

Marcy led Ariel to her "pride and joy," the vegetable garden. "We've got endive, escarole, petits pois, courgettes, and haricots verts. This year I grew all French vegetables, and next year I'm going to do all Japanese. To go with the rock garden."

The vegetables were perfect, oversized and sparkling with dew. Ariel felt one of the endive leaves to see if it was real or plastic.

The men walked around the barns and the machine shop.

"You know, I've been wanting to get into farming for a long time," Bill Conrad said. "And now that I am, I can't tell you the feeling of satisfaction it gives me." They watched John, the woodsman, splitting logs with an old-fashioned ax. "It's a hell of a lot of hard work, but it's worth it. Here, John, let me give you a hand," Bill said, taking the ax from him. He split two logs and then handed the ax back. "There's nothing like chopping wood to get the old blood running. Marcy wanted to get one of those silly hydraulic log splitters from Hammacher Schlemmer. But I wouldn't have it. I guess I'm too much of a purist."

Dinner was served. Bill took Morganstern down to the wine cellar to help him with his wine selection. He pulled out a bottle of 1972 Châteauneuf du Pape. "What do you think?" He deferred to Morganstern's judgment.

"*Parfait,*" Morganstern responded tonelessly.

"It's about the only thing we can't grow ourselves." Bill chuckled. "You know what I like best about this life, Matt? It's that feeling of total self-sufficiency. We grow our own fruit, vegetables, have fresh eggs, smoke our own hams, even raise our own wool. If there were a war or a famine, or if, God forbid, the market should crash, we'd be able to survive beautifully right here on this farm. And that's a great goddamn feeling, I'll tell you."

"How's my painting going?" Marcy asked Morganstern during dinner.

"Painting? What painting?"

"The one I commissioned. The five-thousand-dollar one."

Morganstern turned bright red. He had completely forgotten about the commissioned painting. "To tell you the truth, Marcy, I've been so busy with the farm I haven't had much time for painting. As soon as things start rolling in September, I'll get right on it."

"There's no hurry," Marcy said. "The important thing is, you shouldn't let the farm interfere with your real life. Bill and I learned our lesson."

"That's right," Bill concurred. "With all the activity of moving into this place, Marcy and I missed a whole month of tennis. I totally lost my serve. Luckily I've got it back now."

"You can never neglect your skills," Marcy cautioned. "Otherwise, you lose them."

"I'll keep that in mind," Morganstern mumbled.

"By the way, Ivan's coming up to the country to see us next weekend," Marcy said. "Maybe we can all drive over and see your farm."

"We won't be there," Morganstern said before Ariel had a chance to reply. "We're going to Bermuda."

"Oh? A little vacation?"

"No, business. There's going to be a convention of goat herders there. It's kind of an annual get-together to compare milking procedures."

"Oh, neat," Marcy said.

Ariel started to say something, but Morganstern kicked her under the table.

"Let's make it a point to get together during harvesttime," Bill said as they got into their van. "As I understand it, that's the real peak season in this area."

"Great," Morganstern said. "I'll have my swineherd call your swineherd and they can set it up." Bill looked confused.

"That was a snotty thing to say," Ariel remarked angrily as they drove down the Conrads' driveway. "Why were you being such a prick? Didn't you have a good time?"

"It was great, if you like Disneyland."

"Oh, come on, Matthew, they have a beautiful farm. You're just jealous."

"You call that a farm? That's nothing more than a country club with a petting zoo and a staff of thousands. It's the phoniest excuse for a farm I've ever seen."

"Well, for your information, Marcy told me that they are really committed to farming."

"Oh, they're committed, all right. They're committed in tax dollars. Don't you get it? The whole thing is just one gigantic tax shelter. It's just a way for them to keep from paying the IRS," he said, forgetting that was the very reason he himself was up to his ears in goats. "And another thing. I bet the IRS disallows the whole thing."

"Why would they do that?"

"A cashmere-goat farm? Come on, Ariel."

"Well, I think it's a lovely place. And they seem very happy."

"They seem very rich, is what you really mean."

"There's no law against having a few conveniences," she said, looking down sadly at her hands, which were rough and red from having scrubbed the kitchen floor with Clorox the day before. She wouldn't have minded having a woman to help with the "tidying up," either, she thought.

"A few conveniences," Morganstern scoffed. "Like a satellite dish? I'm surprised they don't have a bird herdsman, just to keep the sparrows quiet in the morning."

"When are you going to do her painting?" Ariel asked.

"I'll do it when I do it," Morganstern snapped.

They were silent for the rest of the ride home. Ariel was lost in a vision of herself. She was Rose of Sharon from *The Grapes of Wrath,* sitting on the back of a truck, her thin legs dangling down, her sticklike arms barely covered by a moth-eaten shawl.

She was suddenly very tired. Tired of the cooking, scrubbing, hand-buffing, the mending, washing, ironing, and penny-pinching. Without realizing it, Ariel had successfully combined the traits of the hardworking, frugal, loyal farmer's wife with those of the beleaguered, martyred, silent-suffering Jewish mother. In doing so, she had created a new female hybrid: the Jewish American Pioneer.

While Ariel was feeling the pain and travails of the rural existence, Morganstern was thinking about the Conrads' silly sumptuous life. He thought back to Bill Conrad's comment about being totally self-sufficient and chuckled to himself. Bill probably couldn't tell the right end of a carrot from the wrong one without his gardener to clue him in. Well, let them have their cashmere goats, their wine cellar and tennis court. Come the peasants' revolution, they'd be singing a different tune. He'd show them what self-sufficiency was all about. He was going to do things the right way, the Morganstern way.

His resolve was strengthened. He felt more confident. The muscles in his arms, which had been tired and sore from long hours of milking, now felt strong and hard. He sat up straighter and gripped the wheel firmly.

"Did you ever hear the joke about the skinny little guy who went up to Canada to get a job as a lumberjack?" he asked Ariel. She shook her head. "Well, the foreman takes a look at this guy, who is all of ninety pounds, plus he's wearing very weird clothes and an earring, and he says, 'Sure, you can have a job, but first you have to pass the test. Just chop down that tree over there.' He points to a big pine.

"The little guy takes a little hatchet out of his tote bag and chops down the tree in one fell swoop. The foreman is amazed. He points out an even bigger tree. 'Okay, smart guy, try that one!' Again the little runt fells the tree with one blow. The same thing happens over and over on bigger and bigger trees. The foreman can't believe his eyes. Finally he says, 'You can have the job, but first you got to tell me, where did you learn to chop trees like that?' And the skinny guy says, 'In the Sahara Forest.' 'The Sahara Forest?' the foreman says. 'The Sahara isn't a forest, it's a desert!' The little guy says smugly, 'Sure it is, *now!*'"

Ariel burst out laughing. Morganstern reached across the seat and took her hand. "We'll show 'em, Ma," he said. "There ain't a thing we can't do, once we put our minds to it."

"I'm with you, Pa. Whip up those horses. I'm hankerin' to get home," she said, squeezing his hand.

They could do it; he knew they could. The two of them together would build the farm, milk the goats, make their life meaningful, profitable, and satisfying. While the Conrads developed tennis elbow and gout, his and Ariel's hard work would triumph, their happiness would prevail.

He was Daniel Boone making his way across uncharted plains, he was the Pathfinder, the Deerslayer (no, not the deerslayer), he was Johnny Appleseed, he was Paul Bunyan with a newly sharpened ax, he was Morganstern, man of the earth, tiller of the soil, milker of goats, foot soldier of the future.

They had been home only an hour when Morganstern came out of the bathroom clutching his stomach. "I think their home-smoked pork had trichinosis," he groaned.

"Don't be silly," Ariel said. "We would both be dead by now. And I feel fine."

In the middle of the night Ariel shook him awake. "Matthew. Matthew. Wake up. There is a terrible smell coming from somewhere."

She was right. There was the most appalling odor coming from downstairs. Had one of the pigs gotten out somehow? Morganstern wondered. He went down to investigate. The smell was coming directly from the cellar. He pulled the light chain and cautiously proceeded down the old slanting stairs. He halted two steps from the bottom. The entire cellar was flooded with sewage. There must have been two hundred years' worth of excrement floating in the murky water.

"Aaaaah, shit!" he cried, and trudged back upstairs.

"What is it? What's the matter?" Ariel asked.

"I think it has something to do with the sewer," Morganstern said, getting back into bed and covering his face with a pillow. "Go to sleep. I'll get one of the Kinderhoffs to look at it in the morning."

"Oh, shit," Ariel sighed, fell back on the bed.

"My words exactly," Morganstern muttered.

Karl Kinderhoff got his cousin Clayton Kinderhoff, "the best

250

plumber this side of the Hudson," to come over. Clayton explained the problem.

"The baffle on your septic tank has rotted. That's why you got this effluvium problem. When I get that fixed up, I can see better what the situation is."

The situation was that Morganstern needed a new septic tank, also a new leach field.

"That one's filled up over the years. It's not a big job," he assured Morganstern. "We drop in a new septic tank, put in a new leach field, and you're as good as new. In the meantime, you got your trusty old outhouse."

The job was estimated at $4,000, barring any complications.

The complications were as follows: the new septic tank was too big for the original hole, so they had to dig another one, and in doing so, they ran into an area of almost solid bedrock. "It's not a big deal," Clayton said, "just takes a little more time." The $4,000 estimate did not include extra labor. Five thousand dollars later the toilets were flushing again. And Clayton gave him a nice break on the main water pipe that had been broken during the digging of the septic-tank hole.

But water continued to be a trouble area.

"Honey, there's no hot water," Ariel shouted from upstairs only a few days after the plumbing job had been completed. "Did you use it all or something?"

"I haven't touched the hot water. There should be plenty."

Clayton got him a very good deal on a new oil burner for the hot-water heater.

And then, two days later: "Matthew, the water's only dribbling out. There must be a leak somewhere."

"This old well lasted a lot longer than most," Clayton said. "The water table being what it is in these parts, you woulda had to dig deeper sooner or later."

"I just wish it would have been later," Morganstern sighed.

"I'll wager you won't have to go any more than five hundred to a thousand feet before you hit water," Karl Kinderhoff said. Karl lost his bet. They finally hit water at 2,500 feet.

"Well, at least we've got the water problem licked," Morganstern told Ariel.

But they didn't. From not enough water one day, they experienced a deluge the next—a torrential hailstorm, "the worst we've had in thirty years," Uncle Kruger remarked.

"It takes a downpour like the one we had last night to really make you appreciate a good copper roof," Mayhew said as they stood in Morganstern's sopping living room. "Hell, you mighta gone for several years without noticing those rotten spots."

251

Building a new roof was going to cost the same thing as getting rid of the old septic system: $4,000.

Morganstern was running low on cash. He made an emergency call to Getty.

"Darling, this commodities thing is very complicated. Can't we get together? It would be so much easier to explain it to you in the flesh."

"I don't need any long, drawn-out explanations. Just tell me why you can't send me a simple twenty thousand dollars," Morganstern said angrily.

"As I said, I've had to use your capital just to cover margins on the contracts. We have to wait for prices to go up in order to make the kind of killing we want."

"Can't you be a little more explicit?"

"These commodities contracts are like beautiful little virgins. You have to bring them along slowly, treat them very gingerly, and wait for the right moment. When they're at their peak, ripe and ready, juicy to the bursting point—"

"I don't mean explicit like that. Just tell me when I can start getting some money out. I need money."

Getty sighed. "As soon as the market recovers."

"Then there are problems," Morganstern said, feeling his heart skip a beat.

"Not problems, just unexpected events. For instance, they didn't have the droughts that were predicted in the Midwest, so the crops are good and the prices are down. All we need is a good long dry spell or a midsummer flood and we're in luck. The market can change overnight."

"You've got all my money invested in something that depends on the weather?"

"But we always have weather. That's what's so beautiful about commodities. Relax, darling. As soon as I can sell, I will."

Morganstern hung up. He was shaking. All his money tied up like some sort of sacrificial virgin. He didn't want to think about it. He couldn't think about it. There was nothing he could do but keep his fingers crossed and try to keep his expenses down to a minimum. He reminded himself that there were only forty-five days left until he was a fully-functioning, milk-producing, money-making dairy operation. Just a little over a month until everything fell into place.

Soon Ariel began to notice that getting her allowance from Morganstern was like pulling teeth.

"Oh, gee," he would say in a way which she found infuriating, "is it a week already?" Then he would dig through his pockets looking for the cash, which he never seemed to have. Finally he would sit down and write her a check. "What's today's date?" he would ask, as if stalling for time. After writing the check, he would examine it as though not sure he had made it out correctly. Only then would he hand it over to her.

Pay to the order of Ariel Hellerman one hundred dollars, not a penny more, not a penny less. Most infuriating of all, at the bottom of each check, in the space allotted for it, he would write the description "For food," as if he dared her to spend it on anything else.

To make matters worse, Ariel was having problems of her own with unexpected expenses. Inspired by Marcy Conrad's garden, she had thrown herself into gardening with a vengeance. The small plot of land where Mrs. Kinderhoff had once grown asparagus as big as a man's leg proved to be less yielding than Ariel had hoped. She spent long hours hoeing and raking and picking out the millions of rocks she found there.

Finally, when the earth was ready, she made a list of her favorite vegetables, bought the seeds, and planted them without any notice of the fact that it was already midsummer.

A brief perusal of Crockett's *Victory Garden Book* told her that black agricultural-grade plastic made an ideal mulch to keep in moisture and keep out the weeds. She purchased several rolls of eighteen-inch plastic and laid them neatly over the whole garden. Then she waited in anticipation for her asparagus, green beans, broccoli, eggplants and endive to come up.

It was Karl Kinderhoff who tipped her off to the fact that seeds had no way of sprouting through the heavy plastic.

"Besides, this late in the season you don't want to be messin' around with seeds. Talk to my cousin Cutworm down at the nursery. He'll fix you up with what you need," Karl said, handing her a coupon which entitled her to five dollars off on the first twenty-five-dollar purchase.

Cutworm helped her pick out already-started vegetables. She was appalled when he rang up a total of $150. But she had already put in too much time and effort to back down now. She charged the seedlings to the farm in the hope that by the time the bill came she would be able to figure out a way to pay it. She was still trying to stay within her budget. Especially now that Morganstern was turning into a scrooge about money.

She punched holes in the plastic and planted everything, then stood back and admired her garden. Beautiful neat rows of baby broccoli, red cabbage, eggplant, tomatoes, and three kinds of lettuce. Not to mention endive, Swiss chard, and of course, celeriac. It was a young garden, full of promise and well worth the money, she thought. Aside from the brilliant and fresh salads, she had a vision of a small profitable vegetable stand. Perhaps Zabar's in the city was interested in opening a farm-fresh-vegetable department.

She hurried back to the nursery and bought a very expensive impact sprinkler (it was too far to haul the water in a sprinkling can from the house), a three-pronged cultivator, a wheelbarrow (to transport the giant eggplants), a pair of hand shears, lopping shears, a beautiful brass trowel, and a Rototiller, because, as Cutworm explained, "You don't want to have to turn over the soil by hand."

She already had, and didn't ever want to repeat the experience. She also bought several bags of fertilizer: bone, foliar, and slow release. The bill came to $2,500, but Ariel felt it was well worth it. Now she had everything she needed to be what Crockett called "the victorious gardener."

The next morning she hurried out, anxious to see how her garden was growing. The plants were gone. Every one of them. Chewed off at the base, as though someone had come through the garden with a scythe.

"Rabbits," Cutworm explained. He sold her one-inch mesh chicken wire, fence poles, and replacement plants. Working like a dog, Ariel managed to have the fence up and the new plants in by sundown.

The new plants lasted a week. Row by row they disappeared, pulled mysteriously down through the plastic. It was like a Bugs Bunny cartoon.

"Woodchucks," Cutworm said.

"But how did they get through the fence?"

"They don't go through, they go under."

He sold her a new batch of seedlings and rented her a very old dog who was purported to be the best woodchucker in the county. "Is this a cousin, too?" Ariel asked, looking down at the bedraggled hound.

"Oh, he's been in the family for years." Cutworm chuckled.

"It figures."

The plants survived, but only long enough to provide feasting for every conceivable kind of pest, from aphids to cabbage worms. It was only then that Ariel threw in the trowel.

She was beaten but not down. She noticed there were big specials at the local produce markets. In an effort to save what she had lost in the garden, she decided to take up canning. And she wasn't interested in canning plain old tomatoes. Why have canned tomatoes when you can have ratatouille? she reasoned.

The recipe called for eggplant (she mourned her long-dead plants), olive oil, zucchini, onions, peppers, garlic, thyme, bay leaf, and tomatoes. Each vegetable had to be washed thoroughly. The tomatoes had to be scalded for one minute and then dipped in cold water, cored, and skinned. She packed the jars with the vegetables and juice and then processed them for forty-five minutes in the new canner she had charged at the hardware. The whole process took her two days. Before sealing, she rechecked the recipe to make sure she hadn't forgotten anything.

She had forgotten something: "The Department of Agriculture does not recommend home canning of the following vegetables: eggplant, onions, peppers . . ." What the hell does the Department of Agriculture know about ratatouille? she thought.

She read on: "Caution: great attention must be paid in the canning of these vegetables to prevent the development of *Clostridium botulinum*, a deadly germ which may be present even though no odor or color changes indicate its presence."

She threw forty jars of ratatouille down the sink.

She had to call Clayton Kinderhoff in again to unplug the sink. "At this rate, I'll be able to retire on you folks." He chuckled; he had the Kinderhoff chuckle down pat.

Ariel waited until he left before bursting into tears. She cried over her pillaged garden, over her ruined ratatouille, over the blisters which gardening had added to her already reddened hands.

Then something snapped in her. What the hell was she doing? she asked herself. A woman of her intelligence, her abilities, her charm, sweating and crying in a hot kitchen over a bunch of poisoned, stewed vegetables. Is this what her life had come to? And if it had come to this, why wasn't she getting paid for it?

In sixty seconds she went through the complete cycle of women's liberation. She recognized her downtrodden role and in doing so realized she had to fight for equal rights, and more importantly, equal pay. The $100 a week food money was translated in her mind into salary. What was she, a former $60,000-a-year copywriter, doing working for a lousy $100 a week? The work was back-breaking. Why should the rewards be so few and far between? She deserved a raise. And that's all there was to that.

"Matthew, I have to have more money. A hundred dollars a week is simply not enough."

She practiced the request for so long that it came out too strong and stilted.

And Morganstern, who was deeply concerned about the state of his finances, the state of the commodity market, and who had just written yet another whopping check to Clayton Kinderhoff, had just the wrong response. "What do you need more money for?"

"Well, I don't think it's out of the question for me to have a little extra beyond the cost of food. I need spending money."

"Spending money?" he snorted. "That's a redundancy coming from you."

"I don't think that's funny, Matthew." She glanced at the check to Clayton Kinderhoff. "The Kinderhoffs certainly don't have any problems getting money from you. I'm the lowest-paid person on the whole staff." She was close to tears.

"Staff? Staff? What are you talking about? You're my girlfriend.

255

My partner. My lover. You're a volunteer, for Chrissakes. Volunteers don't get paid."

Ariel glared at him.

"Come on, honey, what are you so upset about?"

"You wouldn't understand." She sulked.

"Okay, tell me how much money you want."

"Sixty thousand dollars," she snapped.

"Oh, Ariel, be reasonable."

"How can I be reasonable when my hands are falling off? I can't even afford to buy a decent hand cream," she wailed.

He took her in his arms. "There's nothing to cry about. We're not starving. You're not walking around in rags. And I don't beat you."

"Am I supposed to thank God for small favors?" she said, pulling away from him.

"Jesus Christ, Ariel. You don't seem to understand we are up to our ears in bills. Do you want to know what the roof is going to cost?"

"It's not my fault the roof leaks."

"I'm talking about bills and unexpected expenses and you're talking about fault. Fault has nothing to do with it. If this farm fails, whose fault is that going to be?"

"Yours," she said all too quickly.

"Great. Thanks a lot," he said, turning away from her.

"Matthew, I'm sorry. I'm just tired."

But there was no soothing him. "You're tired? What do you think I am, ready to go dancing? Here," he said, taking a fifty-dollar bill out of his billfold and flinging it at her.

Ariel picked it up. "I don't want it," she said, flinging the fifty back at him.

He picked up the bill and crumpled it in his hand. "You take it and you go into town and you buy anything your little heart desires," he said between clenched teeth. He stuffed the fifty down the front of her T-shirt.

Ariel stared at him for a long time, her light-green/light-blue eyes flashing. Then she turned on her heels and walked out of the room.

Morganstern spent the rest of the day trying to calm himself. Sure, money was getting tight; sure, there had been some unforeseen difficulties, but they were three weeks away from becoming an efficient, highly productive, totally automated operation. His commodities were bound to pay off. Things were going to start looking up. You had to expect a few mishaps. It was all part of being a farmer, Morganstern told himself. There was no reason to take it out on her.

Ariel had a terrible time with the fifty dollars. She drove into town with the express intention of blowing it on the most frivolous, most unnecessary thing she could find. But she was out of practice.

After several hours she realized she was unable to spend it. She came home exhausted, the fifty still stuck into her French-lace bra.

They kissed, and though they didn't quite make up, they at least managed to make do.

"Let me just explain something to you," Morganstern said, "so you know where we're at. I've sunk almost every available penny into this farm. Plus, as you know, I've borrowed over eighty thousand dollars to fix up the place. Now, I've got a lot of money tied up in investments that should be paying off any day now. In just three weeks the farm will be operational. And we'll be riding easy. I just don't know if there are going to be any more unexpected expenses before then."

Ariel thought of the bill from the nursery.

"We've got a lot of money going out right now, and nothing coming in. Even with my limited experience, I know that's not the most ideal situation. When we become an official dairy operation, we'll be in very good shape. But right now I'm somewhat uptight about finances. So, I'm sorry if I jumped down your throat. Of course, you can have as much money as you need. I'm just asking you to watch it, that's all."

Morganstern had made his speech in a calm, reasoned tone. A tone that surprised even him. Ariel was impressed. "Don't worry, I'll manage with the hundred," she said. She wanted to be fair. She didn't want to make problems for him. Still, she couldn't quite shake the feeling that Labor had just lost a big concession to Management.

They had experienced a failure of sewers, a leaking of roofs, a drying-up of wells. The next mishap could only be chalked up to human error. The old Bendix wringer-washer stopped wringing and Tinker Kinderhoff was called in to look at it.

"Goddamn son of a bitch," Tinker screamed from the basement. The motor had slipped, smashing his thumb. Morganstern was very sympathetic until Karl came to talk to him about it the next day.

"Boy, Tinker is in pretty bad shape. But I guess your insurance'll cover it."

"Cover what?"

"He's going to sue you for ten thousand dollars. The doctor says he can't work for six months."

"But I don't have any insurance."

"You don't? Oh, yeah, I guess since you bought the farm outright you didn't need to get any. You might be able to settle out of court. But I don't know, he's pretty pissed."

"Can't you talk to him? He's your cousin."

"Nah, I could never talk to that bastard. He's got a real stubborn streak."

257

Stubborn streak or not, Tinker finally agreed to settle out of court for $2,000, which practically depleted Morganstern's cash supply.

"I think the whole family's ripping us off," Ariel said.

"Don't be absurd. Why would they want to rip us off?"

"Oh, it's not malicious, it's only for the money. They're running a monopoly out here. We've never gotten prices from anyone else but the Kinderhoffs. How do we know they aren't overcharging? How do we know we really need all the things they tell us we need? And how do we know Tinker really smashed his thumb?"

"Hell, you could see it was smashed. Didn't you notice his cast?"

"I'm sure his doctor is a Kinderhoff too."

"Come on, Ariel. We're new at this. We have to trust someone."

"Do we have to trust a family of chronic chucklers?" she said.

Morganstern didn't respond. He had other things to think about.

A call to Getty produced the ominous report that crops and weather were doing better than ever and the prices of goods they needed to trade were at the bargain-basement level. He thought about setting fire to his corn, starving his pigs, but he knew that wouldn't make a dent on the world market. He had to face the possibility that he might end up with zero profits from all Getty's speculating. The money he had made on the market had never seemed that real to him. But now the need for it was very real indeed. More than ever, he had to make the farm work. He couldn't depend on the commodities; the farm was his only chance.

He started worrying about finances as he had never worried about them before. He stayed up late every night projecting his potential farm profits and trying to figure out a way to cut his losses. Staring at ledgers and figures until his eyes burned with fatigue, he realized how he had come full circle, leaving the city and his obsession with money, only to end up here on the farm, hundreds of miles away from Wall Street, trying to calculate how to get his cash flowing again.

And when was he ever going to find time to paint? He worried that when he finally did get back to his easel, his eyes would be so damaged by all the late-night accounting he wouldn't be able to see. Maybe he should get a green eyeshade? Was it possible that he was going blind? If so, shouldn't he conserve his waning vision for his art? Was there a market for the work of a blind artist? All he could think of was Mrs. Chase's friend Blinky Lord. There was always hope, he thought hopelessly.

Meanwhile, Ariel felt as if she were the wife of a big corporate executive. Morganstern was up and out early in the morning before she even opened her eyes. And she had no idea what time he came to bed at night.

She flashed back to the early days of their relationship, when she and Morganstern worked at home. He painting and she theoretically writing her novel. She remembered her feelings of frustration and nonproductivity. She remembered how she resented his enthusiasm, energy, and talent. She had those same feelings now. She felt useless, ineffectual, directionless, unmotivated, and unproductive. Only this time she couldn't blame it on him. She could, however, blame it on the farm. And she did.

"Matthew, wake up," she said one night at dinner.

"What? Is it time to get up," he asked, looking around confused.

"It's time to eat your dinner, unless you want tuna casserole for breakfast."

"When did I fall asleep?" he asked, yawning.

"About one minute after you sat down. Matthew, I miss you. It seems like I haven't seen you in weeks. Don't you think you're working a little too hard?"

"It'll ease up. As soon as the barn is finished and—"

"And the goats are on automatic milking, everything will be back to normal," Ariel finished. "I don't think normal is possible on this farm. I know that sex is certainly out of the question."

"Sex? What does sex have to do with anything?" Morganstern asked, pushing his plate away.

"Nothing. Forget it. It's just that we certainly don't seem to be having much fun anymore."

"I'm not doing this for fun. I've got to make this farm work."

"Why? Because the world needs more goat milk?"

"I told you. Everything I have is tied up in this place."

"I thought you wanted the simple life. You can't possibly call this the simple life."

"Tax shelters are never simple."

"Tax shelters?"

"This has to be a real working farm. Not a play farm. Otherwise I don't get the tax breaks that a farmer is entitled to."

"Silly me. I thought this could be a love nest."

"It can be."

"I know, I know. As soon as the barn is finished and the goats are on automatic milking, we can have an orgy."

"Speaking of orgies, I got the bill from the nursery today. May I ask exactly what you spent forty-three hundred dollars on?"

"Where do you think I got all the plants and stuff? They don't grow on trees."

"They sure as hell didn't grow in our garden, either."

"That was a cruel thing to say." Ariel's eyes filled with tears. She got up and took the dishes into the kitchen.

Morganstern was too tired to follow her and too annoyed to apologize. By the time she brought out the apple brown Betty, he had his head down on the table and was fast asleep again.

On the surface, Ariel and Morganstern went on as usual. But an interior battle raged. He felt that he was doing everything humanly possible to make the farm work and to ensure their future and that she didn't even begin to understand what that involved.

Ariel, on the other hand, felt she had been a peerless helpmate, an uncomplaining trooper; she thought she had undoubtedly aged several years from sudden exposure to intense housework and gardening and that he didn't even appreciate the sacrifices she'd made.

He had put all his efforts into the farm so they would be provided with a steady income in a serene setting that would enable them to explore each other and their own potential.

She had expended incredible energy in the house and around the hearth to create a nurturing and harmonious environment so that their relationship could grow and prosper.

Their objectives were, in essence, the same. It was the means to gaining those objectives that seemed so disparate. His primary focus was the farm, hers was the farm couple. Each felt very much in the right and consequently terribly wronged by the other.

While Morganstern continued putting in his long hours in the barn and on the books, Ariel retreated into a world of catalogs and ladies' magazines. There was quiet, but it was a sullen, heavy quiet, the kind army observers must have experienced before the button was pushed at Los Alamos.

And yet, in those next few days they found time to make a lot of love. It seemed that every time their paths crossed they had sex. No words were exchanged. It was the type of intense quick coupling people have when they first meet or when they're about to break up.

6

Midmorning two weeks later, Morganstern, trudging back from the barn, saw Ariel standing on the front porch with one of her suitcases at her feet.

"I'm going away for the weekend," she announced.

"But you *are* away for the weekend. This is the kind of place people make reservations for months in advance," he said in a stiff attempt at levity.

She didn't smile. "I need a break, Matthew. I'm spending the weekend with the Conrads."

"Oh? Is it time for the sweater harvest already?" he said angrily.

"It's Marcy Conrad's birthday. I told you weeks ago we were invited, but you said you didn't want to go, remember?"

"Your timing continues to be flawless," he said.

"What do you mean by that?"

"I mean, every time things get tough, you pack up and run to the Conrads. What in the world would you do without them?"

"At least I have someplace to go."

She was right. He wished he had some Conrads of his own to spend the weekend with. But he couldn't go anywhere. He had to attend to things on the farm. They were scheduled to start pumping milk in less than a week.

"What about the peaches?" Ariel had bought six bushels of peaches the week before. She had planned to make peach pies and peach preserves, but they were still sitting in their baskets, softening and bruising on the back porch.

"Maybe you can write them off," she snapped.

"And how are you planning on getting there? I can't drive you. I'm in the middle of my chores." He was throwing every conceivable obstacle in her way.

"Don't worry about it. Ivan is picking me up."

"Ivan is coming here?"

"The Conrads invited him up for Marcy's birthday."

As she spoke, a new cream-colored Mercedes sports sedan came zipping up their road, scattering ducks and feathers in its path.

"Watch out for the goddamn ducks," Morganstern yelled.

Ivan got out of the car and stretched leisurely. He was dressed all in cream to match the car: Western pants and a bleached buckskin shirt. Gold chains gleamed through the fur on his chest. He slid his aviator glasses back on his head and looked around. "This must be God's little acre. And you must be the Future Farmer of America," he said, extending his hand toward Morganstern.

"How are you, Ivan?" he asked coldly, keeping his arms folded tightly on his chest.

"How do I look?" Ivan stretched out his arms. "I know it's hard to believe. But I am richer, handsomer, and more successful than ever. Except now I can accept it all gracefully."

"I'll just get my purse," Ariel said, hurrying into the house.

"Don't you want to show me around the back forty and the bunkhouse and all that crap?" Ivan asked, still smiling. Morganstern chose not to respond. "So, what else are you raising out here besides dust? Yuk, yuk." He bent down and picked a small stone and threw it in the direction of the barn. "I don't need to tell you, Matt, that this kind of commune-farm crap went out with the sixties. The back-to-nature movement went out with the seventies. This is the

261

eighties, old boy. It's reality-testing time. You're living in a fucking dream."

Ariel came out of the house and kissed Morganstern quickly on the cheek. "I'll see you in a few days," she said.

"Have a *super* time. And don't overdo the tennis," Morganstern snarled.

Over the weekend, he barely thought about Ariel. He had other problems. Cash-flow problems. He had been so busy writing checks he hadn't had time to balance his checkbook. When he did, he discovered that because of an error in subtraction he had $2,000 less than he thought he had. Meeting that month's mortgage payment was going to be tricky. He had to get some money, and get it quick.

On Monday morning Morganstern began trying to get hold of Getty. He left his number several times at the Bartlett office, but she never returned his call. It was D Day minus sixty hours. Ariel still hadn't come back from the Conrads'. Finally, around five P.M., the phone rang. It was Getty.

"I need to cash in on some of my commodities," he told her.

"I told you things aren't doing too well right now," Getty said, her voice sounding uncharacteristically flat. "You would take a bit of a loss, which is fine if you need a write-off."

"How much of a loss?"

"Well, the price of soybeans is down to eighteen cents, hog bellies are—"

"How much of a loss?" Morganstern asked again, his voice rising. There was a long pause, and then Getty said, "A very substantial one."

"Getty, how much money do I have left?"

"If you sold all your contracts today? Five thousand dollars."

"What! How could I lose that much? That just isn't possible!"

"It's a very up-and-down thing—"

"What are the chances of it going up in the next few days?"

"To be perfectly honest, I don't know. Do you want me to sell everything off?"

"Why are you asking me? You're the fucking expert. You're my goddamn stockbroker."

Getty sighed. "If I were you, I wouldn't touch anything. Things have to get better. I don't see how they can get any worse. I'm sorry—"

Morganstern slammed down the phone. He pounded his fist into the wall. One of Ariel's favorite finds, a hand-painted Teddy Roosevelt commemorative plate, crashed to the floor. He was furious at Getty, at the whole stock-exchange, commodity-exchange world. Now he understood what "exchange" meant. You gave them your perfectly good money and they swapped it for worthless paper, for meaningless contracts. Fucking hog bellies!

It had never occurred to him that his investments would ever fall below their original value. He had thought of his stocks and his commodity contracts as currency, as sound as the dollar. He had done so well in the stock market, how could he lose it all now? Except for the $20,000 that went for the farm, he had never seen a penny of his profits. It was as if they had never happened. Then he remembered James's words: "You don't put more than one-fifth of your capital in the market. Haven't you ever heard of the crash of twenty-nine?" He thought back to his own stock certificates, the ones he had been issued the day he was incorporated. He remembered the eagle with the arrows in one claw and the piece of foliage in the other. He understood now. The arrows were shafts; the branch, a branch of poison ivy. What a fool he had been. He punched the wall again. He was wiped out, a ruined man.

No, wait. He wasn't ruined. He was down. But he wasn't out. Not by a long shot. He still had the farm. That certainly counted as an asset. And in two days it would be an official dairy, an income-producing business. He left the house and walked around the property taking inventory. It occurred to him that every single goat, every drop of goat's milk, every egg, every pig, every chicken, every piece of machinery, ear of corn, and stalk of wheat had to be made to count now.

Ivan was right. This was reality-testing time. Money was no longer a vague concept. It was a precise, specific thing which had to do with the price of eggs, of goat's milk, of anything he could squeeze out of the land. It was a little late in his life, but Morgan-stern finally understood the value of a dollar.

Maybe it was just as well that he had lost everything in the commodities market, he thought. The money had never seemed real to him. The farm, that was real. Automatic milking was scheduled to go into operation in forty hours. The vision of the Alamo Surge pulling the milk out of the goats through the pipes into the stainless-steel vat and out into the local distributor's waiting trucks reassured him. The crops were almost ready to harvest, which meant he could stop paying the outrageous prices for feed. The house was in good shape. Barring any unforeseen circumstances, he would have no difficulty taking care of his mortgage payments and turning the farm into a real profit-making enterprise.

Then he thought about unforeseen circumstances and he started getting nervous all over again. Until now, all the minor and major mishaps, the unexpected expenses, hadn't shaken him. He had a cushion to fall back on. Now, with his commodities contracts practically worthless, he had nothing to fall back on but the cold, hard ground.

Had everything that could possibly go wrong gone wrong? Or had he somehow missed something? He ran through a list in his mind.

263

Earthquake? Drought? Typhoon? A plague of locusts? He knew that any act of God, of nature, or of vandalism could ruin him now. He had a sudden flash of just how precarious a farm shelter really was. It was about as safe and secure as a grass shack in hurricane season.

The farm made his previous corporate existence seem like a snap. He felt like a man who, having miraculously survived a head-on car collision, suddenly decides to take up high-speed racing as a hobby.

He stood on the front porch surveying his empire. This is it. It's all I've got. And I'm going to make it work, he vowed. He was on the cutting edge. A man responsible for his own fate, for the future of his farm. From here on in, every penny had to be accounted for. No more waste. No more reliance on the price of hog bellies in Topeka, Kansas. He would make his fortune the good, old-fashioned John Houseman/Smith Barney way. He would earn it.

Ariel returned very late Monday night to find Morganstern on the back porch sorting out peaches.

"One rotten peach can spoil the whole barrel, huh?" she said, watching him pick over the fruit.

"You know, over half of these will have to be thrown out," he said, not looking at her. "It's like throwing money in the garbage."

"Matthew, for heaven's sake. Those peaches cost all of four dollars a bushel. It's not exactly going to break you, is it?"

"Every penny counts," he mumbled. The last thing he wanted to do was tell her about his commodities loss. He was much more comfortable talking about rotten peaches.

"Honey, stop that for a second. I have to talk to you."

"If I finish this tonight, then you can start your preserves in the morning." He examined a peach, took a knife, and removed one small bruised spot. Ariel grabbed the peach from his hand and threw it into the yard. "Please, we have to talk. I did a lot of thinking while I was at the Conrads'."

"That must have slowed up the old tennis game."

"Matthew, if you don't let me talk, I'm going to cry."

"Okay. You did a lot of thinking at the Conrads'. Go on." He stood up slowly, clutching at the small of his back.

"We've got to get out of here. This just isn't for us. Let's admit we made a mistake and go back to the city, where we belong."

"You've got to be kidding."

"I've never been more serious. Look at you, you're a wreck. I'm a wreck. You haven't painted a picture since we came out here. And I can't say these last few weeks have been the happiest time of my life."

"Oh, I see. Your weekend with the Conrads makes this place seem like slumming, is that it?"

264

"No, that's not it at all. The Conrads certainly have the ultimate farm. But I got to see that even the ultimate farm isn't for me. And it's not for you. You're killing yourself. And for what?"

"You think I can just walk away from this farm like it's some kind of fucking hobby that I got bored with? We have a commitment to this place."

"You have a commitment. And I don't think it's to this place or the goats or the goddamn goat milk. I don't think that has anything to do with it. I think you're in so deep you just can't see straight anymore."

"And you can?"

"Yes, I can," she said quietly. "If I felt we were good at this, if I thought this was good for us, I'd say fine. But we've got no business farming. People like the Kinderhoffs have been doing this all their lives. That's why they're getting rich off us."

"The Kinderhoffs have a right to make a living."

Ariel laughed. "Make a living? They're making a killing. But that's not the point. Why shouldn't they profit from our mistakes? The point is, we just don't belong here. You belong behind an easel, and I should be back doing what I do best."

"And what's that?"

"Making money. I realized I like making money. It makes me feel good. Painting makes you feel good. So what in the world are we doing out here in the middle of nowhere? You, a fantastically talented artist picking through a bushel of peaches like one of your bag ladies."

"In approximately two days this farm will be a fully automated, money-making, self-running operation. Two days, Ariel."

"That's a joke. It may make money. But it will never run itself. Never. You'll end up a withered, weathered old man, an old goat working your fingers to the bone for a bunch of nannies. I'm right. Why can't you admit it? Let's go back to the city."

"You can't take a few setbacks and a little hard work, that's your problem."

"I can take as much hard work as the next person as long as it's for something I believe in."

"You're asking me to decide between you and the farm? This farm was for you, for us."

"I think you really believe that. Maybe it even started out that way. But it's not true now. Please, we've got to get out of here."

"You're free to go anytime you want. But I'm not leaving. I've got a dairy to run."

"And what then? What happens then? I'm telling you, the longer you stay out here, the worse it will get. You'll forget you ever even knew how to paint."

265

"Ariel. If you don't want to be a part of this, then you can clear out. The sooner the better. We don't need you."

"We?"

"The goats and me. We can manage just fine."

"I want you to go with me."

"I'm not leaving."

"That's your final word?"

"That's it."

It took Ariel only a few hours the next morning to pack all her things. There seemed to be nothing left to say. The anger was gone. In its place, Morganstern felt a great sadness. He drove her to the train station and unloaded her bags from the van while she bought her ticket.

"Matthew, please change your mind. Come with me."

He shook his head. "I guess this is good-bye, peach pie," he said in a tight, strained voice.

Ariel sighed deeply. "I guess it is. Take care of yourself."

"Sure, sure. You too."

He turned and walked toward the van. He didn't even look back as the train pulled out. They had lived together for almost five years. They weren't beginners. A relationship could go through only so many ups and downs before the shock absorbers just finally gave out, he reasoned. He felt numb. He forced himself not to think about her, or them, or what had gone wrong. He knew it wouldn't do any good. And he needed all his energy to think about tomorrow. Tomorrow was the big day.

The country was in its August ripeness. He was surrounded by living, breathing animals. The night air was crowded with sounds of crickets and katydids. But he might as well have been on a deserted island. He had never felt more alone in his life.

When he finally fell asleep that night, his head on Ariel's still-fragrant pillow, he had another one of his nightmares about falling from a high place.

7

D Day, the official opening of Morganstern's fully automated dairy and goat farm. Despite all the recent catastrophes, Morganstern awoke early in the morning with high hopes. This was what he had been waiting for. If only he could hold on, it would turn everything around for him. He could start selling his milk at regular market prices, the farm would begin to show a profit, he could begin to paint again, and maybe, just maybe, he could show Ariel how wrong she was.

The barn was beautiful. It looked like the interior of a modern factory with its bright red stanchions, stainless-steel milk lines, and shiny new Alamo Surge. The floor had been lowered, the platforms built and Astroturfed, and everything had been painted a fresh white gloss.

It was all hooked up and ready to go, with the exception of the goats. Mayhew was there to make a dry run. A flick of the switch and the Alamo Surge surged on, the vacuum hummed, the pulsator pulsated, and the claw suction cups sucked. It was a finely tuned machine.

"Give me a call if you have any problems," Mayhew said.

That afternoon at milking time, Morganstern and Cowpie separated out a group of thirty-six goats and herded them into the new barn. They found their way into their own stalls. Morganstern hooked up the milking attachments as Mayhew had shown him. One claw with four suction cups for every two goats. Everything was set. He switched on the Alamo Surge.

That was when all hell broke loose. The goats kicked. They squealed. They shuddered. Their eyes rolled back, showing the whites. They tried to get away from the milking attachments. They were terrified. He was terrified. He was afraid they would rip their udders. Cowpie was hysterical. Morganstern ran to turn off the motor. He quickly unhooked the goats, and they stampeded out of the barn, their udders still filled with milk. Cowpie ran after them.

Morganstern tried to collect himself. Obviously these were preindustrial goats. Having been touched only by human hands, you had to ease them into it, he thought. He let them graze for a while until they quieted down.

But when he tried to get the same group of thirty-six into the barn a half-hour later, they scattered through the fields. "Come on, girls, I won't hurt you," he shouted, "it's just a milking machine." From a safe distance they looked back at him skeptically.

He called Mayhew. "These goddamn machines aren't working."

"What do you mean, they aren't working? I checked everything out myself."

"The goats won't stand still for the milking. They hate the machines."

"Oh, they're just spoiled. You got to be firm with them. Can't let a bunch of goats call the shots. Just get out there and tell 'em who's boss."

The goats weren't available for the announcement. The entire herd had broken through the neighboring fence and were grazing in a far pasture. Cowpie was with them. Morganstern wasn't sure if he was following the goats or leading them astray.

Perhaps he should have prepared them way in advance. Some

sort of memo from management: To all nannies, commencing September, work hours will be reduced, pay increased . . .

He called Mayhew again. "Yeah, yeah, these things can happen. Sometimes a whole herd'll stubborn up on ya."

"What the hell am I supposed to do?"

"I'd say sell 'em. Get yourself another herd. Either a younger group that ain't been milked yet or one that's used to machinery. Actually, if I were you I'd go back to cows. I never thought Dad's goat idea was too smart in the first place. They're too damned independent. You're practically all set up for cows anyway. All you got to do is lower the platforms some, raise the floor, widen the stanchions—"

"What the fuck are you talking about?" Morganstern screamed. "I just spent thousands of dollars converting the barn for goats. You've got to be out of your mind."

Morganstern stared at the empty barn. He was in a state of shock. Suddenly he was reminded of a science-fiction movie he had seen as a small boy. It was one of the most frightening films of his life.

The earth is invaded by strange creatures from Mars. People from a small town are captured, one by one. Crystal pins are put in their necks, which cause them to go through a total personality transformation. The good, warm, small-town folks become cold, mean, evil killers. Morganstern always remembered the one scene where the mother comes to collect her terrified little boy at the police station. The desk sergeant, the audience has just learned, is wearing one of the crystal pins, so the mother has arrived just in the nick of time. The boy runs into her arms. He is glad to see her. The camera shows his face: happy, smiling, relieved, and then it pans around to show the face of the mother: cold, mean, evil; it is the face of a killer mom.

Had Appleville been invaded by Martians? Were the Kinderhoffs sporting little crystal pins in their fat pink necks? There was more solace in that explanation than there was in the possibility that he might have misjudged the entire family, that Ariel, in fact, might have been right.

He remembered his first fears when he had learned about winning the sweepstakes. The unsettling feelings of paranoia, the fear of being mugged and maimed. He knew now that he had been absolutely right to be afraid. But he had anticipated disaster from above, from afar, from a stranger. The windfall syndrome. A falling boulder, a flick of the almighty fingernail, lightning bolts. And all the time, the trouble was there, right there in Kinder-city, from none other than the good, down-to-earth, all-too-kindly Kinderhoffs.

He shook his head. No, they were not going to do him in. They were not going to get his farm. He had to figure out a way. He could sell the milking machinery, which was useless on the goats, and use the money to buy a herd of cows. But then he wouldn't have the machinery to milk them with. What about his feed bill? He could sell the goats to pay for the feed, but then what would he do with the feed? He could end up with a lot of well-fed goats who weren't paying their way, or with some fancy milking machinery and nothing to milk. Or with a new herd of cows and no way to milk them. And what about the mortgage? How the hell was he going to meet his next payment?

And then he remembered the peat moss. "That could be your real money-maker," Senior Kinderhoff had said. He wished he could wait until it turned to coal, but he didn't have that luxury now. He knew better than to consult with the local nursery. It was Kinderhoff-controlled. He called in a man from a nursery several miles away.

"You give me your best price per pound, or, if you prefer, we could settle on one sum for the farming rights," he said when the nurseryman came out. The man looked perplexed.

"Farming of what?" he said.

"Oh, sorry. The peat moss. There must be a couple of thousand tons there." He gestered toward the bog. Morganstern and the man walked down the hill and into the swamp to examine it more closely. Their feet made sucking noises in the spongy wet earth.

"Nope, not quite peat yet," the man said, flinging the slimy black mud off his fingers. "I'd let it set awhile if I was you." He laughed.

"Senior Kinderhoff told me it was prime peat moss."

"Oh, Senior. He's a good old man, but he's got silage for brains." His laughter broadened into big phlegm-filled guffaws. "Yhaw. Yhaw. Yhaw. What you got here is muck. Muck has to set a long time before it becomes peat."

"How long?" Morganstern was the straight man the nurseryman had been waiting for all his life.

"To be on the safe side, about two hundred years," he said, exploding in laughter, "and if you're not in a real big hurry and got about five hundred years to kill, you'll have yourself a real fine bed of coal. Yep, I'd just let it set awhile. Best to let sleeping bogs lie. Yhaw. Yhaw. Yhaw."

Long after the nurseryman had left, Morganstern stood on the hill staring down at the swamp. Little puffs of clouds floated against the brilliant blue sky. High above him a hawk soared, pulled up by an invisible air current. The trees swayed softly in the warm afternoon breeze. He was upwind from the smell of chicken and pig shit, and the air carried the sweet fragrance of ripening corn. Get me out of here. Somebody get me out of here, he screamed silently.

He made his decision. He called Uncle Kruger to tell him. "I

269

won't be able to meet my mortgage payment. I'm selling the farm. What's the procedure?"

"Are you sure you want to do that?" Uncle Kruger asked.

"Absolutely one hundred percent sure."

"Well, it's better to find out sooner, rather than later, if you're not cut out for this kind of life," Uncle Kruger said in his warm, chuckly way.

Morganstern was not going to be sucked in. "I want to get the best possible price for the place."

"Well, sure you do. Here's what happens. We put it up for auction. Advertise it in the local paper. And hope for a good crowd."

The crowd was good by Kinderhoff standards. Every single member of the family showed up, plus a few other local people. The farm went to Karl Kinderhoff for $110,000, the same price Morganstern paid for it.

Morganstern grabbed Karl Kinderhoff by the arm. "You can't do this," he yelled. "After everything I put into it, this place has to be worth at least $190,000."

"Then I guess I got quite a deal," Karl said.

"I've been screwed," he shouted.

He had been screwed. Royally, rurally screwed. They had probably fucked him from the very beginning.

"Now, cool down, Matt," Karl was saying. "You got to admit the place has gone down considerably in value. The goats just didn't work out. Dad was wrong about them. He'll be the first one to admit it."

"Well, I'll be the second one, at any rate," Senior said.

"You people were out to get me from the start, weren't you?" Morganstern said, enraged.

"No, sir," Uncle Kruger said solemnly. "You paid more'n you should have, and Karl paid less than he had to, that's all. Business is business. And profits ain't easy to come by in this world of ours."

"All the equipment you sold me, all those improvements, the Harvestore, the new milking barn—you were just selling me a bill of goods."

"We were sellin' 'cause you were buyin'. Ain't that the American way?" said Kaddy.

"You got to understand our position," Senior said. "We got our expenses, our financial commitments, and a corporation to protect, just like everybody else."

Uncle Kruger spoke again. "You see, young man, we been in this county for three generations. Long enough certainly to learn somethin'. The farmin' part was easy. But that don't amount to a hill of beans in today's world. You got to know when to diversify, when to liquidate, when to amortize, and when to economize. If a fella don't know how to consolidate his debt or negotiate a long-term loan, then I don't care if he's the best damn farmer in the world, he's still a fool."

"And what about all the crap about farmers being the foot soldiers of the future?" Morganstern yelled.

"It's true." Uncle Kruger nodded. "But you got to know: money is the machine gun."

"When do I have to vacate the premises?" Morganstern growled.

"Oh, there's no rush," Karl said. "Dad's takin' the whole family to Disney World for a month. Goats'll be sold off and the crops harvested, ain't nothing for you to do but relax."

After paying off the $75,000 remaining on the mortgage, Morganstern was left with $35,000 from the sale of the farm. Well, at least I'm not back to zero, he said to himself. He wondered why he wasn't able to make any plans, either for the money or for himself.

He realized why the following day when he got a call from Bartlett.

"We need your check for $30,000 by close of business tomorrow," said a man who identified himself as Getty Milford's supervisor.

"What are you talking about?"

The supervisor went on to explain: "Well, before Miss Milford went on our executive-retraining program, apparently she neglected to terminate your commodities contracts. Consequently, your contracts continued to follow the market down, thereby incurring a debt on your part of the sum of $30,000. I took it upon myself to terminate your account as of yesterday. I hope that meets with your approval."

He wasn't even surprised. He just felt blank, numb and dumb. He wanted to be able to blame Getty or the Kinderhoffs for everything that had happened to him, but he couldn't. Neither could he blame the system, or the economy, or the times, or the President.

He couldn't even conjure up a decent case of self-pity. Who in his right mind could feel sorry for a man who had won $250,000 through a fluke and then lost it all through sheer stupidity, gullibility, and greed?

He had been in such a fucking hurry. He had rushed into a corporation, thrown his money in the stock and commodities markets, and then made a mad dash for his safe little tax shelter in the sky. Ariel was right. The farm hadn't really been for her or for their relationship, but simply and finally for the preservation of money that he had never even earned in the first place.

He had made a quantam leap from a simple, aesthetic life of no credit cards, no money, no debts, no knowledge of or interest in the world of business, to this: this six-figure, tax-sheltered, overly mortgaged, precariously structured financial fiasco. Who did he think he

271

was, Alan Greenspan? He had been so busy "sticking it to the IRS" that he hadn't seen that he was screwing himself.

The Kinderhoffs hadn't done him in. He had managed that all on his own.

Is there a moral in this someplace? he wondered. Is there a lesson I can learn? Is there anybody out there with a brochure or a seminar on how to survive stupidity?

And what was he going to do? Where was he going to go? His money was gone. The farm was gone. And with it, his tax shelter. For all he knew, he probably owed back taxes now to the IRS. What would they do to him if he couldn't pay? Send him to federal prison? A debtor's prison? Or, God forbid, a prison farm?

The day had turned dark and dismal. It looks like rain, he said to himself. And then he remembered that the weather, whether there was a deluge or a drought, was of no concern to him anymore. He walked over to the big blue Harvestore and looked up. Funny, he had never climbed to the top before.

Halfway up the silo, he remembered why: his overwhelming fear of heights.

The wind was blowing steadily. He gripped the metal ladder tightly and looked down. It was a long, long way. He was frozen with fear. Then he was dizzy with fear. He was afraid to climb up and he was afraid to climb down. How long could he stay where he was?

He took a deep breath and continued his ascent, one shaky foot at a time. What will I do when I get to the top? he wondered. Don't think about it, he answered himself, just keep climbing. The higher he climbed, the colder it got and the stronger the wind blew. His face ached from the cold wind and his hands hurt from gripping the metal ladder.

When he reached the top, he looked down once again. Sixty feet. How many stories was that? Figure twelve feet to a story, twelve into sixty . . .

All the nightmares he had ever had about falling from high places came back to him. Was this what they meant by a self-fulfilling prophecy? Did dreams take up where reality left off?

If he jumped, would it kill him? If it killed him, would anybody care? Would anybody miss him at all? Ariel would. For a while, anyway. They had spent too many years together for her not to mourn him just a little.

And then he thought: I don't have to jump. I could always climb back down and pick up the pieces of my life. That's what they do in all the best tragedies. But he knew that what had happened to him couldn't even remotely qualify as a tragedy. What had happened to him was nothing more than the appropriate and predictable ending to his story: "M. Morganstern, reaper of windfalls."

He took one last look at his former empire. From the top of the Harvestore he could see for miles around. Fall had come early to the area. The trees, bypassing the brilliant foliage period, were dropping their dead green leaves like so many used ticket stubs. How desolate it would be in the winter, he thought. But then, he didn't have to worry about that. He wouldn't be there in the winter.

For the first time, the awesome ugliness of the place hit him: the decrepit farm buildings, the scraggly trees, the goat-gnawed crab-grass, and the dried out cornfields. Even the birds were an eyesore: moth-eaten sparrows, sun-faded crows, and an occasional buzzard littered the sky. And for the first time he had a clear view over the ridge that ran adjacent to his property. He hadn't even realized that in the valley beyond the ridge was the town dump. There were tattered Lazy-Boy loungers, rusted-out carcasses of cars, the insides of old washing machines and air conditioners, and mountains of tin cans, old cardboard cartons, and dead food.

And then all at once the idea for a picture simply and suddenly popped into his head. His mind had been so stuffed with the business expenses and write-offs, stocks and shelters, silage, spoilage, butterfat, sewage and muck, there had been no room for anything else. But now that his head was as free and clear as a paid-off mortgage, images were able to move right in and fill in the empty space.

He began to laugh. He laughed so hard that he almost lost his balance. Then, still laughing, he climbed down the silo as quickly and easily as if it had been a four-foot stepladder.

He had almost a month before the Kinderhoffs returned from their trip. And he had about $5,000 left to his name. He went into town and bought a dozen brushes of varying sizes and twenty different shades of high-gloss-enamel paint. The tin roof of the barn provided the largest, smoothest uninterrupted space in which to work. He rigged up a scaffolding and found some old drop cloths to hang so that the work would be covered up until it was finished.

Working all day and at night, with the aid of floodlights, he managed to finish the mural in just three weeks. A week before the Kinderhoffs were due back. When he was done, he packed up the van and then took one last look at his work.

The painting was Morganstern's conception of life on the farm: farmers wearing pinstripe suits drove huge pocket calculators through fields of waving stock certificates and savings bonds, while a herd of fat four-legged digits grazed peacefully within the coaxial-cable fences. In front of the farmhouse, farmers' wives dressed in designer outfits worked at a long table canning jars of bright green currency. Shining down on everything was a warm noonday sun, the center of which featured a digital readout indicating the Dow Jones average.

273

He had done the painting in a fairly primitive style, but had paid special attention to the faces of the people working on the farm. The resemblance to the Kinderhoff family was unmistakable. Taking into consideration that he had been working in a new medium (Benjamin Moore high-gloss) on a difficult surface and against the clock, he was very happy with the results.

He didn't know if the Kinderhoffs were art lovers or not. If they weren't, they could always paint over the mural. But it would take a good base coat plus several coats of enamel to cover it up. Or they could get Mayhew to put on a new roof. Being family, he'd probably do it for cost.

The thing he liked best about the painting was the fact that it was clearly visible from almost a mile down the road. He had always wanted to paint big. Well, this was certainly big. He thought it was probably the best work he had ever done. He felt exhilarated, excited, and powerful. He felt like a painter again. If he could continue painting like this . . . well, then, anything was possible.

Epilogue

From the New York *Post*, November 16:

MAD ARTIST INVADES HARLEM

The owners of an abandoned building at 102 E. 148th Street want to bring criminal charges against M. Morganstern, 36, an unemployed artist who has begun work on a huge mural on the outside wall of their property. The owners, Trumball Management Corp., charge Morganstern with defacing private property . . .

From the New York *Times*, December 10:

ARTIST PAINTS BUILDING

. . . Living and working out of his van, the artist-in-residence refuses to leave until his mural is completed. . . . Owners of the abandoned building have failed to obtain an injunction, but they insist that Morganstern is "nothing more than a highly ambitious graffiti artist."

From an editorial in the *Amsterdam News*, January 3:

NEIGHBORHOOD SUPPORTS CONTROVERSIAL ARTIST

. . . We applaud Mr. Morganstern's efforts. As a one-man crusade to beautify the blighted areas of this city, we think he deserves all our support. If the absentee landlords of this city would just sit down and . . .

From "The Inquiring Photographer," the *Daily News*, January 15:

Q. "Are you for or against paintings like Matthew Morganstern's?"

A. "I don't know anything about art, but I know what I like. And I think it's great."—Pamela Dubowsky, Cashier.

A. "I say, leave the guy alone. At least he's not mur-

275

dering anybody."—Maureen Broglia, Social Worker.

A. "I know the building. And I'll tell you this, it's pretty hard to deface a pigsty like that."—Angelo Diaz, Former Superintendent of 102 E. 148th St.

From *The Village Voice*, February 20:

GRAFFITI OR GREAT ART? CRACKPOT OR CRACK ARTIST?

. . . Morganstern's epic work on East 148th Street has not only caused a city-wide controversy, but it has created a turmoil in the neighborhood as well. Residents have picketed the building, preventing demolition crews from going in. They have also instituted a fund-raising drive to keep him in food and painting supplies . . .

From *New York Magazine*, March 10:

SLUM ARTIST MAKES HIS MARK

Matthew Morganstern, urban artist, has taken a pot-shot at the city's biggest banking institution. His building-size mural on East 148th Street, entitled *Money Is Like Manure, It's No Good Unless You Spread It Around,* captures quite accurately the interior of the main branch of New York's Metrobank. The painting shows Metrobank customers dressed like farmworkers lined up to make deposits, with wagons and wheelbarrows filled with manure. . . .

From an article by Sidney Adams, art critic, in the March issue of *Art News Magazine*:

FROM MINIATURE TO MONUMENTAL, AN ARTIST FINDS HIS SPACE

A rather interesting phenomenon has been observed on the New York art scene. In a work of epic proportions, Matthew Morganstern, a relative unknown and former painter of small-size canvases, depicts an inside and rather irreverent view of one of the city's major banks. The work, executed in Benjamin Moore latex with the use of oversize brushes, displays a refreshing juxtaposition. Done in a style reminiscent of Early American primitives, it deals with a very modern-day subject. . . .

From "Talk of the Town," *The New Yorker* magazine, April 1:

We dropped by the painting site on East 148th Street to have a look for ourselves at Matthew Morganstern's thousand-square-foot work-in-progress. We talked with the artist, an attractive man in his mid-thirties, as he stood on his scaffolding adding last-minute details to his controversial work. We asked him why he chose to apply his art to the side of a condemned building rather than the conventional medium of canvas. "Canvas is very expensive these days," Morganstern told us, "and so far, I've gotten this building for nothing." Mr. Morganstern denied the altruistic motivations attributed to him by the press. "I don't care anything about beautifying the city," he said. "I just like to work big and I like to work outdoors." We then asked him about his future plans when his present project is completed. "I have my eye on one of the Twin Towers," he said with a quick smile, "but I'm not saying which one."

Morganstern was putting the final touches on his mural. The sun was just going down and his light was fading fast. He quickly painted the initial M in the upper-right-hand corner and he was done. He couldn't believe it. After months and months of backbreaking work, it was finished. His first reaction was to step back and look at the work in its entirety. And then he remembered where he was: on a scaffolding hanging from the fifth floor of a condemned building. He began to replace the lids on the Benjamin Moore paint.

It was then that he heard the shouts and applause. Choruses of "Bravo! Bravo!" "Well done!" "Great work!" "Artist! Artist!" drifted up to him. He looked down. There was a huge crowd gathered on the sidewalk below. He was used to crowds by now. People had been coming by in increasing numbers as the painting came close to completion.

But this crowd was different. They were all dressed in evening clothes and they were toasting him with glasses of champagne. He began to recognize faces. Zero was there. And Ivan. The Conrads and Mrs. Grace Chase. Blinky Lord was caressing the side of the building with both hands. There was Cornwall, and Stuey, and Mr. Shallot. And even Getty. And there was his mother. And there was his father. And there were the Kinderhoffs, every last chuckling one of them. He couldn't believe his eyes. He thought he was dreaming.

"How much do you want for the painting?" someone shouted up. It was Ariel, smiling and looking spectacularly beautiful in a red satin dress. He hadn't seen her since the day he put her on the train.

277

"Oh, my God," he gasped. He thought he was going to fall off the scaffolding. Somehow he managed to lower himself to the sidewalk.

People slapped him on the back and reached out to shake his hand. He embraced his parents and then turned to Ariel.

"It's a surprise party," she said, her eyes sparkling with tears.

"It seems that way," he choked.

"Here's another surprise," she said, handing him a piece of paper. It was a check written out to him for $50,000.

"What's this?"

"Funding for your next project. It's a combined grant from Benjamin Moore Paints and the Urban Art League. They want you to do more buildings."

"Oh, my God."

"Benjamin Moore? The Jewish Benjamin Moore?" his father asked.

"Leave your son alone," his mother chided. "Let him be rich in peace."

Hours later, after leaving the party in his honor at Grace Chase's and after dropping his parents off at the Waldorf (where, amazingly, they consented to being put up), Morganstern and Ariel took a long walk through the quiet city streets.

"Wow, what a night," he breathed.

"You deserved every minute of it," Ariel said, squeezing his arm. "Listen, Matthew, I have a proposition to make," she said, stopping him at the corner. "A sort of barter arrangement."

"What sort of barter?"

"I get *you*. In exchange, you get my heart, my soul, my undying love. My admiration, my dedication, my appreciation, my understanding, my support, my paycheck."

"Your paycheck?"

"Yes, I'm back at work making big bucks, as they say in the ad business."

Morganstern furrowed his brow. "It's an interesting proposition."

"I was even thinking we could make it legal," she added.

"You mean you want to incorporate?"

"Actually, I was thinking more along the lines of a mad, passionate marriage."

He shook his head. "It would never work, Ariel."

She looked stricken. "If I can overlook the fact that you're a dedicated, driven genius," she said, "you should be able to forgive me for being an incurable capitalist."

"It's not that. It's the tax problem."

"What tax problem?"

"Financially, it doesn't make sense. There's every reason to believe that I'll be making a lot of money from my paintings. With

278

both of us earning at such a high level and what with filing jointly, it would be suicide, tax-wise."

"I see your point," she said, smiling.

"Besides, do you really think that two enormously successful, extremely wealthy individuals could find happiness together?"

Ariel thought a minute. "I don't think it would be easy. But we could try." She threw her arms around him. "Oh, Matthew, I love you so much." He held her close and squeezed with all his might.

He thought back to the evening and the party and his parents and all the people that were there and his big, beautiful finished mural and the hefty check in his pocket and the generous woman in his arms.

And then he thought: Of course I could have a massive coronary right now and drop dead in my tracks, and that would be the end of everything.

But he didn't. And it wasn't.

5465 178
5